A WEST COAST ROMANCE

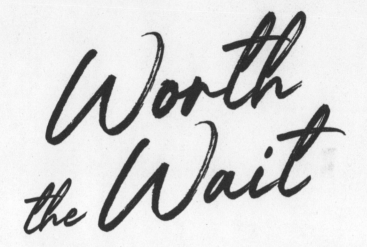

Worth the Wait

LUCILLE JAMES

Cover Design: Ink and Laurel

Edited by: Andrea Davidson

Contents

Dear Reader,   VII

Dedication   IX

Prologue   XI

1. Chapter One   1

2. Chapter Two   11

3. Chapter Three   17

4. Chapter Four   21

5. Chapter Five   29

6. Chapter Six   39

7. Chapter Seven   45

8. Chapter Eight   49

9. Chapter Nine   55

10. Chapter Ten   59

11. Chapter Eleven   67

12. Chapter Twelve   77

13. Chapter Thirteen   87

14. Chapter Fourteen   93

15.	Chapter Fifteen	95
16.	Chapter Sixteen	103
17.	Chapter Seventeen	107
18.	Chapter Eighteen	115
19.	Chapter Nineteen	137
20.	Chapter Twenty	147
21.	Chapter Twenty-One	173
22.	Chapter Twenty-Two	183
23.	Chapter Twenty-Three	189
24.	Chapter Twenty-Four	197
25.	Chapter Twenty-Five	223
26.	Chapter Twenty-Six	233
27.	Chapter Twenty-Seven	239
28.	Chapter Twenty-Eight	247
29.	Chapter Twenty-Nine	257
30.	Chapter Thirty	271
31.	Chapter Thirty-One	279
32.	Chapter Thirty-Two	291
33.	Chapter Thirty-Three	299
34.	Chapter Thirty-Four	307
35.	Chapter Thirty-Five	311
36.	Chapter Thirty-Six	319
37.	Chapter Thirty-Seven	325

38. Chapter Thirty-Eight   331

39. Chapter Thirty-Nine   337

40. Chapter Forty   349

41. Chapter Forty-One   355

42. Chapter Forty-Two   359

43. Chapter Forty-Three   367

44. Chapter Forty-Four   375

45. Chapter Forty-Five   385

46. Chapter Forty-Six   387

47. Chapter Forty-Seven   395

48. Chapter Forty-Eight   399

49. Chapter Forty-Nine   405

Epilogue   411

Acknowledgements   420

About the author   423

Follow For More   425

Dear Reader,

Don't be fooled by the sweet cover, Worth the Wait is a hockey romance that contains open door/explicit sexual situations; it is written for adult audiences only. Please keep in mind that while Worth The Wait is a happy love story it does contain mentions of drug use, addiction and loss of a loved one; proceed with caution.

-Lucille James

Dedication

To all of you who watch hockey with hearts in your eyes;
I see you.

Prologue

News Break:

"Boy, do we have a story for you this NHL holiday break. Roman Graves, captain of the Los Angeles Knights, is in hot water over a series of intimate pictures of him being leaked, flooding the internet. The woman in the photo you see behind me has come forward, demanding a settlement from the Los Angeles Knights captain. Claims of emotional distress and depleted self-worth are being thrown around in the media this Christmas Eve. Looks like Roman Graves will be seeing a lot less mistletoe this holiday and a lot more legal paperwork."

Chapter One

It was the first day of the NHL holiday break and Roman Graves was on his couch. He was *not* wearing a suit. He was *not* at a fancy holiday party or charity event. He did *not* have a beautiful model on his arm. In fact, this marked the first time since he was drafted to the LA Knights that he wasn't going to any lavish parties, holiday feasts or intimate family gatherings. No, this holiday break he was wearing his classic Adidas joggers, his feet were bare, and his Instagram feed was a constant reminder of why he was 'grounded' for the next three days.

After the news broke about his sex scandal, Roman's PR team called an emergency meeting to discuss how they would manage the situation. The situation being several pictures circulating the internet of Roman asleep in bed, butt ass naked with a smiling blonde next to him. These kinds of things did not sit well with the NHL. The girl in the picture, whose name he didn't even remember, was now demanding a settlement due to 'emotional distress'.

In his mind, the amazing sex they had and the multiple orgasms he gave her should have been payment enough. Right?

Apparently not for this woman. She said he never called her the day after. Of course he never called the day after, he didn't even have her fucking number. He didn't have her number because he didn't even remember her name. He didn't remember her name because he made it clear that it was a hookup, nothing more, nothing less. It had been two consenting adults, enjoying each other's company for *a* night. It was not unheard of. People all over the world were having one-night stands at the same exact moment as Roman and the blonde. The only difference was that Roman was a professional hockey player, and that made him a target for gold diggers, or as they were known in the hockey world, puck bunnies.

These women were nothing new to Roman. He always tried to play it safe. He always wore protection when he fucked them. He always got undeniable consent and he always made sure they knew–*without any doubt*– that this would not lead to anything outside of sex. He didn't date. He didn't commit. His life was busy, and his focus was on the Stanley Cup.

But his luck had run out, and his sexual appetite had finally caught up to him. So now, he waited. He waited alone over the holiday break for his PR team to call him with the details of the press conference he would have to do to smooth things over.

The NHL liked to have a clean reputation. Good men played for the NHL, and the ones who weren't always good–the ones like Roman–were expected to keep their indiscretions under wraps and out of the headlines. They were selling hockey, *not* sex, drugs, and rock-n-roll.

But Roman knew that sex *always* sold. He knew that no matter what he said at this press conference, women would continue to lust after him, men would continue to idolize him, and the NHL would survive another scandal.

There was no such thing as bad press, right?

Roman's phone rang and his heart raced when his assistant's name appeared.

"Talk to me Melissa," he said, hitting mute, the image of him with blurred out nudity still sat in the small box in the corner of the TV screen, mocking him.

"Well, it's not good," she said.

"Okay." He sat up on the couch, giving his assistant his undivided attention.

"But it's not bad either," Melissa paused, her voice even toned, "So, your girl," she started.

He cut her off, "She's not my girl."

"No, obviously. How rude of me to imply you have feelings." Her eye roll was almost audible, sarcasm laced her every word. "Your one-night stand, however, is claiming that you were a real gentleman. She said you even let her shower after–how kind of you. She claims typically after a hookup, the men just call an uber and kick her to the curb. So, when she found you asleep she took it as an invitation to snuggle up next to you and as we both know, snap pictures of your junk. Which was wrong, but she said–and you can't make this shit up Roman–that she thought you two had some kind of *soul* connection, and when you never called her the next day, it broke her heart and she wants you to pay for her emotional damage."

Roman let out a frustrated sigh. "The only connection we had was my–"

"Ew," Melissa cut him off, "Listen Roman, you can't fly off the handle with this one. I know what kind of connection you two had and I personally would rather *not* know the details, but the thing is, the NHL is cracking down on this sort of thing. So, this sleeping around shit has to stop. Find a nice girl. Stop fucking these clout chasing influencers. Settle down. Try monogamy on for size. You might find it suits you, babe."

Roman couldn't disagree more. In fact, he hated the idea of all of it. What had monogamy meant for his mother? Nothing. Roman knew firsthand that wedding vows meant nothing, because nothing was sacred. Nothing was fair. Except for winning hockey, and even that could be tainted by a crooked ref.

"So, what's the next step?" he asked, defeated. He knew long before this headline dropped that he was toeing a line that could cost him everything by sleeping around so recklessly.

"So, the good part is that she openly said you were a gentleman and that she consented to the whole thing. The bad part is that I know you, and I know you won't want to admit any fault or pay her any kind of settlement. Here's the thing babe, sometimes we have to swallow our pride and do what's best for the team, NHL, and ultimately, the reputation of Roman Graves, which for the most part has a pretty clean slate outside of being a well-known ladies man. I don't want to see you ruin it all over a piece of ass."

"Do you think her demands will hold up in court? Would they actually make me pay for breaking her heart? Is that *really* something you can sue someone for?"

"No, it absolutely will *not* hold up in court. It's laughable, and she knows that. But this was never about the lawsuit or money, it was always about her fifteen minutes of fame. I did some digging on the girl and she has a bit of a history with this sort of thing."

"Of course she does." Roman said, raking frustrated hands through his hair. "I'll do whatever I have to do. But you *do* realize that admitting fault *will* leave a stain on my reputation?"

She let out a sigh of defeat. "Yeah, babe, I know. But it's the only way and Coach Hibbs wants it done this way. The NHL wants this nipped in the bud ASAP."

He knew this was the only outcome. He didn't like it, but he didn't like letting down his team even more.

"Send over what you want me to say. I'll read it through. I mean, I *do* have plenty of time on my hands considering you grounded me," he teased.

"It's for your own good to stay home for the holiday break. The last thing we need is pictures surfacing of you out at parties while 'your girl' is crying to anyone who will listen about how you broke her heart."

Roman knew it was a good call. He knew everything Melissa said was right, but it was going to be a long three days. He sat up and stretched his body, his back popping from laying on the couch all morning.

"Roman, you still there babe?"

"Yeah, I just realized I'm starving, and I need to go for a run."

He could hear Melissa multitasking in the background of the call, "Okay, here's what you're going to do," she said firmly, "go for a run on the treadmill. I don't want any pictures of you getting out until after the statement is released. After your run, I'll have dinner delivered, how does Thai food sound?"

"Sounds perfect," he agreed.

"Good, because it's already ordered," she said, matter-of-factly.

"You're too good to me, Melissa," he said with every ounce of sincerity he could muster.

"I know babe, but I love you and you pay me *really* well, so it's worth it."

He chuckled, "Enjoy your holiday, Mel."

"Thanks Roman, and don't get in your head over this. It's not as big a deal as it seems, okay? We got this babe."

Roman knew he would be ok. The NHL and its PR team were stellar, the best at what they did. They were no strangers to cleaning up a player's dirty laundry, he just couldn't stand that it was *his* dirty laundry that needed cleaning.

Roman pushed himself hard on the treadmill after his call with Melissa. He pushed his run in hopes that he could also push away the anger that was bubbling in his gut. Owning up to any fault just didn't sit right. But this was his life. He chose to be a professional athlete and with that came compromise and discipline.

He ran faster.

Discipline with his body, with his diet, with his relationships, and even with his indiscretions.

He ran faster.

He loved women. He loved the thrill of someone new. He loved the game, the chase, and the catch.

He ran faster.

He loved sex. It was his drug of choice. It was like an addiction, his only way to relieve his stress. Why had he never considered that if *he* could be addicted to it, these women might be that way too? He never wanted to hurt anyone.

He ran faster.

But he had always made it clear what the arrangement was. Pleasure for the sake of pleasure. No feelings, no emotions, just pure enjoyment.

He ran faster.

But wasn't that what an addict said the first time they tried a drug they thought would be recreational? Just this one time. Just once, they wanted to feel euphoric and high.

Faster.

He knew that's what he was for these women. And he knew, even with all his boundaries and consent he somehow missed that sex wasn't emotionless for everyone. Everyone he slept with didn't fear commitment or intimacy. He was *their* drug. Of course they wanted more. He was rich, he was fit, he was famous—he was their brand of heroin.

He slammed the emergency stop button and fell to the floor beside the workout equipment. His heart felt like it might explode.

He wouldn't apologize for the picture and he wouldn't admit fault. This woman needed to check herself into rehab and get over her addiction. You can't blame the drug if *you* choose to take it.

The food Melissa had delivered came just as he finished his shower. He put on a fresh sweat suit, raked his fingers through wet brown waves, and went to get the food. When he opened his front door a gust of Santa Ana winds hit him, and standing in front of him was the delivery girl, with an absurd amount of bags of food dangling from her arms.

He couldn't help but laugh. He *was* starving, but this was enough food to feed a small village.

The delivery girl scowled and held out her arms firmly for him to take the bags.

"Sorry," he said, taking the food from her hands. "I wasn't laughing at you, it's just, this is a lot of food is all."

"Is this all for you?" she asked.

"Yeah, my assistant ordered it for me. She always overdoes it."

He could see the girl peeking into his home, taking in the lavish lifestyle he lived while she was out on Christmas Eve delivering food.

"Why are you alone during the holidays?" she asked, perplexed by his empty house.

"Why are *you* delivering food on Christmas Eve?" he flirted back. His stomach fluttered at her simplicity. She was naturally beautiful. A small dusting of freckles spread across her nose and rosy cheeks. She didn't have much makeup on or fancy clothes. She was the girl-next-door kind of beautiful. The kind of girl you grow up with, never realizing how perfect they are, always friend-zoning her and treating her like one of the boys until it hits you that you're in love with her, and it's usually too late.

"Isn't it obvious?" she asked, "Why else would I be out delivering food on a holiday?"

Roman felt like it *should* be obvious why she was out delivering food on Christmas Eve, only, it wasn't to him. He had never lived an obvious life. He had never worked a real job. He had always just played hockey. Even before he was drafted, all he did was play.

"I'm sorry, it's *not* obvious. Surely you have someone to spend the holidays with?" he said.

This made her huff in annoyance, causing Roman to smile even more. And not because he was a dick that liked to annoy people, but because he was finding himself genuinely intrigued by her.

"Surely *you* have someone to spend the holidays with," she said back, and he was fairly certain she was *not* flirting with him.

"It's complicated."

She rolled her eyes, not buying his copout and shrugged her shoulders again. "I'm an intern who makes shit money, happy? I deliver food for this place when I'm not at my internship. Although, I don't recommend food delivery this time of year. People's wallets are exhausted from the holidays and the tips suck." He watched her cheeks flush and she instantly began to backtrack. "I shouldn't have said that. It's obvious you're loaded. I'm not trying to make you feel sorry for me. It's just, well, it's true..."

Roman leaned into his house and set the bags of food on the floor by the front door, "It's fine. Even if you *were* hinting that you want a good tip I wouldn't be offended because you're right, I am rich, and I know that sounds arrogant, but it's facts. I can say it without feeling bad because I worked hard for this house *and* the ability to tip really well—even during the holidays."

The girl smiled just a hint before rolling her eyes at his blatant arrogance. It was the cutest thing Roman had ever seen, and maybe, just maybe, she *was* flirting back. He wanted to make her smile more, hell, he wanted to make her roll her eyes more. Something about this slightly awkward and incredibly beautiful woman's reaction to him made his entire body tingle in a goofy, puppy love sort of way.

"Well, if you wouldn't mind, I would actually like to tip you really well, for working on the holidays, and because my bank account *isn't* exhausted."

She took a step back, distancing herself from him at the mention of a tip. A gust of Santa Ana wind hit her, causing her shoulder-length brown hair to blow into her face and for a second he wondered if the wind might just sweep her away. Sheltering herself from the winds, the delivery girl stepped forward again, back into the entryway of his lavish modern home. It took everything in Roman's power to stop himself from stepping toward her to brush the unruly curls from her face.

"No." she said assertively. "No generous tip. The standard tip will suffice. I don't want your charity."

It was in this moment Roman realized he would do anything to steal a few more minutes of her time. He had been grounded for less than

24 hours and he was already grasping for any kind of female attention he could get, like a true addict.

Maybe he *was* the problem.

"What's your name?" he asked intently. He genuinely needed a name to put with her face.

"Grace," she said, followed up with another simple shoulder shrug.

Grace. How pure, and perfect, and fitting.

Her phone buzzed and she scrambled to pull it from the pocket of her oversized sweatshirt.

"I gotta go. I have another delivery," she said. Another text came through and she instantly looked annoyed after she read it, "Ugh, the bad part of town. Wish me luck..." she paused, hinting at not knowing *his* name.

"Roman," he said, realizing for the first time since she had shown up that she had no clue who he was, "Roman Graves," he said, this time adding the last name to see if it rang a bell. Because in Los Angeles, Roman Graves was a household name.

She just gave him a nod of approval and went to leave. She had no clue who he was, and he *loved* it.

She turned back to him. "Happy Holidays, Roman Graves. Enjoy your feast," she said with a bashful grin.

"Be safe out there Grace."

She shrugged her shoulders one last time, as if saying, 'I'll try' and then she was gone.

Roman took the bags of food to the bar in his kitchen and began to eat. It wasn't until he got the text from Melissa asking if his food had been delivered that he realized he had somehow *still* managed not to tip her.

Chapter Two

R oman woke the next day to a string of text messages from teammates wishing him a happy holiday accompanied with a lot of inappropriate jokes about Santa, memes, and even a few last minute offers for him to come celebrate with their families. He also received the typical, generic text message from his father, thanking him for the gifts–Melissa, his PA had sent–and wishing him a happy and healthy holiday.

He spent the remainder of his morning on the couch watching Sports Center until his face was plastered on the TV screen again with the reporter covering his nudes leak. He knew it would be in the headlines over the holidays. With hockey on break, it would be the best news they had to cover.

His mind wondered, leading him to think of Grace, his delivery girl and what she might be up to today. Would she be with her family, or her boyfriend? He could see her dating the sweet, intellectual type. Maybe a nerdy guy; like her. Not that nerdy looked bad on her, she was gorgeous, and she didn't need all the makeup and fillers, and bleach to make her that way. He liked the way she looked so comfortable in her leggings and high-top converse and an oversized hoodie. He couldn't help but wonder if she had stolen the hoodie from her boyfriend. But if she had a boyfriend, why would she be delivering food on Christmas Eve? What kind of jerk-off would let their girlfriend work on a holiday?

Did that make Roman a jerk-off in turn? Ordering takeout on Christmas Eve? He didn't know, and he wouldn't let the idea of it stop him from looking up the restaurant to see if they were open to order food again–despite having tons of leftovers from the night before. If they were open, he had to take his chances at seeing Grace again. This time he wouldn't forget her tip.

He called the restaurant and placed his order, making sure to thank the woman for being open on the holiday.

The wait began.

He put on Scream and watched as Drew Barrymore was hacked up on her front lawn. Her hair was short, like Grace's, except Grace was a brunette and she didn't have bangs–so not really like Grace at all, but that didn't stop him from thinking about her.

Roman had never really been into short hair or brunettes for that matter. Or maybe the way he grew up, and the women he was constantly surrounded by, had misconstrued what he truly found beautiful. His mother was tall, blonde, and thin. The women he usually slept with were tall, blonde, and thin. Grace was the opposite of that. She was just tall enough that if he let himself consider it–and he did–he could imagine her fitting perfectly against his body. Her curves pressed against his hard lines.

The food came quicker than he expected. He pressed pause on the movie and stopped to check his appearance before he opened the door. If it was Grace, he wanted to impress her. Usually, he only had to confess he was a professional athlete, and the women were putty in his hands, but he didn't want to use that angle on Grace. *That* angle had already gotten him into enough trouble.

When he opened the door, he found Grace standing there, her arm held out with a single bag of food, and a knowing smile on her face. She wore an old Dodgers baseball cap tonight to keep her hair from blowing in the insane winds they were having, her hair tucked behind her ears did a sort of flip out at the ends. She was wearing the same oversized sweatshirt as the night before, only tonight she had thick fluffy socks on with a pair of worn-in Birkenstocks.

"You again," he said, taking the bag of food, but not without giving her his most flirty smile. A smile that had all of its teeth, which was a treat considering he had been in the NHL long enough to have lost a few by now.

"Sorry to disappoint you on Christmas," she said, her eyebrows raised accusingly, but the smirk on her face showed that she was amused, maybe even a little charmed.

"Disappointed?" He asked, "This is the best Christmas gift I got this year."

She shook her head in mock disbelief. "You must not have gotten many gifts if take-out is the best one you got."

His smile fell from his face, and in all seriousness, he said, "I wasn't talking about the food, Grace."

This statement alone seemed to knock the breath out of her lungs. She was clearly taken aback by his outright flirting. He wondered what it would be like to actually date a girl like Grace. So far, he had gathered the obvious things about her; she was beautiful, a bit feisty, and a hard worker. And the best part, she didn't have a clue who he was.

What would dating a woman who didn't care about a loaded bank account look like to a man with a reputation like Roman's?

His conclusion: He would break this sweet girl's heart. Girls like Grace, who delivered food on holidays and blushed so easily, did not belong with guys like Roman. Roman knew guys like him should never have a girl around longer than one night at a time. He knew there was a generational curse lingering in the dark corners of his life, a curse his dad had bestowed upon him; the curse of infidelity.

She finally spoke up, breaking the silence that had formed between them. "Can I ask you something before I go? If I don't, I think I'll wonder about it for the rest of my life."

"Ask away." he said, leaning into the doorframe.

"I'm just curious why someone with a house like this," she paused. He watched as her cheeks grew rose-colored, "And a face and body like that, is alone on Christmas ordering takeout?"

Roman considered being honest. Letting her know it was because his naked body was now searchable on the internet. And because he was in trouble with the NHL. And because he slept around and hurt women in the process. But he didn't. He took the easy way out, because despite knowing that tonight would most likely be the last time he would see Grace, he didn't want her to leave thinking less of him.

"I just needed some time alone and this was the only time I'll have off for a while. So, I'm laying low," he lied. Well, half lied. Or maybe, he didn't lie at all, he just withheld some truth.

"I get that entirely. I can't remember the last time I allowed myself to slow down."

"You should treat yourself to a break sometime," he said.

She just shrugged off his suggestion. He knew she would leave soon and the second she was gone she would have saved herself from getting tangled up in his bullshit.

"One day I'll slow down," she said, taking a deep breath, her chest puffing out with pride, "But for now I gotta keep pushing through this season of life," she started to leave, and then turned back to face him, the smile on her face was simple, and sincere. "Enjoy your food, Roman Graves."

He called out to her, remembering the tip. "Wait, I have a little something for you," he reached to grab the envelope off the entryway table, the name *Grace* scribbled in his best chicken scratch on the front.

He handed it to her, and she looked down at it with confusion, her nose scrunched up, her smile gone.

"What's this?" she asked.

"Just a card I had left over from last year, and a small, *reasonable* tip for keeping you out on Christmas," he lied with a wink.

"You didn't have to do that," she protested.

"I know, but let me, okay?" he asked, his eyes softer, and pleading.

"Fine," she agreed and shrugged her shoulders, which he was finding to be her signature move. She put the card in the front pocket of her oversized hoodie and patted it for safekeeping.

"Merry Christmas, Grace. I hope you get a chance to take a break sooner than later."

"Merry Christmas, Roman, I hope you figure out whatever it was that caused you to spend the holidays alone."

Me too, Roman thought, *me, too.*

Chapter Three

After her final delivery on Christmas, Grace Fairchild took the order of sticky buns gifted to her from the owners of Thai Spoon up to her loft above the restaurant where she lived. She put her favorite Beatles album on–Rubber Soul–to play in the background as she ate her dessert with a hot cup of tea.

The loft was quiet when her roommate, Jess, wasn't around, and Grace was grateful for the sounds of John, Paul, George, and Ringo that filled the small space while she was alone. She had been invited to go with Jess to her family's house for the holidays, but Grace needed the money from deliveries, so she opted to work instead.

She settled into the old broken-down couch she had thrifted to relax for the remainder of the night when she felt a crunch in the front pocket of her hoodie. She pulled the Christmas card from Roman out and her heart began to hammer inside her chest at the very thought of him.

She knew she would never see him again, now that she was done delivering for the holidays, but she could allow herself to enjoy the few moments they had spent together on repeat in her mind for a little while. That should be okay, *right*? She could let her mind linger on the way his smile was so genuine when he was standing there tonight. She could allow herself just this small token of romance to hold her over until she was ready to start dating again.

She opened the envelope from Roman and was shocked to find a beautiful Christmas card inside. It was a variation of blue and silver foil snowflakes that glittered under the lights of her modest Christmas tree. It dawned on her that it was the only Christmas card she had received this year, causing her heart to ache for something she didn't realize she was so desperately lacking.

Her aunt and uncle, who had raised her since she was eleven, had called to wish her a Merry Christmas but that was it. They didn't have much of a relationship since she had moved to LA. To be honest, they hadn't had much of a relationship before that; just because someone raises you doesn't mean they feel like family.

When she went to open the card from Roman several bills fell into her lap. She held the money in her hands and was shocked to find that it was not a modest tip at all; even rich people knew that four hundred dollars was an absurd amount of money to tip the delivery girl. At first, Grace felt pure joy at the sight of the money. She couldn't recall the last time she had hundreds of dollars that wasn't already spent on a bill, or a textbook, or food. Before she even let herself get too excited about the money, her rationale kicked in and she knew this was absurd. There was no way she could accept this kind of gift, or tip, or charity, or whatever it was this Roman character was playing at.

She could kick herself for saying the tips had been bad during the holidays. She didn't say it with the intention of him doing *this*. It was just a slip of the tongue. She was certain this insane amount of money to her was nothing more than pocket change for a man that lived in a house like that, but that was beside the point. She didn't need charity.

She wasn't some good deed for some handsome rich guy to get off on, filling his own cup, and playing the hero.

Tomorrow she would give the money back. It would hurt to see it go, but she couldn't live with herself if she kept it. She would always feel a lingering sense of obligation to him. She had worked too hard and come too far on her own to take handouts now.

If he wanted to tip her for the two nights of deliveries, she could do the math for him. Twenty percent would suffice.

Annoyed with her inability to do anything about the tip at this hour, she turned off the record player, deciding to call it a night. Christmas was never a holiday she celebrated anyway. What even *was* Christmas when you didn't have anyone to celebrate it with?

The next morning, Grace woke up early despite it being her day off from her internship. She knew it was a losing game trying to go back to sleep for many reasons, the first being she had never been great at wasting time, the second being Roman and the four hundred dollars he had given her last night.

She considered keeping the money one last time, it would be a huge financial relief for her. When would she ever have money fall into her lap like this again? Because it had literally *fallen* into her lap from the card. But the deciding factor on whether or not she would return the money was one she wasn't proud of, but she had never claimed to be perfect. That factor being: If she returned the money, she would have a reason to see him one last time. It wasn't her finest moment, but she was human, and humans were needy creatures if nothing else.

She got ready quickly, not wanting to talk herself out of going to his house unannounced. She put on a pair of high waisted jeans, her black high-top chucks, and an oversized hoodie. She pulled a mauve beanie over her bed head to keep her hair from blowing all over the place in the wind, and looked at herself one last time on the way out only to realize she could have tried harder not to look like a poor intern. Only she *was* a poor intern. That's what had gotten her into this mess in the first place.

Her car still smelled like Thai food, and she hoped it wouldn't cling to her clothes like it normally did after a long night of deliveries. She put his address into her phone and pressed play on a Beatles mix to try and calm her nerves. Only, her favorite songs didn't help this time, and the Beatles *always* helped.

When she finally arrived, his house managed to be far more impressive in the daytime than it had been the past two nights. She took in the expensive landscape, the perfectly manicured hedges, and beautiful array of seasonal flowers. The fine details in the home's architecture made her reconsider one last time if she should return the money; he clearly didn't need it. What did this Roman character do to afford this house, a doctor or a lawyer or some kind of Hollywood movie guy perhaps.

She nervously made her way to the grand front doors of his home. The enclosure of it saved her from the deathly Santa Ana winds that wouldn't stop. Before she could talk herself out of it she rang the doorbell, then nervously stuck her hands into the front pocket of her hoodie. The feeling of the hundred-dollar bills keeping her company as she waited for the door to open.

Chapter Four

Roman wasn't expecting anyone over. Melissa hadn't told him of any visitors on the calendar for today. It *could* be paparazzi but that wasn't likely. Sure he was in the NHL headlines, but NHL gossip rarely crossed over into actual celebrity gossip; he wasn't a fucking Kardashian.

He paused his workout and went to check the monitor in his gym to see who was at his front door, at nine in the morning, the day after Christmas.

Standing on his front porch was Grace, his delivery girl. She was looking down at her feet, avoiding eye contact with the doorbell camera, her hands tucked away in the pocket of her pullover.

He knew instantly why she was there unannounced, and he was certain it had nothing to do with Thai food and everything to do with the Christmas card he had given her.

He wondered last night if it was too much. Then after thinking about it, he *knew* it was too much but Roman, being Roman, didn't care so he gave her the large tip anyway. He knew it might piss her off, or get under her skin, but he definitely didn't anticipate *this*.

He pulled a white t-shirt over his bare sweaty chest, and made his way from his personal gym to the front door. Her eyes shot up to meet his when he opened it, and then, without her even realizing what she was doing, he watched as her eyes left his and raked over his body on display, his sweaty hair, the cotton tee clinging to his sweaty chest, the way his athletic shorts hugged his thighs.

He smiled. Sweet, *sweet*, Grace. It was evident she liked what she saw. He just stood there, with a cocky grin on his face. He watched as she physically shook her head, as if snapping herself out of a daze and put her 'angry' face back on. He found her angry face to be less intimidating than it was cute, the way her full lips puckered a bit, as if she were pouting.

"What is *this*?" she said, pulling out the crisp bills from her pocket.

Roman leaned into the door frame, crossing his arms over his chest nonchalantly. "A tip," he said, a coy smile on his face.

"No, no. A tip is four dollars on the low end, and twenty if you're lucky. Four hundred dollars is what you would pay someone that delivers more than food, if you know what I mean," she huffed.

She was *undeniably* cute when she was mad.

"Grace," he started.

"Don't you *Grace* me. You can't go around giving people four hundred dollar tips, *Roman*," she said.

"And why not?" he asked, the smirk on his face only infuriating her more. He found it all rather amusing and not in the least bit problematic.

"Because it's rude," she said, and crossed her arms over her chest. However, *her* arms crossed over *her* chest were far less nonchalant than his, and more of a stance of dominance, which Roman found to also be extremely cute and not intimidating in the least.

"It's my money. I can do with it as I please," he said, even-tempered.

"Well, I don't need your pity," she said, *uneven-tempered*.

"I don't pity you. In fact, I admire you." he offered.

"Well, I don't need some strong, rich, handsome man admiring me right now. I'm too busy. And I couldn't live with myself if I kept it." she admitted.

"Why won't you let me be generous?"

Now *he* was starting to get frustrated. He just wanted to take care of her, to show her he appreciated her. He knew it was a lot of money to a lot of people. He wasn't a stupid or naive man, but he wasn't trying to *buy* her. He didn't need to buy women for sex; women would sleep with him just to say they had slept with him. He just wanted to do something good before he released his statement tomorrow about the sex scandal. Because he knew what he was about to say, and after he said it there was a good chance no one was going to see him the same way again.

"I don't need your generosity Roman," she said, and he knew it was a lie, she had told him that she was a struggling intern. She absolutely needed his generosity, but he could tell somewhere in her life her pride had grown to be as thick as his, he knew that kind of pride all too well.

"Fine," he said, taking the money from her hands. "Fine, no generosity Grace, I get it. I see now that I've crossed a line with you, but that's only because I don't know anything about you."

She took a timid step back, her face flushed with all kinds of uncertainty.

He continued, "Tell me who you are?"

"I'm Grace," she said, adding her signature shoulder shrug. "I'm just Grace, and I have to go. I have a lot to do today." she started to step away.

"Wait, that's not what I meant. I know your name–which I find to be the most fitting name for a person I've ever met– but that's not what

I mean. I want you to tell me something about yourself," he asked, and he knew he shouldn't.

He wasn't supposed to see her again. He wasn't supposed to get the opportunity to know her. He wasn't a good man, and she was *everything*. She was a girl who worked on Christmas and returned four hundred dollar tips. But he knew what tomorrow held. He knew what his reputation looked like in the headlines, and Grace was two Google searches away from finding out exactly what kind of man Roman Graves was.

But he asked anyway.

"One thing, tell me *one* thing about yourself Grace."

She hesitated, and then, as if in a moment of weakness said, "I'm really focused on my future right now. And as you've now learned firsthand, I'm extremely prideful and hard-headed."

Her face relaxed a bit, and he watched as her arms fell to her side, easing up on the dominant stance she had tried to pull off and failed.

"I didn't mean to offend you Grace," he said gently. A peace offering, an olive branch of sorts.

"Well, I don't know what kind of company you usually surround yourself with, but if they're easily inclined to take your money then, spoiler alert, you might not be hanging around with the right kind of people."

"You're probably right," he agreed, and noticed her take a step back further, looking over her shoulder towards her car, an old green Toyota Corolla.

"I should really get going though. It's been..." she paused, "It's been kinda strange, hasn't it? The last few days?"

"Yeah, I think so," he agreed.

"Take care of yourself, Roman," she said, and began to walk away.

"Can I take you out to dinner?" he shouted after her before he could remind himself that it was a bad idea. He didn't date, but something about Grace made him want to try.

She turned back to him, and he knew she was thinking about it. She frowned a bit, scrunching up her nose. "I just don't think it's a good time for me to, you know, get distracted."

Roman hated how surprised he was by this. He hated that there wasn't a doubt in his mind that she wouldn't say yes. And here she was, saying *no*.

"When's a good time then?" he asked, taking a few steps forward to close the gap she had put between them.

"I don't know, I'm just really busy."

"Next weekend?" he asked.

"I'm busy." she shrugged.

"Two weeks? I'll be back in town again in two weeks." he pleaded, wracking his brain when his team would be home after their long road trip on the East Coast.

"Busy," she said again–no hesitation.

It stung a bit, and now *his* pride was under fire.

"A month? Surely, you're not busy in a month."

Grace shrugged her shoulders, and he knew, he *knew* what it meant. Over the course of three days, that shoulder shrug had meant many things, but today, he knew it meant *no*.

"I can't. I'm just really busy," she said again, and disappointment lined *her* face.

If she was disappointed, why didn't she just say yes? Find time? Go on a date with him?

"When are you not busy? You tell me when and I'll wait. And if you don't want to go on a date with me then, I won't ask you again. You have my word."

Grace looked down at her hands and fidgeted with a simple gold ring she wore on her pointer finger. Roman held his breath.

"Four months?" she asked hesitantly, drawing her shoulders up nervously. Because she knew four months was a ridiculous ask, but he gave her the option to be ridiculous, and her answer said it all.

She *really* was busy.

Roman knew she was an intern somewhere. He knew internships could make or break your career, and he would respect that, he had to, because he gave her his word, and because if anyone understood being unavailable, it was professional athletes.

This was for the best.

"Four months, huh?" he asked playfully, and her shoulders eased up a bit.

"I just can't afford to be distracted right now, and you seem like you could be very distracting," she said, her simple smile back on her face. The word *distracting* laced with so much more meaning than your typical kind of distraction—a phone call during a movie, a baby crying during a flight—the way she said it meant so much more than that.

Roman liked the idea of distracting her. He liked it so much he agreed to her terms and made empty promises.

"Okay, four months," he said.

He held out his hand for her phone and she hesitantly handed it over.

"You better not bail on me in four months Grace," he said, punching in his number, pausing before he added the last name Graves.

He handed her phone back and she put it in her pocket.

"Text me so I have your number in four months, okay?"

Grace smiled and shook her head. "I will," she said, turning to leave. Looking back over her shoulder she added, "*Four* months Roman."

He knew he wouldn't wait for her, and it made him feel sad. She was worth it for sure. But hopefully four months would cure him of his little obsession with her that would only end in her heart broken. In four months, he would be balls deep in playoff hockey, and the shock of his scandal would be water under the bridge, and he would be back to his old ways indulging in his sexual endeavors, and Grace would be a distant memory.

But he agreed, looking down to punch something into his phone, causing him to miss the last moments he had with Grace, as she walked away.

Chapter Five

R oman cleared his throat and sat up straight at the press table, the Los Angeles Knights logo behind him on the wall. Melissa adjusted his mic and while leaning in to fix his tie she whispered, "Just stick to what I wrote up for you, try and steer the conversation back to hockey, and how it's your number one focus. If they ask personal questions about you and her, go back to hockey. And whatever you do, don't let them get under your skin, babe."

He cleared his throat again, it suddenly felt extremely dry. Roman had done more interviews than he could count; post-game, pre-game, you name it, but he had never been in the hot seat like this.

Over the holiday break he had thought about this interview a lot, and he knew it would be a different vibe than all his other interviews, but he didn't expect *this*. He looked around the room, so many people had showed up to hear his apology. He had dealt with press before, but this was *negative* press; it made his heart race. He ran his hand over the nervous sweat on his brow, then wiped it on his pants. He could do this, he had to. He just had to tell them what they wanted to hear and it would be old news.

He cleared his throat again, and without asking, Melissa brought him a bottle of water.

"Are we ready to go?" he asked, looking over at Coach Hibbs. His coach gave him a thumbs up and Roman cleared his throat one last time before he leaned into the mic and began to speak.

***

Grace sat at the tall bar table with her roommate Jess, and Jess's best friends, Chris and Mia, who had become Grace's friends by default. It was packed with college students, but tonight it seemed louder than normal. The televisions all had sports on, but music played over any sound coming from the TV.

Today marked the first day back to her internship with The Los Angeles Drug and Alcohol Recovery Center. Grace needed four months worth of full-time hours to get her certification to become a CADC. When she got to the facility that morning, she had been blindsided to discover she was assigned a new mentor. And after working with him for one day she already felt defeated. He was good, *really* good at what he did, but he kept contradicting her, and making her feel like she was the patient, not the intern. She started seeing patients on her own under her last mentor before *he* showed up. Now, he came in and wanted to see her "skill set" and it drove her crazy, it felt like a major setback. She hated being doubted, or treated like she was stupid, and that was exactly how this new guy had made her feel. The last person she worked under, Dr. Meredith Williams, had treated her like an equal. This new doctor, Dr. Wayne Gandy, gave off toxic masculinity vibes.

She couldn't wait to be done with her supervised work hours so she could do this on her own. Without the pressure of having to prove herself to anyone.

Grace knew she was going to be a great counselor once she got her certification. She had even gotten her master's degree in behavioral science at UCLA before she started her internship. She knew she was going to be a good counselor because this wasn't just a job to her. She was doing it for her dad—or the memory of him. She had seen firsthand what drugs could do to a family after losing her own father to addiction, and she vowed to spend her life helping others avoid that same fate.

Grace sullenly picked at a chicken wing, defeated from her day, as Jess and her friends shared animated stories of their holiday break.

"How was your holiday, Gracey?" Jess asked.

Grace sat the chicken wing down, her appetite nonexistent with the stress from her day lingering.

"I just worked. Delivered food for Thai Spoon." Grace said. And while she gave her friends the bare minimum of details about her holiday, she secretly wanted to scream and shout about meeting her mystery man, Roman.

"You should have come home with me," Jess said, shoving cheese fries in her mouth mid-sentence.

"Maybe next year," Grace said with fingers crossed, because next year she hoped she would have a full-time job at the Los Angeles rehab facility, and enough money to stop delivering food during her free time just to be able to survive.

Grace felt her face blush, and her body sank down a bit, before adding, "I did meet someone?" she said with uncertainty.

Jess squealed and Chris finished his beer, slamming the cup on the table as they all began to encourage her to tell them *everything*–they were a dramatic group. They were instantly excited for some steamy gossip from Grace. Only Grace wasn't sure it was all that steamy, unless they considered steamy to be really rich guys with tight white shirts sticking to sweaty abdominal muscles. In which case, yes, her interactions with Roman were pretty steamy.

"It's not a big deal. Nothing happened." Grace said unenthusiastically. She really didn't want to make this out to be something bigger than it was, especially with Jess being who *she* was, and her ability to blow everything out of proportion for the sake of entertainment.

"Okay, but you *did* meet someone?" Jess pried.

Grace couldn't help it. She couldn't contain it. She thought of the three days and her smile grew wide as her cheeks flushed with the memory of Roman.

She began, "Okay, so I was delivering for Thai Spoon—"

"Yeah," Mia cut her off, "skip the boring part. Who is he and when are you going to see him again?"

Grace laughed, because it *was* truly laughable. All of it. The whole past three days, when she thought about it.

Grace cleared her throat and began, "So, I get a huge delivery on Christmas Eve in the Hills, and I'm expecting it to be a bunch of rich people drunk at a holiday party."

"Ew, " Chris chimed in, "the worst kind of people. Tell me more."

"Well, I show up and this house is, like, insane. It's not huge, but it's LA huge, does that make sense?" she asked.

"Yeah, we get it, he lives in the Hills. Get to the sex," Jess demanded with an exaggerated amount of anticipation.

Grace rolled her eyes, and shook her head. "Spoiler alert–this story is PG-13 at most, and that's only because one time his feet were bare, and that seemed oddly intimate," Grace said, and they all agreed.

"Okay, so I show up to this mini mansion and I have to maneuver about ten bags of Thai food in my arms."

"That's me every time I get groceries, honey," Chris said. They all laughed, and Grace went on.

"I manage to get all the food in one go and head up the long driveway to this house, fully expecting to be greeted by some drunk rich housewife, but when the door opened, it was just one guy."

"Sounds like a horror movie," Mia said in her overly monotone voice.

"Tell me he's super-hot, and shirtless with washboard abs, please, lie to me, Grace." Jess pleaded playfully.

"It's better than that," Grace teased, and the whole table of her rambunctious, and slightly drunk friends went silent with anticipation.

Grace made them wait a beat, playing into their dramatics, then she dropped the bomb.

"Tight. Gray. Sweatpants." she said, breaking up each word into its own statement.

Her friends went wild. Chris began to fan himself dramatically. Mia held her cool beer to her warm cheeks as Jess began to shake Grace frantically. They recently had the conversation of how gray sweatpants were possibly the hottest thing a man could wear if done right.

"So, there I am, wind blowing my hair in my face, bags of food in my arms, looking like a whole mess, and he just takes the food, and we start to casually talk. He was smiling–a lot, and looking at me–like, *really* looking at me? Like, maybe he thought I was cute? Which is bonkers because I looked like I had just rolled out of bed."

Chris snorted. "Honey, don't lie, you know you *had* just rolled out of bed."

"Okay, I *had* just rolled out of bed," she corrected. "He asked for my name, and then when he said it–and I may have imagined this–but he let it roll off his tongue like it was some kind of sensual moment. It was–*hot*? He was hot. Like, absurdly hot. And a little cocky. He knew he was rich and flaunted it a bit. He said he wanted to give me a 'good' tip and I told him just a standard tip would do. But then I left, and he forgot to tip me anyway."

No one responded, they just looked at her like they would stab her if she didn't go on.

"The next night, I got another delivery to the same address. I secretly hoped it had nothing to do with the food and everything to do with this man wanting to see me again. When I showed up it was just him again. We ended up talking a bit, and I had my guard up, as I often do, and when I went to leave, he gave me a Christmas card. I was certain it was the last time I would see him because he didn't ask for my number or anything."

"Please tell me he put his number in the card. Please tell me you have plans to fuck him in every room of that gorgeous house of his?" Jess begged.

"Nope, not his number," she said, leaving them on a bit of a cliffhanger.

"A bloody finger?" Mia asked, "No, no, his ear?"

They all laughed, and Grace went on, "No, not body parts, thank god. When I got home, I opened the envelope and when I pulled out the card, money fell out of it."

Being that they were all broke college students or interns they gasped at the mention of money.

"I quickly realized it wasn't ones, or fives, or twenties even. He gave me four hundred dollars. And the card just read, `A tip for Grace. Love, Roman.`"

"Roman? What a strong manly name," Mia said.

"Right?" Grace asked, "That's what I thought too."

"So, he didn't give you his number?" Jess asked.

"No, and that didn't even disappoint me at the moment. I didn't really expect anything to come from it. I mean, I'm in no position to meet new people. You know how swamped I am."

"You make yourself swamped because you *don't* want to meet new people," Jess corrected her.

And Grace knew there was truth in that, but she was also genuinely busy.

"I didn't even expect his number, so when I saw the money, I just got mad. I felt like an idiot. It made me feel like he hadn't been flirting with me to begin with, like maybe he just pitied me, or something."

"Please tell me that at the end of this story you kept the money." Chris asked, doubt lined his every word.

"Please," Jess said, rolling her eyes, "This is Grace, we all know how this story ends."

"You donated it to charity?" Mia asked, "Please tell me it wasn't the red Salvation Army bucket in front of the Sprouts. That guy is a fraud."

"No, I didn't donate it. I went to his house yesterday and gave it back."

They all gasped in disbelief.

"This isn't a romance story; this *is* a horror story. Mia, you were right. Now who's going to buy us another round if you didn't keep the money." Chris pouted.

"You're right. I didn't keep the money, but when I went back he *did* ask me on a date. More like, he begged me to go on a date."

"He *is* a murderer. I knew it. Hot rich guys don't beg unless they have bodies decomposing in vats of acid in their garage," Mia said.

"Mia, you're morbid, and I think you need to talk to someone about it," Jess said.

"It's Netflix, I can't stop watching murder documentaries," Mia admitted sadly.

"So," Jess pressed, "When's the date?"

"It's..." Grace paused, knowing damn well they were all about to give her hell, "It's in four months. I told him to call me in four months." She slouched into her chair as her friends began to shout at her.

"Four months? What is wrong with you, Grace?" Jess demanded.

"I'm busy with my internship. I can't take on any new distractions."

"But this isn't the worst kind of distraction to have, Grace. When was the last time you went on a date? Let someone care for you?" Jess asked in all seriousness.

"I don't know—never?"

"So, did you get his number? Has he communicated with you since?" Jess asked.

"I have his number. I haven't texted him yet to give him mine. I'm afraid if I do, he'll ask me out again and I won't be able to say no."

Jess aggressively reached across the table. "Give me your damn phone."

Grace, under the pressure of Jess's aggressiveness, obliged, and handed her phone over.

"Roman...Roman..." Jess said, as she opened a new text message thread, "Roman *Graves*?" she asked, her face suddenly less aggressive and more shocked.

"Yeah, Roman Graves," Grace confirmed, and everyone at the table looked at each other like they were all in on a joke that Grace was on the butt end of.

"What?" Grace asked incredulously.

"Roman *Graves*?" Mia asked again.

"Yes, why?"

Jess pointed up to the TV screen directly behind Grace. "You mean *that* Roman Graves?"

Grace slowly turned around, afraid of what she might see, and staring back at her from the TV screen was the man she had spent the last three days flirting with. He was giving some kind of press conference on television, and while she didn't know much about sports, she knew it was the Los Angeles Knights hockey logo plastered behind him. In the corner of the TV screen was a box with a picture in it, and in the picture was a beautiful blonde woman smiling a toothy grin, wrapped up in a bed sheet, and asleep next to her was a *very* naked, *very* blurred out image of Roman Graves.

Chapter Six

"I would like to start by saying that I have nothing but the utmost respect for my team and the NHL. Those two things alone are my main focus. My only priority is leading this team to victory. Recently, I spent the night with a woman I am not in a relationship with. There was complete consent by both parties involved and I thought that was enough. At the time, I did not consider that her feelings or emotions could have become tethered to what we did together and for that I am sorry. The NHL does not, and never will tolerate the disrespect of anyone regardless of their sex, ethnicity, or religion. For that I apologize to the NHL, my team, and my coach for putting a negative light on our organization and stress on our game. I came here to apologize to the woman who..."

Roman paused, his eyes became blurry with rage, and his heart hammered in his chest as the sounds of the press room became a distant ringing in his ears. Why did *she* get an apology for a picture *she* posted of him for all the world to see? Why was he the one apologizing when he was the one that had intimate pictures of himself leaked by *her*?

Fuck that.

He wouldn't do it; he wouldn't apologize for something he wasn't in the wrong for. He wouldn't tarnish his reputation because some puck bunny caught feelings.

"You know what, on second thought, I don't apologize to her. That woman took an intimate picture of me while I was asleep and shared it with the world. I asked for her consent before we had intercourse and she gave it. I told her it was a one time thing, and she agreed to those terms. I made it extremely clear that I don't date, I have no intentions on dating and she told me she understood. I made it very clear that it was sex for the sake of sex. The only thing that did not have consent that night was the pictures that were taken of *me*. If it had been me that had taken a picture of her, naked in bed after having had relations, I would have been canceled. So, no, I won't apologize for something *she* knowingly did. I won't apologize to her for something she did to *me* that has been detrimental to *my* team, and the NHL, and ultimately my privacy. I'm sorry if that isn't what you all came to hear, but if anyone still sees me as the problem then that's on them. I refuse to accept fault here, and I refuse to offer a settlement for the bogus claims this woman has made against me. Accepting fault will only allow others to think they can do the same thing and get away with it in the future, and I refuse to have any part in signing off on that kind of abuse. Thank you all for coming, I can't wait to get on the ice tonight and secure another win for the city of Los Angeles."

***

Grace and Jess sat curled up on the couch, watching Roman's press conference on YouTube for the third time. Graces' insides burned with disappointment. This wasn't the same guy she met over the weekend. He was so kind, and easy, and he asked her on a *date*. Did a date with him just mean casual sex? A one-night stand?

She wanted to punch something for allowing herself to think she might have met a good one, and she hated how much time she had already let him occupy her mind.

"I made it extremely clear that I don't date, I have no intentions on dating and she told me she understood..."

Grace growled. She *literally* growled listening to him. He sounded so pompous and arrogant. Yet, while she wanted to believe he *should* be apologizing, she had to agree that the woman did an awful thing leaking intimate photos like that. Who took selfies of a naked sleeping person against their will? It did seem a little gold digger-ish if Grace was being honest. But something about his stance on it, the way he so boldly declared he was not interested in anything long term, just sex, something about that rubbed her the wrong way. Apology or not.

She pulled out her phone, and Jess swatted it away. "Oh no Grace, not now. You need to sleep on this. Don't fly off the handle and say something stupid or mean. He's already going through it."

"*He's* going through it? What about the girl he just refused to apologize to?" Grace argued.

"Oh, the one who posted naked pictures of her and Roman with obvious intentions to seek out her fifteen minutes of fame? That girl?" Jess demanded.

"She didn't even release her name."

"She didn't have to, Grace. Anyone who watches Sports Center has seen her face by now. What difference does it make if they don't know her name?"

Grace didn't know why she felt so mad about it. Maybe it was because she knew she had lost the image of him being this perfect man. Maybe it was because hearing him say those things about women and dating and sex made her feel a little misled or betrayed. Or maybe, it was because she really hoped this would be her fairytale ending–as desperate as that sounded.

She pulled out her phone from her back pocket, "I should text him."

Jess gently pushed it back into her lap, "You should give it a few days. It looks like your guy might have had enough negative attention today."

"He used her for sex, Jess." Grace stated matter-of-factly.

Jess shook her head in disbelief, "It was a one-night stand, Gracey. People do it all the time. It's just harder for guys like Roman to do it and not get caught. Women seek out men like him. If anything, *she* was using him."

Jess was right. Grace knew all of this already. But somewhere between her shitty day at her internship with her new shitty mentor, and finding out who the *true* Roman Graves was, left her feeling bitter.

She knew in the end; it didn't matter anyway. He was never going to text her in four months–not if it was just a booty call he was after. She opened up her phone, and decided that she needed to cut all ties here and now. If she didn't, she would spend the next four months thinking of him, being distracted by him, and that was the whole reason she said no to his date proposal in the first place. She needed to end things on her terms–for the sake of not being distracted.

Hey Roman. It's Grace, the delivery girl. I think it's best if you didn't text me in four months, like we agreed. You probably wouldn't have anyway, but in case you considered it, I think it's best you know that I'm probably not what you're looking for in a woman considering you don't date. Good luck this season.

She hit send, and then she deleted his contact information.

Chapter Seven

"Wat the actual fuck was that Graves?" Coach Hibbs said, storming the locker room, pressing a surprisingly strong finger into Roman's chest.

"It was me not compromising who I am," Roman said with no signs of regret.

"You put your whole team in a hard place tonight. We have a game to play and now the only thing anyone can think about is that stunt you pulled back there."

"I did what I had to, Coach. How could I sit there and tell people on such a huge platform that what that woman did to me was okay?"

"Sometimes we lie, Graves. Sometimes we fake it. You signed on to fake it," coach said, his finger stabbing into Roman's chest with each forceful word, "You have one job: Win. If this team loses because you can't keep your dick out of the headlines you might just find yourself jobless. You got that?"

Loud and clear, Roman thought.

However, Roman called his coach's bluff. They wouldn't fire him or trade him. He was the face of this franchise; this city loved him. He had led the Knights to a Stanley cup two times in the past five years.

His teammates were his family, and he, their valiant leader. He knew, however, that he absolutely needed to stay out of situations like this because he would *never* apologize. Not when he did nothing wrong. Not when he watched his father go through life never having to apologize once for the way he had treated his mother.

He just wouldn't do it. He refused to become like his dad; a man who walked around in public with so much pride, while he secretly fucked around on his wife in the shadows. A man that lived by the saying 'Do as I say, not as I do.' A man who lied so much he believed the lies, he *lived* in them. Roman would *not* become his father.

He could feel the presence of someone behind him before he heard a familiar voice ask, "Need a hug?"

Roman shook his head. "I need us to win tonight, that's what I need."

Roman's best friend, and the best right winger in the NHL, Liam Harvey stood behind him.

"It's Anaheim, of course we'll win," Liam said with complete confidence.

"It's going to be choppy out there tonight. Emotions are high. And it's always a tough win against rivals, you know that."

"Yeah, but, it's fucking Anaheim," Liam said matter-of-factly.

Roman turned to face his best friend. "Coach is pissed," he said, feeling better already getting that off his chest. He didn't like to disappoint Coach Hibbs; he had been like a father to Roman since he was drafted to LA.

"Yeah, no joke. We all saw him lay into you."

"I couldn't apologize. It felt wrong. I couldn't even apologize to Coach. I just couldn't."

Liam put a big hand on Roman's shoulder. "The boys agree with you. Don't worry about them. If anything, it has them shaken up because they're wondering if they're next. We all know it's a gamble every time we sleep with a puck bunny. This just brought to light what these women will do for their moment in the spotlight. We all have to be more careful."

"We can't just blame the women though. I think that's the biggest takeaway from this. Sure, Jane Doe shouldn't have outed that picture of me, but I don't think any of us take their emotions into consideration." Liam started to cut Roman off, but he put up his hand. "Let me finish. I know we all make it clear we're only looking to hook up. But I was thinking about it over break."

"When you were grounded?" Liam teased.

"Yeah, when I was grounded. I thought about how these women might feel afterward. I know all they signed up for was a one-night stand. I'm sure they know that's all it will ever be when they approach us at the bar or club. But emotions happen and sex is intimate, even if you're drunk and don't know the other person's name."

"Roman Graves did you...did you just express emotions?" Liam teased.

"I don't know. I'm just saying I won't apologize for the picture, but I might lay low for a while. Try and avoid any more drama for our team."

"Our team *and* Coach. He was ready to murder you."

"Don't remind me," Roman said, pulling his Knights Jersey over his head, the bold C on his chest reminding him that he was the captain of this team, and he had that to be proud of. That C on his chest was the very reason slowing down with women wouldn't be so hard if he just focused on his game, on the cup, and...

A thought raced through his mind: *Grace.*

He pushed it away; it was game time.

"Let's go boys. We have a fucking game to win!" he shouted, all the other men in the locker room began to shout too, and rally behind him as they made their way to the tunnel to hit the ice.

Chapter Eight

The win against Anaheim didn't come easy. The boys were all battling hard for the puck. The hits were punishing, and it was evident to Roman that this was their way of saying, we stand with you. Which was exactly how he wanted the alliance.

The locker room felt back to normal after the win, and there was no lack of conversations about New Year's Eve buzzing around.

"I heard McKinnon is having a party," one player said.

"Fuck McKinnon," another player shouted from across the locker room.

McKinnon was a big-shot player for the San Jose Threshers, another one of their West Coast rivals. On the ice, he liked to chirp, but off the ice, he was a good guy, and a lot of the players on the Knights would party at his house when they were in San Jose.

Roman just kept his head down and listened. LA had an away game the afternoon of New Year's Eve in San Jose, and the next day they had early flights to Vancouver. He would usually be all for a party after the game, especially if they won, but he felt drained. And besides, when he took away the potential of meeting a beautiful woman to kiss when the clock struck midnight, the appeal of going out on New Years Eve was lost.

Roman didn't drink often. He didn't do drugs. He had never been interested in those sorts of highs. It could have something to do with the way his father's breath always reeked of scotch on the nights he would come home from his affairs, or maybe it was because Roman found his brand of high through sex and winning.

"Graves, are you going out on New Year's? San Jose has lots of beautiful women to take from the Threshers after we destroy them." a player asked from across the locker room.

Roman tossed his jersey in the bin, and cleared his throat. The room went quiet, "You all know we have a game the next day against Vancouver, right?"

"Yeah, but it's New Year's, Cap." a younger player chimed in.

Brave of him.

"Yes, it's New Year's, but above all, it's hockey season. We can't afford to lose two points against Vancouver. And you know San Jose is on fire right now."

A few of the boys coughed into their arms, and it sounded an awful lot like, "*Choke, choke.*" Some of the team laughed at the jab about the Threshers, who had a bad habit of choking in the playoffs. A glove flew across the locker room smacking a rookie in the head.

"Shut the fuck up," Liam shouted. "Cap is talking."

Roman waited for them to settle, he wasn't mad, they had every right to be hyped after a win against Anaheim. Any time they won against a West Coast team the victory felt sweeter.

"You boys played a good game tonight and you deserve to be proud. You worked hard out there. New Year's Eve is just another night to party, but the next day, in Vancouver, that's another two points on the line. Those points can ultimately be the deciding factor if we make it to the playoffs, every point counts. So, I'm *not* going to say you can't go out, but I am going to tell you to be smart if you do."

Roman felt like such a hypocrite saying these things when only hours ago he was at a press conference for his own bad behavior. But he was still the captain of this team, and that meant saying what had to be said, even if his doorstep wasn't the cleanest at the moment.

"So, make sure the women leave their cell phones in their cars?" Nikko Hart—Roman's biggest pain in his ass on the team, and ultimate pot stirrer—said under his breath.

Deciding he might as well address the elephant in the room, Roman squared his shoulders and said, "Make sure the women sign a fucking NDA if you must. I know I fucked up. I know what happened between me and her could have been avoided. I know I don't always think before I do stupid shit. I know I let you all down recently by putting our team in the hot seat. None of you deserved to be associated with my indiscretions this week, but you were, and because of that, I will apologize to *you*. But I'm still your captain, and it goes without saying that if you party on New Year's Eve that's on you. You're all grown-ass men in this locker room, but if you show up to Vancouver hungover, or unable to play your best game, you can expect the worst practice of your life the next day. Do I make myself clear?"

The locker room all agreed in different ways, grunts, the smacking of hockey sticks against lockers, *yes sirs*, and even a few disgruntled huffs. The boys all showered, dressed and slowly the locker room cleared. Roman made his way to the parking garage with Liam.

"I'm happy you addressed what happened," Liam said, pulling his car keys from the pocket of his fitted suit pants.

"It had to be done."

"So, are you really laying low for New Year's? We missed you during the holidays, man."

This made the image of Grace pop into his head again; her smile, her effortless beauty, her awkward shoulder shrugs. Because of Grace, he hadn't missed anyone during the holidays.

"I think I might join Jason and Claire. They're having food catered. Super low key." Jason Kidd was the goalie for the LA Knights. His wife Claire was a saint for putting up with all of Jason's weird superstitions, but Roman always enjoyed their parties and gatherings.

"How come I wasn't invited to their fancy party?" Liam asked, pretending to be wounded.

"Because you're a fucking wild animal," Roman said, and Liam just shook his head in agreement.

"So, are you really going to settle down? Stop going out as much? Stay away from the puck bunnies?"

Roman felt his phone vibrate. He pulled it out and saw a text from an unknown number.

Grace?

He put his phone back in his pocket, deciding if it was her, he wanted to read her text in private. "I just want to focus on Hockey," Roman said.

Liam clicked the lock on his black Range Rover and slapped Roman on the shoulder.

"It's going to be weird not having my wingman with me at parties."

"I'll still go out. I'm not dead. Just, rethinking what fun needs to look like this season."

They parted ways, heading to their cars, "That's why you'll be a hall of famer," Liam shouted across the parking garage.

Roman couldn't help but smile; he sure fucking hoped so.

"Don't jinx it, man," he shouted back, lowering himself into his Mercedes S65 AMG.

He pulled out his phone and took a second to settle before he opened the text.

The press conference flooded his thoughts. He played back his words in his head and wondered what that would sound like to an outsider, to someone who didn't know him, and his integrity, and his reasoning for not wanting to apologize for something he didn't do.

He wondered what it would have sounded like to someone like Grace.

He read her text.

He got his answer.

Chapter Nine

It had been two weeks since Grace had asked Roman not to contact her. And while it seemed like the right thing to do at the moment, she was kinda *sorta* beating herself up for it now that she was lonely, and discouraged with work, *and* a hot blooded woman who had not failed to notice how beautiful Roman was. It had *also* been two weeks since she watched him declare on television that he didn't date or do relationships after she had very optimistically agreed to a date with him, leaving her to feel like a complete idiot.

She threw herself back into work at the facility. Wayne Gandy, who was supervising her for the remainder of her internship had turned out to be as bad as she had pegged him to be. Every day she worked with him, or should she say two steps *behind* him, was hell. He constantly found ways to make her feel stupid or doubt every word she said during her sessions with her patients.

The last two days Wayne had managed to wear her down with his constant scrutiny. So much so that Grace decided enough was enough; it was time to confront him. She couldn't continue like this, walking on eggshells, and leaving the facility feeling defeated.

"Hey, Wayne, do you think we can talk before you leave?" she asked timidly.

"I have plans tonight, Grace, can you make it quick?" he said sternly, as if she were a little child asking for something insubstantial.

"I can make it quick," she said.

He reluctantly opened the door to his office, holding out a hand for her to enter, his face lined with annoyance. She really couldn't stand him.

"So, what is it?" he asked, as he began to tidy up his desk, not making eye contact with her, not even willing to sit down and give her a moment of his time.

"I feel like maybe we got off on the wrong foot," Grace said, deciding she didn't want to automatically put him on the defense.

"I don't think so," he said, nonchalantly.

She should have been shocked by his inability to admit any fault, but she wasn't. He had proved day after day to be insufferable, and arrogant.

"I just feel like, maybe I did something to bother you?"

"Nope," he said, with an air of confidence that only made her feel stupid, like he often did.

He would give back nothing in this conversation, Grace should have known. He wasn't bothered by her. He wasn't bothered by *her* being bothered by *him*. He was a fucking narcissist. Dread crept in, the next few months were going to be him gaslighting her and breaking her down until she cracked.

She didn't understand it. She didn't understand how a man that was trained to help addicts who were in the worst shape of their lives could lack humility or compassion towards his pupil. He was supposed to be training her, and all he was doing was breaking her down.

"It's hard to believe that you can't feel the animosity between us, Wayne." she said using every ounce of courage she had to call him out.

"I don't. It's all in your head, Grace. Buck up. It's not about *you* when we're on the clock. It's about our patients. So, if you can't keep your emotions in check maybe you should reevaluate if this is the right profession for you. We work with addicts, Grace. We are a high-end facility that treats people who spend a lot of money to be here. So, if you're going to come in here day after day and think everything I do is a personal attack against you, then maybe you should talk to Dr. Williams about putting you in a different building, maybe one with less intense cases? Because I'm here for our patients' needs, not to babysit some intern who internalizes the way I carry myself," he said firmly. No sign of emotion present on his cocky face.

Grace felt her body begin to tremble with anger. Her emotions were always in line, it was just getting harder and harder not to question every word she said around this man when he constantly cut her off, or corrected her, or finished her thoughts in a pompous manner.

"You don't know anything about me," she said, trying to keep her voice from cracking, "or why I'm here. Maybe if you took the time to get to know me, you would know where my passion for this profession came from."

Grace turned to leave, but his next words stopped her at the door. "I know why you're here, Grace. I know about your father's overdose when you were a young girl. I know that you see this as your personal mission to save people from the war on drugs, so other young girls like you don't lose their parents too. Dr. Williams filled me in before I took you on as my intern. But if I'm being honest, and I always am, I don't think your dad being an addict makes you any more fit or worthy to work with these people than the next UCLA student. You think your sob story and a fancy degree makes you worthy of my respect, and it just doesn't. I think you're too emotional and who's to say that when you're on your own one day with a particularly hard patient, you won't let your emotions dictate the advice you give?"

Grace turned back to face him, and she hated that her body betrayed her as it began to tremble with anger, because it only proved that she was emotional–no, no–not emotional, but she *had* emotions, unlike him.

"You wouldn't know genuine human interaction if it hit you in the face, Wayne, and that's why I don't think *you're* cut out for this work," she said, her voice shaking with rage.

There was a moment of silence between them, and she could see, as her insides fell apart, that Wayne was only growing stronger under her insults.

"One day, Grace, a man is going to walk through the doors of this facility and remind you of your father, and when he doesn't make it, when he doesn't complete the program, and you find out he's dead in a ditch somewhere, you're going to wish you would have taken my advice and rethought your life choices, because I can tell you right now, all those emotions brewing in your gut are going to tell you it was your fault the first time you lose a patient. It's going to tell you that *you're* the reason they didn't make it, and you will never be able to forgive yourself." he said, his voice steady and cruel; it infuriated her.

"I'm asking to be reassigned to a new mentor," she said.

"Good, I don't think you can handle my truths."

"I can handle your truths, Wayne, what I can't handle is your inability to see your faults."

Chapter Ten

The Knights were playing in Seattle, and already down by two. Roman could hear the boys banging their sticks on the boards, letting the team know their power play was coming to an end. He watched from the corner of his eye as Sergey Petrov came flying from the penalty box, well rested. Roman found the puck behind the net and was greeted by a hard check into the boards by Petrov at full speed. Roman lost the puck to Petrov who sent it flying across the ice.

Icing was the call.

Roman made it back to the bench after puck drop and watched as his third line played sloppy, slow, hockey. They were going to lose this game. But that's what happens when no one shows up to win. Roman watched as his defense allowed one of the Seattle players to take the puck and skate it up center ice like this was some kind of team effort to let Seattle win.

Roman slammed his stick in frustration.

"We fucking needed one on that power play," he said to Liam.

Liam, still out of breath, just shook his head, pissed; they needed the win tonight. Their road trip had been a bust, losing three out of five games on the East Coast. The team was defeated; but Roman felt no sympathy. They were playing sloppily. Defense was slow. And no one would...

"Shoot the fucking puck," Coach Hibbs shouted.

They did *not* shoot the fucking puck. Instead, Roman watched as his third line tried to make fancy passes in front of a very hungry, extremely aggressive Seattle defense.

Roman readied himself for his next shift. He needed a goal tonight. He needed to give the boys hope that they could still win this, since they all seemed to have left their will to win at home.

Roman jumped over the boards, with Liam by his side and Petrov on their heels, but Roman kept control of the puck, passing it to Liam. Roman watched as Petrov stuck his stick between Liam's legs causing him to trip up.

Roman waited for the whistle.

No whistle.

No fucking whistle?

"Are you fucking kidding me?" Roman shouted as he skated after Petrov—dirty rat bastard.

Petrov was fast, and the split second Roman took, waiting for a penalty call had cost them the game. Petrov took the shot and scored.

***

Grace sat at the local bar with Jess, Chris, and Mia. She was trying, and failing miserably, not to watch the LA Knights game that was playing on four out of five of the big screen TV's.

It was hard not to watch because she knew a month ago, she had that man—who was very angry at the moment—asking her out on a date while he was *also* preparing himself to face negative press for a sex scandal.

She wondered if Roman had told her about his life, and what he was going through when she met him, if she still would have felt so angry towards him. She was fully aware that at that moment, he didn't owe her any explanations, they *had* just met. But what if he *had* told her? What if he had been upfront about his career and the situation he was in? It had to have crossed his mind. Surely, he knew she would eventually find out about the whole 'Roman Graves, the playboy' scandal, and whatever else the headlines had said about him.

Would she have become another one of those women, taking any kind of attention he would give her, and then dumped the day after; a single use serving size?

"Gracey?" Jess asked in a concerned voice, "Are you watching hockey?"

Grace's gaze snapped back from the TV to her friends in front of her. "I can't *not* watch now that I know who he is. I've watched every game. I know what icing is—*icing*! I'm pathetic."

"You're not pathetic. You're a bit stupid, for deleting a professional athlete's number from your phone, but you're not pathetic," Jess said.

"Can you not remind me? Besides, what if I hadn't deleted his number? What would that even do for me? It's not like I could text him, 'Hey, Roman. It's me, Grace, the Thai food girl. I know I told you not to contact me for four months, but now that I know you're a hockey player I've changed my mind,' yeah, no thanks."

"He is hot though," Mia chimed in, "even when he's brooding."

Grace looked up at the TV screen, he was back on the bench, and he *was* gorgeous when he was brooding. Grace watched as the other team skated the puck down the ice and scored. The cameras zoomed in to catch Roman's reaction; he slammed his stick into the boards and Grace was certain she saw him mouth the word, *fuck*.

"Your boy's team is playing awful," Chris added.

"How would you know, all you watch is RuPaul's drag race and cooking shows," Jess teased.

Chris rolled his eyes dramatically. "Gay men can enjoy sports too."

Jess returned his eyeroll with one of her own. "Yeah, because the players are hot."

"Only the ones with all their teeth," Chris admitted.

Grace looked up at the TV, auto-generated captions were provided, and she read along as a very pissed and defeated Roman gave a post-game interview.

His face was sweaty, his brown hair was shorter than when she had seen him last, but it wasn't lacking the natural waves that she found so sexy. His forehead was red from where his helmet sat throughout the game, and she could see that the slashing call against the Seattle player, Sergey Petrov, had left him with a fat bottom lip.

The reporter asked, *"Can you tell us what happened out there tonight, Roman?"*

Roman just shook his head, his face lacking any real emotions, unlike when he was on the bench during their loss. The Roman she saw on the TV screen now, the one being interviewed, was calm and collected. Grace could only imagine he had done this plenty of times in his career—which she had learned after late-night insomnia Googling of him, was five years playing for LA, after a first-round draft pick.

Roman answered the reporter with what Grace found to be a very generic response. *"We should have played better defensively, got more pucks in deep."*

The reporter shook her head in agreement, her smile—despite the loss—never faltering. *"Do you think the recent losing streak for LA has anything to do with your own personal setbacks?"*

Grace watched as Romans entire demeanor changed. He went from cool and collected, to obviously annoyed. He ran his hands through his hair, and across the stubble that lined his sharp jaw. *"I think if my team can't win because of some bad press, then we don't deserve to win."*

She agreed, and went on, *"How do you feel about making the play-offs? Does that still look like something achievable for this team?"*

Roman responded, and this time when he spoke there was no doubt present on his face. *"I feel good. This is a good group. I think we've hit a low, but we just have to review the games and get better."*

The reporter thanked Roman, and he just gave her a nod of approval. The man behind the bar changed the TV to a soccer game.

"Grace," Jess asked again, "are you okay?"

Grace wanted to be okay. She was usually *very* okay. She avoided drama. She stayed focused on her goals. She didn't date. She didn't party. And she was usually the favorite at work, but all of that seemed like a distant version of herself.

Since the holidays, it seemed like it had all been downhill for her.

Roman felt like a distraction she thought she had dodged when she deleted his number, but instead, she found herself obsessing over him. Watching his games, and his interviews. Googling him and finding out that he had a reputation for sleeping around long before this woman leaked the pictures. But now, she couldn't look away. She was too invested. She had to know how the season ended, and right now it was not looking good for the Knights.

"I just really hate Wayne Gandy," she said, turning the focus away from hockey and the secret pining she was still having towards Roman, redirecting it to her prick of a supervisor.

Grace had felt a constant veil of loneliness over her since her father had passed away. She had never known her mother, so when her father lost his life to addiction when she was eleven, she ended up with her Aunt Linda and Uncle Keith. Keith was her dad's much older brother who never wanted kids and it showed. She spent the rest of her childhood years feeling unwanted, like a ripple in someone's existence. And it wasn't that her aunt and uncle treated her badly, it was that they didn't treat her in any kind of way at all. She was provided for, given food, and money for things like clothes, or dances, or movies. But there were never any real emotions involved, no hugs after a hard day, no words of affirmation or congratulations. It was just a roof over her head that she shared with strangers.

Over the past few weeks it felt like that veil of loneliness she always carried had been exchanged for a much heavier cloak. She could feel its burden on her shoulders constantly and when she finally laid down, slowed down, and tried to shut her brain off, she realized she wished she had someone to be with in those late hours of the night.

"Wanna talk about it?" Jess offered.

And she did. She wanted to talk about it. About Wayne's gaslighting, and his insults. She wanted to talk about how she was denied being moved to work under a new mentor. She wanted to tell her roommate so badly how much she was struggling every day at her internship. She wanted to say 'I think I might be lonely,' but the thought of speaking the words out loud felt like more energy than she had to offer.

"No. I think I'm going to head home, get some rest. You staying out late tonight?" Grace asked.

"Not too late, I have school tomorrow morning and an exam in my afternoon class," Jess said.

Grace stood to leave, giving Chris, and Mia a hug goodbye.

"See you later then?" Mia asked.

"Yeah, I'll be around. Good luck on exams." Grace waved and then headed home to sleep off the yucky feeling she couldn't seem to shake.

Chapter Eleven

R oman was running half an hour late, but no one would mind. This was LA, everyone was always running late in this city. He had noticed Liam acting differently during their East Coast Road trip; slipping away to talk on his phone, smiling more when he checked his messages, even staying in when the rest of the team went out for drinks.

At first, he thought maybe Liam was staying behind to keep the newly celibate Roman Graves company. But then, Roman started to suspect otherwise when Liam invited him to an 'intimate dinner party' as Liam had called it.

"Just a few close friends, good food, and wine. Super low key. You should bring a date," Liam had told Roman.

Liam had been Roman's best friend since his second year playing for the LA Knights, and Roman had never known Liam to do anything 'low key'. It was common knowledge that parties at Liam's house were the kind that got you in trouble, left you hungover, and with a giant dick drawn on your face if you fell asleep. So, the idea of an intimate dinner party left Roman guessing what this could be about.

Roman could hear mellow music coming from Liam's eleventh floor penthouse when he arrived. He let himself in and realized there was a whole ass mood set. The lights were dim, and the smell of savory food lingered with that of the sweet burning candles that lined the grand marble entryway.

This level of fancy was so far from Liam's norm, Roman couldn't help but wonder if he had missed the reason for the party. Was it someone's birthday? Was it *Liam's* birthday? Roman wracked his brain, Liam's birthday was during the summer. Roman suddenly felt under-dressed in his slim fit plaid pants, white button up, and fresh white Balmain B-Court lace-up sneakers; this felt like a suit and tie kind of dinner.

Roman made his way to the living room and found a few of his teammates there with their wives or girlfriends, as well as Liam's older brother and his wife. Everyone was standing around with wine in hand, a gentle murmur of adult conversation being had; this was the opposite of the ragers Liam was known for. The lighting was dimmed, and more candles were lit. Roman noticed the place looked spruced up a bit, it had a woman's touch to it that it never had before and suddenly it all made sense; Liam had met someone.

Roman was greeted by everyone and handed a glass of red wine. He took it and found Liam standing on the other side of the living room with a beautiful woman pressed against him, a glowing smile on her face, a nervous one on his.

"Fancy party," Roman said, interrupting the conversation Liam was having with a fellow teammate and the mystery blonde on his arm.

Liam's smile widened instantly at the sight of his friend and pulled Roman in for an embrace.

"How does everything look?" Liam whispered in Roman's ear.

Roman laughed and gave him a nod of approval.

Liam pulled the beautiful woman back into his body and Roman could see her face anticipating her introduction. When Liam missed his cue, Roman seized the opportunity and filled the awkward silence. Roman held out his hand to the woman, and she received it with a smile that belonged in magazines; perfect white teeth, full red lips; she was stunning. Roman–who considered himself overly confident–almost felt his confidence falter at her beauty.

"I'm Roman," he said. "And you are?" he asked, causing Liam to smack his forehead in realization that he missed the opportunity to introduce them.

"I'm Ava, Liam's girlfriend. Nice to finally meet you. Liam speaks highly of you." she said, placing her hand on Liam's chest, looking up at him with love and adoration in her bright blue eyes.

"Is this the reason for the dinner party?" Roman asked.

Liam laughed nervously. "Yeah, I've been wanting to formally introduce Ava to everyone, so she helped me plan tonight. I even hired a chef; he's making surf and turf."

"It looks good in here, man," Roman said, taking the place in. "Looks like Ava definitely had a hand in this, because there is no way you did this on your own."

Ava laughed modestly. "I helped."

"She makes everything better," Liam said, pulling his girlfriend in closer.

"So, I take it *she* is the reason you've been staying in with me during our road trips?"

Ava looked up at Liam, awaiting his confirmation. "*She* is the reason for a lot of things. Aren't you, baby?"

Roman watched as Ava leaned up on tiptoes to kiss his best friend who was so obviously pussy whipped, or smitten, or even in love? Roman had never seen Liam act like this over a woman. He almost felt embarrassed witnessing it.

"Happy looks good on you, man," Roman said.

"She makes me *so* happy. I never thought I'd want to settle down, but Ava brings out the best in me. Don't you baby?" Liam beamed.

"You bring out the best in *me*, baby," Ava said, leaning in to kiss him again.

The guests began to take their seats around the dinner table. Roman noticed the place settings; an arrangement of dusted gold and pale pinks, Ava's fancy work no doubt. Sitting on the corner of the plates were name cards, each guest's name written in elegant calligraphy. Roman found his name on the card next to Ava's. She patted the back of the chair, encouraging him to take the seat next to her.

"Would you like me to pour you some more wine?" Roman asked, reaching for the bottle in front of him.

"Yes, please. I must admit I'm more nervous to meet you than I expected to be," she said, holding up her glass for him.

"Yeah? And why is that?" he asked, pouring himself another glass of wine as well.

"You're Roman Graves," she said, as if he didn't know this about himself.

"That's me," he confirmed with a cocky smile.

"It's just, I've been following your career since you were drafted." She blushed, bringing her plump red bottom lip between her perfectly straight teeth.

Roman hated where his mind went when he found out she followed hockey, but he couldn't help it. Not after the mess he had found himself in during the holidays. Was Ava a puck bunny? She couldn't be. Liam knew better than to feed the stray cats.

"Is that so?" he asked, seizing the opportunity to get to know her a little more, and dig into her motives with Liam.

"Yeah, my father is a season ticket holder. We have a box. I grew up watching hockey."

This caught Roman a little off guard. A box? That must mean she came from money, and if she had money of her own maybe she wasn't a puck bunny after all.

"A box, huh?"

"Yeah, my dad is kind of a big deal in Los Angeles," she said, rolling her eyes, and taking a drink of her wine.

"So, how did you meet Liam?"

"Photo shoot. I'm a model. He was taking pictures in the new 'retro' jersey, I was modeling the women's one, the rest is history," she said with a wink.

"I hate that jersey," Roman said, taking a sip of his wine. "So, how long have you two been official then? That photoshoot was before the season started."

Ava covered her mouth and laughed a bit, as if she were about to say something embarrassing.

"Well," she started, "after the photoshoot we would *meet up* from time to time and it was good, but there were no strings attached. Eventually we realized we missed each other when we were apart, so we made it official," she said.

This shocked Roman, Liam was the worst at keeping secrets. He was the kind of guy that told you what he got you for Christmas, and he had somehow managed to keep a whole ass relationship a secret? It was out of character for his best friend, but Roman didn't press the subject. "I should have suspected something was up when he stopped going out to party after a win. He would stay back at the hotels with me since I've been laying low. *I've* been a good boy since Christmas. I just assumed this whole time he was staying behind for moral support."

This made Ava laugh, the idea of Roman Graves being a 'good boy.'

"So, it's true," she said. "I thought maybe Liam was only telling me you had taken this insane vow of celibacy to keep me from worrying he was out meeting other women with you on the road trips."

"Not celibate per se. Just *not* hooking up. If an opportunity I couldn't resist presented itself, I wouldn't deny myself. I am still a man with needs," he said. He could feel the wine coursing through his body; he felt hot, and easy, and oddly aroused. It had been a while since he had let loose, had a drink and enjoyed conversation with friends. It had been a while since he had felt the high that came with the attention of a beautiful woman.

Ava leaned in closer to Roman. Too close considering the boyfriend she had sitting next to her was *also* Roman's best friend. She brought her red lips within an inch of his ear and whispered, "What would an opportunity you couldn't resist look like, Mr. Graves?"

Roman felt his cock twitch at the purr of her voice and the heat of her mouth so close to his ear. Shame flooded his body instantly knowing this was Liam's girl. Had it been any other woman at the dinner party he wouldn't think twice about excusing himself for a quick fuck in the bathroom, but that wasn't the case here, and this conversation had somehow taken a turn leading them to discuss things that were off limits with your best friend's woman.

Roman cleared his throat and leaned back in his seat as the first course was placed in front of him with perfect timing.

"Well? Go on." she said, changing the tone of her voice back to a more playful one effortlessly.

"I guess I don't know what that would look like right now," Roman lied, because if it weren't for Ava being Liam's girl, an opportunity he couldn't resist would look exactly like Ava. "I think I'm too focused on this season to worry about women. I don't need to make any more headlines unless it's one about me winning the cup."

Ava rolled her eyes at his 'boring' answer and turned back to Liam who was talking to his brother in the seat next to him. Roman watched suspiciously as some kind of switch was turned off in Ava and she went from being some kind of seductive deviant, to a sweet adoring girlfriend in the blink of an eye. Her ability to change so quickly was giving him whiplash.

Or maybe Roman had read her wrong. Maybe she wasn't being flirty with him at all. Maybe, Roman just needed to get laid.

He thought of Grace. That happened a lot these days.

He instantly pushed her from his mind, hating that she wouldn't go away. That she wouldn't leave his brain, like any other woman before her would have done by now. He wondered if it was because *she* had turned *him* down. Being told no was not something he was used to. He was Roman Graves. Hell, if he wanted to leave this dinner party with Ava, he could. So that had to be it, that was the only reasonable explanation why a girl like Grace could completely ruin his want for anyone else. Her denial had cut his pride deep, and he didn't like it.

He had a few regular hookups he could call. Women who also worked in the industry, models, actors, influencers, who weren't looking to settle down. He could call one of them for sex. They were safe. But even safe didn't sound good. He missed the chase. He thought of what Ava would look like naked under him. He thought about fucking her and making her call him by his best friend's name and then instantly hated himself for thinking that. He wasn't that kind of guy, he didnt get off on fucking his friends' girlfriends. He was disgusted in himself.

He was undeniably drunk. He had to be.

The thoughts infiltrating his brain made him feel like his father, who had no issues fucking other people's women.

He excused himself in a panic. He had to get the fuck away from Ava and clear his head. He rushed to the bathroom noticing the second he was on his feet that he was in fact far more drunk than he thought. He splashed icy water over his face. This wasn't who he was. He would never, *could* never hurt his friend. The lack of sex *was* making him crazy.

He pulled out his phone and opened a new text thread. He hit 'G.' Several names popped up as an option. He hit 'R'. This narrowed down the list. He hit 'A'.

There was knocking at the door.

He put his phone away.

"Roman, you okay man?" Liam's voice came through the door.

"Yeah, just, needed to piss," he turned off the sink and met his friend in the hallway. "I haven't had a drink in a while, the wine hit me pretty hard."

"Yeah, you've been walking the straight and narrow since Christmas."

"Yeah," Roman agreed, trying to mask his guilt for the way he had allowed himself to think of Ava.

Liam looked behind him to make sure they were both still alone, and leaned in a bit closer to Roman, his eyes glossy, a tell- tale sign that Liam was two drinks away from being drunk. "What do you think of her?"

Roman's stomach dropped at the idea of giving his best friend the honest answer; *I think she's fucking hot. So hot, I considered what it would be like fucking her, and while we are on the subject, I'm almost positive she was flirting with me over the first course.*

"She's great, man. I'm happy for you," he lied.

"She's the real deal, man. I can just tell. She's all out for me. Like, all-the-way out for me," Liam said, making an explosion hand gesture over his head as if his mind was blown.

Roman's heart sank a bit for his friend, because if this was what 'all out' looked like, it was a prime example of why Roman didn't date and didn't trust anyone with his heart. But it wasn't his place to burst Liam's bubble, because for all Roman knew she was '*all out*' for his best friend and Roman was the real asshole here thinking every beautiful woman he met wanted to fuck him.

So, he smiled his best smile, and tried, despite his reservations, to be happy for his best friend's new relationship.

Chapter Twelve

Grace sat on her bed, legs crossed, laptop open in front of her, eating a day-old Panera bagel, while she shamefully watched the LA Knights game. And while she had done amazing during her last observation with Wayne, and had some major breakthroughs with her new patients, she continued to feel like she was drowning at her internship.

She was so close to completing her hours, with only one month to go to be completely certified as a CADC. All she wanted was to land the job at the Los Angeles facility and make enough money for her to stay in LA. But, with there only being one spot available for a full-time position at the facility, and Wayne having a say in who got it, she was not optimistic it would go to her.

She watched as Roman hit the ice. She couldn't look away when he had the puck. In the bottom of the screen, she could see that the Knights were on a Power Play, giving them the extra man advantage.

She knew all this because she couldn't stop watching hockey. At first, she felt like a stalker, but now, she just genuinely liked it. It was fast, and exciting and it was a nice distraction when she was home. It helped keep her mind off how stressed she was over the whole Wayne situation.

The thing was, if she didn't land the job in LA she would most likely have to go back to Northern California with her aunt and uncle for a while. She couldn't afford Los Angeles without a decent job, and The Los Angeles Drug and Alcohol Recovery Center was the highest paying facility in the city. They treated high-profile clients–not that that mattered to her–but mostly, she just loved it there, or she *had* loved it there before Wayne transferred. She loved the rest of the staff, her patients, the facility, and how close it was to her apartment.

Sure, her apartment always smelled of Thai food, and sure, there was traffic noises, horns honking, race cars revving, and loud music rattling her walls until ungodly hours of the night, but she had found her footing here and she didn't want to go back. She needed to land this spot at the facility. She needed to get Wayne on her good side and win him over. Tomorrow, she should bring him a bagel from Panera. Who didn't love Panera bagels?

Grace heard the wail of the Knights horn come from her laptop and looked over to see Roman skating towards his teammates, a huge smile on his beautiful face, and his team hugging him and patting his helmet. Roman had tied the game and she felt oddly proud of him. She didn't know him, not really. The moment they shared had very obviously been a fluke, a thing of the past, but that didn't stop her from wanting the best for him, and secretly allowing herself to daydream about what it might be like to still–despite her asking him not to–receive a text or call from him when the four months were up.

***

The game was tied up, and the LA fans did not disappoint. The arena was electric. *This* was why Roman loved playing in this city. These moments when the whole building shook with the cheers and chants of their fans, *Go Knights Go! Go, go, go.* Roman looked up at the jumbotron from the bench, his teammates still patting his back when he saw the replay. It was a sweet goal, might even make the highlights. He needed a goal like that, one that reminded him who the fuck he was.

The last few games had been bad. They somehow managed to lose against Anaheim despite Anaheim's building being damn near empty and their goalie, Max Miller, being completely off his game. They needed a win. This was the closest season they had come to not making the playoffs since Roman started playing for the Knights, and after what happened in December, Roman knew this was not the year to fail. The next month was their final push to clinch a coveted playoff spot and he would fight tooth and nail for it.

His next shift came, and he hopped over the boards and battled for the puck behind Arizona's net, their star player and captain, Milo Yavitch came up behind him pushing his body into the boards.

"If you get any closer, we'd be fucking, Yavitch," Roman chirped.

"But I thought you are nun now, no?" he said snidely through his thick Russian accent.

Yavitch won the puck and passed it to the front of the net, another Arizona player took the shot, and the fans lost their shit when Jason Kidd practically stood on his head to save the Knights from being down by one again.

Roman skated to the blue line to face off with Yavitch. "You should be happy I'm celibate. Maybe you'll have a chance with a few ladies now," Roman said.

"I don't need your sloppy women, Graves. That is why I date Russian women. They don't post pictures on social media to get attention. They just cut off your balls. Is nice. Good accountability," he said with a cocky wink.

"So, your balls are long gone, I take it?" Roman asked, leaning down for the puck drop.

"No, I am better at women than you. I don't get caught."

The puck dropped. Yavitch won and skated off with Roman on his heels. Roman watched in what seemed like slow motion as Yavitch passed the puck. The receiving Arizona player took one shot with perfect form. Kidd fumbled in front of the net, and the puck flew over his left shoulder. The Knights were down by one, again, with six minutes left in the game.

Six minutes was a lot of time with hockey, Roman told himself. Six minutes for him to tie it up again. Six minutes, and they could take it to overtime, win two points best case scenario, or walk away with one which was better than zero. But they needed points, they needed any points they could get. He refused to let his season end this soon.

He needed hockey more now than ever. He had always filled his time so easily, parties, women, and travel. But since Christmas, he had the realization that he was pretty fucking lonely, and now with Liam dating seriously, he had lost his best friend too.

He *needed* hockey, he told himself as he pushed himself on the ice.

He *needed* to score a goal, he told himself as he battled for the puck.

He *needed* to make it to the playoffs, he told himself as he lined up a shot in front of the net...

"Fuck's sake, Roman," Liam said, aggressively smacking his back in the locker room after their loss. "You need to get laid, man. The no pussy rule is hurting your ability to score."

He knew he *needed* to get laid. He knew hockey wasn't enough. He needed human interaction that wasn't ass slaps in the locker room and his body being crushed into the boards on the ice, he needed to feel the release he felt with a woman below him, and not just his hand in a hotel room shower.

"You going out tonight?" Roman asked Liam, as he untied his skates, his shoulders sagging with defeat.

"Ava's in town, we *were* going to hit up a bar if we won. But after that loss, I'm thinking I might just let her lick my wounds," Liam said, painfully rubbing his hands over his wounded heart.

"No, let's go out. Tell Ava to bring a friend."

They ended up at a rooftop bar downtown. A VIP booth with a view. Ava knew someone who knew someone.

"Ava knows everyone. Her dad practically owns L.A.," Liam bragged as they sat at the leather lounge seats waiting for Ava and some friends to arrive. "It also helps that she's a model. She's doing the new Adidas photo shoot with you. She's modeling the women's stuff."

Roman's heart raced at the mention of Ava being at his upcoming endorsement photo shoot. She was trouble when she was fully clothed; he couldn't imagine being around her half naked. His nerves amplified just thinking about it.

"Maybe this is a bad idea," Roman grumbled.

"Of course, it's a bad idea. We just played a brutal ass game, and got our asses kicked. We're six points behind Ari-fucking-zona. My body hurts, my ego hurts and technically it's bedtime fifteen minutes ago, but my man, you need this. It's been too long. And I respect the reasons behind not wanting to go out and meet women, but if a man could die of blue balls, I would recommend you start writing your will."

When Ava arrived, she was solo. Liam stood to greet her with a kiss and a firm gripping of her ass. Roman stood too and offered a weak hug to Ava as well.

"Where's your friends?" Liam asked a little too hastily.

Roman watched as Ava put on a fake puckered-lip sad face. "Don't be mad at me, but I couldn't wrangle a single girl. There was a big party in Malibu tonight–that I ditched, for you," she said, leaning in to *boop* Liam's nose, making him grin like a fool.

"Sorry Graves, looks like Malibu is hotter than you these days," she teased.

Roman took a seat and a long swig of his beer. He would finish his drink and let Liam live out his plan B of letting Ava lick his wounds, because Roman was not in the mood to play third wheel tonight of all nights.

"Sorry about the loss," she said, and Liam shook his head, warning her to not go there. "Too soon?" she asked, and Roman took another drink, he needed to get out of there.

Liam pulled Ava close. "Babe, are you sure you can't call someone? There has to be at least one chick free tonight. The entire LA modeling scene can't be at this one party."

"It's fine," Roman said, his tone grouchy and annoyed. "If I want to hook up, I'll find someone. I don't need anyone's help."

Ava leaned over Liam's body and gripped Roman's knee–a little too tight–in encouragement. "I'm just happy you came out. Liam's been missing you."

"I'm just going to finish this beer and leave you two love birds to it," he said, shrugging away from her touch.

Liam raised his hand for the server and she rushed to their table, her eyes lingering over Roman before settling on Liam. "What can I get for you?" she asked, her smile perfect, big lips, blonde hair pulled back in a sleek high ponytail, her body tall and fit, just how Roman usually liked his women.

"Another round," Liam said.

The server looked back at Roman, a twinkle in her eye. "Same for you?"

"No," he began, and Ava interrupted him.

"He'll have the same. Thanks, babe," she said, letting the server know she was excused.

The server took her cue and left to get them another round.

"See, that's why you shouldn't leave." Liam said, pointing in the direction of the woman.

Ava rolled her eyes. "She's trashy."

"How so?" Liam asked, and Roman knew Liam was asking because had he not been there with Ava, he would be considering taking the blonde home for himself.

"She's a server," Ava said, as if it were obvious.

"And?" Liam pried.

"*And* girls get jobs like this to meet celebrities to fuck. She's trashy."

Roman cleared his throat, commanding both their attentions.

"What?" Ava asked, clearly on the defense.

"It's just, not everyone gets to sit in our seats," Roman started. "Someone has to serve us our drinks."

Ava rolled her eyes again and sat back. "So, I'm a bitch for thinking she's trashy? As if I don't know someone has to serve us our drinks. I know how it works, but she's trashy because she is clearly trying to fuck Roman, and every other celebrity that she serves tonight."

Liam pulled Ava into his body. "Chill babe, if she's trashy, so is Roman. He came here with the same intentions tonight, to meet someone to fuck. It's the circle of life, babe, cut the girl a break."

Ava loosened up and took a drink of whatever clear bubbly she had in her champagne flute. "I still think Roman can do better than a woman that's going to smell like cheap vodka and Abercrombie perfume at the end of the night."

The server came back with the drinks and while Roman had no real intentions of hooking up with this girl, he flirted anyway. He flirted because he was pissed they had lost. And he was pissed that 'allegedly' not even one of Ava's friends could come. And he was pissed because of the way she had squeezed his leg a beat too long.

And he flirted because for some reason Ava didn't sit right with him, and he wanted to get under her skin. He wanted to get under her skin so deep that she revealed who she really was, because right now he didn't trust her. And if he didn't trust her, that meant Liam shouldn't either, and Roman wouldn't sit around and watch his best friend get screwed over.

After several rounds of drinks, and far too much talk about the playoffs, Roman decided to call it a night. He flagged the pretty server down for the bill.

"You sure I can't get you anything else?" she asked. Roman smirked, knowing that come on all too well; he had heard it a million times. *Can I get you anything else,* always meant, *wanna hook up when I get off?*

Roman, despite not really wanting to hook up with her, played the game a little more. "I know this is your job, so forgive me if I'm being rude, but would you be interested in sharing your number with me? I would love to text you sometime."

Ava rolled her eyes and audibly let out a sputter of disapproval.

The blonde's face lit up. "Oh, yeah, umm, yeah, absolutely."

She fumbled with the pen, writing her name on the bottom of the receipt, nervously ripping the paper to hand it to him.

"My name's Roman, by the way," he said, taking heed to run his rough hockey fingers over the soft skin of her palm as he took the small piece of paper from her. This caused her to blush and a small sheepish giggle escaped her.

"I know," she admitted. Roman caught Ava rolling her eyes at the girl. "You're, like, the best hockey player ever."

Roman beamed at her. "Thank you...Sorry, I must have missed your name earlier."

"Whitney," she giggled.

"Thank you, Whitney. You're like, the best *server* ever," he teased.

"Okay, well, thanks, babe," Ava cut in, passive-aggressively excusing Whitney yet again. The woman left, but not without looking back over her shoulder to smile at Roman one last time.

"Babe," Liam groaned at his girlfriend.

"What? She knows who he is, and was totally looking for her fifteen minutes of fame. Be smart, Roman, toss her number on the way out."

Roman just shrugged, as if he didn't see the problem in it. He shrugged like Grace had done back in December. The server was beautiful, sure, and he had her number, so why shouldn't he text her or call her when he got home? But the bigger question was why the hell was he thinking about Grace again?

He overdramatically put the piece of paper in the front pocket of his suit jacket, making damn sure Ava didn't miss it, and he stood to leave.

"You getting a driver?" Liam asked.

"Yeah, I already have one on the way. Are you two staying here or heading back to your place?"

Liam looked at Ava, who was obviously still annoyed by Roman's interaction with the server–not that it was any of her damn business.

"I guess we're heading home," Liam said.

"Be safe."

"No, *you* be safe," Liam winked.

Roman winked back and patted his suit pocket where the number was, in a final attempt to piss off Ava, and left.

On the way out, he took the number from his pocket and tossed it in the trash. He wasn't ready, not tonight, he just hoped he wouldn't feel like this forever.

Chapter Thirteen

"Grace, I called you into my office today to discuss your future with us at this facility," Dr. Meridith said calmly.

Grace knew that Meridith had the final say in who got the position at the rehabilitation center, but she knew without Wayne backing her, Meredith couldn't give her the spot.

"Okay," Grace said. "Let me have it."

"Well, Wayne thinks you show promise," Meredith started, catching Grace completely off guard. "But, he thinks Ryan Hughes, the other intern, is a better fit here. While Wayne praises your work ethic and your drive behind wanting to become a certified CADC with us, he thinks you resist change, and you struggle to be a team player."

"That's not true and you know it, Meridith. He just refuses to let me do my job. You mentored me for the first half of my internship. You know I'm adaptable, easy going, and the first in line for constructive criticism. But *his* critiques are things like, I smile too much, and that my body language is too inviting. What does that even mean, *too* inviting? I want this more than anyone, Meredith, you know that, but Wayne is being unreasonable." Grace pleaded.

"Grace, I know he can be hard to work with. But he has a say in this too, and he doesn't seem to think you are the right fit at the moment, which is why I'm bringing it up before it's too late. Maybe you can make some adjustments, try and get on the same page as him."

"How? Smile less? Meredith, he's known me for two months and in those two months he's hovered over me like I'm the patient. I can't catch my footing around him because he's always contradicting me. If he would just back up and let me do my job..."

"Grace, if you fumble under the pressure of supervised work experience then how will you do under the pressure of being on your own?" Meredith asked.

"You've seen me with my patients. You know I'm damn good at this. I've lived with an addict. I've seen it firsthand. I've lost the person I love the most to addiction. I put in the hours here. I came in with my masters. The list goes on. What does Ryan have that I don't have–besides a dick?"

This made Dr. Meridith pause. Grace knew she was being out of line and all the things Wayne had accused her of being. She took a deep breath, regained composure and apologized. This wasn't who she was and she refused to let her emotions take control of the situation.

"Grace, I'm not saying you still can't land this spot. But I am saying you need to prove to Wayne what you proved to me."

"I honestly don't know how I can do that at this point. He's had it out for me since day one, and maybe I am too emotional sometimes, and maybe I do smile too much, but only because I genuinely care about these people. I've seen patients come here two clicks away from overdosing and watched them leave this place with hope for a better future. I'm good at this, Meredith, but I can't convince Wayne to like me."

"No one's saying you're not good at what you do. Not even Wayne. I'm only saying that you might want to start considering other rehab facilities after your hours are done here and you have your certifications. I don't want you to put all your eggs in one basket, Grace." Meredith said, with conviction, and Grace knew at that moment that Wayne had gotten to her. Got in her head and convinced her that Grace wasn't the best fit.

"Will you at least write me a good recommendation letter when I leave?" Grace asked.

"*If* you leave. I still want you to try and show Wayne how good you are. You still have a month to prove him wrong."

"If you're telling me to keep giving it my all while I finish my hours here you don't have to worry. I'll always give it my all when I'm here. I know I might be the final hope between life or death for the patients, Dr. Williams, so even if you told me today it was certain I wasn't getting the spot at this facility, I would still come in here every day and fight for my patients."

***

It was Roman's last night off in LA before the Knights' last road trip of the regular season. They needed to win to secure their spot in the playoffs. Right now, they were in, but that could change if Arizona kept up on this insane winning streak or if Anaheim's goalie, Max Miller, pulled his head out of his ass, poor guy couldn't stop a puck to save his life.

Roman had contemplated going out with the boys for drinks but found himself at home, ordering from Thai Spoon. He knew Grace wouldn't deliver his food, but that didn't stop him from holding his breath when he opened the door only to find a young man standing there with his order.

He took the food, and handed the guy a tip, and although he knew he shouldn't, he asked anyway, "Hey, does Grace still do deliveries"

The delivery guy just looked at him blankly and Roman knew it was for the best. She didn't want to hear from him. She was off being 'busy' without him and his drama. He knew it wasn't easy to date a professional athlete. He heard the horror stories in the locker room and saw the emotions on the road from the men on his team that were married, had kids or serious girlfriends. He saw the toll it took on them and their families. Between away games, getting traded and exhaustion; being with a professional athlete could be lonelier than being single.

He sat at the bar in his kitchen to eat his food, turned on the TV and instantly saw the face of Anaheim's Goalie, Max Miller, on the screen. He turned up the volume and nearly shot Thai food out of his nose when he heard what the sports announcer was saying.

"Max Miller of the Anaheim Condors has been put on medical leave until further notice. It has been said that he is being treated for an unknown medical condition. Anaheim's coach feels optimistic that Miller will be back on the ice in no time..."

Roman muted the TV to check his phone. The team's group chat was already popping off.

Can you believe this?

So sad.

Not sad news for us. Now Anaheim has to put Brown in.

That's not good news for us. Brown is a fucking brick wall. I can't believe Anaheim didn't put him in sooner.

Miller is a good dude, weird, but good a guy, I feel bad for him.

Anaheim has a good rookie in the minors they can pull up, too.

Yeah, the kid they have in the minors is killing it.

Poor Miller.

I like Miller...losing. IDGAF, a rival is a rival.

Don't be a dick. I want to win as much as the next guy, but I won't celebrate someone's career potentially being over.

He's just out on leave, not dead.

Miller must be losing it, he's already a fucking weirdo.

All goalies are weirdos.

But Miller is next level weird.

Poor Miller.

Fuck. Anaheim must be sweating it.

Fuck Anaheim.

Yeah, I agree, poor Miller, but fuck Anaheim.

Roman put the group chat on silent and went to his contacts. He stared at Grace's name. He didn't call. He didn't send a text. He knew he was only thinking of her because he was lonely, and horny. But he also didn't text her or call her because he said he would wait four months, and he would keep his word...and he would respect her wishes.

Chapter Fourteen

G race sat with her patient, Rose. She was a rich kid with a celebrity father. The patient's mother had checked her into the facility after an accidental overdose on pain meds. Painkillers were a common addiction with patients that grew up with money. They often used prescription pills with the illusion that if they took medications prescribed by a doctor it wasn't as bad as street drugs. What they often didn't understand was that heroin was heroin no matter what form you took it in. Addiction couldn't be masked by a doctor's signature on a prescription pad.

Grace knew that all too well.

Her father was all the proof Grace needed. He had never done a drug in his life before his accident. He didn't even keep over the counter pain pills like Tylenol or Ibuprofen in the house. But surgery after surgery on his back, and prescription after prescription of pain meds led him to an addiction he didn't even know he had. Then the doctors cut him off, and said he would be fine without them. He was left to fend for himself as he detoxed, cold turkey, from something just as addictive and powerful as street-grade drugs. Grace watched as her father slowly lost himself to the pain meds. She watched firsthand as he crashed and burned from the drugs he acquired on the streets when he had run out of prescription refills.

She watched her dad go from bad to worse.

He stopped providing. He stopped working. He stopped waking up. Until he never woke up again.

This was a cycle so many others went through. A slip and fall; pain meds. A car accident; pain meds. A work-related injury; pain meds. Surgery; pain meds. It's the fix for the pain, but no one talked about the fix you need, *for* the fix from the pain. No one warned a naive dad, and his eleven-year-old daughter of the possibility of addiction to something that should be safe, right? A doctor gave him the pills, so they *must* be safe, right?

Grace sat back and let Rose tell her story.

It was the story of a girl raised around rock stars. It was the story of a young girl exposed to a lifestyle built and designed by over-indulgence. It was the story of finding your dad's bottle of pills with a group of your high school friends and saying, "Just this once," but loving it so much you end up chasing that high until that high kills you, or *almost* kills you. Now it's a story of a young girl, who will battle addiction for the rest of her life. An addiction so severe sixty percent of people who battle addiction with *this* drug will relapse, and never fully get the monkey off their back.

Grace hated the statistics. So, she fought every day to help another patient become one of the twenty percent who make it out alive, who live a full and happy life, and who never, ever go back to the drugs.

Chapter Fifteen

R oman arrived at the photoshoot fifteen minutes late, because LA traffic was the worst. He knew it would be a long photoshoot because it would be on and off the ice. Adidas would want action shots, still shots, and then some of him and the female model.

The idea of having a photoshoot with Ava didn't sit right with him. Since he had met her, he went from being slightly jealous of his best friend's relationship to worried for his best friend. Ava just seemed a little too involved in *his* life considering she was dating Liam. She was always finding ways to cock block him at engagements they all went to. She asked inappropriate questions about his sex life when Liam wasn't around, and her hands always lingered a little too long for comfort on his body.

He wanted to tell Liam about his reservations with Ava, but he didn't know how to go about it. How do you tell your best friend that you think his girl is flirting with you?

Hey man, Ava always asks about my sex life when you're not around. Hey man, Ava is always finding ways to put her hands on me, or whisper in my ear. Hey man, your girl is always cock-blocking, I think she wants to fuck me.

Yeah, *no*.

When Roman thought of the things he wanted to say to Liam about Ava, it always left him sounding like an egotistical asshole. Because where was the proof? How could Roman even be sure it wasn't all in his head? He was the one who was sex deprived and possibly going crazy.

When he entered the arena, the camera crews had their lights set up in different areas and Roman could see that the photo shoot was already in motion. They sent him to makeup and wardrobe where he was lightly touched up, his hair styled and he was given his first outfit of the new athletic leisure line. They made sure his joggers were snug, accentuating his massive thighs and bulge. They hugged his hips and ass, and he couldn't deny that it was a good-looking pair of joggers.

He was led over to the locker room where he took a few photos solo, his abs had been covered in an oil to make it look as if he had just gotten out of the shower or off the ice. Modeling used to be so hard for him. He was awkward and always felt stupid when he heard the directors say things like, *'Now flex, but keep your face soft.'* Now, he was used to it. They wanted hard muscles, with soft smiles. They wanted fierce and sexy. They wanted the clothes to look both comfortable and durable.

He felt hands cover his eyes and he knew who it was before she had time to say, "Guess who?"

He pulled Ava's fingers away and turned to greet his best friend's girl. He couldn't deny that Ava was stunning. Her skin was perfect, her body long and fit. She was hard to look away from. She made it hard to think with his brain and not his *other* brain—even knowing damn well she was off limits and then some.

"Hey, Ava," he said, greeting her with less enthusiasm than she had for him.

"*Hey, Roman,*" she said back, mocking his lackluster tone. "What has you all grouchy?" she asked, bumping her shoulder into his.

"Not grouchy, just done this one too many times. I want to get the shot and go."

"We're up next, so at least you have that to look forward to," she said, her voice flirty and teasing.

"Do you know what we're wearing yet?" he asked.

"I'll be wearing booty shorts and a sports bra; you'll be in briefs. It's the new active underwear line, and let me tell you, it's *hot.*"

Roman felt his stomach drop, he let out a sigh of frustration.

He did not need to be half naked with Ava, oiled up while three months celibate. He couldn't stand the girl, but try telling his dick that.

"Oh, come on ya' big ol' grouch, it could be fun," she said in a low purr. "I've always wanted to see you in your underwear."

Roman could smell the perfume she wore, or maybe it was all the fancy hair products they used, but the way his body responded to the femininity of it all made his head fuzzy. He took a step away from her and she instantly dropped the sultry act and started laughing.

"Oh, wait," she said, her voice playful now, her smile wild, "I already saw you in your undies–on the news!"

Romans heart raced at the mention of the sex scandal. His face must have said it all, because Ava stopped laughing, her face dropped to something more serious, something challenging, something he both wanted to act on and run from all at once. Before he could respond to her well-played little jab, the director showed up and escorted them both to the lockers for their next wardrobe change.

Ava had been right. Roman sat on the locker room bench in his black boxer briefs, his thighs so thick the elastic pulled tight at his skin there. Ava stood to the side of him, ass popped out, and her arm draped around his neck. While what she was wearing was far from sexy in comparison to some of the things he had seen women in, it didn't stop his dick from threatening to pop wood right here in the middle of the damn photo shoot.

He felt angry at himself. He knew it was a job. But his body responding to her this way; he hated himself for it. He wanted this to be over. He wanted to be as far away from Ava and her flowery smell, and her soft skin that was–in the name of endorsements–all over his oiled skin.

"Now," the director said, "I want you both to straddle the bench, facing each other. Ava, scoot in closer, so that your body is up against his."

Roman grit his teeth and tried not to love the way it felt to have her intimate parts brushing against his. He tried to stay professional, to keep his eyes on the director of the shoot, but out of the corner of his eye he could see her eyes on him, burning into his soul, encouraging him to look, begging him to like it.

And he did like it.

And for that, he would make a new vow. Tonight, celibacy was a thing of the past, Roman Graves was getting laid. And Ava, well, he had to find a way to get rid of Ava because no woman should look at her man's best friend the way she was looking at him right now–not even in the name of professionalism.

"Now, Ava," the director said, "Lean back and place your hands behind you on the bench, pop your body towards Roman's. And Roman, I want you to hold your head as if you're resisting her."

And sadly, he *was* resisting her. He was resisting with every fiber of his being. The temptation to give in, to enjoy the closeness, and to possibly fuck her the second they called wrap on this photo shoot was too real. The thought of it alone felt like a betrayal to Liam.

"Nice," the director said as Ava arched her body like a dancer. His dick regrettably stiffened as she intentionally rubbed against him, pretending to 'adjust' to make the shot.

"Roman," the director said, "just need you to hit that pose now."

Roman realized he was looking down at Ava instead of focusing on the task at hand. He pulled his hands up to his hair and tried desperately to refocus, to hit the pose the director wanted all while reminding himself that he hated this woman.

"*That's a wrap,*" came after three more poses in the underwear line, and Roman stood to hit the showers without saying goodbye to anyone. He knew it wasn't the best manners for a big endorsement, but he had to get away from Ava. He had to get his head on straight, and he had to get all this fucking oil off his body—he looked like the hockey player version of Edward Cullan.

When he got to the garage, he found Ava leaning against his car looking at her phone.

Why was she still here? And why did he feel a terrifying thrill knowing that she had stayed behind? This was dangerous territory. He heard his father in his head telling him to *be safe*, and while it felt like good advice in the moment, he knew all too well just how much he *was* like his father, despite trying his whole life to be nothing like him. He knew damn well that he had a problem saying no to sex. Sex was his addiction. Sex was the only thing that ever made him forget about hockey and his dreams and his morals.

"What are you doing here?" he asked, clicking the locks, loading the massive duffle full of new Adidas gear into the trunk.

Ava made her way to him and leaned against the back of the car, her body looking loose and welcoming to his eyes.

"Wanted to know if you were coming to the after-party," she asked.

Roman closed the trunk and made sure to avert his gaze back to her eyes.

"What after-party?"

She moved closer and he was hit with the scent of her again—blood rushed to his dick.

"The one we all discussed while you were off in the shower being grouchy and rude," she said. "You know, I don't get it."

"Get what?" he asked.

"I don't understand how you got a taste of the most forbidden fruit in your life today, and you still managed to be grouchy at the end of it. I mean, you got paid to eye fuck me, Roman, what do you have to be grouchy about?"

Roman hated that she was right. He would never tell her that the reason he left without saying goodbye was because he loved eye fucking her. He loved her body against his. And he hated himself for it. He hated how good it felt. And he knew he had no right feeling that way toward her for more than one reason. Sure, Roman had fucked models he met at photo shoots, but they were never his best friend's girlfriend.

"You're Liam's girl, Ava. Do you really think I liked what I had to do with you today?" Roman asked.

Ava leaned in. She was close, much too close for comfort.

"Roman, you can play the good boy act all you want for the team, and the NHL, and your coach, but your dick didn't lie today. You want me and you know it."

Roman had two options.

Option one: Take her into his car and fuck her.

Option two: Get into his car alone and leave.

One of these options was not as fun as the other. One of these options was harder to choose. One of these options would prove that he was *nothing* like his father, and the other would prove he was a carbon copy of him.

He went with option two.

"Ava, you need to sort your shit out real quick. Because I'll be the first to admit–to my best friend even–that I struggled today. That I fought off a boner. That I was unprofessional. I can own up to that. I can blame not having sex for three months until I'm blue in the face because that *did* contribute to it, but I can also admit that it *was* partly because you're beautiful–you know you are–and we were in compromising positions today that any man would have struggled with. But *you*, on the other hand, need to admit to yourself that you're intentionally egging me on. If you don't stop fucking with me, you're not going to like what happens next," Roman said, his voice trembling with emotions, with sexual frustration, with anger *and* restraint.

Ava let out a wicked laugh, teasing him, calling his bluff. "And what would you do, Roman? What will you do if I don't 'sort my shit out'? Huh? What will you do that I won't like?"

His heart raced.

He thought to himself:

Option one: I'll fuck *you*.

Option two: I'll tell my best friend that *you* want to fuck *me*.

"Go home Ava." Roman said, and got into his car without giving her another glance, because glances with Ava had proven to be lethal and dangerous. He hated his father, and he hated that he was like him to the core, and he knew that if he didn't leave, option one would win, like it had so many times before.

Chapter Sixteen

Grace's time was coming to an end at the rehab facility. Her intern hours would be completed the second she clocked out on Friday, so she wasn't surprised to find an email from Dr. Williams asking her to stop by her office. Grace had seen her last patient of the day, ran a workshop with her group about sobriety outside of sober living, and tidied up her desk before she went to meet her fate.

"Come in, Grace. Have a seat." Dr. Williams said, gesturing to the chair in front of her desk, the smile on her face unreadable.

Grace took the seat, noticing the perfect stack of papers sitting front and center on Dr. Williams desk. It was fifty-fifty at this point. Grace had done all she could do to prove herself. It was up to Dr. Williams and Wayne—who thankfully was not present—to decide if she made the final cut.

"How did your workshop go?" Dr. Williams asked politely.

Grace shrugged her shoulders and gave her a nervous smile. "It went well. I think they enjoyed the Minute to Win It games we did at the end, it was nice to see my group smiling and excited."

Dr. Williams beamed. "I'm proud of what you've accomplished here. You weren't afraid to think outside the box and create safe spaces for our patients. Being in rehab, away from family isn't easy, but you made them feel like they were home when they were with you. Especially the younger patients. You have a way with them."

Grace tried to stay optimistic, but something about these particular compliments coming from her supervisor felt like a goodbye.

"So, Friday is the big day." Dr. Williams went on.

"Yeah." Grace agreed, her smile weak with nerves.

"Will you go out to celebrate completing your hours?"

Grace nervously spun the single gold ring on her pointer finger, "Depends."

Dr. Williams' easy smile faltered at her response. "On?"

"On whether or not I get the spot. Obviously I'm going to be proud of myself for completing my hours and getting my certifications. But I think it might be hard to celebrate *not* getting the job."

"Grace," Dr. Williams said, it sounded like a warning, "I want you to know that had there been two spots open myself and Wayne would have hired you on, no questions asked."

"But there *aren't* two spots." Grace managed, her voice low and shaky. She felt her heart begin to race in her chest. She knew this might happen. She came into this office expecting one of two outcomes, but no matter how much she prepared herself for it, this was always going to hurt.

"That is correct, there aren't two spots. And with that being said, we *have* decided to move forward with the other intern."

Grace felt her eyes begin to gloss over; she really didn't want to cry. She was always so strong. If she could just make it out of this office without letting her emotions get the best of her she could allow herself to let go, and finally break in private.

"And where *is* Wayne?" Grace asked, trying like hell to keep her voice steady.

"I thought it best if he wasn't here for this. I know your time with him hasn't been easy, and the two of you didn't always see eye to eye, so I wanted to respectfully let you know without him present."

Grace huffed out a small laugh. Not because it was funny. Nothing about *not* getting the job was funny, but the niceties of it all made Grace laugh nervously.

"I appreciate that. Thank you." Grace managed.

Dr. Williams nodded politely, pushing the stack of papers forward on the desk. "These are all of your certifications, proof of hours spent here, and letters of recommendation. I know of a few facilities outside the city that would love to have you Grace. I speak nothing but praise of your work ethic and capabilities as a CADC."

Grace smiled and shook her head in agreement with the compliments, while pushing back tears of disappointment. "Thank you for everything, Meredith. I appreciate my experience here more than you'll ever know."

Dr. Williams stood and circled around her desk, pulling Grace in for a hug, and despite feeling disappointed and upset, the hug felt good. She didn't realize just how badly she needed one.

"Your father would be proud."

Grace's body trembled in Dr. Williams' arms as she fought back her emotions to not lose it completely at the mention of her dad.

Dr. Williams took a step back, and handed the paper work to Grace, on top was a card with Grace's name written on it. "A little something from us here at the facility, to say thank you for your hard work."

Grace took the paperwork and the card, "Thank you."

"Congratulations, Grace. You're going to do great things." Dr. Williams said, and Grace couldn't agree more, she *would* do great things, but that didn't mean this part didn't feel awful.

The second the fresh air–well, as fresh as air can be in LA–hit her face she let the tears fall. Her heart was absolutely broken. So, she cried. She let it happen naturally, and she didn't try to stop it as she walked the busy streets of downtown. Years of being so strong coming to a halt at this very moment. Years of holding it together, a thing of the past. She was done carrying around the weight of life without allowing herself to process what it all meant.

She went to the only place she knew where money could buy happiness–Panera.

After ordering herself half a dozen cinnamon swirl bagels with a tub of honey walnut cream cheese she headed home. The only way she could possibly imagine swallowing the news of the rejection was with a mouth full of bagel and The Beatles playing on repeat.

Chapter Seventeen

"It's going to be down to the last few games," Roman said to Liam as they both stripped down from their uniforms after an embarrassing loss against the Seattle Sounds, the worst ranked team this season.

"I don't get the disconnect happening on the ice. The boys all get along. Everyone is training, reviewing, and putting shots on net. We can't even buy a goal lately."

Roman lowered his voice, leaning toward his best friend, "Do you think it's me?"

Roman wasn't a superstitious man, but he couldn't help but wonder if his little incident in December had landed his team in some kind of bad luck spiral.

"No, don't be a hero Roman. You know damn well your game has been on. In all honesty, I don't know how we're not winning. We played a full sixty minutes tonight. We're making the passes. It doesn't make sense to lose, especially to teams like Seattle."

"Right?" Roman asked. "How do you get that many shots on goal and not one goes in?"

"You cursed us with your celibacy. You need to get off so we can get off...this *fucking* losing streak," Liam joked, but Roman didn't laugh.

Nothing about this was funny to him. He had made the playoffs every year since he was drafted and he didn't know if he could carry the weight of not making it on his shoulders; they already felt so heavy these days. Heavy with feeling like he let his team down, and this different kind of weight he was carrying since the photo shoot, the weight of knowing what his best friend's girl was capable of—what *he* was almost capable of too.

Guilt flooded him. Every time he thought of the photo shoot—and what happened after—his stomach dropped. He knew the right thing to do was tell Liam. Clear his conscience. But how do you tell your best friend something like that? His suspicions about her had been there since day one, but it was never concrete enough to say anything. After the photo shoot, it was clear that Ava was coming on to him but that didn't make it any easier to tell Liam. Especially with the way the team had been playing, Roman knew he needed to carry this secret a little longer. He had to carry it until they clinched a playoff spot at the least.

He wished he had someone, anyone to talk to about this. Someone outside of the hockey world. A friend that didn't know everyone on his team. For the first time in a long time, Roman wished he had a safe place outside of the NHL.

***

"I honestly don't know what we're celebrating. I didn't get the job," Grace said, lifting her Dr Pepper to toast with her friends at the local bar.

"We're celebrating you completing your intern hours! Even if you didn't get the position–and they're idiots for not hiring you–you still deserve to be celebrated," Jess said, tapping her glass of beer against Grace's plastic cup of soda.

Grace knew she deserved to be celebrated. She just didn't feel as proud as she thought she would. She really didn't plan to leave L.A. She always anticipated getting the position. And now instead of celebrating, she was anxiously playing out how she could stay, keep her apartment with Jess, and not have to go back up North with her aunt and uncle.

The appetizers arrived and they all ordered another round of beer. Grace stuck to Dr Pepper and picked at the nachos while everyone around her happily celebrated. She looked up at the TV across from her and saw the L.A. Knights game starting on the screen, the camera zoomed in on Roman, his face handsome and serious.

"Knights are playing," she said mindlessly.

Jess smiled up from her giant heap of buffalo wings. "Still pining?"

"You can't pine after someone you hardly knew," Grace lied, because she absolutely was still pining over Roman Graves. She was absolutely still regretting the text she sent. And she, most importantly, regretted deleting his number.

It had been nearly four months.

Four months.

Holy shit, it *had* been four months.

"Wasn't he supposed to ask you out again pretty soon? Like, didn't you give him a ridiculous waiting period?" Mia asked.

"Yeah," Grace said, blushing at the mention of it all.

"Do you think he'll actually text you now that it's been what...?" Chris asked.

"Four months," Grace answered. "It was four months. And no, he won't. I told him to delete my number after I saw his press conference."

Jess shook her head in disapproval. "I still don't think he was in the wrong," she said, sucking the meat off the bones of a chicken wing in a very unladylike manner.

Grace just shrugged. "I don't either." she admitted.

"Are you kicking yourself for sending that text now that you've had time to realize it wasn't that big of a deal," Jess pried.

"Maybe."

"Maybe?" Jess asked. "Maybe my ass. You've watched every game since you met him. You know hockey better than any guy I know."

She watched as Roman skated the puck up the ice. He was so fast, graceful even, she couldn't look away. She never seemed to be able to look away when he was on the ice. He shot the puck–no luck.

"How are they doing?" Jess asked, shoulder bumping Grace.

"How's who doing?"

"The Knights, *obviously*, how are they doing?"

"Not well. They have to win tonight *and* Thursday against Arizona to advance into the playoffs," Grace said, shocking even herself that she knew that much about a sport.

"Do you want them to win?" Chris asked.

Grace found that to be an odd question, but she found it even more odd that she felt slightly offended by it. A weird sense of loyalty towards the L.A. Knights had formed over the last four months of watching them play and she hadn't even realized it. Of course she wanted them to win. She wanted them to win because they had somehow become *her* team. She wanted them to win because now, with her internship over, she didn't know what else she had to look forward to. She had oddly become dependent on hockey to fill her time with something she quite frankly had grown to love.

"I don't care either way," she lied, and Jess laughed under her breath.

"Sure, you don't," Jess said, calling her bluff.

"Lies for sure," Mia agreed.

"Okay, it's a lie. I think I kinda love hockey," she admitted, with a slightly hidden smile on her face.

"You love who plays hockey," Chris teased.

Grace shrugged her shoulders. "I'm not saying they're not good to look at."

"Neither am I," Chris agreed, and they all laughed.

Grace managed to enjoy the rest of her night, her friends serving as a pretty good distraction from the day's bad news. They ate their appetizers, laughed, and cheered for Roman everytime he was on the ice—which felt nice to finally feel free to celebrate him.

As the night went on her anger towards Roman seemed to fade. Whatever it was he had done in the past that upset her had become water under the bridge. She watched proudly with her friends as the L.A. Knights won the game that Roman had deemed a 'make or break' two points towards a playoff spot. Grace's insides felt warm and fuzzy. She felt happy for him, and the Knights, and despite not getting the job, she felt happy for herself.

***

"That was a big win for you tonight, how'd you pull it off?" the interviewer asked.

"We knew we had to test their goalie early on. Take short shifts, finish our checks, and just play our game," Roman answered, his entire body buzzing with excitement from the win.

"Speaking of Anaheim's backup goalie, how does your team feel going up against the unstoppable Jack Brown?"

"He's been great in front of the net. To come in during the playoff push to cover an amazing goalie like Max Miller is a tough spot to fill, but he has definitely shown up for Anaheim. I'm sure that's made Miller's recovery a little easier knowing his team is in good hands," Roman said, wiping the sweat from his brow.

"Anaheim clinched their spot last week, so this game wasn't as important to them as it was to the Knights. How do you think that affected their game tonight?"

Roman took a second and then spoke, "Anaheim showed up tonight, they played hard. It's always going to be chippy this time of the season, especially in these rivalry games. But we played our game and got the puck in deep, and we got the two points we needed."

"What's it going to take to win in Arizona, Thursday?" the reporter asked.

Roman knew this question was coming. He knew it was coming because they *had* to win Thursday. If they didn't, they were out.

He wanted to tell her, *A lot of luck,* or, *Who the fuck knows, this season has been a shit show of bad breaks,* but he resorted to the only answer that would suffice. "Just gotta get pucks in deep, play a full sixty minutes."

The reporter turned back to the camera. "You heard it from him, pucks in deep and a full sixty minutes." She turned back to Roman. "Thanks for the interview Roman, and good luck next week."

"Yeah, thank you."

Roman was on a high. The win in Anaheim was one of the biggest wins in his NHL career, and Anaheim hadn't made it easy. Most of the team was going out after the game. Liam would likely bring Ava with him, and Roman wanted to stay as far away from that woman as physically possible until he could talk to his best friend about the bullshit she had pulled at the photo shoot.

Roman decided against going out. More often than not these days he went straight home or back to the hotel after a game, but after this big win his body felt electric, he felt optimistic and unstoppable. He wished he had someone to celebrate with. He wished he could call his dad or his mom to talk about the win. He wished he could celebrate with Liam, his best friend, and for the first time in his life, he found himself wishing he had someone special to come home to. A constant. Someone who congratulated his wins and tended to his wounded ego when he lost.

He changed from his game day suit into sweats and flopped onto the couch and turned on the TV just in time to catch the highlights from the game. The commentators were surprised by the win, and not hopeful that the Knights would beat what seemed to be an unstoppable Arizona team come Thursday night and he couldn't blame them.

Arizona was living a true underdog story this season. The worst team in the NHL coming from the bottom of the rankings during Thanksgiving and fighting their way to a spot in the playoffs.

Roman knew the next three days he needed to stay focused, he needed to ride his team's ass at practice, keep spirits high, and keep everyone's eyes on the prize.

A reminder alarm went off on Roman's phone.

He looked down to turn it off and noticed what the reminder was set for: **FOUR MONTH MARK.**

Chapter Eighteen

Roman stared down at the reminder on his phone. He didn't even remember creating the reminder to text Grace about the date she had challenged him to. But now, sitting alone in his expensive L.A. home, post-win and on a high, he couldn't help but be grateful that the Roman four months in the past really didn't want to forget about this girl four months into the future.

He pulled up her message, a reminder of why he shouldn't even consider doing what he so desperately wanted to do. He wondered if over time she had forgiven him for not telling her about the scandal. If she had googled him after she found out who he was, inevitably seeing his most intimate body parts. He wondered what she thought when she learned that he was considered a 'player' in the NHL world, and the most *un*available bachelor in L.A. because of his adamant stance on marriage, and how he didn't see himself ever settling down.

If he ever got the chance to tell her the *why* behind his stance on dating and marriage, she might still consider him a decent guy. Could he be transparent with her about his relationship with his father and his father's relationship with his mother, and all the infidelity and hurt and trust issues he had? If he did share those things about himself, would she see him as a wounded bird or a lost cause? Would he be someone worth fighting for?

Was he someone worth fighting for?

He couldn't be sure, but he found himself desperately wanting to find out.

Roman was filled with waves of adrenaline. Tonight's win, the reminder of Grace, the want to text her just to see if she would respond...the fear of her rejection.

His fingers and brain and heart were all on different playing fields. His fingers slid over the phone screen, his brain telling his fingers to stop, his heart encouraging him to hit send.

His heart won.

His heart *never* won.

Roman:

> I had a reminder on my phone go off. It said FOUR MONTH MARK. Do you have any idea what that might mean?

Roman sat up straight on his couch, his body tense as he held the phone like a desperate teenager, constantly touching the screen to refresh it.

Grace:

> No clue.

His heart sank, that didn't seem like an optimistic response.

His phone pinged again.

Grace:

> **Maybe you need an oil change?**

Roman let out the loudest sigh of relief he had ever experienced. She texted him back, and she was absolutely joking with him. *Right?*

That was a good thing. *Right?*

He decided at that moment that he hated text messages. How was he supposed to know what she meant without seeing her face, or hearing her voice? He would even settle for an emoji or two to help him sort out how to take her response.

His phone pinged again. He held his breath and read it.

Grace:

> **Now that I think of it, probably not an oil change reminder. I'm sure a famous hockey player like you has the kind of car that does its own oil changes.**

Was that a dig at him being a hockey player? Was she being snarky or funny? Did she hate guys that had expensive cars? Why didn't people just call each other anymore? Not that Roman ever answered his phone. In fact, up until this moment, he preferred text messages. And when did he get so insecure? He was Roman Graves, captain of the L.A. Knights.

He needed to respond.

Roman:

> **Are you busy?**

He decided to skip the uncertainty and cut to the chase. He *was* Roman Graves, and he *did* want to ask her out again. And he absolutely wanted her to know that.

Grace:

> **Depends. Is this a booty call?**

Yup, she was definitely still on the fence about him, and he knew this was her way of letting him know.

Roman:

> Nope.

> Not at all.

> I promise.

He responded quickly. Sending short, frantic texts, afraid he might lose her attention if he took too long or kept her waiting.

Roman:

> Exact opposite.

> This is a guy who fucked up, made bad choices, withheld crucial information about himself, and sabotaged any chance he had with the one girl he's ever been genuinely interested in outside of a booty call.

He had to do it. He had to be transparent with her. He knew it was the only way she would ever trust him.

He waited for her to respond knowing damn well he had just blindsided her with his honesty.

He waited some more.

He waited for what seemed like an eternity–or possibly seconds–then his phone dinged again.

***

Grace sat on her bed reading and re-reading the last text message Roman had sent. She was trying to be intentional with her words. Her first instinct was to respond quickly–she couldn't help it; she was excited he reached out after four months, but she also didn't want to seem too eager. Which was hard considering she was both of those things all at once.

She read it again. An admission of his faults she did *not* see coming. Her defenses flared, warning her that this was the line any good man-whore would feed a woman. Her stomach dropped as the memory of his interview played out in her mind. She thought she had moved past it the other night, but that was when she was considering him as *Roman - the hockey player*, not Roman - the man, texting her. She was a skeptic, there was no doubt about that, but she couldn't shake the underlying feeling that he was being sincere. She weighed out all scenarios.

Why would a famous man like Roman Graves ever beg or lie or put on a front to get laid? He obviously, and famously, had women throwing themselves at his feet.

Why would a man like Roman Graves want a woman like her? She didn't even know who he was when she first met him. Maybe that's exactly what he needed; a woman who didn't care about his celebrity status or his money. Which she didn't, but she also would be lying if she said she wasn't a little star struck by what was transpiring between the two of them at this very moment.

She settled on playing it safe.

Grace:

> Did you really set a reminder on your phone?

His response came instantly, which made her cheeks grow warm. She wasn't entirely savvy with the dating world, but she had been told more than once that men were awful at texting back, and Roman was proving that theory wrong.

Roman:

> Yes. I set it that night. It felt like a challenge. One I couldn't pass on.

Grace:

> Thank you for keeping your word and waiting.

Roman:

> I promised.

Grace:

> I asked you to delete my number though.

Roman:

> **Are you angry at me for not listening to you?**

Grace let out an audible giggle and brought her hands to cover her mouth. She felt like a schoolgirl with a crush. She wanted to hate how much she loved talking to him, but she couldn't manage to deny herself the immense joy she was experiencing–she deserved it, even if nothing came from it.

Grace:

> **No. I'm happy you didn't listen to me. I sent that text in the heat of the moment.**

Roman:

> **Did you delete my number?**

It felt like a dare to answer this because the truth would reveal so much. But she was firm in her belief that honesty was the best policy, and she kind of liked the idea of having some kind of upper hand on him.

Grace:

> **I did.**

Roman:

> **Ouch. Do you still hate me?**

She bit her lip as she considered whether or not she ever *really* hated him. Hate was such a strong word.

Grace:

I never hated you. I just had my guard up after I saw your interview.

Roman:

Did you ever regret deleting my number?

Now it was getting personal, and Grace felt exhilarated at the idea of laying emotions on the table for someone else to feast on. She had always been so reserved; keeping everything to herself. Something about being honest with this man made her feel oddly alive and in control.

Grace:

I did.

Roman:

You could have come to my house and asked for it if you wanted it again. You know where I live.

Grace:

I was busy.

Roman:

Oh, right. You were busy.

Grace:

Four months, remember?

She pulled her blankets up to her throat and got cozy. She was invested in this now. She was flirting with Roman Graves, and she was almost certain he was flirting back. It was like no time had passed.

Roman:

> Silly of me to forget.

> I thought of you a lot over those four months.

Grace felt her entire body tremble at his confession. It wasn't anything earth shattering. It wasn't a profession of love, or marriage, hell, it wasn't even the offer of a dick pic, which she knew was a common thing these days, but something about the easy way he admitted to her that she was on his mind made her body come to life.

Grace:

> I like that you thought of me.

Roman:

> Did you think about me at all? Or was it out of sight out of mind?

Grace:

> Hard to be out of sight when the person you are trying to forget is Roman Graves.

Roman:

> So, you did think of me? ;)

Grace giggled at the silly winky face he sent along with his text. She liked this version of Roman that sent emojis, a version of him that made him seem less celebrity and more human.

Grace:

I started watching hockey. At first, I watched because I was intrigued by you, but then I started to learn the game and before I knew what was happening, I was hooked.

Roman:

You're a Knights fan, right?

Grace:

Maybe...

Roman:

Grace, now is not the time to play games. Tell me you're a Knights fan.

She was—holy hell had she become a fan. She had watched every game she could. She felt the pain of the losses, and the excitement of the wins. She covered her eyes when the players fought, but she peeked through her fingers to make sure they were okay. She absolutely was a Knights fan, and if nothing else came out of this, she would always have Roman to thank for giving her this newfound love of hockey.

Grace:

I am indeed a Knights fan.

She finally hit send.

Roman:

Thank God! I thought this was over before it even started…and I waited four months to talk to you.

Grace:

Guess what?

Roman:

Chicken butt?

She couldn't help but chuckle. Roman was more silly than she remembered. Her heart hammered in her chest at the easy exchange between them.

Roman:

No, but really, what?

Grace:

I know what a power play is!

She giggled as she sent it, half joking, half bragging, a flex, nonetheless.

Roman:

Tell me more.

Grace:

I know what offsides is!

Roman:

> **Talk icing to me Grace!**

Grace couldn't help but burst out in laughter, only a few texts in and things had already escalated to hockey kink sexting–if that was a thing.

Grace:

> **Roman Graves, I know what icing is!**

Roman:

> **That's it. I'm coming over. This is officially a booty call…or text, or whatever the kids are calling it these days.**

Grace wished she could be so bold. She wished she could agree, and tell him, yes, yes this is most definitely a booty call now.

However, she could not. She hadn't been with a man in so long the thought of it escalating that quickly made her stomach clench with nerves.

Grace:

> **Speaking of booty calls, great game tonight!**

Roman:

> **That has nothing to do with booty calls… but thank you.**

Grace:

It was such an intense game. Knowing that you HAVE to win.

Roman:

Yeah. It's been a weird season.

Grace:

One more game is all you need.

She encouraged him—and waited. His response seemed to take longer now that they were talking hockey—in a non-hockey kink kinda way.

Roman:

Sorry you became a fan during a shitty season. I wish I had met you when we were at our best.

Grace:

I think I'm happy I met you on an off season.

Roman:

And why is that?

Grace knew he would pry. She half wanted him to. But now that she had to answer the *why*, she suddenly didn't feel so sure of herself.

She answered anyway.

Grace:

> Because I think—and I could be wrong—but I think that I met you at a pivotal time in your life, and I'm not sure you would have given me a second thought if you weren't going through what you were going through. The rough season, the whole 'sex scandal' thing, I think it made you realize you might need something more than the lifestyle you were living.

She hit send and immediately regretted it. She didn't think anything she said was mean, or wrong, but maybe it was too forward for something so new, and she wasn't even sure if *this* was *something* at all.

Roman:

> I don't know. I'd like to believe that even if I met you at the peak of my career, I wouldn't have been able to forget you. You *are* kind of unforgettable, Grace.

She pulled her blankets over her head and let herself hyperventilate for a few seconds before she pulled herself together to respond.

What the actual fuck was going on? And why the actual fuck was she allowing it to go on so easily? This man had a very public reputation, and that should scare her. But at the same time the things he was saying to her just didn't line up with the things she read online. And if those things were true–him not wanting to settle down, him being emotionally unavailable, him being a player, and a heartbreaker–she had to ask herself if she was the kind of girl he was willing to change for? To break his rules for?

Was *she* worth changing for?

***

Roman waited for her to respond. He knew he was being forward, and he wouldn't be surprised if this was catching her off guard, hell, it was catching him off guard. But the last few months alone, celibate, and losing games, had opened his eyes to the things he was missing in life, and every time his brain went there, to show him what he was missing, it was Grace staring back at him.

The win tonight made him feel unstoppable, and Grace was in the line of fire for this high he was riding. He could only pray that it wasn't the win against Anaheim making him say the things he was saying. That tomorrow when he woke up with the receipts of tonight's texts, that he would still want Grace as much as he did at this moment.

Roman:

Did I scare you off?

Grace:

No. I'm just a little surprised.

Roman:

Why?

Grace:

Because guys like you don't say things like that to girls like me.

Roman:

Maybe you haven't been around the right men.

Grace:

I guess not.

Roman:

So, Grace, are you still busy? Or was four months not enough time for you to get everything done that kept you so unavailable?

Grace:

It was a busy four months, that's for sure.

Roman:

I would love to hear all about it.

Grace:

Okay. But I have to warn you, it's not that exciting. It's not 'professional hockey player' news.

Roman:

Honestly, I like the idea of that.

Grace:

Of hanging out with a boring girl?

Roman laughed, she was a tough one. She wasn't going to give him anything easy.

Roman:

Boring sounds nice.

Grace:

Then you're in luck, because I am definitely boring.

Roman:

I've been known to make the most boring situations fun.

Grace:

Oh, I have no doubt that is true.

Roman:

I'm happy you responded.

Grace:

I'm happy you texted.

Roman:

I should probably get some sleep.

Grace:

Same.

Roman:

Goodnight, Grace.

Grace:

Goodnight, Roman Graves.

Roman got himself ready for bed; a newfound glow on his face. He did it. He texted her. And she *didn't* hate him. And he was going to see her again. Only, he wasn't sure when that was because he had somehow managed to forget to ask her out. He rushed back to his phone on the bedside charger and texted her again, before it got too late.

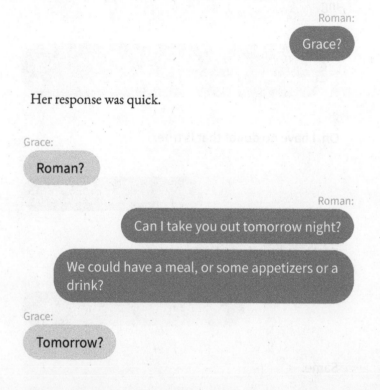

Roman:

Grace?

Her response was quick.

Grace:

Roman?

Roman:

Can I take you out tomorrow night?

We could have a meal, or some appetizers or a drink?

Grace:

Tomorrow?

Romans' hearts raced. Was she turning him down again, after he had waited four months for her to say yes?

Roman:

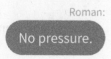

No pressure.

Grace:

I want to say yes.

Roman:

Please say yes.

Grace:

But…

Roman:

Please no but…

Grace:

But I'm going to be honest…

Roman:

Please don't tell me you have a boyfriend.

Grace:

No. I've been busy for four months, remember?

Roman:

Yes, four months, I remember, but what is the but?

Grace:

I'm super nervous. I wouldn't know how to dress. I don't own anything nice and I haven't been on a date in a really long time.

Roman:

It's fine. I'll take you somewhere where you can feel comfortable no matter what you wear. Just say yes.

Grace:

Don't you have to like, hide from paparazzi and stuff?

This made Roman laugh. He genuinely loved how out of the loop she was with celebrity status.

Roman:

No, I might get stopped for a selfie with a fan, but I'm not Justin Bieber famous. So, what do you say? Can I take you out?

Grace:

Fine.

Roman:

Fine? Just fine?

Grace:

Yes, fine. I'll go out with you, Roman Graves.

Way to twist my arm.

;)

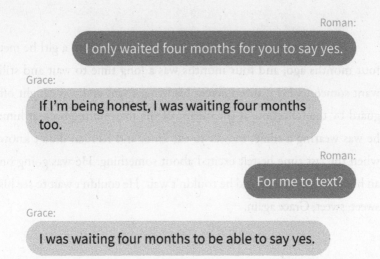

Roman:

I only waited four months for you to say yes.

Grace:

If I'm being honest, I was waiting four months too.

Roman:

For me to text?

Grace:

I was waiting four months to be able to say yes.

Roman felt his heart race and his body warmed from head to toe. His brain tried to remember every detail of her from the short time they had spent together all those months ago. If she was as beautiful as he remembered her to be, he was the luckiest man alive.

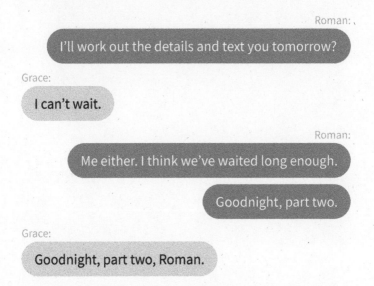

Roman:

I'll work out the details and text you tomorrow?

Grace:

I can't wait.

Roman:

Me either. I think we've waited long enough.

Goodnight, part two.

Grace:

Goodnight, part two, Roman.

He was going on a fucking date. A real date. With a girl he met four months ago, and four months was a long time to wait and still want someone. He glanced across his living room and was caught off guard by the reflection in the mirror of the man staring back at him; he was wearing a smile, the ear-to-ear kind, and Roman didn't know when the last time he felt excited about something. He was going on an honest-to-God date and he couldn't wait. He couldn't wait to see his sweet, sweet, Grace again.

Chapter Nineteen

G race woke up to a good morning text from a man. A very handsome man. A professional athlete. She woke up to a good morning text from Roman Graves. She audibly squealed, this was actually happening. It was really, *really* happening. Sure, she told him to fuck off. And sure, she made him wait four months to contact her. And sure, most of all, she expected to never hear from him again. But she had to admit, his text couldn't have come at a better time.

Roman:

> I don't want to bother you. But I couldn't start my day without saying good morning.

> So, good morning, Grace.

> Question, what's your favorite food?

Grace wiped the sleep from her eyes and read the texts over again. She wanted to enjoy this moment, his good morning, his need to know more about her. The smile on her face was so wide she could feel it in her ears. Is this what mornings could feel like? This was the first morning since she didn't get the job that she hadn't woken up nauseous with disappointment and anxiety.

She wondered what he meant by that; what food did she like from a fancy restaurant, or did he mean a food you could eat anytime? Was this a rapid fire, getting to know you type of question, or was there a reason behind it? Maybe to better help him prepare for tonight's date?

Grace typed in the only food that she could ever imagine eating every day for the rest of her life, because she sucked at dating, and flirting, and she was really good at over-thinking, so she went with her standard, go to answer in this situation.

Grace:

> Panera's cinnamon swirl bagels, of course.

Roman:

> Of course?

She laughed because Panera bagels were a thing people didn't understand unless they'd had them. She wondered if he ate unhealthy foods outside the holidays, when he had no problem ordering enough Thai food to feed an army.

Grace:

> If there is one thing I'm certain of, it's that Panera cinnamon swirl bagels with honey walnut cream cheese is the best food ever.

Roman:

Never tried it.

Grace:

Well, you're missing out.

Roman:

Noted.

Grace:

What's your favorite food?

Roman:

Thought you would have guessed it.

Grace:

Smoothies and protein packed power bowls?

Roman:

So, you're funny too?

Grace:

Not often.

Roman:

Doubt that.

Grace:

Thai food?

Roman:

Only when you deliver it.

Grace:

Flirt.

Roman:

I have four months of lost time to make up for.

Grace:

We both do.

Grace felt heat flush through her entire body. This man had waited for her. She had always had men express interest, but none were willing to put up with her crazy schedule and stress, but Roman had waited, and now, four months later, she didn't know if she could make him wait for anything ever again.

Grace:

Those four months gave me plenty of time to pine.

Roman:

I thought you hated me?

Grace:

I think I was maybe a little irrational in how I reacted.

Roman:

Hey, you said it.

Grace:

I'm sorry I overreacted.

She waited impatiently for him to respond.

Roman:

I'm happy you did. It made me realize how much I needed to change.

Grace:

Hey, *you* said it.

She laughed, already addicted to this playful banter they had so easily established.

Roman:

Send me your address.

She reluctantly sent it. She wasn't ashamed of where she lived, but in comparison to his mansion it may as well have been a hovel.

Roman:

I have to practice this morning, but I was thinking I could pick you up at seven?

Grace:

Seven works.

Roman:

Can't wait. Enjoy your day.

Grace:

Enjoy your practice.

She sat there for a moment, a bit amazed by their whole exchange. He seemed so...normal? And sure, professional athletes were people too, but he was nothing like what the headlines had painted him to be in December, and everything she hoped he was.

She had just gotten out of the shower when she heard a knock at the door. She slipped on her robe and looked out the peephole. She didn't recognize the face, "Sorry, we're not interested," she shouted.

"I'll just leave it on the porch," the young man said, before turning to leave.

Grace watched out the window as the young man got in his car and left before she opened the door only to find an iced coffee sitting next to a box of Panera bagels.

She had never had a man send her gifts, flowers, or jewelry, but she was willing to say this was way better than any of those things.

She pulled out her phone.

Grace:

Thank you! It's all I need in this life...bagels and coffee!

Roman:

If bagels are all you need, what am I good for? ;)

She wasn't sure how to respond.

Correction–she *was* sure how to respond. She just didn't know if she was brave enough to do it.

She typed, and untyped, and typed her response again.

She hit send.

Grace:

I can think of a few things that have nothing to do with bagels and everything to do with you.

He left her on read, and she thought that she might actually die.

Grace had spent the last half hour both trying on everything in her closet and catching Jess up on what had happened when she got home from the bar.

"You said what?" Jess asked, her mouth wide open in shock.

"I said, I can think of a few things that have nothing to do with bagels and everything to do with you. And then he left me on read and I've basically been dying all day. I couldn't even focus on my job search."

"You're going to marry a rich hockey player. You basically don't even need a job or a degree anymore. You just have to look pretty and learn hockey terminology."

"I *do* need a job. I can't afford this place without one, and the other rehab facilities anywhere near here won't pay enough for me to make rent, Jess."

"No, it's way easier now. You are going to marry Roman Graves and become a trophy wife. Live an easy life. You *will*, however, have to bleach your hair blonde to fit in with the other hockey wives," she teased, as Grace tried on her third outfit, hating everything she owned.

"God, I know. Why are all their wives model beautiful?" she asked, ripping off another shirt that she usually loved, but suddenly found all the reasons it didn't work on her body.

"I kinda love that you look nothing like the typical hockey wife; you and Roman are going to stand out" Jess said, handing her a pair of high waisted jeans.

They hugged her ass in a very flattering way, accentuating how small her waist was. "Please stop joking about that. I haven't seen the guy since December. With my luck he'll see me and realize I'm not his type and never text me again."

Jess handed her a white racerback tank top. She put it on and tucked it into the high wasted jeans, adding her high top chucks. It felt *too* simple so she doctored it up with some gold bracelets and a gold chain necklace–compliments of Jess's jewelry box– and while it wasn't something Grace would wear to a fancy steak house, it was flattering. She looked hip, and felt confident.

"A. You look super cute, and B. He waited four months to text you, just like you asked. The fact that he set a fucking reminder in his phone is all the proof I need that he was into you then, and is into you now. Also, might I add–bagels! He sent your favorite food. How cute is that," she squealed.

"So cute!" Grace blushed then turned to look at herself again. "Are you sure this works?"

"Totally sure. Your body is perfect."

"My body is curvy and thick, and my chest is flat, and my ass is..."

Jess cut her off. "Your ass is my dream ass. If he hasn't been with a curvy girl before you, he's going to have his mind blown when he sees the way your ass is currently eating up that pretty little thong I noticed you're wearing."

Grace threw a pillow at her. "He's not going to see my ass tonight."

"Oh, so you wore your best panties for no reason at all?"

Jess wasn't wrong to question it. There was always the 'what if' factoring in. What if they had a few drinks? What if they ended up at his house? What if she didn't overthink it and they *did* end up having sex. Would that make her easy? Would that make this a booty call? Would she become another notch in his hockey stick? Or, maybe, it would mean none of those things, and Grace would just be a woman with needs, allowing herself the opportunity to accept pleasure without overthinking it.

Yeah, she kinda liked the idea of that.

But she would never admit it. "I'm not having sex with him tonight,"

"Sure," Jess said sarcastically.

Chapter Twenty

Roman pulled up to the curb outside Grace's apartment, ignoring the "no parking" sign. This was a date. A real date. There was no way in hell he would send her an "I'm here" text like he had done with women he hooked up with in the past. He put his car in park, crossed his fingers he wouldn't get towed, and nervously headed up the steps.

He wiped nervous palms on his jeans and took a deep breath. What if she wasn't what he remembered? Would he still be attracted to her after all this time? Would she still seem mysterious and hard to get now that he had convinced her to go out with him?

He had never had to ask himself these sorts of things. He never cared enough to. But tonight, he felt a weird sensation in the pit of his stomach. One often associated with an important game, or the draft, or trade deadlines. He was nervous, and excited, and he knew none of those emotions were going away anytime tonight, so he knocked.

Roman could hear someone racing to the door and was confused to find a woman that wasn't Grace greeting him. The woman was tall, slim, and her nose a bit long. Thick purple framed glasses sat on her slim face. She was pretty, in a 'weird girl in high school' kinda way. Roman wondered if maybe he had the wrong apartment.

"Hi," she said, offering a hand. "I'm Jess, the roommate."

He took her hand. "I'm Roman, the—"

"Hockey player," she cut him off.

"I was going to say date, but I'm not unfamiliar with my hockey playing being something people know me for." he said, giving her a wry grin.

"Better than me saying, 'the guy who got caught naked in the sheets with some gold digger," she teased.

A startled laugh burst from Roman's lips. "That too," he agreed, feeling a newfound relief that enough time had passed since the incident that people could joke about it.

Jess grinned and let him into the apartment. "Sorry it smells like Thai food, it's part of our identity now."

"I like it. If it wasn't for Thai food, I never would have met Grace," he admitted.

"She just needs a second to finish getting ready." Jess leaned in to whisper animatedly, "She's really nervous."

Roman smiled. "I'm pretty nervous too."

Jess beamed. "Four months is quite the wait."

"Yeah, no kidding."

"She's worth it," Jess said before leaving to get Grace.

He knew she was right. The past four months were messy. It had been a time of self-reflection and growth. It was the worst hockey season of his career and because of that he had to face other things in his life he was not great at, like being honest with himself, and realizing that maybe, his father had done more emotional damage on him than he had realized.

Roman stood in the center of the small apartment living room and took in the chaotic clutter that felt like literal happiness in the form of decorations. Colors, and art, and books jumped out from every corner–his house suddenly felt so sterile in comparison. He turned to look behind him to find a small wall covered in papers, papers with grades on them–exams.

"It's the wall of our finals," he heard from behind him. A voice he was worried he may have forgotten but knew instantly belonged to Grace. He turned to face her, and the air was knocked from his lungs at the sight of her. She was just as he remembered.

"Every time we got a passing grade, we hung it, in an attempt to keep us motivated," she said, her cheeks rosy with nerves, maybe. He couldn't be sure, but he knew one thing for certain: he wasn't wrong in remembering her classic beauty. She was the girl next door every guy secretly loved, but never dated because they knew she was too good for them. And maybe she was–too good–but Roman was willing to try and be better to deserve her.

"Did it work?" he asked.

She shrugged her shoulders, and scrunched her nose in a smile. "I graduated last year with my master's in behavioral science. Top of my class... So, I guess?" she said modestly–and his heart raced in his chest. That shoulder shrug, how could he have forgotten? It was her thing, and he loved it. It was nothing at all and yet the cutest thing he had ever seen.

He smiled. "So you're smart *and* beautiful."

"I guess it pays to be busy," she said.

"I guess it does. I'm happy being busy paid off for you."

"Almost. Some things didn't go as planned, but I'll figure it out."

"I'm sorry to hear that."

"It's fine, it was just a long four months."

"I agree. We made it though. I'm here," he said, giving her a sweet, inviting smile.

She dropped her head shyly, trying and failing to cover her blushing grin. "Thank goodness you set a reminder," she said looking up. "I hope I'm still what *you* were expecting."

He shook his head and she pulled back her shoulders in question.

"No, you're better than I was expecting. I thought I might have exaggerated over time how beautiful you are."

Grace blushed and averted her gaze from his, shying away from his compliments.

"Should we go?" he said, opening the door, and she shrugged her shoulders again, only this shrug had affirmation behind it, and he wanted to learn them all; what every one of her secret shoulder-shrugs meant.

When they got to the car, Roman rushed to get to the door first. He held it open for her and then went around the car to hop in quickly.

"You know this isn't a legal parking spot, right?" she asked incredulously.

Roman looked around, acting surprised, a boyish grin on his face. "Oh, shoot. It's not?" Grace rolled her eyes, and he gave her a playful wink.

"Nice car though," she said.

"I like it. I'm not a car collector like some of the boys I play with, though."

"Car collector?" she asked, buckling up with nervous, shaky hands. He placed his hands on hers, trying to steady them with a gentle touch.

"Yeah, some of the boys on my team have car collections. Most of the single ones. The married ones, not so much. But cars have never been my thing." He took his hand from hers, giving her a reassuring smile, then signaled to get over. The car behind him laid on the horn in typical L.A. driver fashion, breaking this small moment they seemed to be sharing.

"What *is* your thing? I hardly know anything about you."

"Oddly, I don't have an expensive *thing*. If I'm being completely honest, I think the things I love the most are career based. I love hockey…"

"Obviously," she interjected playfully.

"Yeah, kinda obvious. Ummmm…," he drummed his thumbs on the steering wheel. "I like to work out."

Grace mimed vomiting.

"You don't like to work out?" he asked.

"No. Not really. Is that a conflict of interest?"

"Not at all. I just get paid to be fit, but I also really like pushing myself, seeing how far I can take my workouts."

"Okay, that sounds like my own personal hell, but I respect it. I'm sure your body is grateful," she said, and he noticed her eyes taking in his physique.

"I also really like scary movies, naps, and pedicures. I'm not all 'gym bro' all the time,"

"Pedicures?" she teased.

"Yeah, gotta keep my feet nice, especially after being in skates all day. What about you Grace? What do you like to do?"

She adjusted her body to face him, and he couldn't help but notice how tiny she looked in his car. She wasn't tall, and for the most part she *was* rather petite, minus her nice big ass and thick thighs that looked amazing in the high waisted jeans she wore.

"I like to listen to old music, especially The Beatles. They were my dad's favorite band. And I like to people watch at parks or coffee shops."

"In a creepy way?" he asked, jokingly.

"Gotta scope out any potentially good organ donors for the black market," she bounced back, and he laughed. "I like to help people, too. I like to listen to them. I'm a good listener. Basically, I'm really boring."

"Well, I like to talk, so we'll balance each other out. And I have tons of problems, and am in desperate need of help, so that works too. Frankly, I'm kind of ready for boredom, Grace. This year has been one of the hardest of my career, but it helped me reflect on some things I need to work on. So, yeah, I think boring sounds nice."

There was a beat of silence between them and Roman hated the L.A. traffic even more than normal for keeping him from being able to stare at the woman beside him.

"So, did I dress okay for what you have planned?" she asked.

"Perfect," he said.

"Are you going to tell me what it is yet?"

"You'll see soon enough." He flicked on his blinker and pulled into the back entrance of the private parking garage at the L.A. Knights arena.

"Are we going to play hockey?" she asked incredulously.

"Not hockey, but close," he said, pulling into a parking spot that had a reservation plaque with his name on it.

"You have your own parking spot?"

"I'm the captain, of course I do." He winked, and got out of the car, racing around to the other side to open the door for her. "Do you know how to ice skate, Grace?" he asked, holding out his hand to her.

"I've never been," she winced apologetically.

"No worries, I'm a good teacher," he said, taking her hand into his.

***

His hands were oddly soft considering his line of work. There were a few calloused spots, but nothing like she'd expected. She wondered if he got manicures too. A silly image of him getting pampered in an overly fancy salon popped into her head, she laughed nervously.

"What?" he asked, taking notice of her secretive giggles.

"I just imagined you getting a mani-pedi."

"And that's funny?" he teased.

"Yes. I can't even remember the last time I got one. Poor intern problems," she said.

"Not for long right? You have a nice degree, and you're interning. Seems like self-care might be in the near future, right?" he asked, as they made their way down a long cold hallway.

"A degree, yes. A job, not so much."

"Why is that?"

"They chose the other intern over me." Saying it aloud still hurt as much as it did the day she found out.

Roman squeezed her hand in a sort of apologetic way. *They were holding hands.* Holy shit, she was holding hands with Roman Graves, how was this even real life?

"I just realized, I don't even know what you were interning for."

They kept walking. This was the absolute longest hallway in history.

"I was interning at the Los Angeles Drug and Alcohol Recovery Center."

"Wow. That's admirable of you, Grace."

"It's important," she said modestly.

"It is. Most people write addicts off. Assume they chose that life, and some of them do, but some addicts are made in ways most people don't even consider," he said.

"*That*," she said, surprised, taking her turn to squeeze his hand back, "is absolutely true. Some people don't see it that way, they don't see the depth of addiction, or the generational curses attached to it. They just dismiss addicts and say it's their fault. And sometimes it *is* their fault, but that doesn't mean they deserve help any less than the lawyer who drinks too much, or the mom who suffered a back injury and got hooked on pain meds."

Grace paused, she knew she was spiraling in the passionate way she often did when it came to this sort of thing. "Anyway, I didn't get the job. They chose the kiss-ass over me. I think one of the leads on staff had it out for me, so I saw it coming. But it hurts, ya know? I gave so many hours of my life to that facility. *And* I won't be able to see my last patient all the way through her program. That part hurt the worst." Roman reached forward to grab the big heavy arena door in front of them. "That has to be hard, not getting to be the one to see your patient to the end."

"It really is," she said, and then, the conversation was halted by the sight of the fresh ice. The cold chill that hit her warm cheeks took her breath away. She never realized something so trivial as an ice rink could be so mesmerizing.

Roman released her hand, and she took a step forward looking up into the stands. Stands that only nights ago were filled with people shouting his name, *Graves, Graves, Graves*.

"This is..." she broke off.

"Pretty cool huh?" he finished.

"Extremely cool."

He pointed at a few boxes that sat on the bench at the entrance of the ice. "I got you skates," he said, picking up a box. "I didn't know your size, so I got several options. I can donate the ones that don't fit to the youth program."

She beamed. On the one hand this all seemed like too much, too showy, for a first date. On the other hand, she didn't really expect anything less from him. She knew he was a famous hockey player, so she knew he would make an effort to impress her if he really wanted to.

"I'm a size seven," she said, and he put the box down he was holding and grabbed the one next to it.

"Your feet are tiny," he teased.

"And probably not up to your grooming standards," she joked, sitting on the bench to slip out of her old chucks and into the brand new, bulky black, hockey skates. "You know you could have at least got me the pretty white ones."

"No way," he said, taking a knee before her, pulling her foot into his lap. "We wear hockey skates or nothing at all," he joked, tugging the laces tighter than she could have done herself. "Does that feel good?"

"I don't know. I've never done this, so I don't have anything to compare it to."

"Does your ankle feel supported while also having room to move?"

"That seems like an oxymoron."

Roman looked up at her through his thick lashes, his smile combative and dark. Grace felt her stomach flutter at the sight of him before her, looking up at her like he might pounce.

"Are you always so challenging?" he asked, releasing her foot and taking the other.

"Only when I'm with you."

He pulled the laces tight with an assertive tug. "Good. I like a challenge."

He took the bench beside her and put on a pair of skates that were waiting for him. His skates were used, worn in places, possibly his game skates. Grace wondered how often he replaced them.

"Are you ready?" he asked, holding out a hand to help her to her feet.

She shrugged, her face unsure. "I might suck."

"That's okay, I'll help you. I happen to be really good at this," he teased.

"Is this how you weed out the girls worth dating; take them ice skating and if they fall three times, you never call them again?"

He took her hand in his and on wobbly skate blades she stepped onto the ice.

"No, I don't call them again if they fall once." he smirked, gripping her hand tight; they both started to push off on the ice.

"No pressure then," she said.

"The thing is, Grace, I know you won't fall."

"How can you be so sure? I might have two left feet." she asked.

"Because I won't let you," he said, his smile sweet, and certain.

Grace beamed. Roman was far more romantic than she ever could have imagined. When she watched him on TV, he was a fierce competitor. Calling out the refs for bad calls, battling hard for the puck in the corners, making big hits, and occasionally dropping the gloves. But right now, on the same ice he was famous for during the hockey season, he was just Roman, her date. "Do you think you can manage on your own without falling for a second?" he asked.

"Are you sure you want to take that risk and blow it all?"

He leaned in, slipping his hand from hers to wrap around her waist. "I'm going to let you in on a secret, Grace," he whispered into her ear.

She looked up at him in anticipation.

"I'm breaking *all* my rules for you," he said, and if her heart wasn't racing before, it might explode now.

"And what if I don't want to fall," she asked, biting nervously at her bottom lip, not sure if she was still talking about the ice, or if she had moved on to matters of the heart.

He took his hand from her waist and pulled his phone from his back packet. "Then you're in trouble, Grace. Because I plan to make you fall harder than you've ever fallen before."

He hit play on his phone and The Beatles' "I Want To Hold Your Hand" started playing on the arena's sound system. He took her hand back into his, his smile proud. Roman knew he had done well; he had listened when she told him she liked The Beatles and had found time to queue it up to play as they skated.

Grace felt fearless with Roman holding her, guiding her, their bodies starting to find a rhythm on the ice.

"You're a natural," he said.

"I used to roller skate as a kid. I think that's helping," she admitted.

Grace beamed; she couldn't help it. The cool air of the rink made the flush of her cheeks bright and cheery, and she noticed that Roman was a confident enough skater that he could do it effortlessly while never taking his eyes off of her.

The song changed, and a different album began to play, this time–*Abbey Road*, the song, "Oh! Darling". Paul's voice echoed through the empty arena, a lament of how he would never do his girl *no* harm.

Roman slowed their skating and pulled her into his arms. "Slow dance?" he asked.

She wanted to argue, she wanted to say this song wasn't ideal for a first dance together. She wanted to tell him not to be fooled by the opening lyrics declaring love and dedication. She wanted to tell him that it ended with Paul McCartney shouting, and yelling about his emotions over his girl telling him she didn't need him anymore, but she decided he would just have to find that out on his own, because she absolutely wanted to slow dance? Slow *skate*? Whatever it was, with this man.

Roman took the lead, skating backwards effortlessly as he held her. It could have been awkward. It *would* have been awkward if two amateurs tried such a thing, but Roman was far from an amateur on the ice, and he managed to make it easy, and to her surprise, extremely romantic.

She enjoyed the moment. His eyes were on hers. His smile, boyish and a little shy.

And then it happened, just as they really began to find their rhythm together...

Paul McCartney lost his shit, screaming out the lyrics, as she knew he would; a story of his woman not needing him any more–*no*, this absolutely was *not* a great song to slow dance to.

They both began laughing. The once intimate slow skate was suddenly over, only to be replaced with uncontrollable laughter.

"That escalated quickly," Roman finally said, Grace still laughing. "Why didn't you tell me this wasn't an ideal song for our first slow dance?" he asked, shaking his head in mock disbelief at her betrayal.

"It was your punishment for not knowing The Beatles," she teased.

"So, was this *your* deal breaker? Me not knowing that this song ended in a man screaming like a maniac?" he asked.

"No... because selfish gain was involved."

"Is that so?"

"Yup. I wanted to slow dance. Skate? With you. So, I kinda let you fail this round."

"Dubious," he teased.

She rubbed her hands together, in an evil villain sort of way. "The dubiousest of all dubiousness."

Roman took her hand in his again, and they began to skate as "Strawberry Fields Forever" started to play. And for a moment, they didn't say anything at all. They just skated, and she smiled, and he gripped her hand tight, as if reminding her this was real, and he *wouldn't* let her fall.

After three more Beatles songs, Roman led her off the ice, "Are you hungry?" he asked.

"I'm always hungry. I'm *that* girl," she admitted, feeling oddly at ease and ready to be authentic.

Roman helped her to the bench to change back into her shoes. "So, are you *that* girl meaning, once you get hungry, I should fear for my life?"

"I don't get *hangry* per se, but I definitely never pass on food. I'm a trash panda," she admitted with a snort. "The effects of being an intern in L.A."

"Trash panda?" he asked.

"Yeah, I'm like a raccoon–trash panda–I'll eat anything. But I love Panera bagels most of all," she said, bumping his shoulder.

He smiled proudly. It was a new kind of smile for her, and she wanted them all, every smile he had tucked away in his arsenal of happiness.

"So, would your inner trash panda like to see the next part of our date?" he asked, standing up, and holding out a hand to help her up.

Her legs were admittedly shaky from the skating, and she felt a little embarrassed by it. Maybe she should work out, so she didn't feel like a ninety-year-old woman after an hour of ice skating with him.

"I'm already pretty blown away with this date, so I'd be lying if I said I wasn't excited to see what other tricks you have up your sleeve."

Roman began to pull her towards the hallway and Grace looked over her shoulder at the skates they had left behind.

"Don't worry about that stuff, I can get it later," he said, as if reading her mind.

They began to walk back down the long hall. Roman, without hesitation took her hand. She really liked the way it felt. It felt safe, and oddly sexy how big his hand was in comparison to hers.

Grace knew she was on the short side. She had always been considered petite in that sense. Her frame and height were dainty, minus her ass and thighs—those showed up to the party. But something about feeling like Roman Graves could pick her up and throw her over his shoulder was causing something to happen deep in her stomach, warm, and exciting.

"So, are there any foods you don't like?" Roman asked.

"Not really. I don't have a super refined palate. I grew up on a lot of beef and potatoes. My aunt and uncle were minimalist."

"They raised you?" he asked, as they rounded the corner of the long hall.

"Yeah, after my dad passed, they were the only option. Even though they didn't want me. They're decent enough people, so they took me in. I grew up knowing I wasn't exactly loved, but taken care of, and I was wise enough to know—even at a young age—that that was more than some kids got in life. So, I tried to fly under the radar, get good grades, stay out of trouble and the second I had a chance I got out of there," she admitted.

"Sounds similar to my childhood, and I *lived* with my parents," he said.

"Really?" Grace asked, looking up at him.

"Really. I know my mom loves me. But she was always such a mess emotionally that she didn't have anything left to give me. I'm pretty sure that's why she pushed hockey, it gave me somewhere to be, an outlet to pour my emotions into since she couldn't be there for me. My dad was..." he paused, figuring out how to word it. "My dad is a big deal. He has a lot of power and money in Canada. And he–in my opinion–abused my mom in a sense. I don't think he married her for love, he married her because the whole 'family package' looks good politically. And I don't think he had a kid because he wanted one, he had a kid because it was the thing to do in his line of work."

"I'm so sorry," Grace offered.

"It's okay, I turned out alright. I used to think I needed them to validate my success, but over time I realized *I* did this. I got where I am because I worked my ass off. They just footed the bill."

"Do you still talk to them?" she asked.

"I consciously try not to. My dad is toxic. He's undoubtedly the biggest hypocrite I've ever met. He's a serial cheater. I don't think he's gone through a month of being married to my mom and not cheated. And my mom, she's a mess. She's so broken down from his mind games and manipulation she actually defends him. She takes the fault in everything. I resent her for that. I know I shouldn't, but I do. I resent her for not being strong enough to leave him."

"What do you think your life would have looked like if she had left?" Grace asked, and Roman didn't hesitate to answer.

"I think my mom would be happy. I think she could have found someone else who genuinely loved her. And I think maybe if I saw her leave that kind of abusive behavior, I wouldn't be so afraid of becoming just like him."

And there it was.

The holy grail of admission.

In that one statement Grace felt she understood this man so much more. His need to sleep around. To keep women and relationships at arm's length. He was afraid he would treat them the way his father treated his mother.

Deep rooted generational curses. She knew about that all too well. It was why Grace feared taking Tylenol for her cramps, or panicked when she felt the least bit buzzed off a beer. She didn't want to like it so much she ended up like her father, and that was exactly Roman's thought process when it came to dating and marriage.

"You know, your mom probably wants out," she offered. "Sounds like your dad might be really good at gaslighting people."

"He's the best at the game. If he met you today, he could convince you the sky was green, and then he would make you feel like shit that you didn't already think it was."

Grace could feel the mood of the date shifting, and it felt too heavy considering it was their first date. She looked over at him with a confused look on her face. "Wait? The sky isn't green?" she asked playfully, lightening the mood.

Roman bumped her shoulder mischievously. "I sure hope you're hungry, Grace." he said, stopping to open a door that led to the club level of the rink. It was carpeted, unlike the rest of the arena she had seen, and had huge picture windows that overlooked the pavilion down below. It had a 'members only' vibe that served as a reminder of just who she was on a date with.

Roman Graves, captain of the L.A. Knights.

Her heart hammered in her chest, because while she was on a date with him, she was still having a hard time believing she was on a date with *him*.

"I could eat," she said nonchalantly, playing it cool despite her giddiness.

The smell of food hit her nose and her stomach happily growled with hunger. She hadn't eaten anything since the bagels he sent that morning.

"How do you feel about snack bar food?" Roman asked, his brow lifted with curiosity.

"I love snack bar food. It's the only reason I go to sporting events,"

Roman smiled, "Good, because I had the whole snack bar prepped for you. And I must say, when I chose to do this, I had no idea you were a dumpster rat yet."

Grace burst out laughing.

"It's a trash panda," she corrected, "not a dumpster rat."

Roman started laughing with her and, god, his laugh was electric. It made her feel things in places she hadn't felt in a while.

"I can't believe you just called me a dumpster rat," she teased.

"Can I make it up to you with the most delicious cuisine the L.A. Knights have to offer?" he asked, stopping in front of the snack bar. It was lit up with neon signs, and fully stocked with concessions. Three people in uniforms stood behind the concession counter, smiling, ready to serve.

"Seriously Roman? You did all this for me?" she asked, walking closer to look up at the menu.

"I did. They came in on their day off to help." he said, shooting the workers a thankful smile.

"I guess we should make it worth their time then?" Grace asked.

"Absolutely," he agreed. "I'll order first," he said, stepping forward, "give you some time to think."

She listened to him list off all the things he was going to get adding a pretzel at the last moment, and then turned back to her. "Your turn."

The young man waiting to take her order greeted her nervously, "Hi, what can I get for you?"

She stepped forward, "I'll have a hotdog and a nacho," she turned back to see Roman's reaction and he smiled at her encouragingly to keep going, "Extra cheese on the nachos," she added, and she heard Roman jokingly say, "*That's right, get that extra cheese*" behind her, which made her laugh.

She continued, "And I'll take a salted pretzel, and a half coke, half cherry icee,"

Roman shouted from behind her, "Oh, make that two, I didn't even think to get an icee."

She took a step back after ordering, bumping into the solid wall behind her that was Roman. She hadn't even realized he was so close, but his body against hers felt warm and inviting. He wrapped his strong arms around her from behind and gave her shoulders a squeeze.

Leaning in to whisper in her ear, the warmth of his mouth so close to her made her body cover in chills. "Where do you want to sit, Grace?"

Her name rolled off his lips like something sensual, she didn't even realize she had closed her eyes.

"By the windows," she said, "so we can see the city lights."

They took a seat at a bar style table that overlooked the pavilion, the neon lights made Romans eyes glow as he kept his gaze on her, a gentle inviting smile on his face. Grace was at a loss for words. She looked out at the pavilion, unsure of what she should say or do in this small moment of silence between them.

Roman, as if reading her panic, reached across the table for her. "Is it okay that I want to hold your hands?" he asked.

"I like it," she said shyly, as he took her small hands into his and began to gently press his thumbs into her palms.

"I'm sorry I didn't take you to a nice steak house or somewhere fancy and upscale," he said.

"What? No, that's not what I'm thinking at all. This is perfect," she argued.

"I could have taken you somewhere fancy," he said. "I even considered it. I considered all the places in L.A. that are known for fine dining, and exclusivity. But I remembered you hinting at not wanting to feel out of place, and not knowing what to wear, and I just really wanted to bring you somewhere we could be alone, have fun, and get to know each other. So, don't think I didn't consider doing the standard, appropriate date, I just really wanted to surprise you."

"You did. Trust me. I am so blown away by everything you've managed to pull off so far. And dinner at the snack bar? My inner dumpster rat approves," she teased, leaving Roman shaking his head in mock embarrassment.

He was kind of beautiful at that moment. A kind of beauty that made her wonder how many people got to see him this way. Unfiltered. No pressure. A carefree kind of beautiful. She didn't know how she got here, but she feared that if he ever took it away, she might die. She suddenly, for the first time in her life, understood what it was like to be hooked–addicted–to something after just one hit.

Roman Graves was her official drug of choice, and after years of training, school and hours served, she didn't even know if she had the right advice to talk herself down from wanting more of him before the first dose was gone.

The food arrived and they had to put some of Roman's order on the table next to them because there wasn't enough room for the obnoxious amount of food they had.

"Ketchup only?" he asked, eyeballing her hotdog.

She eyed his messy relish covered dog disapprovingly. "You have room to talk. Would you like some bun and weiner with that relish?"

This made Roman burst out laughing. "You know, you're pretty funny," he said.

"Thank you, I make up for my stature with my amazing humor," she teased.

The conversation was light, and easy, and Roman asked her a lot of questions, which felt reassuring. They were this far into the date, and he was still interested in finding out more about her.

"So," he said, wiping his mouth after he finished the last of his nachos, "what's next for you now that you're done interning, Grace? Are there other rehab facilities on your radar that you're considering?"

"I got a lot of financial aid, and scholarships for school, so I graduated in a much better place than most students do, but L.A. was too expensive to save money while being a full time student and intern, so I am in a pickle for sure. If I want to stay local I have to land a job that has comparable pay to the facility I interned at. So, worst-case scenario, I have to move back up North when my lease is up. Best case scenario, I land a job that pays the bills, and I get to stay here in L.A."

"There has to be plenty of rehab facilities to consider, right?" he asked.

"There are several other facilities I could get hired at, sure, but the facility I interned at was high end. It dealt with a lot of high-profile clients, so we made good money–hush money. But I'm going to stay optimistic until I've exhausted all my options. I haven't had time to job hunt since I was let go from my internship, but I love it here, and I'll do everything I can to stay."

Grace picked specks of salt off a pretzel she had hardly touched, she could see Roman working her situation out in his head.

"And if you end up having to move back up North with your aunt and uncle, do you see yourself being happy?" he asked, his face sincere.

"Not really. That place harbors a lot of bad memories. But we all don't get the spot we want. There was one opening, and I didn't get picked. So, I have to head back down to the minors," she said, trying to speak his language.

"Well, I'm definitely crossing my fingers for the best-case scenario. And it's only mildly for selfish reasons," he said, reaching across the table to give her hand an encouraging squeeze.

"Me too," Grace admitted, realizing she had never considered *this* happening. She never considered that Roman, the NHL player, the guy with the leaked nudes, and more Stanley Cups than seemed fair, would consider their future past the first date.

Roman sat back and rubbed his stomach. "Well, I think I ate too much," he said, taking notice of her barely touched food. "And I see you didn't," he teased, lightening the mood back up.

"I think I'm too nervous to eat around you," she admitted, because why not.

"Why would you be nervous?" he asked playfully.

"Oh, I don't know, maybe because I'm on a date with a super famous, super good looking hockey player." she blushed, bringing her icee up to cover her face.

"What? I'm famous?" he teased, pulling her icee away.

She rolled her eyes at his ridiculous flirting. But she knew he loved the idea of her not giving a shit about his fame. Grace liked him before she knew all that, and she was quickly realizing that while him being a hockey player *was* pretty hot, it wasn't the thing she found the most attractive about him.

"So, Grace, how do you feel about getting out of here with a super good looking hockey player?" he said, a cocky grin lining his handsome face.

She took his hand with no hesitation, and when she stood, he pulled her into his arms. She smiled up at him. "Don't let it go to your head, Roman Graves." her breath uneven with the close proximity of him.

Was this the moment, she wondered, was this how their first kiss happened? She wasn't opposed to it, but she would rather they both didn't have hot dog breath. She thought about Jess teasing her over her choice of underwear and she suddenly realized her roommate was absolutely right, if the night ended with anything more than a simple goodbye kiss, she would absolutely allow it.

"Too late, it went to my head the second you said it. You think I'm a super famous, super good looking hockey player," he said with a wink.

Roman's hands found hers, and just when she thought he was going to give her a hot dog breath kiss, he pulled away and led her to the exit of the arena.

***

Roman had never really been in situations where he wanted to hold someone's hand, but this might be his new favorite thing. He found himself oddly surprised that sex, while on his mind, wasn't the thing he wanted most from Grace. He really just wanted to spend more time with her. He knew dating a hockey player was hard in and of itself. So, if he was really going to do this, he knew he had to make every moment count.

"So, I want to ask you to come over tonight," he admitted once they were back in the car. The smile that lit Grace's face made it ten times harder to say the next part, the words feeling foreign to him. "But, I think the right thing to do is to take you home. I really like you, Grace, and I really want to take this as slow as I can."

He watched as her face seemed to fall with disappointment, which only caused his impatient dick to twitch. She *wanted* him to invite her over. She wanted to break her own set of rules and let *her* guard down, it was evident in the way she was looking at him. He wanted to reach out and take back the words he had just said, but she broke the silence.

"I think it's probably for the best as well," she agreed.

And that was that.

The drive back was relatively quiet. There was a sense of calm between the two of them, an easy silence. He had so much he wanted to ask her, and so much he wanted to share, but for some reason, it felt like he was learning so much more about her—and about himself—in this moment that involved no words at all.

He pulled up in front of her apartment and got lucky for the second time with parking, and wondered if it was a Grace thing. If for some reason the universe was pulling everything into alignment for them to work out. But if that was the case, why didn't she get the job? He couldn't lose her. He had only been on one date with her, and already he was coming up with crazy game plans to keep her in the city, close to him, hell, in the city *with* him.

"This *still* isn't a legal parking space," Grace said, and okay, maybe he hadn't gotten lucky with parking, maybe he had broken the law twice in one night to park as close to her apartment as possible, but he was feeling optimistic about it all, and that had to stand for something; parking ticket or none, right?

"I know. I'll just pay the ticket if I get one," he said, and regretted how much it made him sound like a douchebag.

She looked up at him in judgment, then smiled and shook her head in disbelief. "Unbelievable," she muttered under her breath, a hidden smile on her face. He raced from the car to get the door for her one last time tonight.

"You probably shouldn't walk me up," she said. "They might tow you."

He reached for her hand, and she willingly gave it. "It's okay. If they tow me, I'll just crash on your couch," he teased. "Besides, there's no way I'm not walking you to the door. I haven't been on any real dates, but I know a thing or two about the expectations."

Grace laughed. "Oh, haven't you heard? Any old-fashioned expectations are out the window since Tinder," she teased.

"What's tender?" he asked, playing dumb.

"Ohhh, right, a fancy hockey player like yourself probably never needs dating apps," she said, looking up at him through her thick dark lashes.

"The only dating app I've used is the one where you order take out during Christmas and ask the food delivery girl for her number."

Grace beamed. "Oh, yeah, and how'd that work out for you?"

"Pretty fucking good," he said, his face as equally smitten as hers. "She made me wait four months, but overall, I'd say it panned out."

"And how was the food she delivered?" she asked, stopping at her front door to face him.

"The food was amazing. Would have been better with company."

"Maybe don't order so much next time?" she suggested.

"Or maybe, next time, you stay and help me eat it."

"Are you suggesting a second date, or did I read too much into that?" she asked, scrunching her nose up in question.

"I absolutely want to go on a second date," Roman said, and then became distracted by the flashing lights of a police vehicle that sat behind his illegally parked car. "And I wanted to kiss you goodnight too, but I think my car is getting a ticket, and I don't want to rush our first kiss, so I'm going to make *you* wait this time. I'll text you when I get home?" he offered, looking over his shoulder watching as the cop got out of his car.

Grace pushed him away. "Go! Go flaunt your celebrity status to get off the hook. And yes, text me," she said, shooing him away.

He made it halfway down the steps then stopped to look back. "And what about the kiss?" he asked. "Would you have let me?"

Grace smiled from ear to ear and shook her head in disbelief at his question because, yes, obviously, yes, she would have absolutely let him kiss her.

"Well?" he shouted at her.

"Did I not make it obvious?" she asked.

"Can you ever just answer my question without a question?" he asked back.

"Go!" she shouted at him, laughing, and pointing at his car, refusing to say it outright. He shook his head at her, giving her the biggest smile, he couldn't help it, he couldn't remember the last time he felt this good, this happy.

He was so fucked. He was so utterly fucked up over this girl.

Chapter Twenty-One

G race fell back against the door of her apartment to catch her breath for what felt like the first time since the date with Roman started.

Roman admitted he had planned to kiss her, and the very idea of it made her insides dance. She could have told him she desperately *wanted* him to kiss her. But she had to leave him guessing. She had to allow herself some kind of control over him, because if she was being honest, she felt like one date had left her spiraling in what could only be described as "feelings" for Roman Graves.

Jess rushed from her room at the sound of Grace getting home, her face red and shiny with some kind of night serum and her hair in a messy knot on top of her head. "Holy shit, you went on a date with Roman Graves," she said, taking a seat on the couch, patting the spot next to her.

Grace took off her high-top chucks and put them in the shoe rack by the door before making her way to sit next to her roommate.

"Tell me everything," Jess demanded, and right as Grace went to talk her phone chimed with a text. "Oh my god, is he already texting you?" Jess asked, and he was.

Grace opened the text. It was short and sweet, and for some reason the simplicity of it made her heart race.

"What does it say?" Jess begged.

Grace looked up at her roommate, trying to contain the excitement she felt over the simple one-word text, "It just says, 'Hi'."

"Hi? That's it? No dick pic that you would most definitely show me if I promised to never tell a soul?" Jess asked.

"There's no dick pic that I would most definitely *not* show you even if you promised to never tell a soul. Besides, if you google Roman Graves naked there's leaked nudes out there, remember? It just says, hi. That's it."

"Grace, he must *really* like you," Jess said.

This made Grace laugh, because she knew she was far from being a romance expert, but someone texting you 'hi' was hardly an admission of love.

"No, really," Jess said, "Hear me out. It takes a special kind of confidence to send something so simple. It says he doesn't feel the need to bullshit. Also, might I add, he didn't take you home. At this point, I'm not sure if he tried to or not, but knowing you wore cute undies and you're home before midnight leads me to believe he didn't offer. I know you're far from promiscuous, but I also know you're a hot-blooded woman who would not have been able to say no to a night with Roman-fucking-Graves. And if he didn't take you home, then he absolutely respects you and wants to take it slow and just..." Jess paused and took a breath, then added, "He totally likes you."

Grace felt all of Jess's rant was valid. She couldn't argue.

"So, what do I text back?"

"Hey." Jess said simply.

"Just hey? But that's almost the same thing *he* texted me," Grace said.

"Yeah, but you're playing a game now. Trust me. Trade him a simple hi, for a hey. It will drive him crazy and make him want more," Jess confirmed.

"But what if I don't want to play games?" Grace asked, because it was true, she had never been a fan of games, that's why dating always went so poorly for her. She didn't want to wait X number of days to text back, or whatever the rules were.

"Trust me, send a "hey" and watch how fast he texts back begging for more," Jess suggested, and who was Grace to argue?

She typed out, "Hey." and hit send.

The text was almost immediately marked as read. He saw her *hey*, and now she had to wait.

Fuck.

It felt like a game even if she said she wasn't playing one.

"Now what?" Grace asked.

Jess settled in on the couch. "Now you tell me every detail of the date until that man makes it home safe and texts you back asking you to marry him of course."

Grace told Jess everything she could remember, some of the night feeling oddly foggy. There were parts of the date that seemed like a blur, or something out of a rom-com. Surely this wasn't her life. Her life was interning. And being broke. And delivering take out. And studying. And not getting the job.

How was she suddenly living some kind of fairy tale? How long could it last?

Her phone chimed. Jess squealed with excitement and Grace opened the new text.

Roman:

> Just got home. I should sleep. I have practice early tomorrow. And if you've been following hockey as closely as you said you are, then you know my team desperately needs a good practice.

Grace and Jess both let out disappointed sighs at his need to go to bed.

"He does need to rest. If they don't win this last game in Arizona, they won't make the playoffs," Grace said, feeling the need to defend him.

Her phone buzzed again.

Roman:

> But who am I kidding? I can't sleep right now. I feel like I'm buzzing and I didn't even drink.

Grace looked over at Jess, reading her the text. Jess's face said it all.

"Go," she encouraged. "Go text Roman Graves in private all night. But just know that if he sends any pics of his abs, I want to see them tomorrow morning," she teased.

Grace made her way to her room, "You can literally just Google 'Roman Graves shirtless', there's only like a million pictures of him on the internet."

"You've totally been Googling him shirtless, haven't you? You are so fucking horny for him, Grace it's not even funny," she teased.

"Goodnight, Jess," Grace said, not even entertaining her room-mate's jabs, because Grace knew damn well, she was right, she was ab-solutely horny for Roman—who wouldn't be?

Grace:

> I really don't want to be the reason you have a bad practice tomorrow.

> I'm kinda invested in how your team does now. I need you to win.

She began to get ready for bed waiting for his text back. She pulled off her jeans, and damn, the underwear she had on *were* hot.

Roman:

> I think you might already know this, but the rest of this week is going to be a little chaotic for me, with practice and then the game in Arizona on Thursday.

> I just don't want you to think it's because I don't want to see you again, or I'm not interested in you. I just have a demanding career.

Grace could whole-heartedly say she didn't mind demanding. She knew eventually she would also have a demanding job. It was about balance and communication.

Grace:

I know what I'm getting myself into.

Roman:

Can I call you? I know I just saw you. But I can't
stay up too late, and I want to talk.

Before she could respond, her phone was ringing. She laughed at
his impatience. "Why ask if you were going to do it anyway?" she said
playfully.

"Always with the questions."

Following his lead from earlier, she offered him a simple, "Hi."

"Hey," his voice was low and sultry and she didn't know that
one word could pack so much punch—-particularly to her lower re-
gions—-but with Roman, anything could be sexy.

"So, that date was amazing," she said, flopping down on her bed
like a schoolgirl with a crush.

"It was pretty fun, wasn't it?" he asked, and it seemed like he was
reassuring himself just as much as he was her.

"So, Thursday..." she said, and she couldn't miss the deep breath
he sucked in on the other end of the phone. "Big game." she added.

"Yeah. I've never missed the playoffs in my NHL career. So, to say
the pressure is high would be an understatement."

"It's okay, you know? To miss the playoffs one year. Obviously,
I don't want that to be the case, but if no one has ever told you, I
guess I'm here to say that you've been amazing this year, and every year
before this one, and no one is going to blame you." she offered, using the
professional voice she often used with her patients.

"The shitty part is, I think I might be the reason we won't make it. After that whole incident, with the leaked pictures, I just couldn't focus. I struggled to act like a leader because I felt like I had let everyone down."

"I can see why you would feel that way, but you have to remember you play with an entire team of men that all have a role, and maybe you weren't the best this season at your role, but neither were they. It takes a whole team to win, not just one person, so you can't carry that burden alone."

"Are you using your master's degree on me right now?" he asked.

Grace giggled. "Maybe? I went to school to learn how to assess situations and give advice accordingly. It's second nature to me."

"Then let me ask you something, and I want you to be honest with me," he said.

Grace sat up a bit, preparing herself for the task at hand.

Roman took a deep breath and then said, "Do you think my celibacy could have messed up my game?"

Grace was taken aback. "Do I think a lack of sex could have thrown off how well you play hockey?" she asked, just to be sure.

"Yes. I've never—and I hate admitting this to you—but, I've never denied myself sex. And then, after what happened in December, I decided I might need to slow down, and not sleep around so much. I don't want to hurt anyone, Grace. And I thought not being in a committed relationship was the only solution. If I don't date, I can't cheat—like my dad—-and no one gets hurt. Only, I realized that I was hurting these women. By sleeping with them and dismissing them like a piece of used up trash. So, really, I was still hurting people, but I was too dumb to see it until it negatively impacted my career."

"Ok, so my initial response is yes, not having sex does affect men differently than women. I know some UFC fighters will abstain from sex before a big fight because it's said that abstaining can increase aggression and testosterone," she offered.

"So, it should have helped me then, not hurt me," Roman said, his voice light on the other end.

"It helps fighters, but they only have one fight that they train for, and when it's over, it's over. But you, you play night after night. It's a different scenario. I mean, did you at least..." she paused, feeling her chest grow hot just thinking about what she was about to ask. "Did you at least... you know?"

Roman laughed on the other end. "Grace, are you asking if I jerked off?"

"Yes," she confirmed, her whole body hot with equal parts embarrassment and arousal. "A release is a release, no matter how you get it."

"This is true," he agreed. "And yes, obviously I jerked off. But it's not the same. I guess it just felt like–and this is superstitious of me, I know–but it just felt like maybe not sleeping around was breaking tradition and it threw my game off."

Grace considered her own traditions: Panera bagels before a big test, hanging the test results on the wall in her apartment, The Beatles when studying, appetizers and beer at the bar with friends after hard days at the rehab facility. She had her own set of superstitions so she could relate, maybe not on an NHL level, but on some level.

"Grace?" he asked.

"Yeah, I'm here, just thinking," she said.

"And what have you come up with?"

She took a deep breath, and before she could stop herself, she said, "Maybe *we* should have slept together tonight, before Thursday's game. Test your theory and put it to bed."

She held her breath waiting for his response. He was oddly quiet which seemed cruel considering she had just asked him to fuck her–for superstition's sake.

"Roman?"

"Oh, I'm here. Just wondering how I'm going to sleep after a comment like that," he teased, his voice an octave lower, and laced with so much lust she could almost feel it through the phone.

She giggled nervously. "See, I can be funny," she said, trying to play it off as a joke.

"So, you were joking?" he asked. "Because I don't think you were. I don't think you're as much of a good girl as you think you are."

She felt breathless, and hot. She *was* a good girl, but god was she sick of it. She pulled her legs together to try and settle the throbbing sensation there. Roman was challenging her, and she couldn't blame him, she had basically offered him sex, what guy would pass on that? Especially if it also might mean a win that would land his team in the playoffs?

"Maybe there's a little truth to that statement," she said, her own voice heavy with need.

She could hear him breathing on the other end and felt her breath matching his, deep and rough.

"I should probably try and sleep before this conversation goes any further," he said, with a husky laugh.

"Yeah, me too," she agreed, disappointment lingering in her tone. She didn't want to say goodbye, not when they had just got to the good stuff.

"I want to see you tomorrow."

And yes, of course she wanted to see him too. Because while he had waited four months for her to be ready, she had also been waiting, wondering, and wanting this so desperately despite everything.

"Okay," she said.

"It won't be much fun," he warned. "Chances of me falling asleep mid conversation are pretty good after the kind of practice I'll have."

"I think we can manage to keep you awake for a few hours." she flirted, and honestly, she didn't even know who she was right now, but she liked it.

"I think so. Can I pick you up after practice?" he asked.

"That sounds perfect. What time do you think practice will be over?"

"I'll text you when I have an idea, is that okay?"

"Sounds good."

"Goodnight, Grace," he said, his voice low, filled with pure sex.

"Goodnight, Roman Graves."

Chapter Twenty-Two

R oman showed up to practice the next day and he felt oddly re-freshed, excited, and optimistic. The adrenaline from his date still pumping through his veins. He felt giddy, like a kid on Christmas Eve. His whole body felt electric. His heart raced, with anticipation for more Grace. He felt equally happy and nervous.

He didn't want to hurt her. And what if he didn't? What if he let this happen and it was good? What if he was nothing like his cheating father? The idea of being a better man than him was intoxicating—he did love a good challenge.

"Why are you smiling at 5:00 a.m.?" Liam asked, his hair messily standing up in the back, and one of his eyebrows pointed in the wrong direction with a deep sleep crease in his forehead.

"Just ready to skate," he lied; it was so much more than that.

"Sure," Liam said, unimpressed with Roman's blatant lies. "Tell me who she is when you're ready to stop busting my balls."

They entered the locker room together and the atmosphere was instantly heavy. Roman knew they were all feeling the pressure to get it right today at practice, to work out whatever kinks the team had that could keep them from winning. It felt like they needed a hockey miracle, especially with the way Arizona was playing, but he wasn't ready to count them out just yet.

"So," Liam said, pulling his pads over his head, "Ava said something about dinner at her place. She won't be able to make the game on Thursday, so she wanted to do a little something before we hit the road. She mentioned inviting you. Maybe you could bring whoever it is that has you grinning like a lovestruck idiot at 5:00 a.m."

Roman looked away, he would *not* be going to Ava's. He didn't have much time to spare, and what time he did have would be spent with Grace, *not* Ava.

"I have plans," Roman said, tightening the laces on his skates.

"'I have plans'? Is that how you talk to your best friend these days? 'I have plans.' What does that even mean?" Liam pried playfully.

"I met someone," Roman admitted, "and I like her."

Liam stopped dead in his tracks. "You like someone? Like, you *like* someone?"

Roman laughed, mostly because, yeah, it was pretty shocking, but also because thinking about Grace made him happy.

"Yeah, I met a girl that I can see myself with. She's different. She's not like the girls I normally go after."

Liam bumped Roman's shoulder. "Is she a lawyer or something? No, let me guess, she's older, more mature. A cougar?"

"She's none of those things. She's just a girl I met back in December when all the sex scandal shit was happening. She was busy, told me to call her in four months, and I did. And believe it or not, she was just as amazing as I remembered her to be," Roman confessed, Liam's jaw hitting the floor.

"Wait, let me get this straight, you waited *four months* for this girl? I don't know anyone I'd wait four months for, not when you're a famous hockey player who could literally fuck anyone you wanted."

Roman considered it. What *had* set her apart? Grace wasn't anything like the models he'd slept with, or the big-name celebrities he'd had a few fun nights with. Grace was worth the four month wait because she was *none* of those things. Grace was worth it because he had spent four months trying to forget her, and when the four months were up, she was the only thing he could think about.

"She's not a celebrity or a model. She's just a normal girl," he said, meaning normal in the utmost honorable way, because Roman was over these fake women, and their agendas. He was sick of the rat race of it all. "She delivered my food over the holiday break. And she was so fucking hot, but in a shy, plain-Jane, girl next door kind of way. It's hard to explain. But she didn't know who I was. She had no idea I was a professional athlete. That was refreshing, considering what I was going through at the time. I didn't know how much I needed that in a woman. Someone who isn't hung up on my hockey career."

"You should bring her to Ava's. She's been asking about you. She doesn't want our relationship to push our friendship apart–she would love to meet your mystery woman."

Roman wanted so badly to shake Liam, and tell him what kind of person Ava really was, but instead he considered bringing Grace around Ava and Liam. He wondered if Ava would finally back off if she saw that he was dating someone.

But he wasn't ready for that brand of drama. Not yet. He wasn't ready to subject Grace to Ava's toxic behaviors. He wasn't ready to introduce her to his friends, but most importantly, he wasn't ready to share his time with her.

"Maybe next time? It's still really new," he said, clapping Liam on the back before skating off on the ice for warmups. Two practices before Arizona. Two practices for the Knights to get their shit together and win one more game. That's all he needed—one more fucking win.

***

Grace woke up earlier than usual with butterflies in her stomach and a smile on her face. The first thing to cross her mind was Roman Graves. She beamed at the memory of cool air on her face while ice skating hand in hand with him. The way he found simple ways to touch her while talking last night, and his smile—god that smile would ruin her. Grace sat up and looked out her window to see the sun already blistering on the busy streets down below. Her day was wide open, she couldn't remember the last time she had a day with no real commitments.

She opened her laptop and typed in "CADC job + Los Angeles, California". If she was going to give this thing with Roman a fighting chance she had to start searching now.

There was no shortage of job openings. Everywhere was hiring. This was a city that moved fast, and hard, and the party scene had easy access to every kind of substance under the sun.

She clicked on the first job opening that popped up; it wasn't even in Los Angeles, but the city of El Segundo. She knew the city; her favorite taco place was there. The problem with working in El Segundo would be the commute. Not to mention this facility's starting pay was closer to minimum wage than some of the local burger joints.

She clicked the next listing. Better pay, but in San Clemente, which was an absurdly expensive beach town, so technically she would break even. She kept scrolling, clicking, and trying to make it work. She could always do food delivery too; Thai Spoon was constantly in need of help.

She scrolled—disappointment settling in—and just when she was ready to start looking in Northern California again, she saw a listing that made her stop. She held her breath to read it again, her heart began to hammer in her chest. She couldn't believe what she was seeing.

Did she believe in fate? Not really.

Divine intervention? Nope.

Meant to be? Hadn't put much stock into it.

But she found herself ready to reconsider all angles. Something about this job listing looked a hell of a lot like a lucky rabbit's foot holding a four-leaf clover with a fortune cookie fortune on top of it that read 'The thing you want is right in front of you.'

Company: Los Angeles Knights
Needed: FULL TIME CADC.
Must have CADC-III certification, master's in behavioral science required, 2+ years experience, flexible schedule.

With shaky fingers she clicked the link to submit her resume.

Chapter Twenty-Three

Practice was more than awful. The team couldn't make a pass. Their goalie couldn't see the puck. Defense was sloppy. Coach was pissed, Roman was exhausted, and things were not looking good for the Knights.

He didn't say anything to his teammates in the locker room. There was nothing to say that they weren't already thinking. Tomorrow they would wake up and do it again. He knew he wouldn't be much for company tonight, but the thought of going home to an empty house after a practice like that sounded much worse than it normally did.

"You going to see your delivery girl tonight?" Liam asked, as they walked out to the parking garage, their hair still wet from their showers, Liam sporting a new gash on his cheek from his visor—a tell-tale sign of a bad practice.

"Probably," Roman lied, because there was no "probably" about it, he would see Grace tonight, even if it ended with him falling asleep in the hot tub.

"You should be a fun date after today's practice," Liam said sarcastically, rubbing his thick hand over his aching shoulders. "Does she know what she is getting into, dating a professional athlete?"

Nothing could prepare her for that, but he liked to believe Grace wasn't naive. She knew what busy felt like. If anyone got it, Grace did.

"I think she has a good head on her shoulders." Roman said.

"Is she smart?" Liam asked.

"She's really smart, has her master's in behavioral science. She's going to be a drug and alcohol counselor," Roman said.

Liam beamed, he was genuinely happy for Roman, and it showed. Roman only wished he could be happy for Liam in return, but he knew too much, and sadly, Roman was preparing for the aftermath that would come when Ava did something to break Liam's heart.

"I'm happy for you, man," Liam said. "I can't wait to meet her."

"Thanks, but first, we have a game to win. Right?" Roman said, and he realized it was just as much a reminder for himself as it was for Liam–*keep your head in the game, Roman.*

"That's right, we got this, I know it. We'll figure it out come Thursday." he said, his attempt at assurance missing the mark.

"I sure fucking hope so," Roman said clicking the lock on his car. "See you bright and early tomorrow."

"Yeah, I'm already dreading it."

Roman got in the car and pulled out his phone.

Roman:

I'm sorry. Practice was hard and long. Do you still want to see me?

He sat in the parking garage waiting for Grace to message him back. His heart raced when he saw her name pop up with a new text.

Grace:

> Do *you* still want to see me?

He laughed, because he knew this wasn't a question fueled by insecurities, *this* was a question for the sake of a question...because Grace never gave a straight answer.

Roman:

> I'm on my way to get you. How does the hot tub sound?

He started to drive towards her apartment and considered if he would be good company tonight. He decided it didn't matter, he liked the idea of being with Grace with zero expectations. Just two people, hanging out, getting to know each other—possibly making out—which he loved the idea of.

Grace:

> Absolutely. I can't remember the last time I relaxed in a hot tub. I'm so excited.

He loved that she was excited about the little things. He had spent so much time with people that took everything for granted, that he forgot what it looked like to have someone in his life that was genuinely appreciative.

***

"Jess," Grace shouted from her bedroom. "Bathing suit emergency."

She could hear Jess' heavy foot fall heading to her room. "Bathing suit? Girl, go nude, you know you're both thinking it," she joked.

Grace stood with her hands on her hips, unamused. "I'm serious, Jess. We're going in his hot tub and I honestly don't know what suit to wear. I'm freaking out because he'll be here soon-ish, depending on traffic, and I'm really nervous because what if he wants sex, and what if *I* want sex. He's a professional fucking hockey player. And it's all getting very real that I'm kinda sorta dating him, or at least we are going on dates, and hanging out, and he wants to spend his time with me after practice when he has one of the biggest games of his life in two days, and...help. Just help me. I'm spiraling and I don't want to fuck this up."

Jess very calmly sat on Grace's bed. "Okay, first thing, take a fucking deep ass breath. *He* is pursuing you. *He* called you. *He* asked you out, and then waited four months. He sent bagels. He is leading the texting, calling, and initiating. Roman is very obviously into you. So, there's that," she said.

"You're right," Grace agreed, walking to pull her swimsuits from a tote that was crammed in a small corner of her even smaller closet.

"I know I'm right, I usually am. Now, let's see your options," Jess said, picking up a deep green one-piece with a look of distaste on her face.

Grace grabbed it. "To be fair, this is sexy for a one piece."

"Okay, I don't care how sexy you think it is, the one-piece is a no. We need skin to show. We need your amazing ass to be on display."

Grace agreed. She knew her ass was one of her biggest assets, and she meant that in the physical sense as much as the literal.

"Okay, so there's this one," Grace said, holding up a floral print bikini. The top was a red bandeau style, which didn't help her itty-bitty-titty situation at all, but the bottoms were cheeky and rode up high on her hips, accentuating her curves.

"No. The top is wrong. It'll look weird if he pulls it down to see your boobies," Jess said very seriously, the word *boobies* making Grace laugh.

"Okay," Grace said, she picked up a pair of black high rise bottoms that had a neon green elastic band. The back was cheekier than she usually wore. She felt undeniably sexy when she had tried it on, so she kept it like a small indulgence. "These are probably my most revealing pair of bottoms," she said, and before she could finish Jess snatched them from her hands and held them up to examine.

"These are the ones. Where's the top?" she asked, digging through the bin.

Grace found the black top, the elastic band also neon green like the bottoms. "It's a halter, and while it's probably a more modest top, it helps me in the chest department the best, so the bottoms and top balance each other out."

Jess held the bottoms up against Grace's body. "I hope you shaved," she began, "because something tells me a lot of ass is going to be showing and Mr. Graves is going to have a hard time keeping his hands off you."

Grace blushed. It had been so long for her, and now that all the stress of school and the internship were gone, she realized she had neglected certain needs.

A text came through.

Roman:

> Would you mind if I didn't come up? I'm parked illegally again.

She texted back.

Grace:

> I'll be right down.

"Okay, he's here," she said, tossing the bikini into her purse. "I'm so fucking nervous. I know for sure he's going to kiss me tonight, and I'm not positive I won't let things go further."

Jess squealed with girlish excitement. "Good! I hope you do. Let loose, Grace. Have fun. Let him make you feel good. And if by chance nothing comes from this, at least you got off with a hot hockey player."

Jess was right. If all else failed, at least Grace would forever have a good story to tell.

"Okay," she said, heading for the door. "Thank you. I love you, wish me luck."

Jess held the door for her, waiting for her to leave. "I love *you*. And good luck times one hundred."

Grace heard the lock click behind her as she headed down the stairs. Roman stood outside his car, his body leaned against the passenger side door waiting for her. He was as handsome as she remembered, only today his cheeks were a bit flushed from the strenuous practice, and he was dressed down, in sweatpants and a tight black Knights tee, with a fresh pair of running shoes on. She couldn't decide which version of him she found the most attractive, Roman in his pre-game suit? Roman in his street clothes? Roman in his sweatsuit? She decided she wouldn't make a scientific conclusion until she saw him in person in his hockey gear, and possibly his birthday suit.

Chapter Twenty-Four

Roman remembered thinking Grace was *cute* when he first met her. She was simple and simple translated to *cute*. Over his years with the NHL he had started to formulate this idea of what the perfect woman looked like; tall, long legs, thin, fit, big tits, nice ass, blonde, done up, plastic. But now, as Grace walked towards him in her high waisted jean shorts–that showed off her gloriously thick thighs–paired with a vintage L.A. Knights shirt—that made him smile like a damn fool—seeing her, in her element, no frills, no facades, he realized those other girls were fuckable, but Grace was someone he wanted to wake up next to. Grace was someone he wanted to take his time with. He wanted to slowly unlace her high-top converse and slip them from her tiny feet, and for some reason, this made his heart hammer and his cock stir far more than any pair of Louis Vuittons ever had.

When she got to the bottom of the stairs, she stopped for a second, shrugged her shoulders as if to say, *I'm here, this is what you get*, and he smiled back, as if to say, *You're everything I want*. It took everything in him not to pull her into his arms and kiss her right here, with his car parked illegally and the sounds of busy L.A. traffic surrounding them.

"Hi," she said, stepping into his space. He could smell the faint sweetness of her shampoo; his body warmed with her scent so close.

He decided against the kiss, not here, not now, and leaned in to hug her. And fuck, she was a good hugger. He didn't know when the last time he hugged someone was and felt the anxiety of hockey slide off his back–which might not be the best thing, considering he had the biggest game of this season coming up–but he hugged her, nonetheless.

"You look..." he paused, his brain had been trained to think this brand of woman was *cute*, but his dick said otherwise, so he led with his dick and said what he was really thinking, "You look fucking hot."

Grace blushed immediately; he wondered how long it would take to make her entire body blush.

She shrugged off the compliment. "Thanks?" she said, in question form.

"Why is everything a question with you?" he teased, opening her door.

"I just don't often consider myself *fucking hot*," she said, mimicking his voice. "So, it felt like a questionable compliment."

"I was going to say cute," he offered, and she nodded her head in agreement, "but then I realized cute is a word you use for a little girl in her Easter dress, and the way my body responded to seeing you in those jeans, and that *fucking* Knights shirt, yeah, no, cute is *not* the word."

He shut her door before she could respond, but he didn't miss out on the pride-like smile she had at the mention of the L.A. Knights shirt. He climbed into the driver's seat and started the car. Before he drove away, he leaned over the center console and kissed her cheek, the skin there warm under his lips. He wanted more instantly, the way Grace let out a small gasp at the small act of intimacy made his every nerve ending come to life.

When he pulled back Grace was looking at him, her face a bit shocked, but the way she was trying and failing to hold back a smile made it clear she had approved.

"So, you liked the shirt then?" she asked.

"Grace, seeing you in that shirt... you have no idea." he said, his voice low, and insinuating.

"I had it long before I met you," she teased.

"Oh yeah?"

"Yeah. Found it in a thrift store. But before, when I used to wear it, it meant nothing to me," she said.

"And now?" he asked.

"Now..." she said, taking her time to think about it. "Now when I wear it, it feels like I have this wonderful secret. I feel like I'm a part of something bigger than just owning a shirt from a thrift store."

She reached over and ran her fingers firmly over Roman's shoulder. The press of her hand against his sore muscles made his breath hitch and she pulled back instantly.

"Did I hurt you?" she asked.

"No, it felt good. Every muscle in my body hurts," he said, reaching to take her hand in his.

"Will the hot tub help at all?" she asked.

"It will, but mostly, I'm just happy I have you with me to take my mind off hockey for a few hours."

***

They talked the entire drive to Roman's house. Conversation with Roman was easy. He asked good questions and she gave good answers. He asked about her day and she instinctively almost told him about the job opening she had applied for with his team but held back, realizing she wasn't ready to go into detail with him about that just yet. She gave him a generic answer and told him she had been job hunting. Changing the subject quickly, she asked about his practice, and he told her how hard it was, and how his best friend Liam had called him out for smiling so much at 5:00 a.m.

Grace beamed, because *she* had done that. She had been the one to make Roman Graves smile like a fool at hockey practice.

When they pulled up to the house, the garage opened on its own, and she wasn't surprised. When you're rich, doors usually open for you. His garage was pristine, organized, and modest. There was a deep freezer in the corner and she wondered if it was full of expensive meat and Costco sized boxes of frozen junk food. Which was what she always considered being rich looked like.

"Do you have a whole cow in there?" she asked, patting the top of the freezer.

"I do," he said. "But I also have every kind of frozen snack you can think of." he smiled, and she appreciated his balance of being a healthy hockey player and a relatable trash panda.

"Do you have bagel bites?" she asked.

Roman looked back at her and very seriously said, "Grace, if you can have pizza on a bagel, you can have pizza anytime."

She snorted out a laugh at his monotone rendition of the Bagel Bites jingle.

When they entered the house, the lights came on as she walked across the marble floor hallway. When they entered the massive open concept living room she took in the stunning decor, simple and clean. The furniture was grand with white coverings; she wondered if he ever ate on them, it seemed like a dangerous game. The majority of the far side of the living room was windows that overlooked the Los Angeles mountains, the winds they had been experiencing had managed to push the city pollution away, leaving the sky clear, and beautiful. She held her breath at the beauty of it all, the city lights managed to look romantic from this high up.

"This view is amazing." she said, slowly walking towards the massive windows.

"Isn't it? It's what sold me on this house."

Roman came up beside her. Her body instinctually leaned into his sudden nearness. "Wanna see something cool?" he asked softly in her ear. She could feel the warmth of his breath on her neck, sending shivers down her spine. He was so close, so warm, so safe; yes, *yes*, she absolutely wanted to see something cool. She wanted to see everything she could with this man.

He stepped forward and pressed his hand on the seam of one of the windows. As he pushed, it glided open, folding into the other window like an accordion. The warm night breeze pushed her hair back off her face, and in that moment she thought she might be able to settle for this and this alone tonight: the Los Angeles hills, the lights of the city down below, and the warmth of the night caressing her bare legs.

Her body was covered in chills just standing in his house, taking in the view; her body responded to its beauty almost as intensely as it responded to the man standing next to her. She had never been so impressed by something so available. She realized she had taken things like this view for granted since she moved to L.A. She had kept herself so busy she had never allowed herself any enjoyment. And now, if she didn't get the job with the Knights, she may not have much time left to really let herself make up for lost time.

Roman tugged on her hand. "Do you still want to go in the hot tub?"

"Hot tub sounds amazing. It's beautiful tonight."

"It is," he said. She could feel his eyes intent on her. He took her hand and tugged her to follow. "Do you have your suit with you?"

She held up her purse.

"It fits in there?"

"Small suit, I guess," she shrugged, biting back a smile at his wicked grin. "Where should I get changed?" she asked, suddenly very aware of how close to naked she would be with Roman, whose body was nothing less than that of a Greek god. What if he didn't find her attractive once she removed all her layers? What if he hated small breasts? And her ass, what if it was too big for him? She had seen the women he had slept with, all the same, the type of women who would blow over in the wind, the type of women who had enough plastic in them that their funerals would probably be held at a recycling facility.

"I have a pool house. You can change in there" he said, leading her out through the large, open window and around to his oasis of a backyard.

"Holy shit," she said under her breath, causing Roman to laugh.

"Nice, right?" he asked.

She turned to face him. "You know it's impressive, don't play modest."

"Get changed, and meet me at the hot tub. I'll go get my trunks on," he said, turning to leave.

She couldn't help but watch for just a second as he walked away, because his ass in those sweatpants was something you didn't sleep on.

The pool house was nicer than most hotel rooms she had stayed in. It felt like a five-star, high end spa, smelling of eucalyptus and mint. There was a massage table and she wondered if Roman had a private massage therapist he used often enough to have a separate little space to get massages.

She went into the restroom and slipped out of her clothes and into the bikini she brought. The lighting was soft and complementary. She looked herself over in the mirror, turning to check out her ass, pulling the bottoms up just so on her hips. She felt sexy, she hoped Roman felt the same.

***

Roman waited by the hot tub and braced himself for the sight of Grace in a swimsuit. Something about seeing Grace in a swimsuit had him stupidly turned on.

She came around the side of the pool house and Roman felt like he was punched in the gut at the sight of her in a little black bikini, with neon green accents—his team's colors. It was modest, but not prudish. The top covered her breasts in triangles, wrapping up to tie around her neck and he noticed her breasts were on the smaller side, but fuck, they worked so well on her body. Her waist was tiny, and her bottoms rose high on her hips, accentuating her curves.

He could tell she was nervous, so he looked at his feet for a few seconds, to give her time without his eyes on her so intently. When he looked back up, she was there in front of him, and he was ruined. She was fucking gorgeous, and her body was unbelievable. He needed to get into the hot tub before his small black trunks turned into a small black tent.

"Hi," she said, nervously. He could tell that she needed his approval, and he had no issues doing just that.

"Hey. You look un-fucking-believable, Grace," he said, taking her by the hand, guiding her to do a small spin. She giggled and went along with it; her body language loosening up.

"Thanks. This suit is new-ish, so I'm still not sure about it."

"You can be sure that *I* like it. Shall we?" he asked, hinting at the hot tub.

"Yes, let's get your muscles feeling better," she said. He held out a hand, insinuating ladies first, but obviously with selfish gain in mind, he had to see her ass in those bottoms.

Her body was perfection. The way the suit wanted to ride up on her ass made him want to yank it up, pull it against her until she squirmed at the tight pull of the fabric on her skin there–maybe she would let him–*or* maybe he needed to chill the fuck out and stop letting his brain go there.

The water was hot, almost too hot, but it felt good on his sore muscles. He felt his body truly relax for the first time in a *long* time.

"This is amazing," she said, gesturing to his backyard, the hot tub, the infinity pool, the view, *him*?

"I'm happy you like it. I don't have people over often," he admitted.

"Why not? If I had a house like this, I would have people over all the time to enjoy it with me."

The glow of the string lights above them showed the small beads of sweat that were gathering on her upper lip–he wanted to lick them away.

"I think so much of my life is public knowledge that I always keep my house to myself. I just need something that's mine and mine only," he said.

"Do you ever bring women here?" she asked, taking him by surprise.

Was she asking because she wanted to know about his past or was she asking because she wanted to know if he set her apart in doing so?

"No. I don't date."

Her face scrunched up with discomfort over the statement, so he backtracked. "I mean, before you, I didn't do this sort of thing with women. You, Grace, are in fact the first woman I have brought here with romantic intentions in mind."

Roman reached for his phone and opened an app, dimming the lights throughout the entire backyard.

"Just like that, huh?" she asked, signaling to the new lighting he managed with one swipe of a finger across his phone.

"What?" he asked, playing coy.

"With the snap of your finger–bam–mood lighting,." she said, a playful sexy smile on her face.

"Is *this* mood lighting?" he asked, his brow hitched, his smile crooked and dubious.

"I think so?" she giggled. "I'm not really an expert on this sort of thing, but it definitely made me feel a bit seduced."

"Would you be mad if I told you, it *was* intentional–the lighting?" he asked, bringing his hand above her shoulder, letting water fall from his fingertips to trail down her neck and across the smooth skin of her breast bone.

She looked down as the water rolled along her body, and then with hooded eyes back up at him. "I think I might be offended if it wasn't intentional," she admitted, her voice low.

Roman could see where this night was headed. He knew where *they* were headed. He wanted more than anything to take things slow with Grace, to prove to her that she wasn't just another puck bunny that he fucked and discarded after he got off. But he wasn't dumb, he knew by the way she looked at him that she wanted it too. Fuck the slow burn, they had already done that for four months. He needed to be open. Fuck, he needed to be transparent. Because he needed her to trust him despite his past.

"I want you to know that your first impression of me—in the head-lines—was accurate," he said, his voice sincere, and steady. He watched as her face fell slightly with disappointment.

"Okay," she said, drawing out the word, asking him to go on.

"That's exactly who I was when I met you. I was a man whore. I was completely shut off from the idea of being in a relationship. I used sex like some people use drugs, and I know you know a thing or two about that...about addiction. I have a lot of baggage in that department. My father did a number on me. I'm so afraid to hurt someone or let someone down because of the immense pressure I put on myself to be a good person, and because more than anything, my fear of becoming like my dad."

Grace pulled her body closer to him, her leg pressed up against his, her face willing and ready to hear what he had to say—things he knew he needed to say if he was going to be with her. He knew he wanted more, but he knew if he expected her to be with him, she should understand what she was getting herself into, the generational curses she would be up against.

"He married my mom young. She was beautiful, any man would have wanted her. But my dad got her, and sadly, he wasn't marrying her for the right reasons. He did it because he was in a position of power and with that position there comes a certain expectation for your lifestyle. Family is huge. It makes you seem stable and committed. So, he married her young, and while it was a love connection for her it was a business transaction for him. Marry the beautiful, prized wife. Have a child. Buy the house. Smile in the pictures. Shake the right hands. Donate to the best charities. When the cameras were gone though, and it was time to tuck me in, and read me a bedtime story, or when it was time to settle in with his wife, ask her about her dreams for their future, tell her she's beautiful; when it was time for him to love us the way a husband and father should, he had nothing left. He gave it all away to his career, and the press, and the parties, and eventually, he gave it all away to his mistresses." Roman looked up to see if Grace was still there, still real, still willing to sit beside him, to press her leg against him, knowing what kind of home he came from and what kind of man he was raised by.

She was still there.

She was still beside him, with her leg pressed against his.

She was still real and willing, and listening.

"Anyway," he continued, "I have this fear that I'll end up just like him. And being a professional hockey player almost sets me on the same path as him. I'm always in the limelight. I'm expected to have a certain kind of life, be a clean cut, respectable, gentleman. That's what the NHL loves to see. But I've been so afraid that if I do that; settle down, start a family, it will only be for the sake of my image in the public eye. For the sake of the NHL's pristine reputation. And in turn, I'll fall short, and do exactly what he did to his family. Love us when it benefited him and do what really made him happy in secret."

He felt Grace's hand on his back, and then in his hair, gently stroking, and kneading–simple acts of comfort. Roman didn't know when the last time was that someone touched him to comfort him.

He relaxed into her touch. He was tired, he was sore, and while he knew it had needed to be said, he had to make damn sure Grace was aware that while he might not be a *bad* man now, he had potential to become an awful one later. He had to let her know because he was certain that he wanted her in his life for more than one night of sex. He wanted to really know her. He wanted to watch her succeed. He wanted to introduce her to his friends and bring her to away games.

Away games.

Fuck.

Hockey flooded his brain. It was always there. Lingering. Especially when in two days he might have the greatest comeback in his history with the NHL, or the biggest letdown of his life. He looked over at Grace, trying to read her expression. Had he scared her away? Her gentle touch said otherwise, but this was new to him, the dating, the being vulnerable, the caring what the person next to him thought.

"Sorry, that was a lot," he said, trying to play it off like it was no big deal.

"It was a lot," she said, and he valued her honesty. "But it definitely helped me understand the parts of you that I didn't like. Parts of you that made me doubt us, whatever *us* is. I just knew going into this that your reputation said that whatever we have going on didn't have much room to grow before you ran, and now, after hearing all that, I think you might be done running. And maybe, I can be someone worth sticking around for. If I *can* be that for you, maybe you can prove to yourself that you are nothing like your father, and that you don't have to follow in his footsteps."

Roman loved the way Grace articulated things. He found her brain as attractive as her face, and her body.

"Good thing I set the mood lighting to blubber on about childhood trauma and shit," he joked.

"I think I might want you even more, now that I know what I'm up against," Grace admitted.

"Baggage is sexy?" Roman asked, half joking.

"No, not baggage. *Honesty*...honesty is pretty damn hot on you," she said, bumping her knee against his.

"Four months I tried to forget you, and the whole time, I was also planning out how I would convince you to trust me, and give me a chance," he said, letting his finger trail across her shoulder.

"And during those four months you were planning how to convince me, I was off being-"

"Busy?" he asked.

"I *was* extremely busy. Yes. But I was also falling in love with hockey, and ultimately, pining over this super-hot celebrity athlete that I had very stupidly dismissed."

Roman let his hand trace up her neck, his thumb brushed along her jawline, her skin was warm from the steam coming off the water, damp with sweat, and colored pink from the heat or maybe from his touch, he couldn't be sure, but he wanted to find out.

"I almost texted you so many times," he admitted, pushing her hair behind her ear, noticing how perfect and soft the skin was under his touch—he wanted to kiss her there—he wanted to kiss her everywhere.

Roman reached out and gently gripped Grace by her hips, guiding her very willing body to his. She straddled him, their faces close enough that he could see the small traces of freckles that dusted her nose.

"Why didn't you?" she asked, running her hands up his chest hesitantly. He could tell that she was still unsure of what she was allowed to do here, and where she was allowed to touch him. The innocence of it all only intensified how badly he wanted to show her that anything—*everything*—was allowed.

"Why didn't I text you sooner?" he clarified.

Grace only nodded her head in response, her eyes carrying the weight of her question.

"Two reasons," he said, his voice low. He let his eyes trail down her body before he answered, her skin a flawless flush of pink, her collar bones begging to be touched, the tiny beads of water on her shoulders a map of all the places his mouth should be.

Grace, without even realizing what it would do to him, rocked forward in his lap, drawing closer to him, aligning them in all the right places. "Tell me," she said, her voice shaky. "Tell me why, Roman."

He brought his hands below the water to her waist where he ran a finger under the elastic band of her bikini bottoms. He didn't miss the way her body responded to something so insignificant in the grand scheme of things. Her eyes gently closed as his fingers traced under the elastic band—his body burned for more reactions from her. His four months of waiting for her had left him hungry for her touch, starved even, but he had never once considered how long it may have been for her since *she* had been touched.

When was the last time this perfect woman was properly taken care of?

He brought his lips to her ear, only allowing the warmth of his breath to whisper across her skin. "The first reason I didn't text you sooner," he said, lowering his hands to gently grip onto her ass, "is because I didn't want to disrespect your wishes."

"And the second reason?" she asked, her eyes remained closed, her head tilting back just an inch, her voice breathless, and needy.

"The second," he said, this time letting his lips brush against her ear. "The second reason was because I wasn't ready, and I knew it. If I had texted you after a hard game, or a bad night, or when I was...needy, I would have ruined everything."

"And now?" she asked, pulling her head back just enough to make room for his lips that were hovering very close to her neck, and her jaw line, and so undeniably close to her mouth. "Are you ready now?"

He was so ready. Fuck, he had never been so ready for something in all his life.

His hand came to the nape of her neck, the other pressed into her lower back, beckoning her to him, filling that last bit of room they had left between them, before their lips met.

He kissed Grace with everything he had been wanting, needing, and carrying for her over the last four months.

Her lips were soft, and salty with the dew of sweat the heat of the water had created on both of their skin. He felt her body hum against his, an electric current, a crackle, a spark, and he encouraged her lips to part for him so he could deepen the kiss. She moaned against his lips, and his body responded like a livewire. He felt every nerve ending from his head to his toes blaze to life over this kiss. Over the way Grace's body pushed back against his, and the subtle way she moved against him, needy, but not showy or overdone.

Was *she* holding back? He knew he was. But he didn't want to push things too far, not tonight, not when he knew they had many more promising nights ahead of them where he could take his time, do this right for once in his life.

He moved his mouth from hers, and she arched her body to make room for him to trail his lips across her neck. He lingered on the smooth skin of her collar bone, kissing away the beads of sweat there, using his nose to push away the fabric of her bikini top to kiss the tops of her breasts. Soft breaths escaped her, letting him know this was as good for her as it was for him. He couldn't help but smile against her warm skin; when was the last time making out was this fun? This satisfying?

He kissed back up to her neck, and let his teeth gently latch to the skin there, nipping her without causing pain. She rolled her hips against him and fuck, if he had any ounce of self-control left it was about to snap at the friction she was causing in all the right places.

His fingers trailed under her ass, gripping her tight, and their bodies were close, so fucking close. He considered pulling away the fabric there so he could touch her, make her come undone.

"I want to make you feel good," he said. Grace's eyes met his, and he saw need in them—he wanted to take that need away. "But I told myself I wouldn't touch you tonight."

Grace nodded, in agreement, but he saw the disappointment hidden there.

"We can just kiss," she said, "We don't have to take it further."

Roman couldn't help but smile. "I do like kissing you."

"Same," she agreed, leaning into him, her lips latching to his earlobe before her teeth nipped at him there.

"But the thing is," he continued, "I still really want to make you feel good."

Grace sat up and looked at him incredulously. "Roman, I do feel good. I'm in a hot tub, making out with you. How could this night get any better?"

He leaned in, his mouth hovering close to her ear, her body covered in chills as his lips grazed her there when he spoke, low and steady. "I could make you come..." he paused, the soft inhale that came from her made his body come to life under her weight. "I could make you come *without* touching you. That way I keep my promise to myself, but I can send you home taken care of."

Grace bit her bottom lip and looked at him with both intrigue and confusion.

"Can I make you come tonight, Grace? Or is that too much too soon?" he asked, he was being sincere. If she wanted to stick to kissing, he would kiss her until every fingertip in this fucking hot tub was pruned.

"I don't know if I'm *actually* supposed to answer that?" she said, an innocent smile of confusion on her face.

"Do you trust me?" he asked.

She sat back a little in his lap to get a better look at him. "I'm still figuring that part out," she admitted, and he loved her honesty.

"Then let me ask you this; when was the last time you had an orgasm?"

Grace blushed a deeper shade of pink than she had been from the heat of the water. "A while," she said with a sigh.

"And if I told you I could make you feel good without touching you, would you let me?" he asked, his voice deep, and sure.

"Sounds like a magic trick," she said, looking up at him, her curiosity heavy.

"One swipe of my finger–*not* on your body–and I can make you come." He brought his lips to hers, kissing her deeply, taking his time while she considered his proposition.

"Or we could just kiss," he said, his mouth still on hers.

His hands found her hips under the water and gripped them tight as her arms wrapped around his neck, pulling his chest flush against hers. Their breathing grew unsteady, he wanted her, and the sounds she was making was all the proof he needed that she wanted him too.

Her mouth pulled away from his, and he thought that was it. She, like him, knew there was no coming back from this if they kept kissing and grinding, and panting like that.

"Okay," she said in barely a whisper, and Roman felt the shock on his face at her words.

"Okay what?" he asked, refusing to move forward with anything outside of heavy petting and kissing without complete and utter consent.

"Show me your magic trick," she said, her voice low and shaky.

"One swipe of my finger," he said, reaching for his phone.

Grace watched as he ran his wet fingers across the phone screen, toying with an app, and then, before she was ready the jets kicked on, startling her.

He sat his phone down and sank his hands back into the bubbling water to find her hips again. "See, magic."

Grace smiled in disbelief. "I was wondering how you were going to pull this off."

"There's a jet right behind you. And something tells me that if I hold you there long enough, you'll come."

He watched as Grace looked behind her, watching with deliberation as the jet caused the water to bubble around her with its pressure.

"What's it for?" she asked, turning back to face him. "Why do you have jets on the bottom of the hot tub?"

Roman gripped her hips tight as he moved his body and hers to the edge of the seat, the stream of pressure from the jet ripping between his legs. "Well, it's technically there to massage sore feet after a long practice. But tonight, it's to make you come. Because once you let me know it's hitting you in the perfect, sweetest spot, I'm going to hold you there until you're begging me to let you go."

***

Grace felt her heart hammering in her chest. She had experienced a decent amount of foreplay in her life, but this, *this* was something new. She was out of her comfort zone here, but her comfort zone had needed to be challenged for a long time now, and Roman had just the right kind of confidence to do it.

She felt his strong hands push her body back towards the bubbling jet, her eyes going wide the moment it hit her ass.

Roman's smile widened at her response. "How does it feel?" he asked.

She bit her bottom lip, looked him dead in the eyes and repositioned herself in his lap, allowing the jet to move from her ass to the front of her body. The pressure of the water hitting her exactly where he intended it to. She gasped audibly at the instant pleasure that rocked through her body as the water thrummed against her sex.

Roman pulled her body closer to his, spreading his thighs wider underneath her, pulling her legs apart for the jet. He leaned in, bringing her mouth to his, stealing one greedy kiss before he sat back, and watched as she rolled her hips to meet the hard pressure of the jet.

Grace, already turned on from just being with Roman, let out a soft moan as her body responded instantly to the sensation there. Grace gripped his shoulders tight, as the water pounded against her clit. Her body began to tense at the sensation. With her orgasm building she fell into his body and wrapped her arms around his shoulders tight, bracing herself against his chest as he held her by the hips over the stream of water.

He kissed her neck and shoulders, nipping and sucking as she moaned into his salty skin.

"Can I move your bottoms?" he whispered into her ear.

Grace moaned. "Yes. Do it."

His hand slid between her legs, pulling her bikini to the side with a quick yank allowing the pressure of the jet to hit her naked clit with blinding force. Her head flung back and she bit onto her bottom lip, trying to contain her moans as the jets pounded against her.

"Fuck this is the sexiest thing I've ever seen," Roman said.

The water hammered against her relentlessly, embarrassment tried to creep in but the sensation between her legs was too strong. Grace felt her body begin to spasm against Roman's, gripping onto him tight as her orgasm hit. "Okay," she cried out, low and husky, bracing herself against him, "Okay, okay, okay," she repeated as she her orgasm came on hard and strong, "ohhhh, fuck."

Roman let go of her bikini bottom and released her thighs. The intensity of the water suddenly too punishing against her sensitive clit. The moment he released her she pulled herself against him and away from the jets as her orgasm rocked through her from head to toe.

Roman held her tight in an embrace as she came, and came, and came.

She loosened her grip on him, but buried her face in the crook of his neck, unable to look him in the eye just yet. "That was not where I saw this date going," she said, bashfully, her body still trembling from her release.

"Me either," he said, kissing the top of her head, a satisfied grin on his face. "But I'm happy it did."

She pulled back to look at him. "I liked your magic trick," she said, smiling timidly, because this could get awkward if they let it–she had just come in front of him–on a hot tub jet, nonetheless.

"Just one swipe of a finger," he teased, before bringing his mouth back to hers for a slow, soft kiss.

Once their fingers and toes were nice and pruney, their lips good and swollen, and the heat of the hot tub had gone from relaxing to miserable, Grace pulled her body away from him, both of them flushed and wet from sweat and steam.

"You know, we can't makeout in here forever," Grace said, her lips puffy and red. "You have practice tomorrow."

"I do. But this was a really good distraction." He dipped down to run the tip of his nose between her breasts, and something about the little ways he found to touch her made her ache for more.

"Happy to be a help, even if you didn't, you know, get to—" she said, her face growing instantly hot.

"I'm fine. It was fun taking care of you tonight."

"You? Take care of me?" she asked playfully. "Sir, I think this one goes to the hot tub jet."

They both began to laugh. "How will I ever measure up?" he asked. And while Grace enjoyed the orgasm and the unique way it had happened, it would definitely be one she would never forget, she couldn't imagine it being better than the real thing with Roman.

He helped her out of the hot tub and Grace made her way back to his house once she changed, the tips of her hair damp from the hot tub making her natural curls spring to life. She sat her converse by the door and found Roman sitting on his couch in a pair of gray sweatpants and a tight black shirt with some kind of athletic branding on the chest. He was peacefully staring out at the city lights, his feet were bare, and she found his toes to be oddly handsome, if that was a thing, possibly from all the pedicures he admitted to getting.

"You look tired," she noted, taking the seat next to him on the massive couch that felt as expensive as it looked. She assumed everything in his life was going to feel extravagant.

He smiled, his eyes were dark and hooded. "Do I look that bad?"

"Not bad. I can just see that practice is catching up to you."

"I usually go to bed right after a practice like that," he admitted.

"Maybe I shouldn't have come over," she said.

"You absolutely should have come over," he assured her. "I was dying to kiss you. It was making it hard to focus on anything else knowing I planned to kiss you tonight."

"It was a good first kiss...amongst other things," she admitted.

"Just good?" he asked, his face cocky.

"Okay, maybe it was a little better than good," she said, deciding not to stroke his ego too much.

"Great?" he asked.

She laughed. "Now you're just being needy."

"Well, it was great for me. Watching you come undone...I'll never be able to unsee that."

"Seems a bit one sided," she said, wondering if he wanted her to return the favor, to which she would have no problem doing, but before she knew what was happening Roman gripped her hips, pulling her on top of him. His eyes were intense, the exhaustion was still there, but it was mixed now with want, and desire, and heat.

"Come to the game on Thursday," he said unexpectedly, the smile on his face wild and boyish.

She leaned back, to get a better look at him. "It's in Arizona."

"I'll fly you there. I can get us a room," he said, bringing his lips to kiss along her jawline.

"I don't know what to say." She tilted her head back to make room for him to keep kissing her there.

"Say yes, it should be an interesting game to say the least," he said, his lips pressed against her collar, his breath warm and satisfying on her skin.

"I don't know, Roman. I don't want to be a distraction or add anything to your plate. It's a big game for you."

"And that's why you have to be there," he said, pulling her in to kiss her nose, and then her forehead, and then her lips. "I want you there to celebrate with me if we win or...if we lose."

"You won't lose. You can't. I'm too invested at this point."

"Well, *if* we do lose—because we might—I want you there to help take my mind off of it." He trailed kisses across her neck. "Can you do that for me, Grace? Can you come to my game and wear my jersey, and cheer me on? Give me a face to look for in the crowd?"

She couldn't believe this was happening. She couldn't believe he wanted her there, in Arizona, at what could be one of the biggest games of the season for him.

"Yes," she said, her voice giving away her excitement. "I'd love to."

Roman pulled her against him and kissed her through his smile.

"I'll have Melissa, my P.A. set it all up tomorrow. I'll give her your number so she can contact you if she needs anything from you."

"Okay."

"But as for tomorrow," he started, "I won't be able to see you. I probably won't be able to see you until after the game, Thursday night. Will you be okay hanging out with my P.A. during the flight and before the game? She's really nice."

"I'm a big girl. I think I'll be able to handle it," she said.

"Good," he said, leaning in to kiss her again.

The slow drawl of this kiss felt like a promise between them, and it was. It was Grace promising to show up, it was Roman asking her to be there. It was committing to the next day, and sharing big moments together, it was a kiss that felt different than all the other kisses he had given her this far. Those kisses were filled with lust, this kiss was filled with promise.

"I should probably get going," she said, pulling away before it got too heated, which was where it seemed to be going very quickly. "You need sleep."

"Yeah," he agreed. "If I don't get you home soon, I'll end up falling asleep *on* you."

"I mean, this couch is amazing, but I might be uncomfortable to fall asleep on."

"Don't underestimate my ability to fall asleep anywhere," he said, releasing her hips so she could stand.

"Thanks for making out with me in the hot tub," he said with a tired grin.

"Anytime," she said, taking his hand as he led her to the garage.

"I remember when you were just a girl on my front porch delivering food, and now you're the girl leaving after spending time with me, and kissing me, and I don't know how that's even possible but I feel really fucking lucky it is."

She couldn't deny that her heart was hammering in her chest. A girl who before December didn't even know who Roman was. A girl who didn't fit the mold. And *he* was the lucky one? She was certain he had it backwards, but she wouldn't argue, not when she could feel his heart hammering in his chest too.

Maybe they were both lucky?

Chapter Twenty-Five

R oman called Melissa the second he got home from dropping Grace off. Excitement about the date, the game and just life in general had him eager to arrange for Grace to come to Arizona.

"What did you do?" Melissa answered, her voice raspy with sleep because it was unlike Roman to call at this hour after a day of intense practice.

"I met someone," he blurted out, feeling a bit silly at the admission.

Melissa gasped. "Like, a *someone*, someone?"

"Yeah, I met a girl, and I like her, and I'm excited, but also freaking out a bit because I don't know what I'm doing, or if I should be doing it at all, but she made me wait four months to call her, and now we are sort of dating, and I need you to help me get her to Arizona on Thursday." he said, quickly, his words a jumble of evident happiness.

"Hold up. You need to back up. I need a little more to go on here," she pried.

So Roman told her everything. "Her name is Grace."

"Grace Vanderbilt? The Victoria's Secret model?" she asked.

"No, she's not like that," he said, realizing he didn't know how to put it.

"Not like what? A model?"

"No, she's not a celebrity. In fact, she didn't even know who I was when we met. She had no fucking clue, Mel."

"Okay, so how does Roman Graves, the captain of the Knights, meet the one girl in the city of Los Angeles who doesn't know him, considering your face is plastered on billboards throughout downtown?" she asked. She had a point, Roman had wondered the same thing at the beginning of all of this.

"Remember during Christmas, when I was grounded?"

"Yes, how could I forget, it was a P.R. Christmas nightmare."

"Well, I met her then."

"How? You were grounded," she asked suspiciously.

"Don't worry, I didn't sneak out behind your back. She delivered my food," he said.

He heard her let out an audible gasp. "The one you asked me about tipping?"

"Yeah. She delivered me food, twice, and I tipped her four hundred dollars because—"

Melissa cut him off. "Was she also delivering pussy? What the fuck Roman? Four hundred dollars? Do you have any idea how insulting that must have been?"

"At the moment, no. But when she showed up the next day unannounced to return the money, I quickly realized that yeah, I may have crossed a line."

"Well, I like that she didn't keep it, shows promise. I would have kept it. I would have been a little offended, but I would have kept it for sure," Melissa said.

"Yeah, so she basically told me that she didn't want my pity, or charity, and I honestly didn't pity her at all, I just felt like it was the right thing to do considering *she* had to work on Christmas because *I* couldn't keep my dick in my pants."

"And?" Melissa asked.

"And I thought she was beautiful and charming. And super fucking gorgeous. So, I asked her out, despite my stance on dating."

"You mean to tell me this has been going on since December and you're just now telling me about it?"

"No, that's the kicker. She denied me. Told me she was busy for the next four months," he said, realizing how ridiculous it sounded after saying it aloud.

"So, what? You actually waited for four months?"

"Kind of? I couldn't stop thinking of her. At first, I thought she would be better off if I didn't contact her again, but I just couldn't get her face out of my mind, so when the four months were up, I texted her, and she agreed to see me, and I like her, Mel. Like, I really fucking like her. And I want her in Arizona."

"Well," she sighed, "It's a big game, Roman. Are you sure you need that kind of distraction?" she asked.

And he realized he didn't see Grace as a distraction at all. In fact, he couldn't remember the last time his brain felt so clear.

"She's the opposite of a distraction, Mel, she's a sounding board." he admitted, causing his stomach to flutter, and his heart to race, because holy shit, he had it bad for this girl and he knew there was no going back.

"Well shit. This is the last phone call I expected tonight, and yet I am pleasantly surprised. You keep me guessing, that's for damn sure Roman Graves,"

"So, can you make it happen?" he asked.

"I can turn water into wine, babe, might as well call me P.A. Jesus," she teased.

"You're the best."

"I know," she said smugly. "Send me her number. Does *she* know I'm doing this?"

"Yeah, she knows," he said, putting Melissa on speaker to send over Grace's contact info.

"Got it," she said. "You should get some rest, Hibbs is going to ride your ass tomorrow at practice."

God, he knew it was the truth. "One last thing," he said, before ending the call, "make sure she has a jersey to wear."

"With Liam's number on it? I hear the chicks dig his baby blues?" she teased.

"Don't you fucking dare," he said through a yawn.

"Note to self, get her the *right* jersey,"

"Night, Mel." he said, flopping down on the bed face first.

"I'm happy for you, babe," she said, and he was asleep before he even managed to say goodbye.

***

Grace woke to a slew of texts from someone named Melissa. She stated that she was Romans' personal assistant, and that she had set up arrangements for Grace to fly out to Arizona for the night to catch the game on Thursday. The last text asking Grace to call her when she woke up.

Not awkward at all.

It was all very intimidating if she was being honest with herself; dating Roman, already planning trips to watch him play, talking to his

P.A. She was very much out of her comfort zone. So, she procrastinated as much as possible. She checked the status on the resume she submitted for the position with the Knights–still pending–and she wondered if she was doing the right thing by keeping it from Roman. She just didn't want to bring him into it, she didn't need his help, nor did she want it. She needed to get this job all on her own.

She took a deep breath and hit call. It only rang twice before Melissa answered.

"Grace Fairchild, I've been waiting all morning for you to call," she said pleasantly.

Grace was caught off guard by Melissa's sunny disposition. "But it's only 9:00 a.m."

Melissa laughed. "I've been up since four. My days start early when my client calls me past his bedtime demanding I arrange for his new girlfriend to be flown to Arizona for the big game."

"I'm not his girlfriend," Grace corrected.

"Yet," Melissa said boldly. "Roman must really like you to be doing all this for you. It's sweet. I've never seen him invite a girl to a game in all my years as his personal assistant."

"I like him too," Grace admitted, timidly.

"You better, he's great and I have prayed for someone special to catch his eye. I didn't think it would be the delivery girl, but what a delightful story to tell the grandkids, am I right?" Melissa went on, and Grace was suddenly very curious what all Roman had told this woman.

"I'm not a delivery girl anymore," Grace said, feeling the need to elaborate.

"He told me a bit about you, but I would love to know more. Which brings me to my next point. I'm flying out with you tonight."

Grace didn't know if that reassured her or made her more nervous. She was just getting to know Roman and now she was going to have to spend the day with his assistant. It seemed like a lot, fast.

"Okay," Grace mumbled.

"Not a big talker?" Melissa asked.

"I can talk, I'm just still a little shocked this is happening. Four months ago I was delivering Roman his dinner and tonight I'm being flown to a different state to watch him play hockey," she said; it was quite surreal.

"Oh, it's happening sweetie, and to be honest, I'm just as shocked as you are. I've known Roman for a long time and the mention of dating to him was always met with a huge 'no', but I don't know... he seems to think you're something special."

"I didn't even know he was a hockey player," Grace said.

"And thank fuck for that. I can't stand puck bunnies."

"Puck bunnies," Grace said under her breath, she had heard Roman use the term too.

"Yeah, tall, model types, trying to score a hockey player husband?" Melissa said, clarifying the term.

"Oh, I know what they are," Grace said. "They're the girls that end up in leaked pictures."

"Ding. Ding. Ding," Melissa chimed before changing the subject. "So, our flight is at 4:00. I'll head over with a driver to pick you up at 1:00, and we can head to L.A.X. Sound good?"

"Sounds good," Grace lied, because it sounded wild, and she was low key freaking out.

"Yay," Melissa said. "Okay, I have a lot of shit to do before we head out, so I'm gonna go. Pack, shower, shave, do all the things, and I'll see you in a few hours."

"See ya," Grace said, and then hung up.

Her heart hammered in her chest.

Fuck.

Fuck.

Fuck?

How was this even real?

Grace showered, packed, unpacked, got Jess's approval, re-packed, and got ready. She added product to her hair to enhance her natural curls. She wore a pair of black high waisted bell bottom jeans, her favorite vintage Harley Davidson shirt, a vintage black belt with a detailed silver buckle, and a jean jacket. She wondered what Roman's P.A. would look like. Most likely sophisticated, high-end clothes, nice shoes. Grace pushed down the feeling of insecurity.

She hadn't had a reason to own nice things. She didn't go to fancy dinners or the theater. She went to school, she interned, and she studied. She knew if she were going to date Roman, she would most likely have to step up her game in the wardrobe department–less leggings and oversized tees and more...more...whatever it was girls were wearing these days.

Her phone chimed with a text from Melissa informing her the car was out front, and Grace took one last deep breath before she plunged into the deep end, into the world of hockey, and flights, and hotel rooms, and new people and most importantly, Roman Graves.

Grace was pleasantly surprised by the sight of Melissa. She was tall and brunette, wearing business casual clothes dolled up with hip gold jewelry and a pair of chunky platform doc martin boots. She was *rockstar* business casual–if that was a thing.

She wore deep red lipstick and had black winged eyeliner so sharp it could cut a bitch. Her skin was porcelain and flawless. Grace wondered how Roman had never fallen in love with *her*.

Melissa eyed Grace as she made her way to the black luxury car and Grace tried and failed to not look as nervous as she felt. She was only a few steps away when Melissa put on a remarkably welcoming toothy smile and pulled Grace in for a hug.

"Well, you're shorter than I expected," Melissa said, teasingly, but it didn't come off rude or judgmental.

"Sorry to disappoint," Grace said, handing her small suitcase off to the driver.

"Disappointed? Babe, you are a breath of fresh air in these parts." Melissa said. "Get in, we have a flight to catch."

Grace got in only to find a gift wrapped box in her seat.

"What's this?"

Melissa just smiled at her. "Open it. It's from Roman."

Inside the box was a white L.A. Knights jersey, on the chest was a bold C, which Grace knew stood for captain. On the back was his last name, Graves, and the number eleven. Under the jersey was a black L.A. Knights pullover hoodie, Melissa chimed in to explain.

"It's white because it's an away game," she said, but Grace had already known that. "The hoodie is to wear under the jersey because it's cold in the arena. Roman's idea."

Right. The arena. The game. Grace had somehow forgotten what she was even going Arizona for in the whirlwind of getting ready and being picked up by a fucking chauffeur in a really nice expensive black car. She wondered how Roman was feeling. How practice was going. And how nervous he must be considering the playoffs were on the line.

"I've never been to a game," Grace said, running her fingers over the hard material of the 'C' on the chest of the jersey.

"Yeah, kinda crazy you didn't know who he was when you met him."

"I didn't know anything about hockey before I realized who he was." Grace paused before deciding to share more. "I found out who he was when I saw the press conference."

Melissa sighed. "Oh, that cluster fuck. Yeah, it was a bad look for him, but I've known him long enough to know he's not a bad guy. He's a man whore–or *was* a man whore–but he would never hurt a fly, not intentionally anyway..." she paused, and looked over at Grace. "I'm not really doing him any justice am I?"

"You don't need to. I see him pretty clearly when I'm with him," Grace admitted confidently.

"Oh, I like you," Melissa confirmed, and Grace felt her heart race at the approval. She had never been big on needing people to like her, but for some reason, this Melissa person seemed important.

Chapter Twenty-Six

Practice was tedious as Roman had expected it to be and he tried his hardest not to wonder how things had gone with Grace. He trusted Melissa with his life, but he wasn't dumb, he had asked a lot of Grace by inviting her to the game. What they had was still so new and here he was, flying her to another state with his P.A. He knew Grace could handle it, but he couldn't help but worry if it wasn't too much too fast.

When he got to the lockers, he pulled out his phone first thing, and sent off a text.

Roman:

> Hey, sorry I haven't been able to communicate with you since last night. I hope Melissa is taking good care of you.

He began to strip away his sweaty gear when a text came through.

Grace:

It's been good. Melissa is genuinely nice. I am still a bit nervous. I don't know why. I just feel like an imposter in your life. It's all very overwhelming.

Roman:

You're not an imposter. You're my date. I want you to be in Arizona for this game. I promise to make all your nerves melt away when you see me tomorrow night.

Grace:

Don't worry about me. You need to focus on winning.

Roman knew she was right, he needed to focus on the win, and when they won—and he fucking planned on winning—he would celebrate the best way he could imagine...with Grace.

Roman:

I have to get showered and get out of here. Can I call you when I get home?

Grace:

Yes. I think hearing your voice would make this all seem more real.

Roman:

Give me a few hours.

Grace:

> Okay, we're landing soon. Then Melissa is taking me to dinner before the hotel.

Roman:

> Order the most expensive thing on the menu for me?

Grace:

> Can do.

His smile went from ear to ear. Grace was in Arizona waiting for him. It was the first time he had someone at a game because *he* wanted them there. Sure, his mom and dad had come to games, but it felt different with Grace, it felt special.

"That smile says you got laid," Liam teased, slapping Roman on the back.

"Nope, just a text from this girl and I'm smiling like a fool."

Liam tossed his dirty practice jersey in the bin. "When can me and Ava meet her?" he asked, and Roman's stomach clenched at the idea of Ava meeting Grace.

"I'm still figuring it all out," Roman said.

"I get that. I remember when Ava and I first started taking shit seriously. I was nervous as hell to introduce her to my friends. She can be a lot. She's so confident, it can come across rude, but she's a good person, and I love her. I'm so happy you and her are getting along. She thinks you're great," Liam said, turning his back to finish getting undressed, "Sometimes she talks about you so much I think she's secretly in love with you," Liam joked, and Roman was grateful his friend didn't see his reaction, because Ava was the worst, and Roman hoped she would reveal herself to Liam before Roman was forced to.

"You want to go get dinner?" Liam asked, before heading to the showers.

"No. I need to get some good sleep. Stay focused. Tomorrow is it. We have to win," Roman said.

"That we do. See you bright and early tomorrow, Graves."

"Yeah, get some sleep tonight, Liam. Don't be reckless."

"When am I ever reckless?" Liam asked, raising a cocky eyebrow.

Roman just shook his head and hit the showers. He couldn't get out of there soon enough.

He called Grace the second he got home. The sound of her voice managed to lessen his anxieties about the game instantly. He had been dying all day to ask how everything went with Melissa. It was weird to think she was already in Arizona.

"Hello?" she said from the other end of the line. He loved the way her voice sounded. It was raspy, and tired—fuck he wished he were there with her.

"Hey, how's the room? How's Arizona?" he asked, flopping down in his bed wearing only a pair of black boxer briefs.

"The room is insane. She booked a suite. I've never stayed in a suite before," she said.

Roman wanted to assure her a suite in Arizona was nothing compared to the places he wanted to take her, but he didn't want to come across too cocky.

"Arizona is oddly beautiful. I don't hate it, that's for sure."

"Good. I'm happy you made it there okay. How do you and Mel get along?" he asked.

"She's great. She's made it really easy. I was so nervous but honestly, she felt like an old friend by dinner."

Relief settled in, and his shoulders loosened up just hearing how well it was going, it was a relief he didn't even realize he needed. Melissa was important to him. She was also the first person he let meet Grace, so knowing they hit it off felt like a step in the right direction.

"How was dinner? What did you order?"

"Dinner was sushi. And I got a basic shrimp tempura roll and wonton soup. I didn't have the heart to tell her I'm not big into fish," she said.

"Do you need to order room service? Are you still hungry?"

"No, I'm okay. I'm still a little shocked that I'm here."

"I'll be there tomorrow. I won't be able to see you until the game though. You have to come down to the ice for warmups, I want to see your face."

"I think I can manage that." she said, her voice teasing.

Fuck, he liked this girl, he liked the idea of her down at the ice while he warmed up. He couldn't wait to point her out to Liam, he couldn't wait to tell his best friend that's her, that's my girl.

"I'm sorry I couldn't take you out to a nice dinner first. I'm sure it's not customary for your first real dinner date to be with someone's personal assistant, but then again, nothing about this has been conventional, has it?" he asked.

"I'm going to let you in on a little secret," Grace said from the other line, in a mock whisper.

"Okay, shoot," he said.

"I prefer Panera bagels and appetizers over steak and lobster. I thought our first date was perfect, and anyone who tried to top it would fail miserably. And, if I had to choose between a fancy night out or pizza and your hot tub, I think your hot tub would win every time."

Roman laughed. "It was the company in the hot tub, and not just the jets, right?"

"The jets get an honorable mention, but you were the star of the show for sure," she said, her voice girlish and playful.

That voice did something to him...and his dick.

"You sound tired."

"So do you," he said, trying to stifle a yawn.

"Should we say goodbye then?" she asked.

Roman felt his body tingle with the anticipation of seeing her tomorrow. "Goodbye then," he teased.

And before she hung up, she said, "Thank you...for all of this."

He hadn't even done much. Hell, he'd spent more money on champagne with women he would never see again, and they hadn't been this grateful. But Grace wasn't like other women, was she? And that both scared him and filled him with a newfound hope.

"Thank you for coming. I can't wait to see you."

She giggled and he couldn't understand how the sound of her happiness made his entire body come alive in ways he'd never experienced.

"But first, hockey," she reminded him.

And yes, of course, first hockey, but win or lose, when the game was over, Roman knew his focus would shift, and he would spend the night, no matter how tired he was, kissing Grace's body from head to toe.

Chapter Twenty-Seven

Grace woke up to her alarm and a chain of texts from Roman and Melissa.

Roman:

> About to take off. I'm nervous about today's game.

> Don't tell anyone I admitted that.

> Also, I can't wait to see you.

Grace was blushing and she hadn't even had coffee.

Roman:

> One last thing…

> In case it wasn't obvious, I like you.

Grace screamed into her pillow. And then proceeded to text him back.

> Grace:
>
> If you see this text before all the hockey madness starts, I wanted to say good luck, I know you can do it, and, I kinda, sorta like you too.

She giggled as she hit send, and then realized how silly her giggle sounded in the massive, luxurious hotel room.

She opened the texts from Melissa, which were a heavy planned agenda for the day, and typed up a response.

> Grace:
>
> Good morning, Melissa. That all sounds amazing. I'll meet you in front of will-call at five. Roman said something about being at the glass for warmups? Do I need a special pass for that?

Grace sat waiting to hear back from Melissa when there was a knock on her hotel door. She threw on a robe, and when she opened the door, she found a man standing in front of her with flowers, coffee and a bag she was very familiar with–Panera.

"Are you Grace Fairchild?" the delivery man asked.

She reached for the flowers, an assortment of different colored roses. "That's me," she said, and she didn't know why she was surprised that this was happening. She realized very quickly that Roman Graves was kind of perfect, and a hell of a lot better at dating than he gave himself credit for.

She sat the flowers down, and then came back for the coffee and Panera bag.

"Someone must really like you," the delivery man said with a wink.

And Grace agreed. He must really like her, and that felt pretty fucking amazing.

***

The locker room in Arizona was eerily quiet for the L.A. Knights. They were usually a pretty lighthearted, rambunctious team. They never took themselves too seriously because up until this point, Roman felt they'd never really had to, not to this degree anyway. He knew he needed to say something. He just didn't know how to tell them it would be okay if they lost tonight. He didn't know how to tell them it would be okay if they didn't make it to the playoffs this one time.

Because it *wasn't* okay.

Roman would never speak those words.

So, he didn't.

As soon as his skates hit the ice for warmups, he heard cheers from all over the arena. He skated over to the glass near the net and found a pretty good-sized crowd of Knights fans huddled there. They had made the drive across the desert to watch what could potentially be the last game of the season for L.A. and that was exactly why he loved his city–they always showed up.

He skated around, got his legs loose and scanned the crowd for any sign of Grace. He didn't see her. Disappointment rose in his chest; he felt needy for her already. He warmed up; shot the puck a few times, made a few passes, looked for Grace again. The boys looked alive, and excited; he needed them to stay this way. Excited was good. He would take excited.

He skated back to the glass and gave a high five through it to a small boy decked out in a Graves jersey. It wasn't until he shot a few pucks that he finally spotted Grace, right behind the net. She looked nervous, but when their eyes met, he watched as her face lit up with the best smile he had ever seen. The white jersey made the blush of her cheeks glow. She was tiny in the oversized jersey, she looked good, it suited her—he could get used to this.

He skated over to her, and winked. She nervously shrugged her shoulders and mouthed, 'Hi,' he mouthed back, 'Hey.' It took everything in him not to just stand there, at the glass smiling like a damn fool for her. She was so sexy, and simple, and beautiful...he didn't know a woman could be all of those things at the same time. He was so gone for this girl, and they had only been on two fucking dates. Two dates, and four months of waiting, and here he was, smiling like a smitten schoolboy through the glass.

Liam skated up to him. "Holy fuck, is that her?" he asked, taking notice of Roman's sudden googley eyes.

"Yeah," Roman said, shooting a puck at Jason Kidd and missing.

"She's..." Liam paused, and thought about it, because the truth was, she was nothing like the girls Roman slept with in the past. "She's fucking hot," he said.

"She's different," Roman said.

"She's definitely not your normal. I think she's better, man. Good job," Liam confirmed, looking over at Grace to wave, she waved back nervously.

The buzzer went off, warmups were over. He shot her one final smile, she mouthed, 'Good luck', and he knew he needed it. Skating off the ice, he made his way back to the locker room where he put Grace on the back shelf of his mind, because it was game time now, and he came to win.

"Alright," he said, his uniform pristine, free of sweat, blood, and tears, "I'm not going to tell you we have this in the bag. You all know that would be a lie and I'm not a fucking liar. You all know we played like trash most of this season, myself included. On paper we should lose. As far as playoff brackets go, we're not on the top of anyone's list, so for that reason alone I say let's fucking win. Let's play the best hockey of our lives starting tonight. Fuck the rest of this season, all that matters now, is this game. So, let's fucking do this!"

The locker room erupted in heavy grunts and shouts and affirmations. There were butts being slapped, backs being patted, hugs being had and testosterone bouncing off the walls. It was time to go out there and win this game. And after he won, he planned to see what that jersey looked like on the floor next to a very naked Grace.

***

Grace's seat was only two rows from the ice, and she was surrounded by a sea of Arizona fans, but luckily, Melissa was with her. She watched Roman line up to take the first puck drop of the game–he won–she felt her entire body warm with pride. That was her guy out there, how that happened she still wasn't sure, but he was hers, and fuck it felt exhilarating.

"Are you nervous?" Melissa asked, offering up popcorn, Grace declined, she was too nervous to eat.

"A little. I'm afraid if they don't...you know," she said, not speaking the words into existence. "If they don't, I'm worried it will have been my fault, like a bad luck thing."

Melissa laughed. "Spoken like a true hockey girlfriend."

Grace winced, she wasn't technically his girlfriend, so she felt weird being called it. "Not girlfriend."

"Sure, *not* girlfriend, just the girl he flew to Arizona to watch him play. Just the girl he put up in the nicest room Arizona had to offer. Just the girl wearing his jersey and getting eye fucked by him during warmups."

"Okay, point taken," Grace said, and her cheeks warmed at the mention of it all.

"Might I add one more thing?" Melissa asked.

"You may," Grace said.

"You're also the first girl he's ever done this for. So, that's got to stand for something."

Roman had the puck and skated it up center ice. Grace pulled the oversized jersey sleeves into her hands and formed anxious fists around them. Two Arizona players came in from the side, but Roman was faster. He kept control of the puck despite their sticks slapping at his skates. The Arizona goalie prepared himself for Roman's arrival.

Melissa gripped Grace's knee and said under her breath, "Come on Roman, you got this."

At that moment, Roman took the shot in the top left corner of the net and the L.A. Knights were on the board.

The rest of the guys on the ice skated over to congratulate him. Grace stood to celebrate his goal. She watched him skate back to the bench and then she looked up at the jumbotron to see him smile directly into the camera.

Melissa pulled her in and whispered, "That one was for you, babe." and Grace loved it. She hadn't received many lavish gifts in her life, in fact a dozen Panera bagels had been the best to date, but she had to admit, she could definitely get used to gifts in the form of goals scored by Roman Graves. That was one thing she knew she would never tire of.

The first period ended and the score remained at one, zero. Grace knew that a lot could happen in two periods, so she remained anxious. She wouldn't let up until the final second was up and the Knights had won.

And they did just that. After two fast periods, a goal by Liam Harvey, and a fight that made Grace's stomach clench, the Knights beat Arizona 2-1, and it was time to celebrate that victory with Roman.

Chapter Twenty-Eight

G race waited anxiously with Melissa in the back hall of the arena. Some of the player's wives were there with kids to celebrate the win. Melissa pointed out a few of the girlfriends, and even some people who worked for the Knights; P.R. people, management, a social media director named Nate that was extremely sweaty, and the head of human resources, Cam Lawndry. Grace shook hands with Cam and gave him her best smile. She knew Cam's name because he was the person she sent her resume to. If she were a braver person, she would have dropped a hint that she had applied for a job with the Knights, but she wasn't, so she just crossed her fingers in hopes that she would be seeing more of him in the future.

The players began to trickle out of the locker room–butterflies fluttered in her stomach. Some of them hugged their wives and kids. Some kissed their girlfriends. Some just left with other players, probably off to celebrate, and drink–they *had* just won, clinching a playoff spot.

Her nerves grew and grew as she waited–what the fuck was she even doing here? How would Roman act when he saw her? Would he just say hi, like she was an old friend? Would they leave side by side, like the two strangers they technically still were? Or would he look at her with the same burning desire he had given her during warmups? Would he still find her beautiful, here, post win?

Melissa bumped her shoulder, pulling her from her spiral of self-doubt. When she looked up Roman was walking straight toward her in his navy blue, tight fitting suit. The smile he had for her–good god that smile–it was just what she needed to set all of her wariness to rest. Before she even knew what was happening, he gripped her waist and pulled her up on tiptoes to meet his lips in a celebratory kiss in front of everyone.

The busy waiting area went noticeably quiet. And then, just when Grace felt nerves threaten to steal this moment from her, everyone started talking again, and Roman began to laugh against her lips.

"Hi," he said, leaning in to whisper in her ear, because *this* wasn't for anyone else, this simple greeting was for her and her alone.

"Hey," she said back, her body suddenly extremely hot in the layers of clothing.

"We won," he said, his smile wild, his eyes strung out–this version of Roman was new to her–she wanted so badly to tap into it in private, pick his brain, experience his excitement of the huge win one-on-one.

"You sure did. Playoffs huh?" she asked, in a mock 'no big deal' sorta way.

"Yup. And the best hockey *is* playoff hockey," he affirmed, bringing his hands from her hips to graze over her ass before coming back to take her hands in his. The simple gesture of his warm hands on her body made her ache for more.

"It'll be my first time watching playoff hockey," she admitted.

"Will you come to all the home games?" he asked, and this felt like a big commitment to make so soon, but, was she not in Arizona? Had she not hopped on a plane just yesterday to come watch him play?

Did it all feel overwhelmingly fast? Yes.

Did she want to take her time? No.

The four months from when she had met him to now had been all the waiting she was willing to give. Grace was finally ready to *take*.

"I'll need a home jersey," she teased, and he beamed.

"I can arrange that. You look good with that C on your chest," he said, his eyes heavy and wanting.

"So do you," she said, nervously biting on her bottom lip.

The tall, extremely handsome blond man came up behind Roman, picking him up by the waist in a brotherly bear hug of sorts. Grace laughed at the sight of Roman being picked up as if he weren't a big, strong, hockey player.

"We fucking did it!" the handsome blonde, who Grace knew to be Liam Harvey, Assistant Captain of the L.A. Knights, said to Roman.

Roman turned to Liam, returning the brotherly bear hug, also lifting the massive man into the air. Grace couldn't help but back up and give the boys room. She loved seeing Roman this way.

"Liam," Roman said, reaching to pull Grace into his side, wrapping a tight arm around her waist, "this is Grace. Grace, this is my best friend Liam."

Liam shot out a rough calloused hand to shake, and offered Grace one of the most striking, friendly smiles she had ever seen. "So, you're the girl?" Liam asked incredulously.

Grace looked up at Roman for some kind of approval, then said, "I might be."

Liam laughed. "No, you definitely are. Trust me. You are *the* girl."

"I guess I am," Grace agreed, wrinkling her nose. "Is being *the* girl a good thing?"

Liam snorted. "It's a fucking wonderful thing. A miracle. I didn't believe I'd live to see the day Roman met someone special enough to wear his jersey, but here we are and stop me if I'm being too forward but, I get why it's you."

Grace squared up her shoulders, and asked, "And why *is* that?"

Roman just shook his head, but let Liam go on.

"Because, Roman was always going to find something special," Liam said.

"Well thank you, I think he *might* be special too. I'll have to get back to you after I get to know him a little better. I'm still deciding if I like him because he plays hockey or if I like him for other, more serious reasons," she joked.

Roman playfully gripped her hips tightly. "I sent bagels."

This made Liam laugh. "Bagels? Grace, if he doesn't serve you a five-star breakfast tomorrow with bottomless mimosas, call me, and I'll find you a better hockey player."

"No way, Panera bagels are my favorite thing ever." She looked up at Roman, "Thanks by the way, for the delivery this morning."

He smiled down at her, and the way his eyes burned into her made her desperate to stop the small talk and get back to their room.

"Well, we're going to head out," Roman said, and Liam smiled a knowing smile. "Good game man," he said, pulling his friend in for a manly, loud, back clapping kind of hug

Grace didn't miss the part where Liam whispered to Roman, "She seems great man, have fun tonight."

Liam pulled her in for a hug. "Nice meeting you, Grace, be good to my boy."

Roman took her hand in his, and gave her a tug. "Should we get out of here then?" he asked, his voice low, laced with foreshadowing of what celebrating this win looked like for the two of them.

"Absolutely," she agreed with anticipation.

The ride back to the hotel was filled with small touches that left lingering side effects on their bodies; warmed skin, quickened heart rates, and blood rushing to particular body parts. His hand on her leg, moving up to her inner thigh, gripping her there. His lips nonchalantly kissed her neck. The heat radiating from his body pressed against hers in the back seat of the car–the promise of sex was heavy all around them.

Roman thanked the driver, tipping him well, and then his hand found hers as they headed into the hotel lobby.

Grace could feel eyes on her. On him. On *them*, walking hand in hand. Roman sporting a smile only winners wore. But she felt it on her own face as well–an undeniable winner's smile–that came with being on the arm of this glorious man.

The elevator dinged, and they entered hand in hand. Roman looked down at her and she could feel his gaze burning a hole through the top of her head. She looked up at him as the door dinged shut and he wasted no time. His mouth was on hers, pulling her body up to him. The kiss was hot and heavy and every indication where the night was headed.

The elevator stopped. Roman broke the kiss. They both stood there panting. Waiting for the door to open. Grace nervously pushed her hair behind her ears, and wiped her lips for any indication of their stolen moment together.

As they made their way down the long hall of the hotel, Grace felt her nerves start to present themselves.

"Will you be tired soon? When the adrenaline of the win is gone?" she asked.

"I'll crash eventually, but even when the high of the game is gone, I'll still be on a high having you here with me," he said, stopping to open the door for them.

"Our room," she said, taking the first step in, the cool air of the air conditioning she had left on full blast hitting her warm face.

"*Our* room," he echoed. "I can't believe you're here with me."

"*You* can't believe it?" she asked, "I can't believe it. How is this even real?"

"I don't know, but I keep asking myself the same thing," he said, and it was hard for her to believe that Roman found himself as lucky to be with her as she found herself to be with him.

He took a step towards her, closing the gap between them, his fingers tugging at the hem of the jersey. "I love seeing you in this," he said, his voice laced with deep, sexy undertones.

"I feel..." she paused, "I feel important in it. It's the first time I've been a real fan of anything."

"I like that you're a fan...of hockey," he said, his hand sneaking under the back of the jersey, his fingertips grazing her bare skin there. "I also like that you're a fan of me..." his fingers trailed up her back, and then down to grip her ass through her jeans.

She couldn't help but close her eyes. Her heart hammered under the heavy team logo on her chest.

He leaned in, trailing kisses up her neck, landing at her ear. "I want you to know that we don't have to do anything tonight that you're not ready for. But, if we do move forward intimately, we go at your pace. Whatever you want Grace."

"And what if I said I want it all?" she asked, her voice desperate with need.

He faintly ran his lips across her jaw line. "Then I'd say, it's about damn time you asked for more than bagels, Grace."

This made her laugh and then Roman began to laugh, and what was once a very sexy situation was now the two of them hunched over in

an uncontrollable burst of nervous, silly, laughter. And she wasn't sure
they were supposed to be laughing right now, when only a second ago it
all felt very serious, and sensual, but it also felt just as good to know they
could laugh like this at any given moment, it felt good to know she could
just *be* with him, carefree, with no expectations.

She could have him both ways; serious and intimate, or silly and
laughing.

That felt like a rite of passage.

"Do you want a drink?" he asked, pulling away, his smile wide and
wild.

"Maybe a beer?" she said timidly.

"I'm having a beer," he affirmed. "A celebration beer is tradition."

How could she forget so soon, this night was about so much
more to Roman than she had been considering on the elevator up here.
Because who was she kidding, all thoughts of hockey were gone and
replaced with the sudden need to have this man naked and on top of her
the second he kissed her.

"A celebration beer sounds amazing," she agreed.

"So, what did you think of live hockey?" he asked, taking a seat on
the couch that faced the beautiful view of nothing, it *was* Arizona after
all.

"I loved it. It was so intense because so much was at stake, but it
was fun. I think I might be a die-hard fan now."

"Good, because if we're really doing this," he said, insinuating to
her and him "there's going to be a lot of hockey in your life. I just need
you to be aware before we take this any further how much of my time
is on the road. How many special occasions I will have to miss. How
much of our getting to know each other will be over FaceTime. It's not
conventional. And I'm already not the best at commitment. In fact, I

don't know if I've ever been committed to anything or anyone outside of hockey. I might suck at this. I can't promise that I won't fail you, but it's been a long time since I've wanted more than the Stanley cup, and that's all you." he said, taking a drink of his beer.

Grace beamed with admiration for this man in front of her. In the short time she had known him he had shown so much of himself to her. His vulnerability was the sexiest thing about him.

"I don't see your schedule being a problem. You being away a lot may be hard for some women, but I'm not like most women. I didn't grow up needing or getting a lot of attention, so to not have that in a relationship wouldn't be a deal breaker because I don't expect it. I want your attention, I want to be around you, but I'm also no stranger to being alone," she paused, then laughed nervously. "God, that sounded pathetic."

Roman took their beers and sat them down on the small end table. "I don't know if I'm any good at this," he said.

"Me either," she agreed.

"So, what now?" he asked.

"We could wait another four months," she teased.

Roman let out a growl and pulled her into his lap. "No fucking way," he said, "So, what do you say, Grace? Do you want to be my girlfriend?" he asked, his face sporting an awkward, unsure smile.

She giggled, and it wasn't funny, not really, but the way he asked her as if they were in some kind of high school romantic comedy was endearing.

"Okay," she said, pulling her shoulder up with uncertainty.

"Okay?" he affirmed.

"Yes," she said more confidently. "Yes, I absolutely want to be your..." she hesitated, the words felt foreign on her lips, almost cheesy. "I want to be your girlfriend."

Roman gripped her hips, pulled her body close and kissed her with a crushing force of his lips on hers. They were doing this. They were official. They were kissing on a couch–a really fucking uncomfortable couch. They were both extremely turned on, and it was evident.

Roman's hands gripped her hips and guided her body against his hard arousal. Too many layers of clothes. Far too many layers of clothes. Grace felt overwhelmed with the need to *not* be wearing so many layers of clothing.

She felt overwhelmed with the need to feel Roman's skin against hers. He kissed her neck, and she couldn't stop the moan that escaped her.

"Do you want to?" he asked through heavy breathing.

"Yes," she said, not even sure *exactly* what she was agreeing to, but yes, yes to all of the above.

Roman stood, taking her hand in his, her heart hammering in her chest as she allowed him to lead her to the bedroom.

Chapter Twenty-Nine

Roman knew that Grace being his girlfriend–*his girlfriend*–didn't mean he had a free pass to her body. He knew it was possible to be an adult, in a hotel room with someone, and not sleep with them.

But...he really wanted to fuck her.

No, actually, not *fuck* her, that felt wrong when being used with Grace.

He really wanted to *be* with her.

He wanted to undress her, and take her apart. He wanted to kiss the soft skin of her body, and worship her from head to toe. He wanted to take his time and make her feel good. Make her feel seen, desired, and beautiful.

He wanted to wake up next to her almost as much as he wanted to make her come. And usually, those two things did not coexist in his life, but with Grace, everything seemed doable. Everything he used to avoid, he suddenly wanted to experience with her.

He brought her mouth to his and kissed her softly, with intent and need.

She ran her hand along the lapel of his jacket, "I like you in your suit," she stated, and he was okay with that, if she wanted him in his suit, he would stay in his suit. "But I wouldn't mind watching it come off," she finished, his lips curled up in surprise.

Her fingers came up to his chest, and button by button she began to undress him. Grace was full of surprises, and he wasn't usually a fan of such things, but when it was in the form of her getting him naked, he would gladly accept any surprises she had to offer.

"I like watching you do this," he said, as she undid the last button and untucked his shirt from his slim fit slacks. She ran soft fingers over his exposed chest, and he enjoyed watching the way her eyes traced across his body with pleasure.

"You're so...strong." she said, with a coy giggle.

"I am," he agreed, loving the way his body made her smile.

She pressed her fingers under the weight of his suit jacket and shirt, gripping his shoulders, and then in one solid movement, she pushed both articles of clothing from his body. He let them fall to the hotel floor with a thud.

One less layer between them.

"My body doesn't measure up," she admitted, as if preparing him for some kind of disappointment. But he had seen her in a bikini, and he had loved every inch of her skin.

"I've seen you practically naked, Grace," he said, running his hands along her arms teasingly, "and I haven't been able to stop thinking of what your thighs would look like wrapped around my face."

He watched as the blush from her neck moved to her cheeks. She bit her bottom lip, and he could tell that those words alone had done her in, she was his.

"Can I?" he asked, slipping his hands under the many layers she wore; the jersey, the sweatshirt, her tank top.

She lifted her arms for him, and he pulled all three layers off in one go.

Three more layers–gone.

They were getting somewhere.

Her bra was modest, her breast size less than a handful. She hadn't worn anything frilly or lacy for him. And he realized he was undressing Grace as she always was. This wasn't a show she was putting on, or a moment she chose to be someone else, she had come as herself down to her undergarments, and it only made him want her that much more.

"You're so fucking sexy," he said, and she just shrugged her shoulders, as if she wasnt entirely convinced.

Well, if she didn't believe his words, then he would have to prove it with his actions. His mouth came down to her neck, and she made room for him there, tilting her head back. He kissed her soft warm skin, trailing his lips across her collarbone and down to the juncture between her breasts. He took in a long deep breath, loving the scent of her; soft and clean, like laundry day, and fresh sheets, and flowers just having bloomed.

Her fingers laced in his hair and as he kissed lower down her body, he could feel the slight way her hands encouraged him down, down, down. He lowered himself to his knees. Every muscle in his body ached, a reminder of the game he had just won. Fuck, what a night, what a victory, what a reward.

He kissed just above the button of her pants, her stomach sucked in as she drew in a heavy breath, a reaction to his lips being so close to her most intimate parts. The trail of kisses across her stomach asking for an invitation to move lower still. His hands trailed up her thighs and found the button of her jeans. He undid them expertly.

Grace's breathing hitched again as he slowly pushed her pants from her hips, his eyes looking up at hers through heavy lids, taking in the way her chest heaved in thick breaths and released unsteadily.

Her jeans fell to the floor with ease, and she kicked them aside.

Victory, another layer was gone.

He sat back on his calves, his body protesting, but he didn't care, the pain of today's game meant nothing in comparison to his need for her. He had to look at her. *Really*, look at her. The soft black lace of her panties against her flawless skin. The goosebumps that covered her exquisite thighs. The way her fingers fidgeted at her sides, suddenly unsure what to do now that she was on display for him, exposed, and so fucking beautiful.

He leaned forward and pressed his lips firmly to where her thighs met. He kissed her hips, and then right above her panty line. With steady hands, he reached up and unclasped her bra. She let it fall from her arms to the floor. The sight of her perfect breasts made his arousal throb, and begged to be freed from his pants, but it would have to wait its turn, because tonight he may have won the game, but he would gladly spend overtime showing Grace how perfect her body was.

He stood to kiss her, her mouth soft and inviting, her perfect pink nipples pressed against his own naked chest sent shivers down his spine. The kiss escalated at the warmth of their skin touching. Her hands found his pants button and unfastened it as their mouths desperately crashed together. His dick ached to be touched by her soft hands.

This was the point of no return, it was evident in the way their kiss had grown harsh, the way her hands were frantic to remove his pants. The way he knew once the layers were gone there was no turning back.

He kicked his pants aside, and Grace's eyes fell to his black briefs, to the way his erection strained against the elastic waistband. Her smile went bashful. She looked back up at him through dark hooded eyes. For the first time since he met her, he was happy she didn't just shrug her shoulders–that might hurt his ego when it came to his dick–instead she pulled his body against hers, her mouth crashing into his, taking control. He groaned under her commanding kiss.

Her kiss was punishing and needy. Roman pushed her body against the bed with his own and lowered her onto her back. She welcomed the weight of him between her legs, encouraging him to stay by wrapping them around his hips and pulling his body closer. He pressed himself against the warmth of her sex, the friction maddening, the last remaining enemy and the only thing that stood between him and the prize was the thin cotton of his briefs and the sheer lace of her black thong.

They kissed like it was their lifeline, only stopping to catch their breath, and then they kissed some more. Grace pushed her hips against him and the way their bodies lined up was perfect. He wanted more. He wanted everything. Her hands pulled at his body and he knew she wanted him too.

His mouth left hers, her lips parted at the loss of him, puffy and red, as he lazily ran his tongue down her neck, stopping to admire her perfectly pink hard nipples. He took the deep pink bud into his mouth before releasing it with a pop. Her body tensed at the sensation and he loved watching her squirm beneath him. Roman kissed his way across her chest, and did the same with the other nipple, sucking it firmly until he felt her hips press up against him again.

His body responded with her every movement, every thrust. His teeth grazed her hard nipple as he slowly pulled his mouth from it, causing Grace to whimper but he didn't let up. He moved right along, down, down, down, stopping at her panties, all that was left between his lips and her *lips*. He had discovered how perfect the kiss of her mouth could be now he needed to know what it was like to taste her sweet, wet lips hidden between her legs.

He looked up at her, his fingers hooked in the thin fabric at her hips. "I'm taking these off now," he said, needing her to know, needing her approval, and eager, so fucking eager to have her completely naked.

Grace nodded her head in approval, lifting her hips to allow room for him to slip her panties off. And down, down, down, they went. Roman let out a low growl of approval.

"Fuck," he said under his breath. Grace squirmed a bit at her nakedness, and he knew just what to do to take her mind off it. "Your body is insane. Your pussy is so fucking pretty, my sweet, sweet, Grace."

Roman gripped her thighs, leaning in to kiss the soft bare skin of her sex. Her breathing faltered at his mouth on her there and if that's all it took to get a reaction, he couldn't wait to show her what came next.

He slid off the bed and with one firm tug of her body he had her at the edge, her legs dangling, a small yelp of surprise escaping her at the act. He looked up at her one last time, her head pressed back in the mattress, her eyes closed, her fists gripping the comforter, and then, without another moment of hesitation, Roman pushed her legs apart, her sex on display; pink, soft and wet—holy fuck was she perfect. It took every inch of his willpower not to come to the sight of her like this.

He held her legs apart and he could feel her body tremble as he moved in to kiss her sweet slit. Grace sighed at the first touch of his lips to her sex. He pulled her legs apart further and pressed his mouth to her entrance and kissed her there, letting his tongue push inside of her. Her thighs tensed around his face, and he loved it, he wanted her to smother him with her pleasure. He slid his tongue out of her sex and then back in, taking his time between her legs, tasting the arousal she already had for him.

Nuzzling his nose against her clit, he pressed the flat of his tongue against her as he licked his way up. He began to suck at her there, rolling his tongue firmly against her sensitive bud. She bucked at the pressure of his mouth there.

He wanted more of her, *needed* to be inside of her.

He slung one of her legs over his shoulder to free up his hand. He gently ran his finger down her wet folds before pressing it inside her, her body rolled against his mouth and he pressed his finger in deeper, curling it inside her.

She was so tight around his finger; his dick begged to be free.

Could he come just from pleasing this woman?

He wasn't sure, but it sure as fuck felt like he might.

He slid his finger out and pressed back in adding another, this time curling them deeper inside her. Grace moaned, low and raspy, as he pushed his fingers into her, deeper, harder, while his mouth relentlessly sucked her clit.

He heard soft whispers coming from her, and he wished she wouldn't hold back. He wanted her to tell him everything she was thinking, everything she wanted, but his mouth had more important business at the moment. He kept his rhythm and was rewarded when he felt her begin to pulsate around his finger inside her, and against his mouth.

He pulled his fingers from her wet core–she was unbelievably tight. And so undeniably close. He pushed her other leg around his shoulder and gripped her ass tight, pulling her body against his face. She rolled her hips against him, her thighs thick and heavy, tensed around his neck as he ate her like a man starved. Her sex spasmed under his lips, he could feel her orgasm building until finally, Grace let go.

She cried out as she came, and fuck if he didn't love her voice echoing off the hotel room walls.

"Roman, oh shit. Oh shit. Ohhhhh. Oh my..."

He continued to suck at her clit gently until her orgasm went from full body vibrations to small tremors. Her legs fell from his shoulders, limp.

Roman kissed her swollen pink lips one last time, and then pressed his face against her inner thighs—he would never tire of his face between them. He pulled his mouth away, instantly missing the feel of her soft skin below them, to crawl up next to her on the bed.

"Hi," he said, looking down at her flushed face, her eyes were wild, dark with post orgasm bliss. "You, okay?" he asked, his lips swollen, traces of her orgasm lingering there, but he was in no rush to wipe it away, it was his reward for making her come so hard and he would wear it like a golden medal.

"Yeah," she said, bringing her arm to cover her face, and he could see the delivery girl he met four months ago in this action. A little awkward. A little shy. Completely strung out in the best way possible.

It made his cock twitch.

Something about her reserve in her post oral bliss, and the way her cheeks were flushed pink with pleasure, and her arm drawn up to cover her nakedness; it made his dick weep to be deep inside her. Most women he had slept with saw sex as an opportunity to shine, to put on a show, and now being with Grace, seeing the natural blush on her breast bone, and the way she hid her face with reserve, despite him just having had his mouth on her most intimate parts made him wonder if he had ever had authentic, genuine sex with a woman.

"Don't hide your face," he said, pulling at her arm. "I love the way your freckles look when you blush."

"That was..." she paused, and he could see that she had a million things she wanted to say, and zero ways to articulate it.

"Fun? Good? Nice?" he asked, and then raised his eyebrow. "Not enough?"

Grace let out a nervous laugh. "It's just been a really long time since anyone has done that. I don't know if I forgot how good it could be or if it's just never been good enough to be memorable."

Roman traced a finger up her bare arm, he lowered his voice, so as not to sound too pushy, "I can think of a few other things I can make memorable for you."

Grace pressed her body into his and kissed him with all she had. He rolled on top of her, pinning her body to the mattress with his weight; she made room for him between her legs. He pressed his boxer brief-covered erection against her naked sex. She met his need by arching her body against him.

One last layer between them.

"Do you want to do this tonight? We can wait. Whatever you want, Grace, it's yours."

"I want it all. I want *you*. I want you to make it memorable."

Roman pushed himself up and didn't miss the way her eyes stayed glued to his body. He hopped off the bed and picked up his suit pants from the ground pulling out the strategically placed condom from the pocket and tossed it on the bed. Grace sat up on her elbows to watch, her chest heaving in anticipation, and so, he gave her what she wanted.

He hooked his fingers into the elastic band of his briefs, his cock straining against the fabric, hard and thick. With one swift motion Roman pulled the last bit of clothing from his body, the last thing keeping them apart, revealing himself to her.

Grace's eyes lit up at the sight of him, the size of him. Roman knew he was on the better end of cock measurements. He gave himself a firm stroke, just to make her blush–and she did not disappoint, a small nervous giggle escaped her. He climbed back up between her legs, running his hands from her knees to her inner thighs, still slick with arousal.

"You still okay with this?" he asked, looking down at the condom in his hand.

"I think I've wanted this every second I've been around you since we met," she admitted.

"Fuck. Even back when you delivered my food?"

"Even then."

He brought the condom wrapper to his mouth and tore it open between his teeth. "I can't wait to be inside you, Grace. I've thought about it so many times."

"Well, what are you waiting for then?" she said, eyeing the condom, and then his dick, encouraging him to put it on.

Her eyes stayed glued on his hands as he rolled the condom down his length, and he loved the way she leaned up further to watch as the protection smoothed over to cover his erection.

He leaned down to kiss her neck and he could feel the way her legs spread wide for him, making room for him. He lined himself up and his entire body buzzed with anticipation. He looked down between them, unable to help himself, he had to watch her body take him for the first time.

Grace let out a shaky breath as he slowly pressed his cock in, rocking against her with slow, intentional thrusts. Her tight entrance made him work for every inch. He wouldn't last long, not tonight, not with the way her walls had to stretch just to make room for him.

"Fuck, Grace," he said in a rumble.

He thrust against her slowly, pushing in a little more each time. Holding his breath, trying to convince his dick not to freak out and come the second he was deep inside her.

It had been so long.

"Damn, Grace. This is so good," he said under his breath.

"I know this is cliche, but you're really big." she said.

Roman laughed and he couldn't remember the last time he laughed during sex, he couldn't remember sex ever being this natural and safe, and he couldn't wait to find out what it looked like once they got over the "first time" hump together.

"Am I?" he asked, thrusting and finally hitting her deep, making her eyes widen at the fullness of his cock inside her. He stopped moving to take a deep breath, then pushed her legs up so he could get a better angle to hit all her sweetest spots. "I think maybe you're just small."

Grace let out a soft purr of a moan, and whispered, "It doesn't matter, I can take it. I want it all."

She gripped his shoulders tight, begging him to be closer, deeper; it was so good, so tight, so beautiful to watch Grace's face relax, her bottom lip between her teeth, her head pushed back against the bed. She was ready for him, and he was almost *too* ready for her. He began to rock inside her, pulling out and slowly pushing back in with more weight behind it, hitting her deep, bottoming out against her body.

"Fuck, I lied. This might not be memorable. Not for the right reasons anyway. I'm not going to last long," he admitted, and Grace pulled his mouth down to hers and kissed him.

"Then make it count while you can."

Roman pulled out to the tip and thrust back in causing Grace to let a soft yelp escape her.

He found his rhythm, his body slapping against hers, her tight sex milking his cock with each thrust. He tried to slow down, he tried to make it last, but she was moaning with each thrust, whispering *Yes* and *right there,* against his shoulders as she held him tight.

He didn't slow down, he didn't hold back, he fucked her hard, using his weight to sink into her and she took him so good, so perfect; *she* was perfect. Roman hadn't even come and he already wanted her again. Deeming between her legs was his new happy place.

Roman felt Grace's body clench around him and he knew she was coming. Her words were now an inaudible murmur of soft moans. He pulled out one last time and when he pushed back deep inside her he came hard. He rocked against her, letting her sex grip him tight. He loved the way he could feel her pulsating around him.

Gently releasing her legs from his body, she let them fall to the bed - dead weight. He stayed there on top of her, his forehead to hers as they both enjoyed the last tendrils of their orgasm.

Roman slowly rolled from Grace's body and he hated how quickly he began to feel the pull of sleep the second he was lying next to her.

He had just had sex with a woman, and he was almost as excited to fall asleep next to her as had been to be with her.

"Why are you smiling so big?" she asked, trailing gentle fingers over his chest and shoulders. He turned to look at her, her face had a softer smile on it after sex. She looked comfortable and safe; she looked like she belonged next to him...because she did.

"I just had amazing sex with an amazing girl, and I already know I want to do it again tomorrow. That feels pretty fucking good, Grace."

She pressed her nose into his neck, and he could feel the deep inhale of her breath there. "Pillow talk. Is that what they call this part?" she asked under her breath. Her voice was beginning to sound as tired as he felt.

"I don't know, I've never made it this far." he admitted, pulling her body closer to his. He could feel her smile pressing against his skin.

"Is this the part where you fall asleep on me?" she asked, noticing his breathing growing heavy.

"Would you hate me if I told you yes?"

She leaned over and kissed him. "No, I think I understand. I only watched you play tonight and I'm ready to fall asleep too."

She reluctantly pulled away from him and sat up. He felt the cool air of the AC hit his warm skin the second she was gone. He never knew how good it felt to have someone's imprint on your skin, your body, and your heart. Now that he had experienced it with her, he never wanted to take her company for granted.

With heavy eyes and his brain threatening to shut down, he still managed to watch as she walked naked to the bathroom to clean up; she was a fucking vision in clothes, but naked, Grace was heaven sent.

Once the bathroom door closed, Roman disposed of the used condom before pulling back the covers for Grace. He waited for her to return, his eyes heavy, his body sinking into the bed, his muscles spent. He wanted to tell her that he was falling pretty hard for her. He wanted to tell her that he thought she was the most beautiful woman he knew. But, by the time she returned, sleep had won. He missed the opportunity to say it all, and most importantly, he missed the opportunity to enjoy her falling asleep in his arms for the first time.

Chapter Thirty

Grace awoke to an alarm going off. Before she could sneak away to make sure she didn't resemble a troll, Roman was sitting his phone back down, the alarm silenced and he was pulling her body back to his. A very evident erection pressed against her ass, and she didn't mind, not one bit.

"Good morning," he said, pressing a kiss to the nape of her neck.

On instinct she pressed her ass against his arousal, causing him to laugh into her skin. "You, Roman Graves, are a snuggler," she said, calling him out.

"I'm not actually. It must be a Grace thing," he said, his lips coming to her neck as he began to trail soft kisses there. His hands began to trace across her ribs, her chest, moving up to cup her breasts. Grace heaved in a heavy sigh as his fingers gave a soft tug of her nipples.

"I'm sorry I fell asleep on you," he said, his voice husky with sleep and arousal.

"I didn't mind. But I'll have you know; you missed our first spooning moment," she said between shaky breaths as Roman's hands began to trail down her stomach to her hips where he encouraged her body to move against his.

"We're spooning now," he teased, as his thick cock pressed against her ass.

"Is that what this is?" she said, closing her eyes. His hands snaked between her thighs pulling her leg up to make room for his hand there.

"Well," he said, pausing as his fingers tickled along her inner thigh, stopping just in time to avoid her intimate parts, "we're also headed towards foreplay, but yes, I would call this spooning."

Grace's entire body ached for his touch, she wanted him, morning breath and all.

"I like spooning," she managed, and Roman took that exact moment to give her what she wanted, trailing a finger gently up her slit–she gasped. "I like this too."

"I didn't get to tell you last night just how much I loved being with you," he said nonchalantly, as if his finger wasn't trailing over her sex in a maddeningly slow and gentle manner. "I didn't get to take care of you the way I wanted to when we were done."

Grace arched her body into his touch, and she felt his smile on the back of her neck.

"I didn't get to tell you that I loved the way you tasted."

This made her blush, but she didn't have time to squirm as his finger pushed between her lips and slid up to her clit.

"And I didn't get to tell you how good it felt," he paused, and she cried out as his finger began to work her sensitive clit. All of her body was still delicate from the previous night, the size of him alone left her with a lingering reminder of how good he fucked her. She anticipated what came next, her breath unsteady, needy–obvious.

He went on, "I didn't get to tell you how good it felt to have someone at the game watching me play."

This caught her off guard. This was not like the other admissions. This felt more intimate without having anything to do with intimacy at all.

The alarm on his phone began to go off again.

Grace pulled her legs closed against his hand, accepting that this wasn't going to happen if they were up against an NHL team's agenda.

"What are you doing?" he asked, pushing her legs back apart.

"Don't you have to like, be somewhere?" she asked breathlessly.

"I do," he said, pushing a finger into her wet entrance. She heaved in a breath and tried to ignore the beeping of his alarm. "But not until I get you off first."

"Oh," was all she managed, because now he had a finger curling deep inside her as his thumb worked her clit. And that simple "oh" turned very quickly into an "Ohhhh fuuuuuck."

Roman's alarm kept going off, and he continued to bring her to orgasm, his fingers matching the rhythm of the alarm. She felt her entire body tense against his. She pulled her legs back together, covering his hand, encouraging him to slow his motions as her orgasm came on strong and hard.

She could feel his breathing heavy against her back, in sync with her own and she loved that he was so turned on by her, and so eager to please her. The alarm continued to beep, and they both laughed when their breathing grew steadier, making the annoying beep more noticeable. Roman gently removed his hand from between her thighs and grabbed his phone. He snoozed again and pulled her body to face him.

"That was the last snooze I get before I have to get dressed to go. We fly out at 9:00, and then we have practice in L.A. when we land," he said, filling her in on his day. "What time do you and Mel fly out?"

"Two."

"Okay, game plan: Snooze is ten minutes, we might have eight left," he said with a mischievous grin on his face.

Grace met his challenge. "Well, considering you only needed around thirty seconds last night I think six minutes sounds more like a marathon and less like a sprint."

This made Roman laugh from his gut, his body shook the bed. Grace began to laugh too.

"Oh, you're a brat in the mornings," he said jokingly "Now I'm going to make you pay."

She watched as every muscle in his back flexed as he reached off the bed to grab his wallet from his dress pants on the floor to recover another condom.

"Is this okay?" he asked, signaling to the metallic package in his hand.

"More than okay, we have four months of lost time to make up for," she said.

Roman let out a silly growl and pounced on her playfully. "I like your thinking, Grace."

He ripped the packaging open and slid the condom over his already erect cock before pulling her to the edge of the bed and flipping her onto her stomach.

"I think I have about four minutes left, and I apologize ahead of time for not being able to take my time with you today, but if you let me see you tonight I can make up for it," he said, pulling her up by the hips to get her into position to take her from behind.

Something about his confidence in sex and the way he maneuvered her so effortlessly made her excited for what came next. She braced her hands in the bed sheets and spread her legs wide for him, arching her back, and pushing her ass up. Roman dropped to his knees in front of her and spread her ass wide so he could drag the flat of his tongue from her front to her back. He pulled away with a playful bite on her thigh, causing Grace to yelp at the sudden sting of his teeth.

Roman stood up behind her, positioning himself against her entrance, his grip on her hips firm. Grace held onto the sheets in preparation for what came next. The sound of heavy breathing and focus filled the silent hotel room.

The alarm began to beep.

"Fuck," he said.

Grace began to laugh.

"Fuck," he said again, this time laughing too. He grabbed the phone to hit snooze. "Okay, one more snooze," he mumbled, and his flustered, horny, demeanor made Grace smile, despite her ass being out and on display. "Okay, for real this time," he said, and before she was ready, he gripped her tight, lined up his thick cock and pushed into her.

"Ohhhh, damn," he managed as he gripped her hips and began to thrust. "How are you tighter today?" he said more to himself.

Grace knew it was because she was swollen, but the burn only made it that much better. He gripped her hips and pounded into her hard and fast. They *were* on a timer and all out of snoozes. She loved the stretch of her sex around him. She lowered her chest and face to the bed to better angle her body and Roman began to let loose on her. He fucked her deep and hard; the sound of his body smacking against hers. His grunts, so animalistic they made her beg for more. She let him know it was good by saying his name over and over.

"Yes, Roman, Roman, yes, harder." and he obeyed her commands.

His strong grip was rough on her hips as he pulled her body to meet his thrust for thrust. "Oh fuck, Grace," he moaned, slamming into her one last time, bottoming out against her ass, and holding her against his body tight as he came.

They collapsed to the bed, his body heavy on hers, his breathing erratic and winded.

"I might die," he teased, pushing up and kissing the middle of her back before helping her to her feet where he pulled her in and kissed her deep.

The alarm went off, and they both began to laugh mid-kiss.

"Fucking alarm." he said.

"Fucking hockey stuff," she teased.

"I want to see you tonight after practice."

"Okay," she said, then thought better of it. "But I also understand if you're too tired."

Roman kissed the top of her head, and headed for the bathroom. She shamelessly watched his ass as he walked away. And those thighs; she had come to the conclusion his body was unbelievable. She couldn't comprehend that a man who looked like that was hers.

She got back in bed, deciding she would wait for him to leave and then shower. He turned the sink on in the bathroom and she heard him washing up, brushing his teeth, and oddly enough, taking a piss, which seemed to make her blush more than anything they had done so far.

She heard the shower come on, and then Roman came out of the bathroom naked. Unabashed by his nudity, she tried and failed not to look at his cock that was soft, but impressive, nonetheless.

He rolled his eyes and shook his head at her when he noticed where her eyes had landed.

"What?" she asked, her cheeks flushed.

"I can see you looking at me," he said.

"How can I not be; your body is insane."

"I want more time to stare at *you* naked," he said, slipping into the fresh pair of briefs he pulled from his travel bag. He continued to get dressed, and motioned to the bathroom. "I started the shower for you. I'm sorry I can't join you this time."

She sat up, pulling the sheet to cover her bare chest, and watched as he put on his suit, and shoes, and ran his fingers through his damp disheveled hair. He crossed the room to her, and she heard the chime of a text come through. He checked his phone and put it back in his suit pocket.

"I gotta get going." he said, taking a seat next to her on the bed.

"Is the team giving you hell for the extra snooze?"

He grinned. "Yeah, but they're not mad, they all knew I was with a girl."

"A girl?" she asked incredulously. "How scandalous."

"I've been known to make headlines," he teased, and she was happy they were past his scandal affecting them negatively.

"I promise I won't post the pictures I took of you sleeping last night," she teased.

He ran a calloused finger along the soft skin of her collar bone, and leaned in to kiss her, their mouths still smiling mid kiss. Grace heard the snap of a picture being taken. She laughed at his sneaky selfie, and Roman pressed her body to the bed and kissed her like he meant it.

"*My* girl." he whispered against her lips.

"Mmmmm, I like that," she said.

"Me too." He kissed her softly one last time and stood to leave, his phone dinged with several more texts. "Order room service, get anything you want. Go to the spa here at the hotel, get a massage, a pedi, whatever you need to recover. And I'll see you tonight."

He shot her an earth-shattering smile and she shrugged her shoulders and smiled back. He bit on his bottom lip and shook his head as if in disbelief that this was real. His phone chimed again, and they both laughed.

"I'll see you tonight, Grace," he said.

"I'll set an alarm as a reminder." she teased.

Chapter Thirty-One

W hen Grace got home from the airport, she was too exhausted to think straight. She imagined Roman out on the ice practicing after the night they shared, and she didn't know how he did it. Athletes were amazing. She had only watched the game last night and she felt like she needed a nap, a basket of french fries and a Netflix binge.

Once she got settled in to watch a documentary about an octopus, she noticed she had several unread emails.

The first few emails were updates on her certifications for completing her hours along with a PDF file to print off her certificate of completion for her internship, which was exciting. She would have to get it framed properly if she got the job with the Knights. The next few emails were bills, an ad about a sale going on if you order more than six meals from a meal kit company, and the last, and oldest email was from Cam Lawndry, the man in charge of hiring for the Knights.

She opened the email, took a deep breath, and couldn't help but squeal with excitement when she read that she had secured an interview with *Roman's* team.

Panic flooded her.

She knew she needed to tell him she was applying for a job with his organization. She knew it was the right thing to do. But when? His first playoff game was Tuesday; she couldn't add that to his plate. And what would she even say, *"Oh, by the way, on top of us dating, I'm trying to get a job with your team, so, I hope that's not weird, and also, I don't want your help."*

Her pride was rearing its ugly head, because at the end of the day, what she needed more than anything was to secure this job entirely on her own. She knew in doing that, she would have to lie—no, *no*—she would have to withhold the truth from Roman.

She would have a phone interview first and then an in person interview would be Monday at the corporate offices for the Los Angeles Knights. She *needed* this job to be able to afford her apartment with Jess. She just hoped that it wasn't a conflict of interest that her and Roman were dating. If it *were* a conflict of interest she would be faced with the hardest decision of her life, her dream job or Roman—her dream man.

It seemed like an easy answer, only when she considered not taking the job because of a man, she wasn't so sure. It went against everything she had always stood for and fought for and worked her ass off for.

Her phone chimed with a text.

Roman:

> I'm leaving the rink. Still up for company?

Grace:

> Absolutely. What vibe are we going for? I want to dress the part.

Roman:

> High school make out vibes?

Grace giggled.

Grace:

Can do.

Roman:

I'll be there in forty-five

Grace headed to the shower and shot him a quick text back.

Grace:

Ok. See you soon.

She couldn't wait to see him. She wanted to care for him. Make him feel good. She pressed her legs together, trying and failing to soothe the wanting ache between them. She could always worry about the interview with the Knights another day when she didn't have Roman around to distract her.

***

Finding parking for Grace's apartment was the worst. And maybe it only annoyed him so badly tonight because he was exhausted, and eager to see her, kiss her, and just *be* with her. He found it hard to focus on practice knowing he had a girl at home, and she was waiting for him. It was everything he feared about commitment, and now that he had it, he couldn't believe he had gone this long in life without ever feeling this kind of certainty. It was a new brand of happiness; it was a new kind of addiction.

He needed someone to pinch him. Grace had somehow managed to uproot his entire reality of the future, and it felt good. It felt promising. When he was with her, he felt himself slow down—it made him realize that he had been tired from doing life alone.

He could smell the Thai food from the restaurant below as he made his way up the stairs that led to her apartment. The smell of the food flooded him with memories of the first time they met. He was so stupid then, so in denial of what he needed. So afraid of what being with someone for more than one night might look like.

His heart hammered in his chest as he approached her door. His excitement to see her only amplified knowing she was a knock away. He was desperate to know that nothing had changed since this morning. He needed to know that even after having sex with her he still wanted her.

The door flung open, and it was like the air was knocked from his lungs at the sight of her. There was something about her like this, in *her* space, in her home, in her pajamas, her face bare, her feet bare, her cheeks still flushed from the heat of her shower.

She was beautiful without trying to be. She was easy to look at. Grace had already managed to feel like coming home when he saw her.

"Hi," she said through a nervous smile.

"Hey," he said back, his smile wide. It was hard to contain when he was with her.

She stepped to the side to make room for him. "You coming in? Or are we gawking in doorways tonight?"

"Reminds me of the first time we met," he said stepping into the tiny apartment, the smell of a sweet candle replacing the spicy scent of Thai food.

"To think that only four months ago I didn't even know you were a hockey player, and now look at me, I have a jersey hanging in my closet and the captain of the L.A. Knights standing in my living room."

"I still can't believe you didn't know who I was," he said, taking a step towards her, pulling her into his body, his grip gentle and inviting on her waist.

"You're not as cool as you think you are," she teased, running her hands up his chest.

"I guess not." His hands trailed down to grip her ass. "I missed you all day."

Grace blushed, which only turned him on more.

"I felt bad for you. Being at practice after last night's game. You must be exhausted? Sore?" she asked.

"All of the above," he confessed. "But things are going to get crazy after tonight. Playoffs start Tuesday, *and* it's an away game so, I don't know how often I'll be able to see you. Which I'm already dreading."

"That's okay. I don't need a ton of attention. I'm a bit of a loner," she said, playfully punching his shoulder.

"I just want you to be prepared going into the playoffs how crazy things get for me. My head is in a different space entirely."

"I knew what I was getting myself into with you. I had four months to consider what it might look like dating a professional athlete. But the thing is," she leaned into whisper, "I have a life outside of you that *I'm* working on, like, trying to get a job, for starters, so I can stay in L.A. So, don't worry about me too much, I'll be busy, just not doing anything as cool as being Roman Graves. It'll be less intense...more Beatles, bagels and possibly a few interviews if I'm lucky."

"Well, since it's out there that we are both going to be busy, which has become a recurring theme in our timeline, can you maybe take me to your bedroom so I can kiss you like I don't know when I'll see you again?" Roman asked with the quirk of an eyebrow.

"I think that's a solid plan," she said, taking him by the hand to lead him to her room. "It's not very big."

Roman looked around, took in the tidy small space, the books on her bedside table, the record player and crate of music next to it, the variety of old teacups on her desk, the full size bed with floral print comforter.

"It's got everything I need in it," he said.

"Is that so?" she asked, fidgeting with the drawstring of her cotton pajama shorts.

"Oh, yeah," he said, closing the gap between them, his arousal very obvious in his black joggers. "It's got you and a bed, and about nine old cups of tea, what else could I possibly need tonight, Grace?"

"Well, sleep, for starters. But I also wouldn't mind a good old fashioned high school make out session before you leave."

"Leave? Am I not allowed to stay?" he asked. He watched as Grace's face filled with panic.

"Oh, I just assumed you would want to sleep at home, what with how busy your week is after tonight."

"Grace, for the first time in my life I have no intentions of leaving."

She pressed up on tiptoes, bringing lips to linger near his. "Well, I guess it's a good thing you brought your pajamas then," she teased, leaning in to finally kiss him. He hadn't realized how badly he needed it, to feel her lips on his. He let out a guttural moan from deep in his chest at the suddenness of her mouth on his; her body taking the lead, pressing into him.

He broke the kiss. "You know I sleep naked, right?"

Grace looked up at him, her face dubious and sexy. "I did, and I think we should get you into your pjs as soon as possible, you know, since it's a sleepover now."

Roman let out a howl of a laugh and pulled her back in to claim her mouth, he kissed her hard, and deep and he could feel how alive and needy her body already was for him by the way her hands were greedy with touch, tugging at his shirt, gripping onto his hips, his shoulders, his ass.

This was a side of Grace he hadn't seen yet. She was setting the tone for what came next, and while every muscle in his body ached and screamed for him to rest, he refused to give in to exhaustion.

Roman's hands slid under the short hem of her pajama bottoms and gripped her ass, his eyes went wide when he found that she was wearing no panties.

Grace giggled. "Can we still make out like high schoolers? Or have we already escalated past that?"

Roman gave her ass a firm squeeze, and whispered into her ear. "You know, high schoolers are going way further than first base these days."

Grace could feel his arousal pressed against her and her entire body warmed. "Second base?"

"Nope. Worse."

She reached between them and slid her hand just below the elastic band of his joggers. "Third?" she asked, her voice low and needy.

Roman's breath hitched. "Depends on what you consider third base."

"I don't know. I wasn't promiscuous in high school," she said, reaching down further, gripping his cock in her hand, and giving it a firm tug, "Would you call *this* third base, Roman?"

"This feels a lot like third base," Roman managed, his head falling back, his eyes closed.

Grace stroked him again and he shuddered at her touch, sucking in a deep breath as she ran a thumb firmly over the pre-come on his slit. Grace pulled her hand away from his erection, Roman let out an audible sigh of disapproval at the loss of her touching him there. She pushed both hands under his tight black L.A. Knights shirt, easing it up his body. Roman helped her out, pulling it over his head. Grace leaned in to kiss his bare chest, admiring how strong and beautiful his body was.

"I thought I could take care of you tonight, since you had to practice all day," she said, hooking her thumbs in the waistband of his joggers, pushing them down his body, freeing his hard cock.

"How thoughtful of you, Grace," he managed, as she pushed him back to sit on her bed, her hands firm on his chest, demanding–he wouldn't argue or resist.

She began to sink to her knees, and Roman's heart began to hammer.

"Wait," he said, stopping her, "I want you naked when you do it."

Grace blushed at his demands. Roman loved that no matter how dirty her mouth was, how willing and ready she was to sink to her knees before him, she was still, underneath it all, his sweet girl.

She took a step back and shrugged her shoulders for him, knowing damn well it drove him crazy, and then in one sweep of her arms her shirt was gone. Her deep pink nipples were hard, and her small breasts sat perfectly on her petite frame. Roman pulled her close, his hands pushing the cotton shorts on her hips down until they fell from her body with ease. Grace brought her mouth back to his and kissed him one last time before pulling away to trail her lips along his body. She lingered on his neck sucking and nipping at the skin there, goosebumps covering his skin.

Her gentle kisses trailed down his hard abs. Her mouth stopped, lingering above his cock. Roman's chest was hammering in anticipation. Grace looked up through hooded eyes, shrugged her shoulders one last time, and took his dick as deep as she could in one swift movement. It took Roman everything in his power not to thrust into her mouth. It took everything in his power not to move his hips.

He gently tangled his fingers in the loose brown curls of her hair as she sucked him hard, pulling off his cock to press the flat of her tongue over his slit. Roman tugged at her hair, the pressure of her tongue was intense, he felt his balls tighten and he didn't want it to end yet. Grace took him in her mouth again and he could feel her throat sucking him deep, and damn she was good, she was so fucking good.

He didn't want it to end. He didn't want to come. Not yet. If he came, that was it. He would fall asleep, and he wasn't ready to sleep. Sleep meant the night was over, and he knew after tonight it would be hard to see her.

He tugged on her hair gently, easing her off his erection. She looked up at him, still on her knees, her lips swollen, her eyes glazed over. "I'm going to come if you keep that up."

"I want you to. That's literally the point of me sucking your dick," she said, giving him a sexy, cocky smile.

Roman let out a groan, because he wanted that too, he wanted so badly to come with her lips wrapped around him.

"Ok." he decided, "But let me get you off first. No one goes to sleep horny in this relationship." he said, pulling her up off her knees, into his lap, his erection *far* too close and far too unprotected for either of their good. He scooted back onto the bed and pulled her down next to him.

Kissing her, tasting his own arousal on her tongue only made him want her more. His body pressed against hers, his dick weeping to be touched. She wrapped a leg around his hip and fuck this was bad, he wanted nothing more than to push inside of her, raw, no barrier between them.

"I want you like this so bad," he admitted, and Grace looked conflicted.

He was sure it was crossing her mind too. Something about not slowing down, not stopping to put on a condom. Something about being intimate with someone with no reservations sounded like the best thing in the world at this moment.

Protection had always been non-negotiable. But Grace was the ultimate temptation. She had been since day one. That's why he was here, in her bed, with the title "boyfriend", when he should most definitely be at home asleep, dreaming of the Cup.

"Do you have a condom?" she asked.

He did. Of course, he did. He came with full intention of being with her intimately tonight. But he knew he had to make her come first.

"I have a condom, but first, I want to go down on you," he said, already making his way down her body. Without pause he pushed her legs apart and lifted her aggressively. With her ass to his face he began to pleasure her with his tongue. He couldn't get his mouth on her fast enough. The hum of his approval buzzed against her sex as she began to roll her hips against his mouth.

Fuck, he would die happy between her gorgeous thighs.

Grace began moaning with each shaky breath she let out. Roman knew she was close, he could feel her body tensing, pulsating against his face. He latched onto her clit and worked it firm and steady, never missing a beat, never slowing down, or easing up until he felt her shatter. Her legs tensed around his face, and he kept licking her there, drawing out her orgasm as long as possible. When the high of her orgasm ended, she loosened her legs enough for him to lower her back down to the mattress.

Roman reached off the side of the bed and got a condom from the pocket of his joggers and climbed up between her legs. She looked gorgeous laying there, waiting for him to have her. Blissed out, lips swollen, wet and still throbbing from the come down of her climax.

"You're beautiful like this," he said, tearing open the condom wrapper with shaky hands. He was amped up, his cock was sensitive, his balls were tight.

"Orgasms look good on me," she teased, sitting up to watch as he slid the condom on.

"One day, I want to have you without a condom," he said, and he didn't know what possessed him to admit such a thing, but the way Grace's face lit up with desire made him happy he did.

"I thought I was crazy for thinking that," she admitted.

Roman growled, "Fuck. I might come thinking about it," he said, pulling her into his lap, her legs instinctually wrapped around his body, his dick hard against his abs. "You want to take care of me tonight, my sweet Grace?" he asked, his mouth below her jaw, sucking at the soft skin there, the scent of sweet shampoo strong on her damp, freshly washed hair.

"Yes, so badly. Tell me how to take care of you, Roman Graves."

He brought his mouth to her ear, and whispered, "Fuck me."

Grace lifted her body from his lap, giving him room to line himself up with her. Her sex slick and wet took him deep with ease as she lowered herself on top of him. Roman's body shuddered as she bottomed out, sitting in his lap; he was filling her so well, she was tight and warm around him. His balls ached for release.

Grace wrapped her arms around his shoulders and began to move.

Roman watched as she closed her eyes, her bottom lip pulled between her teeth. Her hips rocked against his body, the movements slow and steady; a tortuous way to feel such pleasure.

Roman gripped her ass in his hands, and he loved that while his hands were big, they were no match for her ass. He guided her body up, and Grace hummed in approval as he pulled her off him to the tip. She lingered there, his dick begging her to slam back down on him.

"I thought you wanted me to fuck you?" she asked, and Roman let out a desperate laugh, because he *had* asked her to fuck him, and here he was trying to call the shots.

"You're absolutely right," he said, removing his hands from her hips, "Go ahead then Grace, fuck me."

Grace slowly lowered herself back down, taking him all the way to the hilt. Bringing her lips inches from his ear she whispered, "I'm the fucking captain tonight."

Roman's entire body reacted to her dominance. If she was the captain, then he would let her take the lead. Roman leaned back against the headboard, his hands at his sides as he watched Grace do exactly as he asked her to do–fuck him.

Chapter Thirty-Two

G race raced to her phone. "Hey," she answered.

"Hi." his voice was low and strained–exhausted.

"I wasn't sure you'd be able to call today," she admitted.

She left out the part about how she thought not seeing him would be easy, but it had only been a day and she already missed him so bad it hurt.

"I called you first thing. If I didn't, I would have fallen asleep." he said.

She could hear him on the other line as he sat back on his bed, putting an arm over his eyes to block out the light.

Grace sighed. "No more sleepovers for a while. I feel like us staying up all night was a setback you won't recover from."

"As much as it pains me to agree..." he started, only to be cut off by a huge yawn.

"No more sleepovers, Roman Graves," she said firmly, fully aware that staying up late on Friday had only sent him off on the wrong foot for all the pre-playoff hockey practice.

"Ok, Grace, you win. No more sleepovers if I have practice or a game the next day. My sweet, sweet Grace, we can call, or text, maybe even FaceTime, but no more sleepovers," he murmured. He was falling asleep. She knew she should say goodbye.

"Promise me you won't ask to see me, because I won't be able to say no to you," she demanded. "I did that once already—had to say no to you—and I don't want to have to do it again."

Roman chuckled, it was a weak and sleepy thing. "I promise...only if you promise a few naughty texts and phone calls."

"Roman Graves, are you asking me to sext you?" she asked incredulously.

"Maybe."

"You think I would send you nudes after what happened in December? You don't have the best track record with intimate photos, sir," she joked.

"Hey, I didn't leak them, she did. Are you saying you might leak my dick pics, Grace?" he asked.

Now Grace was laughing. "Are you saying you're going to send me some?"

"I might, if that's something you're into..." he trailed off.

"I've never received a dick pic, so I don't really know how I feel about them. Would you want a vagina pic in return? Is that how it works?" she asked, only half joking, because really, would she be expected to send one, she was so new to all this.

"I think the standard for a female is a tit pic, but I would die a happy man for a nice picture of your ass."

Grace blushed, because while this started as him suggesting phone sex, it very suddenly felt like it was escalating *to* phone sex. She could hear his breathing growing heavier on the other end.

"Roman, are you falling asleep on me?" she asked.

"Not anymore."

"Do you want to, maybe..." she paused, and Roman cleared his throat.

"Say it Grace," he said, amused.

"Do you want to like..." she paused again.

"Go on..."

"Do you want to maybe fool around on the phone?" she finally managed and felt equal parts lame as she did aroused.

"Would you be mad if I said I was already palming myself over my sheets?" he asked, his voice low, and steady.

"No, but I should warn you, I've never done this before," she admitted.

"Masturbated?" he asked, shocked.

"No, of course I've done *that*. I mean I've never had phone sex."

"Well," he asked, "do you want to use your hand, or do you have something to help you out?"

Grace hadn't even considered using a vibrator. That would make it so much easier.

"Hold on," she said, hopping off her bed to retrieve her purple toy from her box in her closet. "Okay, I'm going with a toy," she said into the phone, realizing this would be easier if she put it on speaker, but then reconsidered, when she realized Jess was in the next room.

"Grace, I need you to stop overthinking this and take your clothes off," Roman said into the phone.

"What if my roommate hears us?" she asked.

"Then she should be so lucky."

Something about that made Grace even more horny than she already was. Somehow the idea of her roommate hearing her and Roman get off together only escalated her need to make him come over the phone.

"Grace?" he asked, his voice a low purr.

"Okay, I'm..." she kicked off her panties and placed the phone on speaker on the pillow next to her, "I'm situated."

Roman laughed. "What did you decide on? Are you going to pretend your fingers are mine or am I going to listen to you come with a toy?"

"Toy." she said, hitting the power button, choosing the setting that buzzed, then paused, then buzzed, then paused.

"Is it a vibrator or..."

"Vibrator," she said, lowering the toy between her legs.

Roman's breathing grew more intense. "What are you doing with it?" he asked, coolly, like this was a normal conversation about the weather.

"What do you want me to do with it?" she asked.

"Press it to your clit. Get nice and wet for me."

Grace pressed the head of the toy right where it counted, and the pulsing vibrations alone made her gasp.

She heard Roman chuckle. "We should really be on FaceTime," he said.

"Definitely not ready for FaceTime sex. What about you?" she asked through gritted teeth. "Tell me what you're doing."

"Well, Grace, to put it simply, I'm jerking off thinking of you."

She laughed because what was phone sex without humor, right?

"I wish you were here," she said, closing her eyes, blocking out the distractions, enjoying the feel of the vibrations.

Buzz. Pause. Buzz. Pause. Buzz.

The sound of the toy only a faint whisper on the other line for Roman. Grace could hear his breathing grow heavier.

"Mmmm, me too," he agreed, his voice strained, and sexy.

Grace felt her orgasm building quickly. She pressed the buzz of her vibrator harder against herself.

"I wish this was your mouth on me," he said into the phone.

"Me too, I want to suck you until you come in my mouth," she said, her dirty talk catching her off guard. She had never said things like this to a man, sure she had thought them, but Roman made her feel safe enough to actually say them.

"Damn, Grace, you can't just say shit like that. Now I'm about to come."

She felt her orgasm gathering in the pit of her stomach. "Me too."

"Tell me I can come, Grace," Roman huffed, and she loved the power he gave her in those few words.

"Roman Graves, I want you to come all over your chest and hand. I want you to think of my lips sucking every drop of you down my throat," she said, and as the final words rolled off her tongue she lost it completely, her body jerked at the overwhelming sensation between her legs.

Buzz. Pause. Buzz. Pause. Buzz.

She pulled the vibrator away and squeezed her thighs together as her orgasm made every muscle in her body tense in the most satisfying way. "Oh, yeah." she whispered, and down line, she heard Roman say the same thing.

She laughed, and she could hear Roman's deep, post orgasm laughs too.

"Jinx," he said, his voice low and husky.

"I owe you a soda?" she asked, and Roman laughed again.

"Something like that," he said, and she could hear sleep creeping back into his voice.

"Well, that was one way to say goodnight," he said. He was rustling with something on the other line, she imagined a tissue box or maybe an old shirt from the floor to clean up his mess?

"That was one hell of a goodnight," he agreed. "I'm going to sleep like a baby."

"Sorry, I kept you up longer than you were planning."

"Don't ever apologize for keeping me up to fool around together. That was hot, Grace. I think we might survive the long road trips after all if we do this more often."

"Who knows, maybe one day I'll be brave enough to FaceTime during," she teased, and Roman chuckled.

"I miss you," he said, a yawn rounding out the end of his sentence.

"Same."

"Stay on the phone with me a little longer," he yawned.

Grace settled back into her bed, and placed the phone on her still racing heart, "I'll stay until I know you're asleep."

"It won't be long," he said, his voice but a whisper.

"Get some rest, Roman. I'll hang up when you start snoring," she teased.

"I miss you, Grace," he said again, his speech growing sloppy. "I miss you all the time."

"Same. So, why don't you get some rest so we can figure out a day to see each other somewhere in the near future, when you're not so exhausted, okay?" she asked sweetly.

She could make out Roman nuzzling into the pillow. "I didn't even get a chance to ask you about...your day..." he yawned, again.

The line went silent for a second, and then Romans words were replaced with low deep breathing, and the occasional snore.

Grace listened for a few seconds and when she was sure he was sleeping she said quietly into the phone, "I had a phone interview with the Knights today for a drug and alcohol counselor position. I have another interview on Wednesday. I need the job to stay in L.A., but I'm afraid to tell you. I need to do this on my own. Please forgive me for keeping this from you."

She heard Roman rustle in the sheets on the other end of the line. "Roman, are you awake? Did you hear that?" she asked nervously. He didn't respond, he only snored louder. Grace let out a deep sigh of relief and hit the end button.

Chapter Thirty-Three

The bar was crowded for a Tuesday night, and it had little to do with the quality of the bar food and everything to do with it being the first playoff game of the season for the Knights. Every TV was tuned in to the pre-show. The patrons were loud and rowdy, the smell of beer and fried food filled the crowded space. L.A. was known for being a fierce sports city with loyal fans and the occasional bandwagoner, but when Grace looked around the bar she felt a sense of pride when she saw the number eleven on the backs of so many people, and above it, her boyfriend's last name *Graves*.

It was a weird feeling, being amongst fans. Wearing his jersey–the one Roman had given her. It was exhilarating being a part of something this big, and even more exciting knowing that in this bar, amongst a sea of Knights fans–*Roman Graves* fans–she was his girlfriend, and when the game was over, she would be the one he called to say goodnight.

Un-fucking-believable.

Jess had come to the bar with Grace. She told Grace she was committed to the playoffs now that her bestie was fucking the captain. Jess had even bought herself a Knights t-shirt.

"How does it feel?" Jess asked.

"I'm nervous for them. Excited. I don't know. It's the first playoff game I've ever watched, and my boyfriend just so happens to be the captain of the team playing." She looked up at the TV, and her smile grew from ear to ear. The sports broadcaster was talking about Roman, a highlight reel from this season playing on a split screen. Grace felt pride in her man. She knew if he was that good on an off season, he must be amazing during an *on* season.

"How does it feel knowing that man–right there," Jess said, pointing to the TV, "is dicking you down regularly while all these puck bunnies drool on their chicken wings over him."

Roman had changed everything when he chose her. Now, in a sea of groupies, Grace was *the* girlfriend. And not just any girlfriend, she was Roman–Mr. I Don't Date–Graves' girlfriend. And that had to stand for something.

"Well, I'm definitely enjoying my little secret," she admitted.

"Not me," Jess said, "I want to stand on a table and let all these thirsty bitches know that my roommate is the captain's girlfriend."

Grace definitely wasn't up for that kind of attention. She knew if this panned out, and they made it through the playoff season, she would eventually get found out, and the public scrutiny would begin, but for now it felt safe in her secret little bubble with him.

"Did you tell him about the phone interview yesterday?" Jess asked.

And no, she absolutely hadn't. She considered it. And then thought better of it. Besides, they had only been able to manage a few quick hellos, a couple I miss yous, and one round of phone sex since he slept over Friday. She didn't want to add any kind of extra stress to his already very full plate.

"Is it really because you don't want his help securing the spot or is it because you're afraid you might not get the job at all?" Jess pried.

"All of the above, and maybe I'm a little worried that working together will be a conflict of interest, and I'll have to choose between Roman and the job," Grace admitted.

"Is Roman an addict?" Jess asked rhetorically.

Grace knew he wasn't, but she also knew how easy it was for a good, level headed person to become one. One bad injury. One car accident. One slip and fall. One too many drinks a week, and Roman could easily land himself sitting across from her in her office if she got the job, and that would most definitely be a conflict of interest.

***

Roman skated to center ice to take the first puck drop of the playoffs for his team. He was met there by the San Jose Captain, Ryan Porter. Roman knew Porter from juniors and grew up in the hockey world alongside him. He wouldn't call Porter a bad guy, but Porter definitely still held a grudge against Roman for getting the first overall draft pick with L.A. over him.

"*You* were the last team I thought we'd be seeing in this playoff series," Porter chirped.

"You should know better than to count me out, Porter. I was born a winner," Roman said, giving him a cocky wink.

Good guy or not, Ryan Porter was the enemy right now, and Roman would use Porter's grudge against him to get in his head and win this puck drop.

The ref took his place. Roman steadied himself. The puck dropped, and the battle to win this game was in full swing. The fans filled the arena with a deafening roar. Roman won, sending the puck across the ice to Liam. Liam skated the puck up the ice, both teams on his heels, San Jose's defense everywhere all at once. A San Jose player won the puck and L.A. was on the defense in the blink of an eye. Both teams battled for control, looking to be the first to get on the board. The San Jose player made a clean pass, creating a perfect scoring chance for Porter, he took the shot and the crowd shouted as Jason Kidd made the save.

It sounded like playoff hockey in the arena. It was electric. The crowd's energy matched that of the players.

Roman took the puck drop again, knowing he needed to create a moment for his first line to get off the ice. They needed fresh skates out there, fresh legs. The puck dropped, Roman lost, San Jose's rookie, Jonathan Pierce got the puck, made the pass to Porter, he took the shot again, it ricocheted off the net, Niko Hart retrieved the puck for L.A. and skated it up the ice allowing a line change for both teams. Roman watched his second line hit the ice with fire in their veins. He watched as Hart handled the puck in the corner with precision, allowing the rest of the team time to set up to make a play. He passed behind the net, San Jose battling hard to regain possession, only to fail. Myers, the L.A. rookie, took the shot in the right corner of the net, and scored.

"Fuck yeah, boys." Roman shouted. "Fuck yeah, that's how we do it!"

The L.A. team banged their sticks and the boys on the ice pulled Myers in for a celebratory dog pile. The crowd's "boos" filled the arena and Roman loved every one of them. Their disappointment only made him want to win more.

***

Grace watched as the Knights started off strong. For every shot on goal the San Jose Threshers got, the Knights got three. Scoring early had lit a fire under L.A.'s ass in the first period. But the second period was a different team. It was as if they went into the locker room on fire and the emergency sprinklers went off, dousing their flames.

There were three minutes left in the second period and Grace sat with her jersey wrapped around her fists, her knuckles white with anxiety.

"What's even going on right now?" Jess said in disbelief. The bar had gone quiet, the pre-game excitement and the first period goal, now a thing of the past.

Grace shook her head. "I have no idea." She watched the captain of San Jose skate the puck up the ice, take the shot, and score, leaving them at 5-1 San Jose before the buzzer went off signifying the end of the second period.

"Your boy looks pissed," Jess said, as they both watched Roman slam his stick against the boards on his way off the ice.

Grace was happy she wasn't going to be in that locker room after *that* period.

"They need to win this game," Grace said, knowing that it would take a miracle at this point.

"It's like no one showed up after the first period," Jess said.

Grace agreed. This had been their biggest issue all season; not playing for a full sixty minutes, not being able to buy a goal, bad puck bounces, and, as much as she hated to say it, a star player who was having an off season. That player being her boyfriend.

"Roman needs a goal." she said. "I just know if he scores the team will rally behind him. If he scores a goal and they lose, the loss won't feel *as* bad, right?"

Jess gave her nothing. Encouragement was hard to find when the Knights were down by four. No silver lining was allowed, because this was playoff hockey, no one got a participation award in the playoffs. It was win or lose. Grace knew she was going to experience a new version of Roman tonight if they lost. She could only prepare herself for the worst and hope for the best.

***

There were two minutes left in the game and they needed to score two points to tie it up. In some sports that would be impossible. But a lot could happen in two minutes in hockey. Roman had seen his team score three points in just under a minute. He had seen bigger comebacks happen.

The puck dropped, Harvey lost the battle, San Jose took the long shot across the ice leaving L.A. to scramble as the timer ran down.

A lot can happen in two minutes, Roman thought... *if you're not the L.A. Knights.*

The buzzer went off, and the Knights had lost.

The San Jose fans all jumped to their feet and cheered so loud that the ice rumbled under his skates. It was a well-deserved win for the

Threshers, Roman couldn't deny they played a better game, but that didn't make the loss any easier.

Game one was over. Tomorrow they had a short practice, and then the rest of the night off to rest before game two at home.

He pulled out his phone when he got back to the locker room and did the only thing he could do that wasn't punching a wall.

Roman:

> Change of plans. I need to see you tomorrow after practice.

He tossed the sweaty white jersey in the linen bin, ashamed that the captain's C landed face up, as if taunting him, calling him out for the shit season he played.

His phone chimed.

Grace:

> I know you're upset. But we had rules in place to make sure you focus on hockey.

He knew she was right. But that was before he realized that seeing her, and being with her, wasn't a distraction, it was his sounding board.

Roman:

> I'm just going to swing by on my way home. It'll be quick.

Grace:

> I'm not on your way home, Roman.

He laughed, he didn't think he would be able to laugh after such a brutal loss. But she was the queen of ball busting, and he loved her for it. It kept him humble.

Roman:

You're worth the detour.

Grace:

Well, if you really want to break the playoff rules…I won't say no. I did that once and it about killed me.

Roman:

You and me both. I have to see you. Fuck the rules we made. We've never done things to plan, why start now? I'll call you when I get back to the hotel.

Chapter Thirty-Four

Grace anxiously waited in bed for Roman to call her when he got back to his hotel in San Jose. She wanted to comfort him after that loss. She also wanted to be comforted; tomorrow was her in-person interview with Cam Lawndry. Tomorrow, while Roman was reviewing the game, watching every bad pass, every missed opportunity, every time he shot the puck and missed, she would be down the street at the team's corporate office trying to get a job. She was nervous and the only person she wanted to comfort her about it was the one person she was keeping the interview a secret from.

Her phone rang, and she didn't hesitate to answer it at once.

"Hi," she said far too quickly.

She heard the thud of the heavy hotel door slamming shut behind him, and the rustling of his bag falling from his shoulder, then his keys being put on the hotel dresser.

"Hey, sorry, my hands were full," he said, his voice was tired.

"I'm sorry about tonight," she offered. It seemed like the wrong thing to say, but she didn't know what the right thing to say was. He didn't respond, so she went on. "I'm sorry I don't know how to treat you right now. I don't know what you want to hear, or how I can be supportive. But I want to do it right, so any pointers would be much appreciated."

Roman let out a heavy sigh. "Take my mind off it."

"How? What do you want to know?"

"How was your day?" he asked. But Grace knew her day was not going to be helpful since it revolved around practicing interview questions, Panera bagels, and stressing over the game.

"It was interesting. My first playoff game as a hockey girlfriend," she said lightly.

"Next," he said, dismissing any and all hockey talk.

She heard the bed groan under his weight on the other end of the phone. "Why don't you tell me something I don't know about you. Tell me about a memory from your childhood. One that makes you happy."

Grace knew what he was doing. She knew the sting of the loss was fresh. So, she would help him deflect.

"One time as a child, after Halloween, I got this great idea to make the ultimate candy bar," she started. She could hear Roman's breathing through the phone—quick and steady. She went on, "So, I put all my favorite candy bars from trick or treating in a bowl; Snickers, Crunch bars, Reese's, M&M's, you name it. If I got it trick-or-treating and it was chocolate based, I added it to the bowl. I should add I was only ten, and my dad wasn't as present as he should have been. He was already strung out on painkillers by this time," she added.

Roman remained silent, letting her tell her story.

"So, I put the bowl in the microwave, and added five minutes to the clock and pressed start. I went to watch TV while the chocolate bars cooked and when I heard the microwave ding, I ran back to see my creation. I was so excited."

"Did you plan on eating it hot and melted or were you going to let it harden?" he asked, and this was good, this meant she had him distracted.

"I'm not sure if my plans ever made it that far, because when I opened the microwave not only had the chocolate melted, but so had the bowl. Come to find out, not all things are microwave safe. I didn't know what to do, so I just left the melted bowl in there. My dad never said anything about it. I remember waiting for him to be mad, or to ground me, but he didn't. He just cleaned it up without saying a word. I think about that moment so much. I wonder why he never mentioned it, why he didn't use it as a learning opportunity. But mostly, I wonder what it would have tasted like, to have all the best candy bars mixed up into one ultimate candy bar."

Roman sighed—it sounded like a sigh of relief.

It stayed silent for a moment, and Grace wondered if he had fallen asleep. Just when she was ready to hang up she heard him whisper into the phone.

"We should try it again," he said.

Grace wasn't sure what he meant. "Try what?" she asked.

"To make an ultimate chocolate bar. We should try it again in a microwave safe bowl."

Grace's chest tightened at the idea of reliving one of her favorite childhood memories with him.

"I would love that."

Roman fell silent again, and then said, "I miss you."

"You have no idea," she said.

Roman laughed. "Oh, I think I have a pretty good idea."

"Will it always feel like I'm suffocating when you're on the road?" she asked.

"I don't know, Grace. I don't know because I've never missed someone before. This is all new territory for me."

Grace felt like she couldn't breathe. Was he holding his breath too?

"Does it feel like you're suffocating?" she asked.

"Every breath feels shallow when you're not around."

Grace fell back on her pillow, closed her eyes, and tried to picture Roman next to her.

"Do you really think it's wise we break the rules and see each other tomorrow?" she asked.

"If we don't, I think we might both stop breathing entirely," he said with a chuckle.

Grace's heart hammered in her chest. Was Roman saying he would die if he didn't see her? Because, if he was, she needed him to know she felt the same.

"Well, for the sake of not dying, I think some rules are meant to be broken," she teased.

"I'll see you tomorrow, my beautiful, sweet, Grace."

Chapter Thirty-Five

The interview with Cam Lawndry was going surprisingly well considering how nervous Grace was to be on Roman's turf without him knowing. Cam started the interview by asking her about her goals, and ambitions and why she felt she would be a good fit with the Knights organization. He was a bit of an odd guy, he laughed at his own jokes and even asked Grace, as part of the interview process, what animal she felt described her work ethic the best. She told him she was most like a beaver, hard working, loyal, organized, with integrity in everything she did. She had nat-geo to thank for that answer.

"Well, Grace..." Cam said, looking down at her resume again and then back up at her, "Grace *Fairchild*?" he asked, distracted by her last name. "Your father doesn't happen to be a part of the Fairchild and Fairchild Law Firm?"

"No. Different Fairchild, sadly." Grace said apologetically.

"Oh, thank god," Cam said laughing, slapping his knees, catching Grace off guard. "Those guys are pricks–pardon my French."

Grace gave a nervous laugh.

"So, I see here you graduated UCLA, top of your class."

Grace smiled proudly, and straightened her shoulders just a bit. "I did. I was there on an academic scholarship."

"And you just recently completed your hours over at the Los Angeles Drug and Alcohol Recovery Center?"

"Yes, under Dr. Meredith Williams and then, later in my internship, Dr. Wayne Gandy. I've attached their letters of recommendation."

Cam flipped between pages, reading a few things before looking back up at her. "I'm going to be straight with you, you don't have the experience we were hoping for." Grace tensed, she knew it was a long shot applying. "*But*, having your master's in behavioral science is a huge bonus for me–especially as a fellow Bruin," he said with a wink.

"Us Bruins have to stick together," she tried nervously, winking back.

She could play this game.

"Are you a fan of hockey, Grace? I see you're originally from Northern California. Can't have a Threshers fan on our staff," he said, jokingly, but she knew there was honesty in that statement somewhere.

"I am," she said, and then added, "just recently became a Knights fan, actually." Her stomach was a ball of nerves. She felt like she was being dishonest. She felt like the weight of keeping this interview from Roman, and now, not being forthcoming about knowing him with Cam was heavy enough to crush her.

"Oh, really. Not the best season to become a fan. You know, we used to be good. The guys are not playing their best this year. Did you catch the game last night?" he asked.

"I did. It was hard to watch."

"You can say that again," he joked.

So, she did, "It was hard to watch."

This made Cam laugh, he leaned forward on his desk, bouncing the ball point of a pen on a stack of post it notes, small dots of ink marking each drop of the pen.

"The truth is, I don't know if you're the best candidate considering your lack of experience."

Grace nodded. "Understandable. I'm sure you have loads of people applying for this job."

"I wasn't finished," he said, clicking the pen shut, sitting it back down on his desk. "Lucky for you, we don't need someone with a lot of experience right now, we just need someone who's a good fit to come on board with our team in that department. I happen to think you're a perfect fit. And being a Bruin helps." He winked again.

And what the actual fuck was happening. Did she just get the job? Grace just stared at him like a deer in headlights.

"So, what do you think, Miss. Fairchild, not to be confused with Fairchild and Fairchild Law firm of course." Cam said, laughing at his own joke.

"I think," she was at a loss for words. "I..." she said before she could stop herself. "Before we move forward, I think you should know that I'm dating Roman Graves."

"And I'm dating Jennifer Lopez," he joked.

"No, really. It's new. But Roman and I are dating. And it felt wrong to keep that from you. In case it's a conflict of interest."

Cam paused, his eyes assessing her. "Roman Graves doesn't date. Everyone knows that. Or did you become a fan *after* the leaked photo?"

Oh, she had been around for the leaked photo all right. But that was Roman four months ago, she had Roman now, and he was nothing like the man she had met then.

"He *didn't* date," she corrected.

Cam looked shocked. "You're serious."

"I am."

"Why didn't you say something sooner?" he asked.

"I don't know. I was worried it would ruin my chances, but then I just felt yucky not saying it, so, here we are," she said, shrugging her shoulders.

Cam's shocked face lightened up a bit. He smiled and shook his head in disbelief. "Why didn't you have Roman talk to me, his seal of approval would have made this decision that much easier."

Grace couldn't believe what she was hearing. "So, it's *not* a conflict of interest?" she asked.

"No, we have two other counselors on staff. I don't think it should be a problem at all," he said, and then under his breath she heard him mutter, "I just saw Roman yesterday, sneaky, sneaky."

"Oh, and could you not say anything to Roman about this," she said, "about the interview, and the job. I haven't told him yet. Been waiting for the perfect time, and with the playoffs and all, I just haven't been ready."

"So, you're telling me you had an opportunity to use Roman Graves, the captain of the Knights, to your advantage here, and you didn't?" he asked incredulously.

"That is correct," she said.

"Makes me like you even more, Grace. An honest hire in my opinion. Ya' got it entirely on your own."

Cam Lawndry stood and offered her his hand. They shook and she thanked him for the interview and for keeping it between them until she had the opportunity to tell Roman about the job herself.

"My lips are sealed," he said, mimicking zipping his lips, locking them up, and throwing out the invisible key.

"Thank you," she said again.

"You should receive your on-boarding email by late afternoon, Grace. Welcome to the Los Angeles Knights organization."

She gave him her most thankful smile and before she left his office, she turned around and said, "Go, Knights!" with a traditional team fist pump.

She headed down the long hallway of the corporate office, and she couldn't believe she would soon be working in such a nice facility. She passed marketing, and H.R.; everyone seemed happy in their offices. Overall, it felt safe and upbeat. She came up to the next office, the door plaque read 'ticket sales'. She peeked in, and was startled to see Roman standing in the small office talking animatedly to a woman who worked there.

Grace raced past the office and slipped into the community kitchen. The few employees who were having a cup of coffee, talking about last night's game in depth took no notice of her.

Her phone rang, it was Roman. Roman who was in the same building as her. Roman, her boyfriend who didn't know she had even applied for a job with his organization, was calling her—from down the hall as she hid in the lunchroom.

She hit end, and frantically typed up a text.

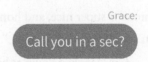

Grace:

Call you in a sec?

She could hear Roman's phone chime when her text went through. She peeked around the corner and saw him standing in front of the ticket office, staring at his phone.

Her phone chimed again and she hurried to put it on silent.

Roman:

> I only had a minute. Just got done running an errand at corporate, headed to the rink for practice now. I'm still going to swing by tonight, is that ok?

Grace peeked around the corner again. He was heading the opposite direction, she let out an audible sigh of relief and one of the girls at the lunch table took notice.

"Which one did you see?" she asked in a thick valley girl accent, catching Grace off guard.

"Huh?" she asked, dumbfounded, looking at the girl confused.

"Which player are you hiding from? All the new hires are star struck at first," she laughed. "You're the first I've seen run for cover, but none of us knew how to act around the players when we first got hired on with the Knights."

Oh, Grace thought.

And then it all made sense.

"Oh, yeah, it was Roman Graves," she said, playing cool.

"Yeah, he's intimidating AF," she said. "But you don't have to hide. They're all really nice, except maybe Milo Yavitch, he's a dick. But Roman is super nice, and honestly if you just ignore them, they ignore you and life goes on as usual."

Grace looked down at her phone, two more texts from Roman.

"Thanks for the advice," she said, peeking around the corner to make sure the coast was clear before heading straight to the exit this time.

Roman:

> Funny thing...

Grace's heart hammered in her chest when she read what came next.

Roman:

> I could have sworn I saw you at the corporate offices today. I guess I miss you so much I'm imagining you now.

She had to tell him tonight. She got the job. She did it on her own. There was no conflict of interest. Tonight, she would finally get this damn monkey off her back.

Chapter Thirty-Six

R oman parked...illegally. He was already breaking his rule about not seeing Grace tonight; he might as well break a few laws while he was at it. Besides, this was very quickly becoming *his* parking spot–if only he could get the police to see eye to eye with him on that.

He pulled a bag from the front seat and bolted up the stairs to Grace's apartment. His muscles ached with every step he took. He reminded himself this was just him bringing her a gift and then heading home. This was not a long visit. He would *not* initiate sex...he would also not deny Grace sex if *she* initiated it.

This visit was strictly oxygen in his lungs.

This was his next fix.

He knocked once and the door swung open. Grace was there. She looked gorgeous. Her makeup was done up more than he was used to; deep burgundy lips, and a small wings of eyeliner–it made her eyes look sexy and her lips look fuckable.

He dropped the bag on the floor and pulled her up into his arms. Grace wrapped her legs around him as he spun to pin her body against the front door.

So much for not initiating sex.

His mouth crashed into hers and he realized not only could he not breathe when he was away from her, but he couldn't breathe when he was with her either.

He kissed her like it was his lifeline. He wanted this kiss to tell her the things he was still too cowardly to say; the way his heart felt, and the way his brain agreed, and the way his dick was on board too—with all things Grace.

A throat cleared loudly across the room. Startled, Roman broke the kiss and let loose of Grace, to find Jess standing in the living room, her eyebrows raised, shaking her head in mock disgust.

"Naughty, naughty," she teased.

Roman laughed, pulling Grace in front of his crotch region to cover his massive erection. He hadn't even considered her roommate might be home.

"Hi, Jess. Good to see you again," he said, clearing his throat.

Jess crossed her arms and smirked. "Always a pleasure, Mr. Graves."

"Sorry," Grace offered.

"Oh, no, don't mind me," Jess teased. "Fuck against the door if that's what makes you happy. Just know I already made popcorn and there's a new episode of the Greatest Chef on, so, you'll have company."

Roman reached between him and Grace to readjust himself before grabbing the bag on the floor.

"Actually, I don't have time for door sex tonight," he said, handing Grace the bag. "I'm just here to give my girlfriend a little something."

"And it's not door sex?" Jess asked incredulously. "Now, she's going to be disappointed."

"There's something in the bag for you too," Roman said, and Jess instantly dropped the sass and perked up.

"Shut up? You brought me something too? Is it Panera bagels, because I gotta be straight with you, I personally think Panera is glorified hospital food."

Grace shushed her. "Don't hate on my love language," she said, pulling out a fresh, black jersey... "Liam Harvey?"

"Oh," Roman said, taking the Harvey jersey and handing it to Jess. "That one's for Jess. The other one is for you."

Grace pulled out another jersey, and all was right in the world; the back had the number eleven and the last name Graves, and the front had the Knights logo and the "C" for captain on the chest. She beamed at Roman and leaned up on tiptoes to kiss him.

"Thank you. I'll wear it to the bar tomorrow night," she said.

"No, you won't," he said, pulling her in and kissing her softly on the lips.

"I won't?" Grace asked, looking up at him in confusion.

"No, because you'll be at the game, in the box," he said.

Jess chimed in, "So, I have to wear the hot blonde dude's jersey at the bar alone? I didn't even like hockey a few months ago and now I have to watch it alone?"

Roman laughed. "No, that's why I got you the jersey. I want you to go with Grace to the game. The box can be intimidating, lots of big wigs will be there, and hockey wives. I thought she could use a friend."

Jess jumped up and down in excitement. "Yes. I knew it would pay off having a friend date a hockey player," she teased, Grace just rolled her eyes at her best friend's inability to play it cool.

"Okay," Jess said, finishing her happy dance. "Thank you times a million for the jersey, and for inviting me to the game, but something tells me Grace wants you to herself. So, out of the kindness of my heart,

I'll postpone my show and go hide away in my bedroom until y'all finish doing whatever you plan to do in peace."

Once Jess was gone Roman pulled Grace down into his lap on the couch to face him.

"I have to go, he said, his lips on her neck.

"Then why are we on the couch starting something we can't finish?" she asked, her voice low and heady—he could tell that she wanted it too.

"I just needed to be close to you."

"Thank you for the jersey," she said, leaning back, creating a little distance, but not too much.

"If we win tomorrow night, I'm going to fuck you in it," he said, matter-of-factly.

Grace leaned in and whispered in his ear, "Tomorrow night *when* you win, you *will* fuck me in it."

Roman let out a growl. "You better fucking believe it."

"You got this. I believe in you," Grace said, leaning back, this time more serious.

"I do too. I feel good about it," Roman admitted.

"Practice went well?"

"It was great. I was worried the boys were already counting us out, but they came hyped. We reviewed the tapes, saw where we needed to shift our game to play San Jose's brand of hockey."

"I can't wait to see you play playoff hockey live. I'm going to be a ball of nerves," she admitted.

"I'm going to win for you," he said.

"Win for *you*," she added, and then her lips curled up in a mischievous grin. "And also win for the victory sex."

Roman gripped her hips and pulled her flush against him, creating a friction between them that neither of them needed, because he knew they couldn't take this any further tonight.

"Where did you go today?" he said, Grace's nose scrunched up at his question. "It's just, you don't normally wear lipstick. Did you have an interview?"

Grace sat up straight, her body language shifting completely from relaxed to stiff, and off putting.

"I didn't mean it in a bad way," Roman sputtered. "I think you're gorgeous without the makeup."

"No, it's not that. It's not that at all. Sorry I got weird," she said, trying a smile. "I *did* have an interview today."

Roman took her hands and squeezed excitedly.

"Why didn't you tell me you had one? How did it go?" he asked.

Grace shrugged. "It went really well."

"Are you not happy about it?" he asked.

"No, it's perfect. It's just... Can we maybe talk about it later? I just really need you to focus on hockey."

"Yeah, we can talk about it when you're ready. I can only imagine it's nerve wracking, the whole interview thing," he said, then added, "but don't ever keep things from me for the sake of hockey, okay? Your life and what you got going on is just as important, and I want to support you, Grace?"

"Okay," she agreed. But he wasn't so sure he bought it. Grace had a wall up about something, her eyes suddenly unable to meet his, and he knew if they were going to do this for real, she would eventually have to let those walls come down.

He leaned in and kissed her nose, and brought his hands up to rub her back. she melted into his body, and he needed that, he needed to feel her crumble into him, to find comfort in his arms.

"I think I like you, Grace Fairchild," he whispered into her hair.

"Yeah?" she asked because she answered everything with a question.

"Yeah," he said. "I do."

Chapter Thirty-Seven

Grace and Jess arrived early to the arena for game two of the play-offs. Her whole body felt on edge, her skin was crawling, her heart was racing; being a hockey girlfriend during playoffs was far more intense than she expected it to be. The anxiety and the need for this team to win wasn't something she anticipated feeling so intensely. But she was invested now. She was all in, as a fan, as a girlfriend, and now, as a part of the franchise.

"Wow," Jess said when they entered the box, "this is fancy."

Grace couldn't agree more. If one thing was certain, it was that the Knights knew how to do things right. Melissa, Roman's assistant spotted them right away and pulled Grace in for a hug.

"Black looks good on you," she said, taking notice of the fresh jersey.

"Thanks," Grace said, nervously scanning the crowded room.

Melissa, as if reading Grace's body language filled her in, "Okay, so a lot of these people are not that important. Those two are heads of marketing, they are probably who gave Roman the tickets to the box. And those ladies are hockey wives. That guy is-" she pointed to the bar, but Grace knew who he was.

"Cam Lawndry," Grace said under her breath.

Melissa looked at her confused. "How do you know Cam?" she asked, and at that moment Cam looked over and mimicked locking his lips, giving Grace his signature wink.

"We've met before," Grace said nonchalantly, and changed the subject. "So, do we just sit wherever?"

"Yeah, you can sit up front, and watch, but most people mingle, and drink, and stand around. It's up to you."

"And the food and drinks?" Jess asked.

"All the food is free, drinks are free, enjoy."

"I'm too nervous to eat or drink anything," Grace said, right as a tall, blonde, model type, wearing a Liam Harvey jersey inserted herself into their conversation.

"*You*," she said boldly pointing at Grace and giving her a less than approving look, "must be a new hockey girlfriend."

"I am," Grace admitted, the blonde gave her another once-over and then turned to address Jess.

"And you, my dear," she said, her voice sickeningly sweet, "are wearing my boyfriend's jersey."

The blonde gave a playful laugh, but nothing about it was funny. The only word Grace would use to describe the whole interaction was awkward.

Who the hell was this chick?

"I'm willing to put money on it that I'm not the only one wearing your boyfriend's jersey tonight," Jess replied with a wink in a playful manner, but it was not lost on Grace that Jess was more than willing to play this bitch's game.

The blonde laughed–overdramatically–then held out a hand to the girls. "I'm Ava, Liam Harvey's girlfriend, and you are?"

"Grace," she said, shaking Avas' limp hand. "I'm Roman Grave's girlfriend."

Ava laughed. "Obviously, you're wearing his jersey."

Grace was so confused about what was going on here. Was this woman for real?

"Yeah, I guess I am. The jersey is a dead giveaway," she said, blushing but trying to play it cool. She had a bad feeling about this chick and wanted to be as far away from her as possible.

"It's funny though," Ava went on, her posture changing to something more accusatory, "Roman doesn't really date, does he?"

Jess chimed in, "He does now. Guess he just needed to find a girl that was worth it."

Ava let out a fake laugh. "You're funny. I guess I'll let you wear my man's jersey tonight."

Jess met Ava's energy and retorted, "Well thank fuck, because I was going to wear it either way. Glad to have your seal of approval."

Ava rolled her eyes and gave another fake laugh. It was getting awkward—fast.

Grace bumped Jess' shoulder, signaling for her to let it go.

"Well, it was nice to meet you, Ava," Grace said. "We were going to sit down. My nerves are shot–new to all this, you know?"

"Yeah, I'm sure your nerves are awful, what with the way Roman's been playing this season," Ava said, lifting an eyebrow as she went on, "You know, with the whole sex scandal thing, and him just not being able to keep his dick in his pants. I know Liam had to stop going around him this season because he was such a bad influence, he didn't want to be around that kind of drama–for the sake of the team. So, yeah, I get it babe, you must be a mess knowing all that shit about him."

Grace wanted to call her bluff. But her head wasn't working properly. Jess took her by the arm and pulled her away from Ava over to the seats, leaving Ava standing there alone, her arms crossed, a sinister smile on her face.

"What the fuck is even happening right now?" Jess asked under her breath. "Do you know that woman?"

Grace sat down, frazzled over what Ava had just said so boldly. "It's obviously Liam's girlfriend. Do you think she's just saying shit to me because she's pissed that you're wearing her man's jersey?" Grace asked, trying to understand what her motives were.

"No. I think she's just one of those awful women who hates to see other women happy." Jess offered.

"I don't know," Grace said, her entire body shaking, her excitement for the game extinguished only to be replaced with a yucky feeling in her gut.

"Don't pay her any mind, Grace. You know Roman. You know him on a more intimate level than any other woman has managed. Don't let her mess up your night."

But did she know him? Outside of a whirlwind romance, a few bagel deliveries, good sex, and a few conversations that felt like some kind of forever, she wasn't sure she *did* know him. She didn't know his favorite color, or movie, or how he takes his coffee. She didn't know his middle name, or if he wanted kids. She didn't know anything about him, and yet her heart ached for him. She wanted to know every detail down to his first kiss...because she wanted to be his last.

She wouldn't let this Ava person ruin her night. Roman was hers. She knew that. He showed her that with every soul-shattering kiss. Whatever he did before her was always going to be out of her control because she couldn't change his past, but she could fight to be a part of his future.

"You okay?" Jess asked.

Grace shook off the yuck Ava had given her, and stood for the national anthem. Her man was on the ice, and she wanted to enjoy this game. She wanted to watch him win, because when he did, she was going to have her way with him in this jersey–because she could–because he was hers, and she knew it.

Chapter Thirty-Eight

The drive back to his house after the big win, with Grace in the passenger seat next to him, felt surreal. She looked natural taking up his space, sitting in his passenger seat, wearing his jersey, holding his hand, celebrating his win. She was the fit he thought didn't exist in his life.

"I want you to meet my mom," he said recklessly, his post-game high making him euphoric and optimistic.

Grace pulled his hand up to her lips and kissed his knuckles. "Okay."

"And my dad. They're a package deal. He's awful."

Grace never took her eyes off him. "You're nothing like him."

Roman squeezed her hand tight. "I could be...still. I don't want to be. But every morning I wake up afraid that I'm going to ruin things with you."

"You can't promise that you won't hurt me, but I know for certain it won't be because you're like him. Maybe this doesn't work out. Maybe we realize we are not a fit—when the new wears off—but I know you would never hurt me intentionally, Roman."

"How?" he asked.

"Because you don't want to. If your press conference taught me anything about you, it's that you stand up for what you believe in and you don't do things because others tell you to do them. I know that even if you decide I'm not for you, you'll end things the right way."

"I'm never getting over you," Roman said, and there wasn't an ounce of uncertainty in his voice.

Grace smiled. "I realized tonight, at the game, that I don't know a lot of important things about you."

Roman looked over at her, the red glow of brake lights in the L.A. traffic illuminated his face fiercely.

She turned her body to face him. "So, since we're stuck in traffic, I think we should do rapid fire questions. You know, the little things that seem insignificant, but can make or break a relationship."

Roman smiled. "Rapid fire?"

"Why not? We have time to kill," she said, hinting at the dead stop, hockey playoff traffic keeping them from the real celebration she wanted to give him.

"I love it," he said. "Who goes first?"

"I'll start," she scrunched up her nose, thinking up a question.

Roman laughed. "I thought it was rapid fire?"

"I know, I know, but once I was put on the spot rapid fire became slow burn."

"Are we considered a slow burn?" he asked.

"I think we qualify for slow burn, although the first four months were their own brand of slow."

"Was that the first question, then?" he asked.

"I guess it was. Okay, I got one," she said. "Middle name?"

"Reginald. I know, super classy and distinguished."

"Obviously the name of your first born," she teased.

He laughed. "Boy or girl. It doesn't matter, it has to be Reginald. What's your middle name?"

Grace playfully pushed his shoulder. "No ask-backs."

"Oh, now there's rules?"

"I make them up as I go."

Roman gripped her inner thigh. "And I break them one by one."

She rolled her eyes, but he didn't miss the heat rise to her face causing her to blush.

"Abbey. Grace Abbey Fairchild," she said. "It's a Beatles thing."

"I love it," he said. "Your turn."

"Your ask-back did not count as a question."

Roman shook his head. "You always gotta bust my balls, don't you?"

Grace laughed. "Oh, balls are not a part of this game, but I think they may have something to do with what comes later tonight."

Roman's hand moved further up her thigh and squeezed. At this rate, by the time they got home he would end up fucking her in his driveway.

"Okay, Grace, I see you." He gave it a thought then asked, "Favorite movie?"

"Easy, Across the Universe," she said.

Roman smiled and asked, "It's a Beatles thing, right?"

"Ding, ding, ding. You?"

"Who's breaking the rules now Mrs. No ask-backs?"

"I thought rules were meant to be broken, Mr. I'll break every rule for you?" she teased.

Roman, finding himself grateful for the first time in history to be at a dead stop in L.A. traffic, took Grace by the neck and pulled her across the center console to meet him halfway. He took her bottom lip between his teeth and gently tugged before kissing her slowly and deeply. The car behind him laid on the horn and they both pulled away laughing.

"I'm going to fuck you so hard when we get home," he said, under his breath.

Grace reached over and gripped his erection. "I'm keeping the jersey on."

"Oh, that's a rule I won't bend on."

She sat back in her seat, then asked, "Favorite movie?"

"Scream," he said without hesitation.

"I'm too scared to watch horror movies," she admitted.

"I'll protect you when we do," he said, giving her thigh a reassuring squeeze.

"Cats or dogs?" he asked.

"Cats," she said, then went on, "but hear me out, that's only because having a dog with how busy my life always is would be cruel. I think a cat would be a better fit for my life."

"I agree. I definitely couldn't have a dog. A lot of players do, but I wasn't allowed to have pets growing up, so I don't think I would know what to do with one."

"Okay, the next question is a two parter. Do you like coffee, and if so, how do you take it?" she asked.

"Good one. I do like coffee and I'm a straight espresso man, but only because dairy before a skate is bad for the gut. If I have a day off and treat myself to something fancy, I like a good, iced vanilla latte. Unless it's basic bitch season, then I'm ordering a pumpkin spice latte every damn time."

"I didn't peg you for the basic bitch type, but it makes me happy, because I too become extremely basic once pumpkin spice hits the shelves."

"Scream movie marathon and PSL date this fall?" he asked.

"Sweaters and fluffy socks are a requirement," she added.

Roman's heart hammered in his chest. The talk of fucking her made him horny, but the talk of a future with her made him optimistic. It was like he had lived his life with a stomach full of cocoons and Grace and somehow managed to turn them into butterflies.

"We'll have to turn on the air conditioning and pretend it's cold because this *is* L.A., and we both know fall in L.A. is just a second summer."

She nodded her head in agreement.

"What's your favorite color?" he asked, and she reached over and playfully swatted his arm.

"That was gonna be my next question."

"Ha, I beat you to it. Now tell me, are you a sad beige girl or do you fancy a bit of color?" he asked.

"I love all the colors. That's why I love thrift clothes. It's why I have so many old sports team shirts. But my absolute favorite color is slowly becoming neon green."

Roman's smile grew from ear to ear. "Care to elaborate?"

"It may have something to do with hockey," she said coyly.

"That's an *almost* answer I can get behind," he beamed, "and before you ask, my favorite color was always blue but now I think it's the color of your eyes."

Grace laughed. "That was the sweetest and possibly cheesiest thing you've said yet. And while we're on the subject, I'll have you know that my eyes are shit brown, so, if you want to change your answer, I'll allow it."

"Nope. Shit brown it is as long as it's your eyes I'm looking into."

This made Grace bring her arm to cover her eyes. "Ok, that was kinda cringy, but also, I loved it and I want to kiss you so bad right now."

Roman scanned the freeway. "Kisses are going to have to wait, because I've almost got you home, and I don't know if you know this, but I kinda won a pretty important game tonight."

"Oh, I don't know if you know *this*, but I was kinda at that pretty important game watching, and when we get home, we are going to celebrate properly."

"One more question?" he asked.

"Shoot," she said.

"Do you want me to eat your pussy with you laying down, or do you want me to eat it while you're riding my face?"

Chapter Thirty-Nine

Roman took off his suit jacket and hung it in his closet. Grace looked around his bedroom, and it dawned on him that he had yet to fuck her at his house, which seemed crazy.

"Your room is nice," she said.

He walked over to her and pulled her close. "Oh yeah? What's nice about it?"

"Well," Grace said, running her hands along his chest, "it has everything I need in it."

"Is that so?"

"Yeah, it has expensive sheets, hotel quality pillows and a great view," she teased.

Roman slapped her ass, and gripped it tight, whispering "You're a brat."

"Sometimes," she agreed.

Roman brought his mouth to her neck and kissed it gently, letting his lips brush her there delicately, bringing goosebumps to her skin. "I've never had you naked in my bed."

She pushed up on tiptoes and kissed his cheek. "It'll be a night of celebratory firsts."

Roman reached between them to unbutton her jeans. "These have to go."

He took his time. He had won the game, and that post game adrenaline had his body alive and ready. And, sure he had to practice tomorrow, but this felt like a recovery of its own breed. Slowly, he pushed her pants and panties from her hips, the oversized jersey hung from her, covering all the good parts; he would have to do something about that.

Grace took a step back and turned away from him. His last name and number on her back looked good. He watched on as she slowly lifted the hem of the jersey, exposing just enough of her ass to make his dick twitch.

"Bend over," he said with a growl.

Grace looked over her shoulders and gave him a devilish grin. She took a step out, spreading her legs wide for him, before slowly bending over like he asked. She tugged on the front of the jersey, pulling it tight across her ass, exposing herself to him.

"Grace, my sweet, *sweet* Grace, if you could see yourself right now," he said, his voice heavy.

"You like your jersey touching me like this?" she asked, pulling it tight against her body.

Roman came to her, grabbing her by the hips, pressing his erection against her ass. With one hand wrapped around her waist to hold her close he slipped his other hand between her thighs.

"You look so good wearing my number," he said, gently running a finger along the soft skin of her sex.

"It's the jersey of a winner."

"And what do I get for winning?" he asked, his free hand slipping beneath the jersey to grip her breasts.

"Whatever you want..." she moaned. "*You're* the captain tonight."

Roman turned Grace to face him. "Undress me," he said.

Grace, willing and eager to do as he asked, brought her hands to his chest and button by button his shirt came undone. She pushed it from his shoulders, letting it fall to the floor.

"I love you in a suit," she said, leaning down to run kisses up his abs, before gripping him through his pants with a slow stroke. "But I think I like you naked best of all."

She undid his belt, and then his suit pants, before pushing them from his body in one swift motion. His erection strained against his black briefs.

Falling to her knees in front of him, she nuzzled her face along the thick line of his cock. Roman's body shuttered at her touch, at her warm breath against his groin. Hooking her fingers under the elastic band of his briefs she pulled them down, along his thick thighs and Grace leaned in to place a gentle kiss to the tip of his cock.

"You look good on your knees, Grace," Roman said, running his fingers through her hair tenderly before gripping it just right; just enough to control her head.

He guided her mouth up his hard length, and she licked him there, running the flat of her tongue along his shaft before taking him deep in one go. He let out a gruff moan; this woman's mouth was too perfect, too eager to take him. She sucked him slowly and deeply. Sliding her mouth back up to his tip where she took her time, pressing gentle kisses to his sensitive slit.

Roman thought he might die if she didn't take him deeper in her mouth soon. He thrust his hips just enough to press against her lips, and Grace, being the goddess that she was, took his cock back into her mouth, sucking him with hollowed cheeks before taking him deep. The sensation of his tip being gripped by her throat made Roman lose control, he clasped her hair tighter in his fist and held her there, encouraging her to keep taking him that way.

Looking up through watery eyes Grace gripped Roman by the thighs as he began to move inside her mouth. She took him well, using his body for balance. Roman felt his balls tighten, and he desperately wanted to come down her throat.

He pulled her back gently by her hair, and she released his cock; her lips making a 'pop' as she freed him, her face hungry for more and disappointed at the loss of him.

"Get on the bed," he said through gritted teeth, helping her back up to her feet.

Grace crawled onto the bed and sat back on her knees facing him. The jersey hiked up around her thighs, bunched between her legs. Seeing her like this, on display for him, wearing his jersey, and wearing it so damn well did things to Roman's entire DNA makeup. Grace may have come across innocent, but right now in this moment, she was playing the role of his hockey slut so well.

"You had me fooled," he said, climbing up next to her, running his hands over her thighs.

"How so?"

"I thought you were a good girl," he said, gripping the front of the jersey in his fist, pulling her body flush against his. The scratch of the Knights' logo on his sensitive bare chest only intensified his hunger for her.

"I *am* a good girl," she said, tilting her head back, making room for his mouth.

"But you're playing the part so well," he said, nipping her skin there.

"What part would that be?" she asked, and he couldn't help but chuckle, even during sex she came back with the questions.

"The part of my hockey slut," he said, not missing the way her body tensed at his words. She pulled his face up to hers, eye to eye. She was fierce–his dick ached to be touched by this new, confident woman in front of him.

"I'm not playing the part, Roman Graves, I *am* your hockey slut tonight."

Before he could react, her mouth was on his, kissing him hard, taking his bottom lip between her teeth and pulling just enough to make him wince. He pushed her down on the bed and covered her body with his, his erection aching to push inside of her. Rolling her over, in one swift move, he gripped her hips, and pulled her body up onto his chest.

With firm hands he encouraged her body to move further up his torso. "My face," he said, "fuck it."

Grace didn't hesitate. She found her place above his mouth, the jersey hanging low on her hips making her most intimate parts all he could see; pink, wet, perfect.

He reached up to grip her ass and pulled her flush down on his face. He could feel her hesitance in the way her thighs tightened, trying to hold her weight up, trying to hover. Roman reached up, took the jersey in his fists, and pulled her all the way down, her legs giving out, her weight fully on him now as he began to show her how badly he wanted this.

His mouth worked her sex, relentless against her clit. He held her tight against his face, the jersey fisted tight, using it as a tether to him as he fucked her with his tongue. Grace's body trembled, her hands slammed against the headboard as her head fell between her shoulders. Unable to control herself, soft moans escaping her lips. Roman encouraged her to rock her body, to move against him. He guided her hips, and she began to roll her body against his face, she began to do exactly what he wanted from her, she began to *ride* him.

With each roll of her hips against his mouth, Grace's moans got harsher, her thighs tightened around him, suffocating him, and he would die a happy man if death came this way, with this woman above him, using his face to come apart. Her body began to tremble, and he knew she was close. Her easy movements became tense and off-beat. She flung her head back, and cried out as she came, her voice booming and deep, her body completely tense, vibrating against his mouth.

He let go of the jersey and Grace tumbled down beside him, her eyes locked closed. Her hands reached down to cup her sex. Her breathing was an erratic song to his ears as he witnessed orgasm quake through her.

Rolling over onto his side, he watched as she slowly came back down to earth. She was beautiful with a pink glow on her face, fine beads of sweat above her upper lip—he wanted to kiss it away with the taste of her orgasm still covering his mouth.

"I can't feel my toes," Grace said with a giggle, her breath still shaky with her come down.

Roman moved down the bed to bring her feet into his hands and began to massage them. "This better?" he asked. "Can you feel them now?"

"Yes, thank god, I thought I'd never walk again after that." She paused, and he watched as she contemplated something before she went on, "This all feels like I'm the one being rewarded when you were the one who had a big game tonight."

"Trust me, you sitting on my face is always a win for me. You get off, and I get...well, I get you sitting on my face."

This made Grace chuckle. It drove him crazy–making her laugh, making her come, making her smile, making her shrug her shoulders, making her do all of that in the same night–he loved being with her.

"Grace?" he said, her name heavy on his lips.

"Roman?" she responded, reaching for him to come back to her. She trailed a finger down the muscles of his arms, reminding his dick that it hadn't gotten *its* end game yet.

"I still really want to fuck you tonight," he said, in all seriousness, which sent them both into uncontrollable fits of laughter.

Who knew you could laugh with someone and still want to be intimate with them? Maybe being vulnerable during sex wasn't just admissions of love, and sweet pet names, maybe being vulnerable during sex was this, laughing, and joking, and honesty. Maybe it wasn't so bad after all.

"What's stopping you then?" Grace asked, the smirk on her face both sexy and cute.

He pounced on top of her and kissed her through their laughter. His dick was unimpressed by the amount of giggling happening and the lack of fucking, but it would have to get used to this new brand of sex–sex with emotions backing it.

"Well then, tell me how you want it, Captain Graves. Do you want me naked? Should I finally take this jersey off? Or did you have something else in mind?"

"Get on all fours so I can see my number on your back," he said, a mischievous grin on his face replacing the playful one.

Grace did as she was told. She was so good at fighting back, but when she was ready to submit it was a beautiful sight to see.

Roman grabbed a condom from the bedside table and rolled it on with ease. He pushed the jersey up on her hips, exposing the curves of her ass and the pink of her most intimate parts. She was perfect.

He pressed the weight of his body flush with hers, the tip of his cock lined up at her entrance. Grace gripped the comforter and looked back over her shoulder, giving him the sexiest smile he had ever seen. With one slow thrust, he pushed inside of her, they both sighed at the fullness, and the stretch and the way their bodies felt so good like this. Grace pushed back against his weight, wriggling her body against his as he bottomed out against her ass.

"God, you look good in my number," he growled as she rocked her hips on his cock, encouraging him to fuck her.

Roman gripped the hem of the jersey in his fists; using it as leverage to push into her harder. He pulled the fabric with each thrust, forcing her body to slam against his. The smack of their skin only made him want to come harder. Grace cried out with each deep thrust, the sounds she made during sex were raw, and real.

"So, hot, Grace," he said, thrusting into her relentlessly. "You're everything."

He was so close. His balls grew tight with his thrusts growing more frantic, more possessive, more punishing, making it harder for Roman to keep his rhythm. Every muscle in his body tensed. Grace's moans had turned to pleas, she wanted more, and he lost it completely. He slammed against her ass one last time, holding her tight against him, pulling the jersey tight across her shoulders as he came, his vision going blurry, his toes going numb.

Sex with this woman made him think that he didn't want to spend the rest of his life just fucking; maybe wanted to learn what it felt like to make love with someone he trusted, and who trusted him in return.

***

When Grace returned from the bathroom, she found Roman in bed waiting for her with the blankets pulled back, inviting her into his space. She crawled into bed next to him wearing only the Knights t-shirt he had given her to sleep in. His face bore a smile that made her heart melt, it was inviting, and calm, and maybe a little sex drunk and sleepy.

"Hi," he said as she nuzzled into his body. She placed her head on his chest and his arms instinctually came up to hug her tightly.

"Hey."

"So, tomorrow," he stated.

Only, she wasn't sure she was ready to talk about tomorrow. She knew it was back to text messages and quick phone calls. And she just wanted to be in *this* moment a little while longer before they moved on to discuss the reality of what came next.

This relationship would always take planning and communication. Communication would be key for them. She thought of her job interview with the Knights and hated how badly she wanted to tell him, and yet, how unwilling she was to do just that.

"Yes, tomorrow," she agreed, looking up at his beautiful face, his strong jaw, his playoff beard stubble present, only making him look more handsome than the clean-shaven version of him.

"We'll be reviewing the game, and practicing. I should get a good night of sleep before it's back to San Jose Friday morning for game three."

"I agree," she said with ease.

"You just make this so easy. I always expected it to be a lot harder dating someone and not being able to see them as often as most new couples do."

Grace's fingers ran gentle trails across his chest, "Well, we did start dating during playoffs, so, that does make it a little more intense than if we had started dating during the regular season. But I think people being able to text *and* call *and* facetime *and* see each other constantly is a huge part of why relationships fail these days. The expectations start so high that people crash and burn the second the euphoria ends."

"I think you might be right," he said. "You also made me wait four months to call you. Imagine all the amazing sex we could have been having." he teased.

She pinched his nipple, and he yelped in pain. "Yeah, but now you're extra needy, it makes it more fun."

Roman laughed. "I've never done this, you know? Slept with a woman and asked her to stay over at my place."

"Well, there was that one time," Grace teased.

"That one time was not in my bed, and I didn't ask her to stay, I fell asleep and was violated with selfies."

"Well, I like your bed, so, I promise not to take any photos of you while you're asleep." she said, pressing up to kiss him between his collar and jaw.

"I could get used to this..." he said, trailing off.

"And that scares you?" she asked.

"Yeah, it terrifies me. To think that right now I want you here more than anything. Knowing damn well I have some of the hardest games of my career ahead of me...its fucking terrifying, Grace, because I know on the other end of wanting to be with you there is this haunting idea that I still might be the man I've always been, and that man doesn't get the girl *and* the Cup."

"I can always go. And we can build up to me staying over. I understand that this is your sanctuary," she said, sincerity oozed with her every word.

Roman let out a relieved sigh and pulled her up to him, her brown curls curtained her face. "But what if you stick around instead?" he asked, his hands holding her body tight against his.

"What *if* I stick around?" she asked. "I think if I stick around it might prove to you that you're nothing like your father." she said, leaning in to press a kiss to his lips.

"And you'll take your chances?" he asked.

"I've had my heart broken before by the man I loved the most in the world, my dad, and do you know what I did after he broke it?" she asked.

"What, Grace, what did you do?"

"I decided to spend my life trying to make sure men like him, fathers like him, would never break their daughters' hearts again. So, I know a thing or two about heartbreak, but I also know how to overcome it. I'm not scared of you Roman. And I'm not worried about what you'll become. I think this version of yourself that you are when you're with me is a version you like too, so, I think we might be okay."

Roman pulled her into his space and kissed her deeply. This kiss felt like an omission of something deeper than pillow talk and sleepovers. Grace knew what was happening here. And she knew that as much as Roman was afraid to hurt her, she was equally just as ready to stick around to prove him wrong.

Chapter Fourty

"How was practice?" she asked, her phone on speaker resting on her chest. It was late, she nearly fell asleep waiting on his call, which she didn't want to make a habit of–waiting around for him while he was off busy doing hockey stuff. She knew once she started working–as a CADC with *his* team–she wouldn't have all this free time on her hands.

"Draining. Frustrating. I don't know. I don't want to speak badly of my team, but it just feels like everyone is already counting us out. The boys were sloppy. One of our rookies was hungover. Liam is so distracted by his fucking girlfriend, Ava, he can't make a pass. I'm sorry. I'm tired and grouchy. Tell me about your day instead."

Grace felt her stomach knot at the mention of Ava. She had managed to not let her comments at the game get too far under her skin but something about her name on Roman's lips made her angry.

"Are you and Ava close?" she asked, trying to sound neutral, "With her being your best friend's girlfriend and all."

Roman huffed out a frustrated sigh on the other end before clearing his throat. "I know her. Obviously, I've been around her because of Liam. But I don't *know* her-know her. She came into his life when I was struggling with my game, and laying low after the photos were leaked, so, I was keeping to myself a lot." he said, and Grace could feel the hesitation in his voice.

"Do you like her?" she pried.

"Fuck no I don't like her. She's my best friend's girlfriend," Roman shot back defensively.

Grace felt her heart hammer. "That's not what I meant" she stated calmly while her insides burned red hot.

"*Oh*, no, I mean, no I don't like her like *that*. I don't know. She's weird. It's hard to explain," he said, back tracking, and failing to convince Grace that there wasn't something more to the story with Ava.

Grace sat there silent, her phone moving up and down on her chest as she tried and failed to take deep, calming breaths.

"You still there?" he asked.

"Yeah," she said, weakly.

"You okay?"

Grace sat up and held the phone in her hand up to her mouth. "It's just... she seemed off at the game."

"What game?" Roman asked, his tone not doing him any favors.

"When I was in the box. Did you not know she was going to be in the box? She's Liam's girlfriend, why would he not tell you that?"

She heard the phone rustle on the other end, she could sense he was sitting up now too.

"We didn't really have a lot of time to hash out our plans for the game and our guest situation I guess," Roman paused. "What did she say? Was she rude?"

Grace hated that she even brought it up, but his defensive manner was not helping.

"She was just weird," Grace said. "She was...fake."

Roman let out a sigh of relief—was he hiding something? It made Grace's stomach drop at the thought that maybe Ava *was* telling the truth about him, that maybe, just maybe she was saying those things because she knew something Grace didn't.

"She *is* fake, Grace. And you know what, I was going to try and keep my mouth shut about her, for the sake of Liam, but fuck that woman. She's drama. Just...avoid her from now on, okay? And don't listen to a word she says because she's full of shit."

Grace wanted to pry. She knew she had every right to ask more questions, to dig. She *was* his girlfriend, and that meant honesty was not only appreciated but expected.

But then she remembered the job. And she knew that she had her secrets too. There would be a time for coming clean, but it wasn't now, not the night before game three.

"Okay," Grace agreed reluctantly, "I'll stay away from her. She seemed really catty."

"What did she say to you?" he asked.

"She just gave Jess a hard time for wearing Liam's jersey," Grace lied.

"That bitch," he said under his breath. "Did she say anything else?"

Grace took a deep breath and lied. She lied and made a secret vow to only do it once—for the sake of the game, *his* game. She lied because right now a lie felt like the best protection she could offer.

"That's it really. She gave Jess shit about the jersey and gave me a limp wristed handshake. Her vibe was just off."

"Her vibe *is* off. I'm sorry I didn't warn you about her."

"It's okay. I'm sorry I brought it up."

"Always bring shit up that bothers you, Grace. It's the only way I'll know what's going on in your life sometimes. I can't always be around, but I always want to be involved."

Grace felt better hearing him say that. She didn't think she knew the full story behind this Ava chick, but she decided to trust that Roman would tell her *if* there was something worth saying.

"I miss you." he said, his voice cracking with exhaustion.

"I miss *you*. I wish I could be at the game tomorrow."

"I can still get you a flight," he said, a yawn escaping his mouth mid-sentence.

Grace yawned too—and remembered her dad telling her yawns are contagious when she was a kid, she wondered if her dad would have liked Roman. She wondered if her dad would have fallen in love with hockey too, watching his only daughter's boyfriend play.

"I couldn't go even if you got me a flight and a ticket. I have this thing I gotta take care of." she said, and it wasn't a lie, she did have things to take care of, like all of her onboarding videos, and paperwork for her new job with the Knights. So, not a lie at all, just, omitting the full facts.

"Okay, I respect that. I respect that you have a life outside of me. It helps me not to feel so bad when I think of how much I'll have to be away from you." he said, another yawn escaping him.

"Roman?" she asked.

"Hmmm?"

"You sound tired."

"So fucking tired, Grace."

"Get some sleep okay?"

"Okay." he agreed, and she heard him settle into his bed.

"And one more thing." she added, and she could hear his breathing growing deeper. "Score one for me tomorrow."

Roman let out a soft chuckle, "Anything for my sweet, sweet, Grace."

Chapter Fourty-One

The next few days flew by in a blur for Roman. An extremely disappointing blur. The loss on Saturday in San Jose was the worst kind of loss. The kind where even the sports broadcasters had nothing good to say about the team.

"The Knights didn't show up."

"They were sloppy."

"Harvey was off his game."

"Graves taking that bad penalty cost them."

Sunday, they spent the day reviewing the tapes and getting their asses chewed out by Coach Hibbs. They ran drills for hours. Then reviewed the tapes again.

Liam was still acting off, quiet and withdrawn, which only left Roman feeling even more unsettled about the Ava conversation he had with Grace. He couldn't help but wonder if Ava had said something about the photo shoot they did together. Ava was trouble, and he knew he needed to be honest with Liam about her sooner than later. He needed to tell his best friend that she had come on to him before it was too late–if it wasn't too late already.

Roman ran to catch up with Liam in the parking garage after practice. Game four was at home tomorrow, and not having to travel would be good for the Knights.

"Hey, Liam, wait up." Roman shouted.

Liam turned to face Roman, and he noticed his best friend looked older than usual. His baby blues were a darker shade of gray, and the bags under his eyes looked like they were carrying the weight of the world.

"Hey, man," Roman asked, "you okay?"

"Just pissed about the game," Liam said.

"Me too, man. Me too," Roman offered.

Liam patted Roman on the shoulder and turned to leave without another word.

"You sure there isn't anything else you want to tell me? Like *why* your game was off yesterday?" Roman called out.

Liam turned back to face Roman. His fingers dug into his eyes, trying to rub away the stress he carried in them.

"It's Ava," Liam said, and Roman's heart sank.

He was too late. He waited too long to tell his best friend that he was dating a cheat.

"Okay..." Roman said, encouraging him to go on.

"She's just acting weird. I mentioned her moving in with me and she blew me off. Like, it wasn't even a big deal to her. But it was a *really* big deal to me. She's just hard to read sometimes. Sometimes I think she's all in, but then sometimes I wonder if she can be trusted. She's really secretive with her phone, which I know I don't have any right to what goes on there, but she gets texts and turns her body away from me to read them. And when I bring it up, she turns it on me, like I'm some insecure fuck boy. She's just, really good at turning shit around on me. It's hard to explain. I don't even know what I'm saying. She's great, and I love her. I'm just in my head over the playoffs."

Roman knew this was the moment. He knew this was technically the perfect opportunity to tell his best friend that the girl he loves had come on to him and tried to sleep with him.

Liam hit the locks on his car.

"Liam, I think you should..." Roman started, and Liam just waved him off.

"Not tonight man. I need to go home and sleep and get my head on straight so I can be on my game tomorrow. Thanks for letting me get that off my chest. I think I just need to be honest with Ava. Tell *her* how bad that hurt me."

Roman froze. He was torn. Tell his best friend everything and risk him not being able to perform at the game tomorrow. Or wait—just until the team was in a better place—so Liam didn't have to process all of this tonight.

He knew it wasn't the honorable choice, but sometimes hockey had to come first. Roman knew that made him a shit friend sometimes, and it might make him a shit boyfriend too, but that's the nature of the Cup. It's the fine line you walk between hockey being your passion, and hockey being your false god.

"Okay, man. Get some sleep though. Don't stay up too late with Ava." Roman said, instantly missing Grace more than he knew possible.

"Same goes for you," Liam said, turning towards his car mumbling, "Roman Graves has a girlfriend, never thought I'd see the day..."

Chapter Fourty-Two

Grace was sitting at the glass of game four of the playoffs because *her* boyfriend was the captain of the home team. She got the job of her dreams; she could stay in L.A. in her apartment with Jess. She didn't know how this had become her life, but it had. Two deliveries of Thai food and a four-month wait had led to this sort of fairytale, and she didn't think anything could kill her high.

Is this what it felt like? To be so high you never want to come down.

"So, what happens if they lose?" Jess asked, shoveling popcorn into her mouth.

Roman had gotten her and Jess tickets for the game, and while she loved being in the box with all the wives and big wigs, she preferred it down at the ice. She felt closer to Roman this way.

"They need to win. Stats show it's almost impossible to come back from a three-game disadvantage in the playoffs, so if they lose tonight it puts them in a bad spot." Grace stated.

"Look at you Gracey, talking stats and shit. You're a bonafied hockey wifey." Jess joked and before Grace could respond a familiar voice chimed in on the matter.

"Hockey wifey? Who got married?" Ava, the bitch, said from the seats behind them. "Better not be you," she said pointing at Jess, "Because that's *my* man."

Jess had worn the Liam Harvey jersey despite the crap Ava had "jokingly" given her in the box. Jess was a pot stirrer if nothing else, and they both knew there would be a good chance they would run into Ava at the game.

"No, not me," Jess said, acting unphased by Ava's arrival, "I couldn't marry a hockey player, I'm too clingy."

Ava did her signature fake laugh and turned her attention over to Grace, "So, are you the one claiming hockey wifey then? Don't want to jinx it, *Faith*." she said, calling Grace by the wrong name.

Grace turned to watch as Ava climbed over the seat to sit next to her.

"Faith?" Grace asked, pushing down the lump of anger that was suddenly lodged in her throat.

Ava mocked the shock on her face, bringing her long-manicured hands to her chest, "Oh, shoot. It's not Faith, is it? Can you remind me again? I'm awful with names."

Jess leaned over, her elbow digging into Grace's thigh, "Let me do the honors," she said, a hint of annoyance in her voice, "Eve this is *Grace*. Grace, this is *Eve*." she said, placing emphasis on the incorrect name she used for Ava.

Ava let out a laugh, "You're funny," she said.

"Did I make a joke?" Jess asked, Grace elbowed her to stop. She didn't want drama tonight, she was here to support Roman, not play games with this bitch.

Ava rolled her eyes at Jess and looked back at Grace. "Sorry, Grace, I knew it was some kind of holy name, I'm just so bad at remembering."

Grace played nice, keeping it short, she just wanted Ava to take the hint and fuck off.

"It's fine. We've only met once," she said. "And, I don't claim to be his *wifey*" she said, cringing a bit at the word on her lips, "That would just be my super funny best friend's way of messing with me. Roman's my boyfriend, and I think I'm satisfied with that."

Ava didn't say anything else on the matter; she just gave Grace a once over and pulled out her phone.

If being on the glass meant sitting next to Ava, Grace might consider asking to get seats in the nosebleed section next time.

***

Roman hit the ice for warmups, the arena was packed and the fans that surrounded the glass held up homemade signs of encouragement; his number on many of them. Little kids that were being held up by their parents banged on the glass with excitement. He made a few laps on the ice before he let himself look for Grace.

She was there, standing in her seat. His jersey on her back and a breathtakingly big smile on her face. She held up a hand to the glass and he couldn't resist placing his against hers in the same place.

She mouthed, "Hi." and he said it back right before a big body slammed playfully into his.

"Look at our girls together. What a beautiful fucking sight," Liam said, and Roman hadn't even realized Ava was standing next to Grace.

Roman looked over at Ava and she waved–it made him sick–but he returned a wave to save face.

"I thought Ava was in the box?" Roman asked.

"She changed her mind last night, so I begged Melissa to give up her seat."

Roman needed to have a serious talk with Melissa about that.

"I take it you and her worked shit out last night?"

"Yeah, she said I'm just in my head," Liam said, giving Ava a nod and then skating off.

Roman turned back to Grace, winked, and skated off too. He took some shots and got his legs moving. They had to win this game. And once again, this season he found his team in the worst spot imaginable.

The buzzer went off, signaling the end of warmups. He gave Grace a final smile, shot one last puck at the empty net, and put her to the back of his mind. It was time to be Roman, the hockey player, and captain of the NHL Knights until he had the win secured, after that he could focus on being a boyfriend again.

***

The first period was explosive. Both teams were playing their best playoff hockey and it showed. Grace could see that San Jose was playing to win, and Los Angeles was playing to *not* lose.

Both teams wanted it, that was obvious, but by the end of the first period it was looking like the Knights wanted it more. The crowd went wild when Nikko Hart scored after a nice rebound off the stick of Sergey Petrov, San Jose's token asshole right before the buzzer went off to end the first period, leaving the game at one-zero, Knights.

Jess stood. "Gotta use the ladies' room, you coming with me?"

"No, I don't think I can walk after that period," Grace said, standing to make room for Jess to pass by her and then Ava, who had been on her phone through most of the first period which struck Grace odd considering her boyfriend was playing.

Once Jess was gone, Ava turned to face Grace, her fake smile in place, only this time it had a cruel curl to it.

"So, have you seen the pictures from the photo shoot Roman and I did together?" Ava said, holding out her phone to Grace.

Grace took it and Ava encouraged her to look, telling her to scroll right.

The pictures were...hot? Sexual? Grace knew it was a photoshoot, but the fact that Ava was taking the time to show her felt vindictive. And Grace wasn't stupid, she knew this was part of his gig, taking pictures oiled up with beautiful models like Ava, but that didn't make it sting any less to see.

"Isn't he sexy?" Ava purred into her ear, and the way she said it was all wrong, it was taunting.

Grace scrolled through a few more pictures, struggling to see the beauty in her man's body with the raging jealousy she felt over the very obvious sexual chemistry the photographer captured between him and Ava.

"He sure is," Grace said, her voice clipped and obviously annoyed.

"The whole crew on that photoshoot thought we were dating," Ava laughed. "Can you believe that? They went on and on about how natural we looked together."

Grace handed the phone back to Ava, but kept her eyes on the ice, the Zamboni making its rounds with a young girl in a Knights jersey, waving at the crowd.

"What does Liam think of that?"

"Of what? Having his best friend eye fuck me on camera?" Ava asked, as she continued to scroll through the photos on her phone.

"Not just that, but of you talking about it like it's something to be proud of?" Grace countered, glaring at Ava.

"Proud of it? Honey, Roman Graves isn't shit in my world and Liam knows that. In fact, Liam knows better than to act any sort of way when it comes to my modeling, he knew what he signed on for dating me."

"And so did you, when you started dating a hockey player, yet you still acted shocked when you saw my best friend wearing your man's jersey," Grace said coldly.

"What's your point?" Ava asked.

"It goes both ways, that's all I'm saying."

Ava rolled her eyes, "Sorry I showed you. You acted so secure in your relationship with Roman when I told you what a player he is..."

Grace cut her off, "*Was*, Ava. What a player he was," she corrected.

"Right. Well, you acted so secure, had I known *professional* pictures of me and him would be the thing to get under your skin I wouldn't have shared them with you."

Now it was Grace's turn to roll her eyes. "It's fine, Ava. They're beautiful pictures," Grace said, her voice monotone trying to drop it before things escalated further.

"And for the record," Ava kept on, "I was joking about your friend wearing Liam's jersey. Sorry your bestie couldn't take a joke."

Jess chose the perfect moment to show up. "What about her bestie?" she asked.

"I was telling Grace that I was joking about you wearing Liam's jersey, she seems to think you took it personally."

Jess pushed her way back to her seat, "Not too personal if I still wore it tonight."

Grace pushed back a smile. She loved Jess's ability to give zero fucks, she wished she possessed that ability, especially now. She had let Ava get in her head, despite Roman telling her not to listen to a word she said. But the chemistry in the pictures was undeniable and she couldn't help but wonder if something had happened between them. Grace knew Roman slept around before they started dating, but she wanted to believe he wouldn't sleep with his best friend's girl.

Chapter Forty-Three

The second period started off on the wrong foot when Roman lost the puck drop, landing the puck on the stick of Ryan Porter, the captain for the Threshers. Porter was known for creating opportunities in front of the net and before the Knights could gain composure in the situation, Porter had the puck in front of the Knights goalie, he took the shot–glove save by Kidd–Roman's heart hammered in his chest. They were still in the lead. They still had this.

The Knights were skating hard, playing hard, making big hits. It was everything he knew his team could do all season but hadn't. It both infuriated him and made him hopeful–better late than never.

Harvey had the puck, and skated it down center ice, took the shot on the Threshers goalie creating a rebound opportunity. Roman got to the puck before a San Jose player had a chance to get it out of their zone. Roman took the shot and scored.

The crowd went wild. The Ramones' Blitzkrieg Bop played loudly at the sound of the horn and every Knights fan sang along, *Hey ho, let's go. Hey ho, let's go,* as their team's goal song played. Grace jumped to her feet and cheered for her boyfriend who just gave the Knights a two-point lead.

Jess jumped up and down beside her yelling, "That's right Roman! That's how we get it done."

Grace's whole body shook with adrenaline as she watched her boyfriend celebrate with his teammates on the jumbotron, catching the moment he looked directly into the camera and winked. Jess pulled her into a soul crushing hug and shouted, "Thats your fucking man, Gracey! That guy right there," she pointed up at the jumbotron. "*You're* fucking him."

The song ended, and the crowd began to settle down when Grace realized Ava hadn't even stood to celebrate the goal.

This bitch was the worst kind of woman.

***

Roman needed that goal, and god it felt good to get. It gave his team the buffer they needed just in case they made a mistake going into the third. Coach Hibbs didn't say much in the locker room. Just a quick reminder to play a full sixty minutes, to not take stupid penalties, and to remember they don't celebrate until they have the Cup.

Roman agreed.

But his team missed the pep talk entirely.

They came out for the third period cocky.

They came out slow.

They came out and took not one, but two bad penalties.

They came out and forgot that they were supposed to play another twenty minutes of this game, because they had two minutes left in the third period and the score was four-two San Jose and they were somehow on another penalty kill.

Roman met Porter at the blue line for puck drop and tried to convince himself a lot could happen in two minutes in hockey. Those were the rules he lived by.

***

Two minutes left in the game and L.A. was on the penalty kill. Grace's heart raced in her chest. She couldn't handle the excitement, stress and anticipation.

Two minutes wasn't enough time.

Roman skated up to the blue line for puck drop.

"You know," Ava said, as the crowd around them rallied behind their team, "I was doing the math on your relationship with Roman, and I'm pretty sure you *weren't* dating yet when we did that photoshoot, so you technically can't be mad about it."

Grace glanced over at her, and then back at the men on the ice. It was so tense in the building she could hardly breathe, so why the fuck was Ava starting her shit up now?

"Why would I be mad?" Grace asked, "It was a job. I can't be mad over his work stuff."

"It just made me realize that what he did at the photo shoot was a little more excusable considering he wasn't dating you at the time."

Grace looked away from the game, and over at Ava. "What the fuck are you even going on about?" she asked, her heart hammering in her chest.

The puck dropped. Grace missed it. The sound of chants and cheers echoed around her, but it felt like she was in a wind tunnel.

"Let's just say he wasn't the best version of himself that day. He was unprofessional—to say the least. He came on to me, Grace...I'm fairly sure he was trying to screw me behind Liam's back."

Grace shook her head. She tried to remind herself what Roman had said about Ava, that she was full of shit, and not to believe a word she said. But was he only telling her that because he knew the truth would come out eventually? It was undeniable there was chemistry between him and Ava; the photos were living proof.

"He warned me you would do this," Grace said, the game raging on in front of her, but her eyes stayed plastered on the woman next to her.

"Of course, he did. He was protecting himself."

"And Liam? Have you told Liam how his best friend tried to sleep with you?" Grace asked.

"No, I'm not cruel. I wouldn't break up their friendship. I'm sure it was just a lapse in judgment that day. He was horny, I was half naked next to him, of course he was going to get a boner for me, who wouldn't? But when he invited me back to his place after the photo shoot, I knew I wouldn't tell Liam. That would have broken his fucking heart. And the last thing I want to do is hurt Liam in all of this. We all know Roman's reputation, Grace. We all know he's a whore. But why should Liam be punished for that?"

Grace looked out at the ice, then up at the scoreboard, fifty-three seconds to go and Roman was skating the puck towards the San Jose goalie. She looked back over at Ava, who was somehow still talking, "Sorry, Grace, but he's not the guy you think he is, and I felt like you deserved to know that."

Grace looked back out at the ice, Roman was right in front of the net, he took the shot, the horn went off, the crowd leaped to their feet to cheer. Jess sprung to her feet beside her, pulling her up to celebrate.

Grace looked out at Roman, at his team hugging him, celebrating his goal.

They only had thirty seconds left in the game.

It wasn't enough time.

And Grace sure as fuck wasn't going to stick around to watch with Ava sitting next to her.

***

Roman gained the puck. Instead of icing it, he decided *fuck it*, and began to skate it up the ice. With fifty-three seconds left in the game, he was willing to risk it all. If he could just score one more, they could pull their goalie, come in hard and battle for one more goal with the last remaining seconds on the board.

He came in fast, the San Jose goalie dropped to his knees, Roman shot the puck in the top right corner of the net–

Goal.

His team rushed in to celebrate. He looked at the clock, they had thirty seconds. Thirty seconds was enough time to tie this up.

He skated along the glass; he knew it was a mistake to mix hockey and romance, but he wanted to see her, to tell her some way that that one was for her, because of her, because he *loved* her?

When he got to the glass where Grace's seat was, he was shocked to see her walking away with her best friend. He looked over to find Ava, sitting in the seat next to Grace's wearing the nastiest, cruelest smile he had ever seen.

Fuck. Fuck, fuck, fuck.

He warned Grace not to listen to Ava, not to believe her. He warned her; but it wasn't enough. He should have come clean about Ava. He should have told Liam everything. He knew how important her trust in him was going to be considering the way they met, and the reputation he held, and now he had messed things up with Grace. His stomach dropped.

If Ava had lied to Grace who's to say Liam wasn't next.

He skated back to the bench; Liam met him there and patted his back.

"Fuck yeah. We can still do this!" Liam yelled into Roman's ear, the crowd still rowdy and on their feet.

"Yeah," Roman said, then added, "Whatever happens tonight, win or lose, I want you to know you're my best friend and I would never do anything to hurt you."

Liam's face looked confused, but he didn't linger in his confusion, the puck dropped, Kidd skated from the ice giving the Knights and empty net, Roman hopped over the boards to join his second line, the timer suddenly seemed to speed up but the chants all around him seemed to echo in the distance. Hart passed the puck to Roman, and as he went to skate it up the center he looked over to where Grace *should* have been sitting, seeing her gone made him falter, his brain went fuzzy. The hit came without him seeing it coming, his body crashed into the ice. The last thing he saw before he got back up was Petrov shooting the puck at the empty L.A. net.

Goal.

The buzzer went off. It was over. They had lost game four and it was his fault. His stupid heart had gotten in the way of his game and because of that they were down by three in the first round of the playoffs.

Chapter Fourty-Four

Roman searched the family waiting area for Grace. He knew he was being hopeful. He knew he hadn't imagined seeing her walk away. And he knew for damn sure he hadn't imagined the look on Ava's face.

"Where's Grace?" Melissa asked, scanning the room of disappointed faces.

Roman looked around one more time, landing on Liam and Ava–his stomach dropped at the sight of her there, next to his best friend, smiling while Roman was left alone, and searching for Grace.

"I don't know Mel. Something isn't right," he admitted.

"Well, what are you standing here for, dumbass? Go find her."

Roman rushed from the room and pulled out his phone to call Grace. It rang once and then her voice mail came on; a generic auto generated one. He called again, one ring and done.

He headed towards the parking garage. If she wasn't going to answer his call then he would just have to go to her house, because what the fuck was even happening? No matter what Ava said, Grace was his girlfriend, *his* fucking girlfriend, she could at least give him the benefit of the doubt.

He hit the call button again and this time he got two rings. She was declining his call and each time she did, it only made him more pissed. He just lost a huge game. He didn't need this shit right now. *This* was why he didn't date. Things always got messy. He hit call again–nothing.

He was about to enter the parking garage when he spotted Jess.

"Ohhhh boy, you're in trouble, mister," she said, shaking her head.

"Where is she?" he asked.

"I have no idea. She took off the last few seconds. I was right behind her, but that snake muttered something as we left so I went down to say my peace. When I went to catch up with Grace, she was gone, but her car is still here, so I'm just as confused as you."

Roman hit call again. It rang once, and then she answered.

"Fucking finally. Where are you?" he asked.

"Don't 'fucking finally' me," she said, her voice visibly upset.

"You're the one who ran off. Where are you?" he asked again.

He heard Grace bang on something, hard metal, a door maybe.

"I–" she paused, and took an audible deep breath, "I think I'm locked in a laundry room."

"You're what?" he asked.

He heard her bang again. "Don't laugh, I'm already embarrassed. I thought it was an exit. I got turned around. I found this laundry room, linen closet type thing and I came in here to scream, and it locked. I'm trapped in here, and I'm so mad at you. And I'm embarrassed. And..."

He cut her off, "Stay put, I'll get someone to help me find you."

"Stay put?" she asked sarcastically. "No problem."

Roman shook his head, and turned to fill Jess in. "She's locked in a closet. I'm going to find a janitor or someone who might know where this room is."

"Who are you telling that to?" Grace asked, on the other line.

"Jess, she's worried about you."

Jess started laughing. "Tell her I'll be waiting by the car."

"Do you know where you were before you entered a random utility room?" he asked, walking down the long corridor of the rink looking for anyone who worked there that might be able to help.

"I was headed to the exit, but I was leaving the way you took me when we were on our date, I don't know, I got so turned around. I was so pissed, Roman," she said, her voice slowly losing its angry edge, melting into the sound of hurt.

"I know," he said, flinging open a random door, only to find racks of buns and chips, and concession bulk.

"Do you see anyone?" she asked.

He flung open another door; toilet paper, paper towels, and cleaning items in bulk.

"No," he said, racing to the next door he saw. "I'm just opening every door I see–"

He flung the door open and sitting on a washing machine was Grace. Her face was so unbelievably embarrassed, or sad, or a mix of both. He stepped into the room, making sure to keep it wedged open with a fresh towel that he found on the ground.

He hated everything about tonight.

She stood, shoulders hunched in defeat. "Did you win?" she asked, her voice weak and nervous.

"You would know that if you'd stuck around to see the last few seconds of the game," he said, and he hated how harsh the words came out.

"I couldn't. I was...it was Ava," she said.

"I fucking told you not to listen to her, Grace."

She played with the hem of the jersey, and bit on her lip. She was nervous, and he was making her that way. But he didn't care. Not now. Not after a loss like that. Not when every instinct in him wanted to accuse her of making it happen.

"She said things, and she showed me pictures and I just...I didn't know how to get out of my head," she admitted, shaking her head.

"You fucking left, Grace."

"I'm sorry!" she shouted. "I'm sorry I freaked out when a beautiful model showed me half naked pictures of you two together and told me how you tried to screw her afterwards."

Roman brought his hands to his face and rubbed his eyes.

Un-fucking-believable.

"It's always a fucking picture isn't it. That's all it takes for you people to make assumptions. You see a picture and instantly I'm the bad guy. Because I used to sleep around, obviously I would fuck my best friend's girl."

"That's not what I said," Grace tried, only to be cut off.

"That's exactly what you said. You said Ava told you I tried to fuck her, and instead of trusting that I wouldn't do that, you stormed off. Why'd you storm off Grace? Huh?" he asked, and now she was starting to cry, and he was incredibly mad and confused and tired. He didn't know if he wanted to make her cry more or walk over and wipe the tears away. "Why did you leave if you didn't believe her?"

"I just...I overreacted. I don't know. I don't *know*," she said, and now she was shaking her head, and the tears were flowing down her face.

"You *know* I don't date. You know I don't do relationships, Grace. But I did with you. I broke every rule of mine for you, and you said you understood the game. You understood that my work sometimes asks things of me that would not be easy for you. But the first time you see a photo shoot of some dumb model and me, you just assume the worst of me?" he paused and mumbled, "So fucking messy. I knew it would come to this."

Grace stepped forward and pushed at his chest. "What did you just say? That I'm messy? That you knew it would come to this? Nice to see that the whole time we were together you were expecting us to fail."

"Well, look at us, Grace. The slightest crack in our armor and you allow Ava right in. You let her lie to you, and you know what happened because of you believing her? After I told you she was full of shit? Do you know what fucking happened when you left?" he asked, his tone loud and intimidating.

"What, Roman. What happened?" she asked, her voice low, and defeated.

"We lost, Grace. We lost because I slipped up. I saw you were gone, and I lost my focus; I tripped up and lost the puck. And *that* is why I don't date. Because the second you lose your focus, the second you depend on someone to be there to celebrate your wins or grieve your losses, you forget that the only person you can ever rely on is yourself, and you just get let down."

Grace shook her head. She was silent. *It* was silent. The linen closet felt smaller, claustrophobic. Being near her felt like a double-edged sword. He didn't know how he could be so mad at her while also wanting to pull her into his body to comfort her, to comfort *himself.*

"Does Liam know?" she finally asked, her words echoing all around him.

"No, he doesn't."

"So, you're standing here, telling me that she lied about everything?" she asked, her voice monotone. He preferred it full of rage.

"I don't even know what all she told you, Grace, that's the problem here. You didn't even give me a chance to defend myself."

"You're right. I'll give you that. I should have waited. And for that I'm sorry. I was wrong to have left. But to blame me for losing the game, that's a different kind of low, Roman."

Roman, despite his better judgment, despite knowing it was wrong, and cruel, pulled up his shoulders, in *her* signature move, and shrugged them at her, as if saying, 'that's debatable'.

Another tear trailed down her face, this one was silent, this one hurt worse to see.

"She said you came on to her. She said you tried to sleep with her. She said that you were a bad influence on Liam, and that's why he doesn't go around you anymore," she paused. "She played into every fear that I brought into this relationship. That you're still a player, and you always will be. And that I'm just another notch in your stick. And the crazy thing is, now that you're here in front of me, I know that I don't believe anything she said. I know you wouldn't do that because I know you wouldn't hurt me Roman. But what I can't for the life of me understand is why you haven't told your best friend that she's like this? You clearly knew something about her was off or you wouldn't have given me a heads up about her. But Liam, he seems so naive to her bullshit. And *that* makes me question everything I thought I knew about you."

She was right. He'd known it for months now; that he should have outed Ava's actions and saved his friend the heartbreak, but he was selfish, and he put hockey first.

His head was so messed up. He was so confused. He didn't want to be like his father, and somehow in this moment, in all his lies, and half-truths—in the name of winning—he was standing in front of the first woman he cared about, and she was crying, and he was the reason for her tears.

He needed to tell Liam the truth, even if it meant losing his best friend.

He needed to tell Grace the truth too—even if it meant losing the only girl he ever loved.

He took a deep breath. "I wasn't lying when I said I would break all my rules for you, Grace. But I was lying to myself when I thought I could do it and not hurt you," he said.

Grace's chest heaved as she cried. No noises escaped her, and he knew she was trying like hell, and succeeding to hold back her sobs. He wanted to pull her into his arms and tell her they were fine, this was fine and they could work it out, but he refused to lie to her again. He knew better. He knew himself too well to tell her things would be fine. "I knew from the beginning it would end this way. And not because I doubted us, but because I know me. It was never going to work because I am who I am. And you were always going to deserve better."

Grace wiped away a tear with the sleeve of the jersey, *his* jersey, and his heart ached knowing that he had ruined hockey for her.

"No, you're right," she said. "It was never going to work. Because neither of us came into this ready to give it our all. We talked about trust and being honest but we both held on to our secrets for dear life because we didn't trust each other to respond like adults. And while I think keeping this whole thing with Ava from me was with good intentions on your end, I think you kept it from me because you knew I would respond this way, and good job on your part, because look at me, I'm reacting exactly how you thought I would. So, yeah, I agree. We had fun. It was good. But at the heart of Roman and Grace, we just don't have a lot of trust to give or take, and that was always going to wreck us."

Roman didn't know what came next. He didn't know because he had never broken up with anyone. He had never had to let someone go that he cared about.

Grace pushed past him and opened the door of the linen closet. "While we're being honest, *truly* honest, I think you should know I had secrets too. I wasn't perfect. I accepted a job with the Knights as a drug and alcohol counselor for your team behind your back. I'll let them know that I've changed my mind. I think it's best if we don't work together. A clean cut is usually how breakups work best."

Roman's heart dropped. She *what*? She had gotten a job behind his back, with *his* organization and didn't tell him?

She was already in the hallway when he grabbed her arm to stop her. "Why didn't you tell me?"

"The same reason you didn't tell me about the Ava thing. I suck at relationships. And I'm too proud. And I wanted to get the job on my own. And because at the end of the day, I didn't trust that you would want me to work for the Knights, and that terrified me, because I knew I didn't want to have to choose between you and my dream job."

He pulled her in, much too close for two people who had just broken up in the sloppiest way. "And what would you have chosen if I told you it was between me and the job?" he asked.

"Isn't it obvious? I was always going to choose you, and that terrified me. And right now, I'm realizing I have to choose anyway. I have to choose by walking away, and by giving up the position," she said, shrugging her shoulders in defeat. She pressed up on tiptoes to kiss him one last time on the cheek. "Good luck in the rest of the playoffs, Roman Graves. I'm sorry I cost you this game–this season–but I know you can do anything you set your mind to."

She turned to leave, and he gripped her wrist tight, just for one beat longer, before he let her go. "Grace?" he asked, and she paused with her back still to him, "was it you at corporate that day? When I thought I saw you?"

She turned to face him, sad, and defeated. "Yeah, it was. Like I said, we've both been hiding far more than we let on."

Chapter Fourty-Five

"**W**hy am I doing this to myself?" Grace asked Jess, staring up at the TV. The bar was crowded and noisy, celebrating the huge win of game five for the Knights.

"Because you *loved* him ya' big dummy," Jess said, tossing a French fry at her.

Grace's heart ached at the use of past tense—*loved*. She didn't know if she loved him, but being told she didn't love him anymore made her question the idea of it entirely. She watched as his team rushed out on the ice to celebrate the win, Roman at the center of it. The cameraman zoomed in on his face, causing Grace to wince at how sad he looked despite just having secured another chance at advancing in the playoffs.

"He looks just as awful and pathetic as you do," Jess said, and Grace agreed.

"Why do I want to text him and tell him how proud I am of him?"

Jess pulled her in for a hug, and Grace let her body fall against her friend's. "Because you *love* him ya' big dummy."

And she did love him.

She still loved him.

But that didn't mean they were meant to be.

"There's no coming back from that fight, Jess. There's no way we can work with our combined daddy issues. We were both already too fucked up to begin with. It was fun. It was a lot of fun while it lasted, but some things are just that."

The camera panned on Roman again, as the rest of the team continued to celebrate. Grace watched as he skated off the ice with his head down, shoulders hung low.

"What are you going to do about the job?" Jess asked.

Grace looked away from the TV, she had seen enough. "I'm going to email Cam this week and decline the position, like I said I would."

"You really don't think you both could work for the Knights as mature adults? I mean, unless Roman falls on some tough times with alcohol or drugs and needs counseling, would you ever really even see him? You would be on the corporate side of hockey, while he's off playing actual hockey."

Grace had wondered this; if she could just keep the job, not tell Roman. There was a good chance that he would never find out she had kept the position, but she was done with lying and secrets.

"No. I said I would decline the job. I'm going to keep my word."

Jess let out a sad moan. "And I'm going to lose my best friend and roommate."

Grace laid her head on Jess's shoulder. "I'm sorry I messed everything up," she said under her breath. And she meant it for Jess, sure, but Grace knew she was really apologizing to Roman, and ultimately to herself.

Chapter Fourty-Six

Roman and Liam sat at the small table in their hotel room in Seattle, surrounded by boxes of pizza and wings devoured from their post win feast.

"Good game tonight, man," Roman said, patting his best friends back. "I've missed this kind of time with you."

Liam beamed. "Me too man, me too."

"We seem to have let women come between us," Roman said, trying like hell to ease into the conversation. One he would rather not have to have.

"We have, haven't we?" Liam asked, his boyish smile breaking Romans' heart over what Roman knew he had to say next.

"Speaking of women," Roman started.

"Yeah, speaking of women," Liam cut him off. "You and Grace had a fight?"

Roman toyed with a napkin nervously, twisting its end. "We did. We broke up actually."

Liam jerked his body back. "What? You broke up over one stupid fight?"

Roman pushed the napkin aside and looked up at his best friend. Liam's shocked face was a direct reflection of how Roman's heart felt at the mention of him and Grace ending things, but that wasn't what this conversation was about. It was about how Roman had failed to trust Liam with information that directly affected Liam's love life, and ultimately his own. Roman had sat back and withheld information about Ava as Liam fell headfirst in love with her. And now he had to sit back and watch as he single-handedly ruined it all for him.

"It wasn't just some dumb fight. It was a pretty valid one, and I need you to know the details. I need you to know why we fought, and why we ended things."

Liam gripped Roman's shoulder and gave it a squeeze. "You can tell me anything, man. I'm your best friend."

This made Roman's heart ache. He knew this about Liam. He knew that he could tell him anything, and instead he hid things from him, because he was a coward, and because of hockey, and ultimately because Roman didn't know if he wasn't partly to blame for the inappropriate interactions between him and Ava.

"Ava isn't who she says she is," Roman started, and Liam began to laugh.

"Yeah, no kidding. She acts so sweet, but that woman is a raging bitch if she's hungry."

Roman shook his head, and the lighthearted smile slipped from Liam's face. "No, Liam, that's not what I mean."

Now he had Liam's attention and Roman could feel the entire mood shift between them, Liam's shoulders tensing as he leaned back in his chair.

"What *did* you mean?" Liam asked.

"Grace and I broke up, and it was partly because of Ava."

Liam ran a hand through his beachy blond hair, trying to comprehend what Roman was saying, "Okay?" he asked.

"Ava came on to me...several times. And I wanted to tell you, but I also wanted to believe that it was all in my head. That I was full of myself and taking her personality the wrong way."

Liam's eyes searched Roman's for any cracks in the foundation, any hint of insincerity, but Roman knew he would find none. She *was* trying to seduce him. She *was* trying to ruin his life.

"The first time was the night I met her. Her vibe was off, but I had drank too much wine, so I couldn't be sure," Roman admitted. When Liam didn't speak he went on, "But there were other times too, and it wasn't always her coming on to me, sometimes it was just a hand lingering on my thigh, or the way she said things. But the day of the photo shoot, she waited for me in the parking garage, and asked me to..." Roman took a deep breath, looking away from his best friend before he said what came next.

"What did she ask you to do, Roman?" Liam asked, and Roman could hear the hints of denial in his voice.

"She asked me if I wanted to sleep with her," Roman admitted.

Liam rubbed his eyes in frustration, or hurt, or any number of emotions Roman couldn't be sure of.

"Did you?" he finally asked, his voice cracking.

"Did I fuck your girlfriend?" Roman shot back, a little too harshly. But he was so caught off guard by Liam even considering he would do such a thing he couldn't help it.

"Yeah, did you fuck Ava? It's a simple question," Liam said plainly.

"No. Hell no! I would never do anything to hurt you."

"If you didn't, why did Grace dump you?"

"Because Ava lied, she told Grace *I* came on to her," Roman said.

"And she believed Ava over you?" Liam asked accusingly.

"No, she didn't believe Ava. She broke up with me because I didn't tell *you* the truth about Ava. We broke up because I failed to be honest with my best friend. And when Grace found out all this was happening behind her back and I didn't tell her she just lost trust in me, and rightfully so. I should have told you the second I realized the games Ava was playing. I should have told Grace, too, before she met Ava. But I didn't. I didn't tell either of you because I always put hockey first, and I was afraid it would mess up your game...I didn't tell either of you because I always put Roman Graves first. That's why we broke up."

Liam took his time processing. And Roman thought this might be the part in his life where he lost his best friend. He had already lost his girl. If he lost his chance at the Cup too would that be some kind of fucked up hat trick?

"You know, I wish you would have told me sooner," Liam finally said, breaking the silence.

"Me too. And I'm sorry. I messed up, man. I messed up things with you, and Grace, and this whole season I messed up on the ice. I wish I could take it all back, go back to the press conference and accept fault for the leaked pictures, and apologize to the girl, and maybe all of this wouldn't have happened."

Liam turned to Roman, his face serious and concerned. "You know, if you really think about this thing between you and Grace, neither of you were the problem, Ava was."

"I kept something pretty serious from her—and you," Roman said. "But Grace was lying to me, too. She went behind my back and got a job with the Knights. So, we were destined to fail. We both have trust issues, and honesty issues."

"Really? She got a job with the Knights?" Liam asked.

"Yeah, she's the new drug and alcohol counselor...or was, she doesn't want to keep the job now that me and her are over."

"Wait, you're telling me she could have used you to get the job and she didn't?"

"Yeah."

"That doesn't sound like a terrible thing to me. Since we were drafted we've been targets for puck bunnies, and you find the one girl in L.A. who doesn't even know who you are, and who is so independent she won't even use you—her boyfriend—as a recommendation for a job, and you let her go that easy?"

"Something like that," Roman said. "We were doomed from the start, man."

Liam leaned in, his elbows on the table. "Doomed or destined? You waited four months for this chick. Are you really going to let her get away after one fight?"

"That whole thing with her, the meeting, and the waiting, it's arguably coincidental. I was celibate, trying to distance myself from any negative press. It just so happened that while I was staying away from other women, I was *also* supposed to be waiting to call her. When we were together it sounded like some kind of fairy tale, but now that I have my rose-colored glasses off, I can see it for what it was."

"And what's that?" Liam asked.

"A reminder for why I stay single."

"So, you're gonna sit here in front of me and tell me you didn't love her?" Liam asked.

"I hardly knew her, man," Roman lied. True, he didn't know how she ordered her burger, he didn't know what kind of lotion she used, or if she liked her eggs scrambled in the morning or fried, but he knew that she made him happy. Really fucking happy, and that felt like something.

"You know what you have to do right?" Liam asked.

Roman *didn't* know what he had to do, because before Grace, he used to sleep around to fill his voids, and after he slept with the women, hockey was enough. He'd always had his drug, his escape, his favorite high, and at first, he thought Grace might be his new addiction, but now he realized she wasn't an addiction at all, she was his escape from needing one.

"You need to text her and invite her to the game," Liam said. "No Ava around this time to screw things up. Just Grace, and you, doing what you do best. *Win.*"

Roman had already convinced himself this was for the best; them not being together. He had already reminded himself why she was better off without him and why he should go back to his old ways, fuck, dispose, repeat. He knew if he just gave up and let her go, he would eventually stop feeling like someone had ripped his heart out.

But Roman wasn't big on giving up. He never had been.

"And what about you?" Roman asked. "What happens next with Ava?"

Liam sat back in his chair and ran hands through his sandy blond hair, "There's a part of me that suspected she wasn't the one. I've even talked to you about it. The way she acted when I asked her to move in, the way she's so secretive with her phone, the writing was on the wall. But that doesn't make it hurt any less that you kept it from me. It's one thing to have your girl try to seduce other dudes, it's a different type of betrayal when it's your best friend. I wish you would have told me right away, so I didn't have to sort out how I feel about you at the same time that I have to figure out what to do about my relationship with Ava. Had you just told me up front, I never would have let myself fall for her so hard. But now I have to navigate a breakup with someone I love, and I don't know if I want you to be the one to help me through it. And that blows. Because I always want you by my side."

Roman's heart sank. "That's fair," he said, guilt lined his every word.

"But I believe you. I believe that she came on to you, I believe that you denied her, and I absolutely believe that she sabotaged you and Grace; Ava is a bitch, I knew that from day one. But she was *my* bitch, so I excused her personality flaws because I loved her. But I don't want to be with someone like her, I don't like the way I feel about myself being with someone who treats servers like shit, and isn't supportive of other women, and most importantly, I don't want to be with someone who tried to screw my friend. I know she has to go."

"I'm sorry, Liam."

"I wish you would have told me sooner," he said, again.

"I do too. I was stupid."

Liam's disappointed frown curled up in the corners just a hint. "Being pussy whipped is a real thing."

"Sure is," Roman agreed.

"Would I be the worst person on the planet if I fucked her before I dumped her?" Liam asked playfully, and Roman was grateful they could still find humor in it all.

"If I'm trying my hand at being upfront about things, I think I would advise you not to fuck her before you dumped her," Roman said.

Liam laughed. "Gah, the pussy was so good."

Roman began to laugh too. He knew what he had done to Liam wasn't forgotten, not yet anyway, but he was optimistic that their friendship could survive it, and that Liam might just get out of his relationship unscathed.

"I'm sorry, man," Roman said again, he needed to say it one last time.

"I forgive you." Liam said, a silly grin on his face. "You know how you can make it up to me?"

"How?" Roman asked incredulously.

"Text Grace right now and invite her to the game."

"I'm nervous," he admitted.

"Nah, you got this. It was just the first of many misunderstandings, man. You don't stop skating when you are down by three, why would you stop skating now with Grace. Fight for her. Fight for your Cup. She's your Stanley Cup now, Roman. But you gotta fight to win her."

Chapter Fourty-Seven

Roman sent the text to Grace the second he hit the pillow. Liam was right, he had given up on her at the first sign of loss, and that went against everything he believed in. If thirty seconds left in a game was enough time to pull off a win, then he needed to believe he could still pull this off with Grace.

Roman:

I think we should probably talk.

Her text came through faster than he expected, and he was grateful that she didn't keep him hanging.

Grace:

I agree.

Then another.

Grace:

> **Congrats on the win. You were amazing tonight.**

Then another.

Grace:

> **I was afraid I'd never be able to tell you that.**

Roman's heart hammered in his chest. He couldn't type out his next text fast enough.

Roman:

> **Please come to the game tomorrow Grace.**

He waited. This time she took longer to respond. He didn't care. He would lay awake until she said she would come.

Grace:

> **Okay. But I don't want to be seated next to her again.**

Roman had so much to fill her in on. How Liam and Ava were over. How he had told Liam everything, like Grace had told him too. How Liam took it well because Liam was a saint. He wanted to tell her how badly he fucked up being mad at her over the job situation, and that it was just him projecting–like his dad always had done with his mom. He wanted to tell her he was bad at this, worse than he ever imagined he could be, but if she would give him another chance, another thirty seconds in their game, he would promise her that while he would continue to fuck up and get things wrong he would never make the same mistake twice.

He said none of those things. Not in a text. Not when he had just gotten her to agree to come to the game.

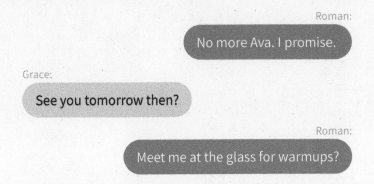

Roman:

No more Ava. I promise.

Grace:

See you tomorrow then?

Roman:

Meet me at the glass for warmups?

He waited, and he knew it was a big ask, but he had something he needed to say to her, and he needed it to be in person, *even* if there was glass between them and hundreds of Knights fans watching.

Grace:

Okay, I'll meet you at the glass.

Now, he waited for the next game knowing sleep would not come easy.

Chapter Fourty-Eight

G race wore her number eleven jersey despite the circumstances. She didn't know what tonight meant for them, but she knew that being here, watching Roman play, she had to wear it. Anxiety consumed her. She was nervous about seeing him. She was nervous about the game. She wanted them to win almost as much as she wanted Roman back.

The whole thing started as a slow burn. *Her* needing him to wait; *him* needing that time to change. What had taken so long to heat between them was suddenly not just a burn but a fucking forest fire. She fell fast and hard, and she knew he did too. Like any fire, with reckless abandon, what they had between them was put out just as fast as it had started, leaving scorch marks on her heart and the lingering smell of smoke and destruction on her skin.

She made her way to her seat. It was on the glass, close to where she had been seated the night all hell broke loose. Somewhere in between their slow burn and quick end, they had managed to skip over the most important part of it all—communication—the one thing she valued the most as a professional counselor. How could she fuck up the one thing in a relationship that she literally spent hours of her life training for?

The buzzer went off, and the clock on the jumbotron began ticking down from fifteen minutes for warmups as both teams took to the ice. She stood, and other Knights fans filled the empty space around her, beating on the glass, holding signs, hoping to get a smile, fist bump, or puck from one of their favorite players.

She watched as Roman skated onto the ice, his face covered in thick stubble, his playoff beard only getting started, making him look older, sexier, and a bit mysterious. He did a few laps, scanning the crowd at the glass with intent, but somehow missing her at first. Then, she watched as Liam spotted her from across the ice, he gave Roman a knowing nod, and pointed directly at her. She held her breath the entire time it took for him to skate over. When he got to the glass, all the surrounding fans fought for his attention, but he only had eyes for her.

He smiled weakly, as if unsure he was allowed to look or act excited to see her, she smiled back, also with reserve, and shrugged her shoulders. This made his smile grow just enough for the girl next to her to notice, bumping her shoulder, saying, *"Lucky."*

Roman put his hand over his heart, over his captain's C, and Grace felt tears threatening to make this whole situation a lot more embarrassing than it had to be.

Without a second thought she held out her hand to the glass, placed it at the thick barrier between them, and mouthed, "Good luck."

Roman, taking her lead, placed his glove covered hand against the glass where hers was, and mouthed, "I'm sorry."

Grace thought she could feel the heat of him through the glass and his gloves, but maybe it was just her body responding to being near him again. And maybe it was her heart racing so fast. And maybe it was all the blood in her body suddenly heating at the simple words he mouthed just for her.

He was sorry.

And she believed him.

"I'm sorry, too," she mouthed back, fighting the urge to break down right there during warmups in front of everyone. Roman pulled his hand away and placed it back over his heart with a knowing smile before skating away to rejoin his team for warmups.

***

Now that Roman had apologized, he felt like a weight was lifted off his shoulders. He felt like he could go out and play tonight without the heaviness of not having said he was sorry to Grace. It was crazy just how heavy he had been feeling with all the secrets he had been carrying. Now, taking that load off, his mental state and his ability to focus on his game seemed so much lighter.

"You apologize?" Liam asked, under his breath, as they all listened to Coach Hibbs go over a few things before they took the ice for game six.

"I did," Roman said, pausing then adding under his breath, "I think she feels the same way I do about it all."

Liam laughed under his breath and asked, "Yeah, and how's that?"

Roman whispered, "Like we fucked up. Because *we're* fucked up. But I think neither of us are ready to call it quits."

"I hope not, especially over something as stupid as Ava," Liam said, and Roman didn't usually condone that sort of language being used against women, but Ava wasn't a woman, she was the devil, so he allowed it.

"Ava, sure," Roman said, and when Coach Hibbs stopped talking, he added, "But we were also holding things from each other. Stupid shit. I think back to the day I met her, and how I almost messed things up then, too, by not telling her who I was, and that I was involved in a sex scandal. I only saw it as the perfect opportunity to *not* tell her the truth, to *not* be transparent with her about my reputation because even then I was terrified of her rejection. I think of how that almost cost me everything. I think of how I forced her to find out who I was through a press conference about my sex life. So, I'll never take it for granted that she allowed me to be a part of her life after all that. And then the stuff with Ava..."

"Man, fuck Ava."

"Yeah fuck Ava, but fuck me too. I made her find out second hand what was happening with Ava when she should have heard it from me first. I don't want to be that guy anymore. I spent four months recovering from that kind of lifestyle, being celibate, laying low, reflecting on my childhood and my dad's actions, and I don't ever want to relapse. I don't want to give anyone a chance to determine the narrative of my life—especially when it comes to Grace."

Liam gripped his buddy's shoulder tight with approval. It was almost game time and Roman was still stuck on Grace. He knew he needed to shift gears, not for long, just 60 minutes, then he could be with her again, win or lose, he didn't care, he just knew he didn't want to spend another day of his life without her.

***

Things were not going well for The Los Angeles Knights. Grace watched in full panic as Ryan Porter, the captain of the Threshers, came around the back of the net and pushed the puck in between Kidd's skate and the posts, leaving the Knights trailing by three. It seemed like an impossible comeback. It felt like the end of this playoff run for Roman, and the Knights, but Grace refused to give up hope until the buzzer said it was over. She glanced up at the jumbotron, the clock said four minutes–four minutes was a lot of time in a hockey game...right?

The camera panned in on the Knights coach, his face told her no, no four minutes was not enough time. She crossed her fingers anyway and said a silent prayer for some kind of hockey miracle.

The game went on. It went so much faster in the last few minutes. L.A. pulled Kidd from the net and Grace watched as Roman and the rest of the first line fought hard. Fought like a team that could still win it. Fought like time was on their side. And, like the rest of the season had gone, they fought a losing battle. A San Jose player took a shot at the empty net and scored. With seconds left on the clock Grace watched for the first time, as Roman skated to the bench as if it were over.

Chapter Fourty-Nine

They needed a miracle tonight and they didn't get one. They had needed a miracle long before this game. Roman was willing to chalk up most of his team's losses to not playing a full sixty minutes. He was willing to blame some of their losses on the nudes being leaked and affecting his game. He was willing to say a few of those losses were bad bounces and the hockey gods working against them this year. He could pinpoint every mistake they made this season, and it wouldn't take away the disappointment he felt entering the press box to give one of the hardest types of interviews a hockey player has to give throughout his career: The last interview of the season.

"We have Roman Graves with us after a devastating loss tonight, leaving San Jose to advance to the next round and the Los Angeles Knights to say farewell to a hard fought first round of the playoffs."

The reporter, a pretty blonde with huge front teeth, turned to face him. "Roman, what do you have to say about this season as a whole?"

Roman took a white L.A. Knights towel from his lap to wipe the sweat from his forehead. "It wasn't our best season. We got into the playoffs fighting for a spot, and we were eliminated from the playoffs fighting for a spot to advance, and it just didn't happen. We fought hard, but we made big mistakes too, so as a team we have to count our losses and come into next year stronger."

The reporter nodded her head in agreement, her smile never faltering.

"What does the future of the L.A. Knights look like for Roman Graves, the captain? What does this summer look like for you?"

Roman knew the answer she was looking for; he knew the answer she expected. It went something like, *"Condition, review the tapes, spend time with the fam, and play some golf."* yadda yadda, but Roman was done with fake interviews.

He thought about the question. Really thought about it. What *did* the future of his team look like? What did his summer look like? A smile grew on his face because for the first time in his life, he had something to look forward to during his off season, he had some*one* to look forward to.

"Well, as for my team, I think we're going to refocus this summer, live in our loss for a bit. We do *not* want to find ourselves back here next season. As for my summer, I plan to spend it with my girlfriend, Grace. She was the reason I showed up and played my hardest this season after my bad press incident. So, I plan to take time this summer to show her how much I appreciate her..." he paused, looking directly into the camera and said, "I want to show her how much I *love* her."

***

Grace watched the interview from the friends and family waiting room. The whole room erupted into oohh's and awww's when Roman said he loved her.

Roman Graves had confessed his love for her on national television. Grace's face grew flushed as he spoke. Her heart hammered in her chest. The cat was out of the bag in a big way, and she couldn't be happier.

He looked beautiful this way. Honest, and in love. It was so much better than the last time she had seen him in person, heartbroken, betrayed and mad.

Melissa swooped in for a side hug. "He loves you!" she said. "I knew you were the one. I'm so happy you two worked through whatever it was that came between you."

Grace hugged Mel back. "Me too," she admitted. "How much longer do I have to wait?" Grace asked, her eyes glued to the door the players usually entered from.

"It's the last game of the season, it might be longer than normal," Melissa said.

Grace's face fell, showing all her disappointment. "I just need to see him. I need to tell him I feel the same way."

Melissa grabbed Grace by the wrist and tugged her towards the door.

"What are you doing?" Grace asked.

"This calls for breaking the rules," Melissa said with a mischievous grin.

Grace followed behind Melissa as she tugged her out of the waiting room, Cam Lawndry gave Grace a wave and then a thumbs up on her way out; thank god she hadn't told him she wasn't taking the job. What a week this had been.

"Where are we going?" Grace asked, despite having a fairly good idea.

"Where else?" Melissa said, holding up her security badge as a flex. "We're going to get your man."

They made it to the corridors that led to the locker rooms and when Grace looked up, the air was suddenly gone from her lungs. Like a punch to the gut, there he was, racing towards her; still in his skates, and uniform, his hair wet with sweat pushed back, a little more curly than she was used to seeing. His forehead was still red where his helmet had been. The smile on his face did not match the disappointment she expected him to be experiencing after such a huge loss.

Was that smile for her and only her?

Melissa let go of her hand and Grace sprinted toward him. He held out his arms for her and lifted her up into them with ease. She wrapped her legs around him tight, and she would never let him go again.

"I'm so sorry," she said, her mouth pressed against his neck, the smell of his sweat heady and manly; it was intoxicating.

His lips found hers and he kissed away her apologies, making her forget what she was even sorry for. He loosened his grip on her and she slid down his body, without backing away, she had to be close to him.

"Roman, I'm so sorry about the game and the fight," she said again, and her concerned face was met with a full toothy grin from him.

"Don't be sorry, Grace. I'm not. I mean, does it suck that we are out of the playoffs? Yes, that'll always hurt. But it wasn't our year. The better team won tonight."

"You played so hard. I'm so incredibly proud of you."

"I gave it my all, but I'm not mad. I realized tonight, when I was being interviewed, that for the first time in my life I have something besides training and golf to look forward to this summer. I have you. And

I want to do everything with you, Grace. I want to go on a vacation–I was thinking Spain...or Greece. I want to make you breakfast, and then lunch and dinner too, all in the same day. I want to golf with you and take naps with you. I want you to show me all of your favorite places and take you to some of mine. I want to fuck you in the morning and make love to you at night. I want to support you on your first day of work with the Knights, because holy shit Grace, you got a job with the best organization on the planet, and I know it's the best," he said with a wink, "because I work for them too."

She couldn't believe what he was saying. Not because she didn't believe him, but because she was in shock. Two days ago, they broke up, and today, in the midst of a huge loss, he was smiling down on her, speaking of their future.

"Roman, you..." she paused, "you said you loved me on live TV," she said, looking up at him, her bottom lip pulled between her teeth anxiously.

"I did, didn't I?" he said, his smile growing wide. "Was that okay?"

Grace pressed up on tiptoes to kiss him, he pulled her body against his thick hockey pads, and deepened the kiss–she wanted more, she wanted it all, and it seemed like she might get it.

"Say it again," she said, letting her lips linger on his. "Tell me again."

Roman brought his mouth close to her ear, and whispered in a low, slow purr, "I love you, Grace. I always knew I would end up loving you."

She hopped back into his arms, wrapping her legs around him again. "I love you too, Roman Graves. Thank you for waiting for me."

"Oh, my sweet, *sweet*, Grace, you were always worth the wait."

Epilogue

NHL Holiday Break

His house looked different with her touches to it this Christmas. Hell, he had never decorated for the holidays at all, he didn't even have a stocking to hang by the chimney with care before Grace. But after a few trips to the thrift store and Pottery Barn, his house had the perfect mix of vintage and faux vintage decorations.

Grace refused to do a trendy color scheme, or as she called it, boring vanilla Christmas so they went with the traditional colors, the tree a beautiful mess of decorations varying from big fat blushing Santas, to rocket ships, to an L.A. Knights ornament, every kind of candy cane they offered and a popcorn garland they had made together one night as they watched hockey. Grace hung the few ornaments she had brought back with her after a trip up North; ornaments she had used in her childhood home when her father was alive.

The house smelled amazing, like his buddies' houses always did during the holidays; like cookies, and sugar, and pine and his sweet Grace, because since she had moved in with him, his house had started to smell a little sweeter, a little homier, a little more feminine.

"Did you place the order? They close a little early on Christmas Eve," she shouted from the kitchen where she pulled a cookie sheet from the oven with a dozen toffee cookies.

"I did. I remembered from last year," he said, memories flooding him of the second night he had ordered from Thai Spoon, hoping Grace would deliver his food again.

Grace set a plate of assorted cookies on a small table near the fireplace. "For Santa," she said with a wink.

Roman loved her this way; messy loose curls of dark brown hair, no makeup, sweatpants and an oversized hoodie–not far off from the way she looked when he had first met her.

"All of that is for Santa?" he asked, as she crossed the living room and climbed into his lap.

"I guess you can have a few after dinner," she teased, leaning in to give him the best Christmas gift he could think of; a long, deep, kiss.

"I have something for you," he said, reaching over to grab a heavy, rectangular gift off the coffee table.

Grace smiled at him and took it. She shook it and balanced it in her hand, weighing it out.

"Stop trying to guess and open it," Roman encouraged, because truth be told, of all the gifts he had gotten her; a thrifted vintage Knights jersey from the 80's, a new pair of slippers, fluffy socks, and a gift card that would cover a *lot* of pedicures–not because she needed them, but because she never treated herself to things like that–this gift was his favorite. He knew he wanted to do this for her since the day she told him this detail about her life.

Grace pulled the red bow off and placed it on top of his head with a smile and then tore into the Grinch wrapping paper. Her eyes went wide as she read the box.

"Roman Graves...is this?"

"It is," he said.

"Where did you? How did you? I can't believe you remembered!" she said, her eyes welling up with tears.

"I remember everything you tell me. But that story especially stuck with me."

Grace looked down at the box again, and read the label aloud, "Grace's Ultimate Candy Bar. Should we try it?" she asked, her face filled with a childlike grin he had never seen before.

Roman's heart hammered in his chest. He wanted to make her this happy for the rest of his life...for the rest of *her* life.

"Are you kidding me? Hell yes we're trying it," he said, encouraging her to open the box.

"But I kind of want to save it forever," she said, pulling it up to her chest with sentiment.

Roman pulled the box away from her chest. "Open it. I had two made, one for eating and one for saving."

Grace ripped into the packaging like a kid looking for a golden ticket in a Wonka bar. She snapped off a piece of the massive chunk of chocolate and handed it to him. He could see traces of peanuts and crunch in it, as well as colored flecks of M&M's. Grace snapped a piece for herself, and held it out. "Merry Christmas Roman Graves," she said, and bumped her ultimate candy bar into his.

"Merry Christmas, my sweet, Grace."

They both took a bite of the candy bar at the same time and began to laugh.

"Oh, shit," Grace said, covering her mouth with her hand.

"I know right?" Roman asked.

"It's awful," she said, swallowing down the childhood concoction.

Roman took the candy bar from her and sat it back down on the coffee table. "It's the thought that counts, right?"

"It was the sweetest gift of my life," she said, leaning in to kiss him. "I finally know how it would have tasted all these years later."

"The mystery of the ultimate candy bar is over."

Roman pulled her body against his and kissed her. The taste of chocolate lingered on their lips. Grace deepened the sugary kiss and moved against him in the best way. His body responded and he couldn't believe he had never had Christmas sex before. He was still shocked by all the firsts they had gotten to experience together and all the firsts they were still discovering they had left to do.

The doorbell chimed and Grace pulled away, "You getting that, or am I?" she asked, but he wasn't ready for her to stop kissing him. He pulled her mouth back to his and pushed her down to the couch, pinning her there. His need very obviously pressing against her as he thrust his hips into hers.

"Roman," she said, with a breathless whimper, "the food..."

He brought his hand between them and pushed under her sweats. "It can wait," he said dubiously, rubbing a firm finger over her sex.

"Roman," she said again, this time more demanding, pulling his hand away, "he's going to leave with the food."

"I already paid." He pushed his hand back into her sweats, the doorbell chimed again, and they both began to laugh.

"Roman, go get the food," Grace said. "The poor delivery person probably wants their tip."

Roman pushed his body up against hers one last time, and kissed her, biting her bottom lip playfully between his teeth. "If they wait, I'll tip them really well."

Grace shook her head, and pushed him from her body. "Go get the food, and if it's a female delivery person, don't fall in love, okay?" she said, and he shot her a glare from over his shoulder.

"I make no promises, Grace. I have a thing for delivery girls."

Grace shouted after him, "And no four-hundred-dollar tips!"

***

Grace met Roman in the kitchen and couldn't help but roll her eyes at the insane amount of food he ordered. She was flooded with the memories of the first time they met and how annoyed she was with him for ordering so much for one person.

It had come full circle.

"We didn't need this much," she said, making a plate for herself.

"Yes, we did, it's tradition."

"Over ordering is our tradition?" she asked.

"Yes. It's the same order I got the night you delivered my food to me."

She paused from serving herself to look over at Roman and appreciate the life she had with him and how important it was for him to create new memories with her, as well as sharing some of his own.

They both sat down on the couch with their plates piled high with several variations of noodles, meats, and rice. Roman grabbed the remote control next to her and hit a button that dimmed the main lights in the living room. The glow of the Christmas tree made him look sexy, and kind, and boyish in the colorful glow.

"So, what are we watching," she asked.

Roman hit play, and the sound of a phone ringing filled the room from the televisions surround sound system. A blonde girl answered the phone on the TV screen as she started making popcorn...

"Scream, silly. It's my favorite Christmas movie of all time," Roman said, and Grace rolled her eyes.

"Your favorite Christmas movie, Roman? Really?" she asked.

"Really. It's also a tradition. This way, I can get you nice and scared so you have to cuddle up to me...and then the cuddling can lead to foreplay, and the foreplay can lead to hot, nasty Christmas sex," he said, reaching over to grip her thigh.

"Deal," she said with a dubious smile on her face. "In the name of tradition."

They both began to eat, and watched as the person on the other line asked the cute blonde if she liked games.

Grace looked over at Roman who was grinning like a fool, "How many times have you seen this movie?"

"I've watched it every Christmas since I got drafted."

"And you never once thought to maybe put on Elf or the Grinch instead?"

"Nope." He turned to face her, his smile a bit deranged. "What's *your* favorite Christmas movie, Grace?" he asked, mimicking the voice of the Ghostface killer from Scream.

Grace laughed. "The Santa Clause, obviously."

"Okay, new plan," Roman said, the scene on the TV just starting to intensify. "After we finish Scream and have our nasty Christmas Eve sex, we watch The Santa Clause, because of traditions and what not."

Grace shrugged her shoulders as he leaned in to kiss her cheek. "You're too good to me Roman Graves."

"No," he said, "I think we're just meant to be."

Grace beamed, because she couldn't agree more. "Worth the wait," she said, taking his hand in hers, giving it an affectionate squeeze.

"Worth the wait." he affirmed.

They both got back to eating as the blonde got hacked up in the front yard.

Grace felt the buzz of Roman's phone go off on the couch cushion.

Then it went off again, and then three more times.

She looked over at him and could tell he was trying to avoid checking it.

"Are you going to at least see why your phone is vibrating harder than a sex toy?" she asked incredulously.

"I have PTSD after last Christmas, I don't want to know what's going on." he said.

"Well, have you been sleeping with strange blondes recently? Screwed any influencers that I don't know about?" she asked, jokingly.

"No. But I don't really care what anyone has to say either. It's my first Christmas with you. I don't want to be on my phone," he argued, eating another bite of noodles, never taking his eyes off the movie.

His phone buzzed again, and Grace picked it up, opening his text messages. Roman looked over at her as she scrolled through his group text with his team, her face intent.

"Well now you have to tell me what they are saying," Roman huffed.

Grace held out her hand. "Gimme the remote."

She turned off the movie and put the TV on the NHL Sports Broadcast. They both read the headline on the screen behind the news anchors, and gasped.

"No way. That's Max Miller, Anaheim's goalie." Roman said.

"When was that?"

Roman sat forward on the couch and watched the replay again, "Last night's game."

Grace watched the TV screen, her face lined with worry. "That's so scary. I hope he's okay."

THE END

Acknowledgements

First and foremost I have to thank my hunky, hockey playing, Canadian husband Jeremy. Your endless amounts of patience, encouragement and hockey knowledge helped keep this book alive whenever doubt creeped in.

My daughter, my dizzy dreamer, my creative little bird; the confidence you have in everything you create reminds me to dream and write with childlike abandon; thank you sweet, sweet girl.

Sara, my sister, best friend and funniest person on the planet, your ears must hurt from all the phone calls about this book. Thank you for listening, and listening, and *listening* so graciously to me as I navigated writing my first novel.

Mom, please skip the sexy parts, but also, thank you for making me feel safe in my role as a woman to write such things. You truly are the best mom on the planet.

Kyle, brother bear, thank you for all the dope new songs you sent along the way, a few of them made the book's playlist.

Dad, I know this makes you nervous, trust me, I'm nervous too, but I got this, I promise. I love you with all my heart.

To my niece, thanks for asking me to tell you love stories at bedtime. You understood love at such a young age, and I admire that.

To my dear friend and fellow author, Jana Sun, honestly, this book would be another unfinished story if it hadn't been for you and your encouragement and knowledge. You walked, so I could run. I'm forever grateful for your friendship, help, daily phone calls, and exposure to boba.

Katie Blowersocks, you have been there since the start of my writing journey. Every plunny, rare pair, sprint and story we've shared helped shape me as a writer, thank you, a million yellow hearts.

Candis, my eagle eyed friend, you saved the day.

To my cover artist, Sam, thank you for taking a risk on a new indie author and delivering my dream cover.

Andrea, my dear friend, and editor, thank you for taking this story in its worst shape and fine tuning it. I have grown as a writer because of your ability to teach as well as edit.

Aunt Janie, thank you for telling me stories about your alien abductions when I was a child. Your amazing story telling paved the way to what would become my passion as a writer.

Thank you to the readers, the book friends I made along the way, my street team, my fellow chaos gremlins, and my arc team. Thank you to the people who didn't have a reason to believe in me, but chose to do it anyway. Your support on this journey will be a memory I carry for a lifetime. Thank you all!

About The Author

Lucille James is a Southern California native who recently relocated with her family to a small Southern town. While she will always love and miss the West Coast vibes; food, beaches, Disney days, Ducks Hockey and the sunny weather, she has come to love the sounds of the South, sweet tea, rural highways, and a slower life that allows her to write more freely.

Throughout her life, Lucille has found stories in her own experiences; from skateparks to cheer squads; hockey games to punk shows; fast food burger joints to Hollywood sound studios; and most importantly, always asking the people around her: What's *your* love story?

Lucille enjoys spending time with her husband, daughter, and pup. In her free time Lucille loves writing, watching Rom Coms, reading, cooking, concerts, coffee shops, and going to the roller skating rink.

Follow For More

If you wish to follow Lucille James for updates on the next two books in her West Coast Hockey Romance series, follow her social media platforms:

Click or scan.

www.lucillejames.com